Light and Shadows

D1565756

Light and Shadows

Karen Batshaw

ISBN-13: 9781798108598

Dedication

This book is dedicated to both the Greek Orthodox Christians of Asia Minor and the Greek Jews of Eastern Macedonia and Thrace.

May their memory be eternal.

Acknowledgments

To my husband Mark, who encouraged me to return to my writing.

To Nadene Geyer, who introduced me to Jacques Frances. It was the incredible story of his family's survival in Volos, Greece, that intrigued me. And so began my research into the little known history of Greece and its Christians and Jews during World War II. My immersion into Greek history led to the creation of *Hidden in Plain Sight*.

To Aphrodite Matsakis, whose knowledge and discussions with me about the post-traumatic stress experienced by the Asia Minor Refugees during World War II, led me to the horrors of the expulsion and massacre of the Orthodox Christians in Asia Minor. Aphrodite also has been a wonderful source of information on Greek culture and customs.

To Marcia Haddad Ikonopolous, the Museum Director of Kehila Kedosha Jannina, who shared with me the annihilation of the Greek Jews in Eastern Thrace during World War II. I am also grateful for her friendship and help in learning about the Jews of Greece.

To Margarita Lazarou, who continues to assist me with all things Greek, including language and Greek Orthodox customs.

To Jack and Daisy Samarias who generously explained details and customs of the Greek Jews.

To Jim Marketos and Jim Stouckler, who shared with me their family histories of the tragic flight from Smyrna in 1922.

To George Mavropoulos who shared his family history of the Pontic Greek refugees.

People often ask an author what was the inspiration for your book? Besides the aforementioned people, there were those who provided that "special spark" which allowed me to take the historical facts, animate my characters and create this story. To Dan Meijer who shared with me the memoirs of his mother, Marianne Meijer, who, as a child, was forced to flee from the Nazis during War War II and as an adult in the United States, became a champion for civil rights. To Jack Samarias, who shared the memoirs of his aunt Naki (Esther) Touron-Fais, whose quick thinking allowed her to escape the Nazis and the death camps.

To Debby Lazar, a great sounding board for my ideas, and my preliminary editor.

To Sharon Cohen-Powers, my final editor, who expertly polished my grammar and punctuation.

To my readers, for their encouragement and support : Marty Hamed, Debby Lazar, Judy Palmer, Margarita Lazarou and Susan Talley

To Andrew Gipe, for another wonderful and evocative cover.

Language Note

Greek and Ladino words or phrases are used within the text. Ladino, which closely resembles the Spanish language, was brought to Greece by the Jews of Spain who fled the Inquisition.

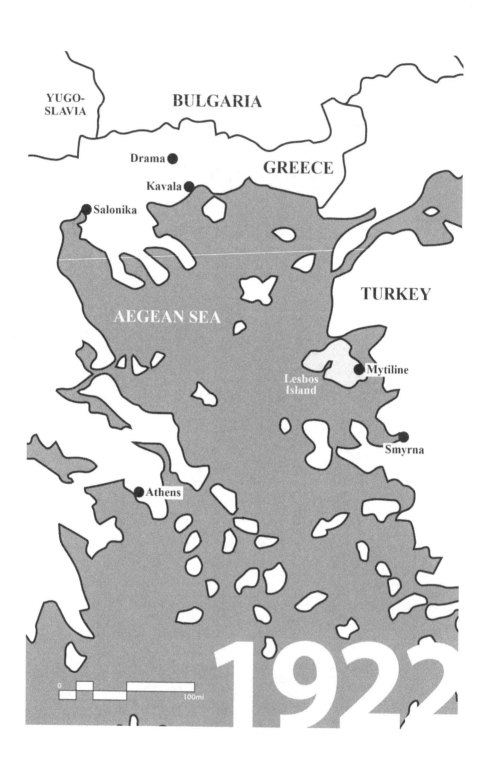

CHAPTER 1

Chicago, Illinois: August 27, 1963

"NO! NO!" THE woman screamed. "Help me!"

"Katerina, Katerina wake up." Andreas tenderly gathered her in his arms. "You're having a nightmare."

"No!" she continued to yell.

"Katerina." He gently shook her. "Wake up, wake up."

His wife looked up at him, her eyes filled with bewilderment. "Andreas?" she breathed.

"Yes, you are safe. You are home with me. You had another nightmare." He kissed the top of her forehead.

"Oh, Andreas," she began to sob. "I'm so frightened."

"You're safe. You are here with me in our home. We're in America." He held her closer, his heart aching for her as he tried to quiet her fears.

"I'm afraid. Every night I have another bad dream. They found me. They found us. What I did was wrong. It was wrong. I shouldn't have done it." She cried tearfully. "I shouldn't have done it."

"You did what you needed to do."

"Every night I'm afraid to fall asleep. Why, after so many years, am I having these nightmares now?"

"You know why. It's because of Maria. It will pass, I promise you. You'll stop having these bad dreams. And I'm here with you. You are safe. We are all safe." He tried to reassure her.

August 28, 1963

Maria, a young woman, sat on a chair in front of the television set, absentmindedly pulling down on her mini skirt. Her eyes were transfixed on the television screen. "*Mamá*, hurry! Dr. King is going to start speaking in a few minutes. You don't want to miss a word!"

She turned to her father who was seated on the couch, a cigarette in his fingers. "Isn't she done in the kitchen yet?"

"Katerina!" Andreas called out and smiled as his wife, dressed in her best Sunday going-to-church dress, walked into the room with a book in her hands.

His wife put down her book on the coffee table.

Maria turned back to the television. "He's about to speak." She breathed with excitement, her eyes glued to the television screen.

Maria sat on her chair and her parents settled into the couch, listening intently to every word spoken by the minister.

"...my four little children will one day live in a nation where they will not be judged by the color of their skin, but the content of their character..."

And then the speech was over and the crowd cheered.

"So many people," Andreas commented in amazement. "Can you believe all those people who have gathered on the mall in Washington? What a sight to behold! America is such a wonderful country, where so many stand up for what is right, for justice, for everyone."

"*Mamá, Patéra*," Maria spoke without turning towards her parents. "This is so exciting. Steven and I have decided to go down South and help register voters."

"You aren't going to do that!" Her father took a sharp intake of breath.

"Yes, we've decided." Maria turned around to face him.

"If I didn't have to look after the boys, I would go with them," his wife announced.

"You would not!" Andreas thundered. My daughter, he thought. I could never let her expose herself to danger. If something were to happen to her, I couldn't bear it. Katerina could not bear it. Not after what happened to their families so long ago.

"Andreas, it's a moot point, because I have to take care of the children." His wife smiled up at him. "But you understand how important it is for everyone to be treated equally. After what happened to our families, it's our duty, everyone's duty to stand up for what is right. Otherwise, we are no better than the Turks." She repeated the refrain they always told their children whenever they spoke about prejudice, oppression and evil deeds.

"I won't permit her to put herself in danger." His jaw tightened.

"I'll be going with Steven," Maria paused, "and Steven and I have been discussing that maybe we would just have a civil marriage ceremony before we go down South. If we leave very soon, we'll be home in time for the fall semester at school. I told you, I promised you, I would finish college after we get married. We could move in together after a civil ceremony and have the big wedding next year."

"What do the Strausses think of this ridiculous idea?" he asked. "A marriage in City Hall is not a marriage."

"Steven is going to tell them tonight before they arrive. Mamá, is everything ready? The food's all done?" she asked.

Andreas knew his daughter was asking a foolish question. Of course, the food was done. Katerina had been baking and cooking for days, preparing for this first important meeting of the two families, their Greek Orthodox family and Steven's Jewish parents. Andreas looked down at his wife. Her eyes were no longer red-rimmed as they had been earlier in the day.

"Mamá, you've been crying," Maria had told her mother this morning as they had sat across from each other at the breakfast table. "It's because of me and Steven getting married, isn't it?"

"I'm trying to accept it, Maria. But it's hard for me and your father."

"Please, please, this will work out. Steven is wonderful. We love each other."

"But he is a Jew and our grandchildren will be Jewish," his wife sighed.

"I don't understand, especially from you, Mamá. You always said prejudice was bad. We must look at who a person is, not how they look, not their religion."

"Maria," her mother said in a calm voice. "Surely you understand the difference between having prejudice as you call it and marrying outside of your faith."

"We've gone over and over this. The wedding can't happen for almost a year because I need to complete my conversion classes and by then you will have grown to accept it."

Andreas had hoped this morning would be the last of the disagreements they would have about this.

And now this afternoon it was time for the first meeting of the two families. His wife rose from the couch.

"Maria, be sure and check the Tribune tomorrow morning," his wife told their daughter. "We must cut out the speech Dr. King gave today. I'll put it in our scrap book. Your brothers at Boy Scout camp need to read it for themselves when they come home next week. And I don't know what access your brother Elias has to American news while he's backpacking through Europe. Maria, put out the cheese and crackers. And I made some *melitzanosalata*. You said they might like my eggplant dip."

"Steven loves it," Maria replied. "You did buy a different cheese than feta, didn't you? I'm so glad you made both Greek and American dishes. I don't want them to feel overwhelmed with all our traditional foods."

"You don't want us to embarrass you with our strange foods?"

"Mamá, Mamá." Maria grabbed her hands. "I didn't say that. You know I love your cooking and Steven likes it. But his parents have never tasted any Greek food."

"And if they don't like my *spanakopita*, they'll want to call off the wedding?"

"Do you want us to call off the wedding?" Maria asked in exasperation.

"Maria and Katerina." Andreas got to his feet and put his hands on his wife's shoulders. "You both need to calm down. We have been over this. Family means everything. There will be no strife about this." He bent down and kissed his wife on the cheek. She gave him a small smile. He knew how hard this was for her. But she was such a strong woman, and she would do what was right.

"Come Maria, we need to put out the appetizers. It's time for them to arrive," said his wife.

As Maria set out the cheese and crackers, the doorbell rang. "I'll get it!" Maria called out.

"I shall go to the door. It's my house." Andreas got to his feet. This is going to work out, he told himself, no matter how great the differences between the two families. Two different religions, even the difference in the education levels of the mothers. Mrs. Strauss had a Ph.D. from the

University of Chicago. Growing up in Greece, his wife had no formal education. Two years ago she earned her GED. And now she had just completed two years at the university.

Other Greek Orthodox families in their church told him they would disown their child for marrying outside their faith. But not in his family. After witnessing the massacre of his entire family by the Turks when he was a child, he would never let anything tear his family apart.

Steven and his parents entered the foyer. Andreas smiled at them and shook their hands in greeting. "Welcome, welcome. We are so glad to have you in our home at last."

Steven warmly greeted them and gave Maria a hug and kiss.

Dinner was a stiff affair. The Strausses stoically tasted all the dishes his wife and Maria had so lovingly prepared; cooking and baking for days. Their faces lit up when the "American" foods, hamburgers and hot dogs, were served. There were a few more relaxed moments when Andreas discussed his work as a doctor at the free clinic and Steven's father expressed an interest in offering his services as an attorney.

When dinner was over, Andreas knew there would be the tense discussion of the wedding. He vowed to do his best to be agreeable for the sake of his daughter. No beautiful church, no placement of the wedding crowns, no candles, no priest. But he and his wife would have to accept it.

"There," said Maria. "Mamá and I baked the *baklava* especially for you." She placed a diamond-shaped triangle with a clove in the center of each dessert plate.

"This *baklava* is quite tasty." Mr. Strauss cleared his throat and put down his fork. "Well, it's time to discuss the wedding. Of course, it is tradition for the bride's family to pay for the wedding. But in this case, Dr. Sefaris..."

"Please call me Drew," Andreas interjected.

"And you should call us Leonard and Estelle, please."

"Yes, of course," Andreas agreed.

"Drew," he paused, "Estelle and I think under these circumstances, we should pay for the wedding."

"Katerina and I appreciate your generous offer. But I must pay for the wedding of my only daughter."

"But it will be a Jewish wedding."

"We understand that. Maria is our only daughter and we will pay for her wedding."

"That is quite magnanimous of you." Estelle smiled at them. "Do you have much family? We have quite a large family and many friends, so it will be a fairly big wedding."

"We have a very small family," Maria spoke up.

"Is your family still in Greece? Perhaps if they have enough notice, they'll be able to come over?" Estelle suggested.

"We have some relatives here in America, a small number. The parents who adopted me in Greece have passed away, may their memory be eternal. My family from Asia Minor is all gone," said Andreas.

"Asia Minor? Isn't that Turkey? You're Turkish? Maria said you were Greek. You're Turks?"

"We are not Turks!" Andreas spat out the words. "My family was slaughtered by the Turks. We are Greek Orthodox. I was born in Smyrna. As a boy, I witnessed my whole family murdered before my eyes. By the grace of God I escaped. We Greeks had lived in Smyrna for hundreds of years before the Turkish army galloped into our city and burned it to the ground."

"Dad," Steven spoke up. "I told you Maria's parents and I have talked long into the night about the evils of prejudice, and why both of them feel so strongly about defending the rights of everyone. They lost all of their families to prejudice and hate."

Andreas's wife was frowning at him. Yes, he knew he had to contain his temper. But to be called a Turk, the worst insult in the world!

"Andreas, I had no idea about your history and of course," Leonard continued, "you know about the fate of the Jews in WWII. The Germans came after the Jews in Germany, France, and Poland."

"And the Jews of Greece as well," Andreas said.

"Greece? I'm afraid you're mistaken Andreas. There were no Jews in Greece. Of course, as a Christian I wouldn't expect you to know about such things."

His wife suddenly leaned across the table, her eyes wide. "No, Mr. Strauss, it is you who are mistaken. There were over 60,000 Jews in Greece before the war."

"Katerina, I am a student of the Holocaust and I can assure you, your information is false. I don't know where you heard such a ridiculous thing. Greek Jews, really?"

Andreas's wife looked over at him. Andreas nodded at her. It was time to step out from the shadows of the past that had been hidden for all these years.

"Leonard and Estelle, my daughter Maria and your son do not have to wait for a year to marry," his wife spoke slowly.

"But of course they do."

"No, they don't. Maria doesn't have to take conversion classes. She is a Jew because I am a Jew. I was born Rebecca Solomon, daughter of Isaac and Esther Solomon. According to Jewish law, any child born of a Jewish mother is a Jew."

CHAPTER 2

Smyrna, Anatolia, Asia Minor: September 3, 1922
Three warships, the British battleships, Iron Duke and King George
V; and the French battleship, Waldeck Rousseau, are all anchored in
Smyrna's harbor.

"SORRY! SORRY I'M late!" The eight-year-old boy ran into his father's study, tossing his school books on a nearby chair.

"Andreas," his father was using his stern voice. "You were in trouble again and had to stay after school?"

"I'm sorry." Andreas looked down at his shoes. He didn't like to disappoint his father.

"Andreas." His mother entered the room holding his baby sister in her arms. "Your father told me that your teacher called to talk about you..."

"I'm sorry," Andreas repeated, trying his best to sound remorseful. Baby Lina reached out her chubby arms to him in delight and Andreas had to stop himself from picking her up. His father wouldn't be happy if Andreas didn't finish explaining what happened at school.

"You are in trouble again." He heard the voice of his sister Maria who was standing next to the new telescope. The new telescope! He wanted to run up to the new telescope and peer at all the wonderful things he could see. At the same time he wanted to kick his twelve-year-old sister in the shins. Just because she was older, she thought she could boss him and he hated that.

"Maria." His father arched a brow in disapproval. "You're not part of this conversation."

"Yes, Patéra," Maria demurred and slid her fingers into a nearby bowl of sultanas. She popped some into her mouth and made a face at her brother.

Andreas was always starving after school. Sultanas from Smyrna were the best in all the world, so sweet. But he knew first he needed to focus his attention on this unpleasant conversation with his father.

"Andreas," his father continued, "your teacher told me you were fighting with Aeolos again."

"It wasn't my fault! Aeolos pushed me down and said I was stupid. And he said I would always be little and never be big like he is."

"And so you hit him? Fighting doesn't solve anything. You know you aren't stupid. Kìrios Thomopoulos told me you are first in your class. And I told you I was also small at your age and now I'm a very tall man."

I don't believe it, thought Andreas. I'm never going to be as big as the rest of the boys in my class. "I know," Andreas tried to sound agreeable as his eyes turned toward the new telescope. "I'll be good. I promise."

"No more fighting?"

"No more fighting, I promise."

"A man is only as good as his word. Always remember that. Now this morning I told you I had a surprise for you."

I know what it is, thought Andreas, as he eyed the new telescope.

"The new telescope has arrived and it's quite wonderful. Come *pitsirikos,* my son, take a look." His father placed a wooden box on the floor.

Andreas hurried up onto the box and eagerly peered through the telescope. "Look at all those ships!" he shouted with excitement. "Why are there so many ships in the harbor today?"

"They have sailed here from all over the world."

"Someday I'm going to be a captain of a big ship just like that. I'll sail all over the world and I'll take our whole family."

"After you have finished your studies at the university and come into the family business with me?" His father smiled at him.

"I'll be a sea captain and help run the family business," Andreas told his father.

"Yes, of course." His father's fingers ruffled his hair. "That's why you must not complain about your Turkish lessons. So someday you will be able to conduct business all over the Mediterranean as my representative."

"Now come, Daphne." His father motioned toward his wife. "Come see all the ships in our harbor."

His mother handed Baby Lina to Maria and peered into the scope. "Are you sure they will keep us safe?"

"Of course I'm sure. These are the ships of the world's greatest powers. We helped the Allies during the war. And now the presence of England, America, Italy and France in our waters will keep the Turks from hurting us. You mustn't worry. I will always protect our family. Andreas and I are the men of this family and, of course, we will be your protectors. Right, Andreas?"

"Yes, Patéra," he answered. He wanted to look through the scope again, but his mother was still standing there.

"All those Greek soldiers walking past our house....where do they come from?" she asked as she left the telescope and Andreas climbed back up on the box. How he loved watching the ships.

"The Greek soldiers are leaving the countryside because of the Turkish cavalry. What happens on the farms, in the countryside, has nothing to do with us here in our great city. Daphne, tonight we will go for a promenade after dinner." His father kissed his wife on her cheek. "You'll wear that beautiful new hat and your lavender dress I'm especially fond of."

"I'm going to take my new parasol!" Maria gushed with excitement.

"We'll get tickets for the cinema. I hear the new picture show is quite good," his father told them.

September 5, 1922

Andreas sat high up on a limb of the stout tree in his backyard; his best friend Petros was beside him, their legs dangling down over the garden. It was a very hot day and this afternoon it was cooler here than inside the house.

"I didn't see Alec in school last week," Andreas commented.

"Haven't you heard? His whole family left Smyrna."

"Left? My father says we're safe. There are more warships in the harbor every day. They are guarding us."

"It must have been his mother, Kiría Tziovas. She must have been afraid. Women are like that, you know, and his father, Kìrios Tziovas, listened to her. So they left."

"When will they be back?"

"In a couple of weeks. I don't know."

"Well, I hope he comes back soon. He's the best at stick ball."

"I know," Petros agreed. "Look, look over there. It's a water buffalo." He pointed toward the large animal plodding next to the masses of people streaming down the street. "I wonder when all those people will go back to their own homes and stop clogging up the streets of our city."

"My Patéra says they are called refugees." Andreas looked down and across the backyard as the long line of women with children, old men, cows, sheep, goats and Greek soldiers riding on donkeys and camels made their way down the street. They didn't look like anyone Andreas had ever seen before. They all looked so sad. He wondered if refugees were another word for poor people. "There are only old men with the women and children. I wonder where all the other men are? The only younger men are the soldiers."

"I don't know, Andreas. It's really hot. Can we climb down and go into the kitchen for some lemonade and *melomakaronas*? Your maid Sophia makes the best *melomakaronas*."

"Sure." Andreas jumped down. "I'll race you."

⚭

Petros had gone home and Andreas was sitting at the kitchen table, nibbling on the last few cookies. Sophia, with her gray hair and kindly face, was bent toward him. "Do you want some more lemonade?" she asked him.

"No, thank you." He smiled at the maid. She was always so nice to him, as if he were her son. She told him once that she never had any children of her own and that in her heart, he and his sisters were like her own son and daughters. Sophia left the kitchen and he remained at the kitchen table.

It was time to do his school work, but he wanted to delay going up to his room. Yes, he was a good student, but he'd rather be looking through the telescope in his father's study. Anyway, because school was closed there was no hurry to finish his school work. He decided he needed to make sure his father knew that the Tziovas family had left Smyrna. Kìrios Tziovas was a good friend of Patéra, so he needed to know. That would both delay him going to do school work and give him a chance to enter the study and look through the telescope. Andreas wiped his hands on his pants instead of his napkin. After all, no one was looking.

He bounded down the hallway to his father's study and knocked on the door.

"Who is it?" his father asked.

"Andreas."

"Come in, son, and close the door behind you."

Andreas walked into the study, eager to count the number of warships in the harbor and hear his father name each ship and its country. He closed the door and started toward the telescope when he stopped in mid step. His eyes widened at what he saw on his father's desk. A gun!

"Patéra, you have a gun! Can I hold it?" Andreas was breathless with excitement.

"I'll let you hold it, if you promise to be very careful. Guns were given to all the Greeks by the Asia Minor Defense League.

"Yes, Patéra. I promise to be careful," he said solemnly, trying not to show how excited he was.

"Here." His father placed the cold metal in his hand.

"Can I shoot it?"

"No, you cannot. But see, this is the trigger and if I must shoot, I pull on this." His father showed him the trigger and then took the gun away from him.

"Why did the League give you a gun?" Andreas asked. Maybe he'd be a soldier when he grew up. Not a soldier like the men dressed in rags, who were trudging through the streets in front of his house. But he'd have a wonderful uniform with a sword and a gun. "Are you going to shoot someone? Those refugee people, are you going to shoot them? Is that why the League gave you a gun?"

"No, I'm not going to shoot a refugee. The gun is just for protection. But we needn't worry. If there's a problem, I've been given papers from the American Consulate for all of us. The papers will guarantee us safe passage out of the city."

"I came to tell you that the Tziovas family left. Did you know that?" I guess, Andreas thought, they didn't get a gun because they were already gone. His friend Kristos would have loved to see a gun and hold it.

"Yes, I know the Tziovas family left. They didn't own any businesses like we do. If a man leaves, his businesses are declared abandoned and the government takes them over. Anyway, we have nothing to fear. In case the Turkish Cavalry does enter our city, I have all my military medals. They are proof of my service and loyalty to the Ottoman Army." He pointed to them, arranged on the desk top. "When I go outside, I will pin them to my suit and I will wear a fez. That will show my loyalty to the Turks."

"The Turks? They live in the Turkish quarter, just like the Greeks live in the Greek quarter, and the Armenians and Jews live in their quarters." Andreas frowned. This was all too confusing to him, and he just wanted to look through the telescope.

"I'm speaking of Turkish soldiers, not our fellow Turkish citizens."

"Patéra, please let's look through the telescope again."

When Andreas had tired of looking at the ships and was about to leave the study, his father stopped him. "Andreas, as the other man in our family, can I count on you to keep this secret about my having the gun? Your Mamá would find it too upsetting."

"Of course," Andreas promised solemnly, his eyes looking at the gun with longing. He wanted to hold it again, but he sensed his father wouldn't be agreeable to that. Maybe later today.

Andreas closed the door and walked down the hallway towards his room. He hesitated as he walked past Maria's room. His father said not to tell Mamá about the gun, but he didn't say not to tell his sister. He needed to tell someone about something so exciting.

"Maria." He walked into her room.

"Andreas! How many times do I have to tell you that you need to knock first. I'm twelve years old now." She put down the fashion magazine she had been holding in her hands.

"You're supposed to be doing homework, not looking at a magazine. No wonder your grades are so bad."

"Is that why you came barging in here, to spy on me?" Maria stuck out her tongue at him.

"Patéra has a gun!" he announced as he plopped down on her bed.

"A gun!" Her dark eyes widened.

"He showed it to me because, of course, I am the only other man in the family. It's for our protection. He let me hold it! But you mustn't tell anyone. Patéra said not to tell Mamá. She would worry. But I did have to tell you, big sister." He smiled at her. Maria could be so maddening. But he loved his big sister, even though she was changing since she'd gotten older and wasn't as much fun anymore. "And Patéra pulled out his medals from the army and the fez hat like the Turks wear."

"Why did he do that?"

"So we will be safe." He tried to recall what his father had said.

"His medals and a fez hat will keep us safe? From what?"

"The Turks," he announced.

"The Turks live on the other side of town. I don't understand."

"Don't worry. Patéra and I will take care of everything." He started to jump up and down on her bed.

"Andreas." She laughed. "You are such a child." She jumped up next to him and pushed him over.

September 8, 1922
Twenty-seven warships in the harbor.

School was suspended because of the presence of all the refugees and Greek soldiers trudging through the streets. Andreas was annoyed that he wasn't able to see his friends and had to stay in the house. It was so hot. He longed to go swimming, but he had not been permitted outside with the "dangerous elements," as his mother had called them.

The family was assembled around the dining table, awaiting the presence of his father before they began eating the lunch that Sophia had prepared. Patéra's step was heavy, his expression worn and tired when he entered the room and Andreas sensed something was wrong.

"Elias?" his mother asked with concern.

His father wearily sank down into his chair, holding a binder in his hands. He slapped the binder down on the table. "Worthless!" he declared. "Absolutely worthless!"

"What happened?"

"I went to see my Turkish friend Badem in his shop this morning. I wanted to pay him for the goods he had sent me last week. The Turkish quarter was bustling with people and everyone was in such good spirits, celebrating, dancing and singing. Badem took me into his back room and told me we must flee the city. The Turkish Army was coming and it wouldn't be safe for the Greeks. He has always been my good friend and he was adamant that for our own safety, we must go. I was quite taken aback and I didn't know what to think. I had read in the paper this morning that there was going to be a negotiated peace between the Turkish Army and our government in Smyrna.

"I went to see Horton at the American Consulate. I waited and waited and was treated as if I was a nobody, as if I wasn't Elias Sefaris, a good friend of Horton. I finally got in to see him and asked what he thought about the situation. He said he really didn't know, but hoped for the best. He believed the Turkish army would enter the city in a peaceful manner, so that the world would see they are a civilized nation. He mentioned the United States Marines had landed to safeguard American property, just in case. I didn't find that reassuring, and I showed him the papers he had given me last week. I asked for additional papers for Sophia which would also provide safe passage on one of the ships if need be.

"I'm sorry," he said. "I'm sorry, but the papers I gave you won't provide space on an American warship. We are under orders to maintain neutrality. We can't offend the Turks, especially their leader, Kemal Mustafa. I'm sorry, Elias. Neutrality is for the greater good of everyone." Patéra took a swallow of his glass of wine. "I do believe he is probably right. The Turks want to present a good civilized side to the world. But if Horton is wrong, I want those papers for our safe passage."

"What will we do?" his mother asked.

"Nothing. We will be fine. There will be a negotiated peace. This is our fine house, one of the finest in the city. We will stay here where we belong. My rug and tobacco businesses are the best in Smyrna. This is our home, Daphne. This is our home."

"Yes, Elias," his mother said and nodded at her husband.

Andreas reached for a piece of bread. He wanted to ask when those refugee people were going to stop filling the streets so he could go back to school and see his friends. But he sensed it was better to remain silent as his father seemed very agitated.

September 9, 1922

The Turkish army had arrived…. sabers gleaming, red fezzes on their heads with silver crescents, forcing the Greek soldiers to shout "long live Kemal." There was no school. No one was allowed to go outside. The doors were locked.

As they gathered around the dinner table, there was a loud pounding on the door. Who was that? Andreas watched his parents exchange worried glances. His father slowly got to his feet and walked to the door as the pounding continued. "Elias!" They heard. "Let us in. It's Khederlarian!"

Patéra opened the door to reveal a large family with five children and two grandparents. Andreas recognized the man as the Armenian with whom his father did business.

"Please, may we stay here? The Turks have arrived, and they are looting the houses and killing people!" The family hurried inside and Patéra bolted the door behind them.

Killing people, thought Andreas. He had heard that the Turks didn't like Armenians. But to kill them…. what had the Armenians done? He was glad he wasn't an Armenian.

His father invited them in and his mother instructed Sophia to provide a fine meal for them.

Andreas looked at the family: a mother, father, four children and grandparents. They all looked so unhappy. No one was smiling and the baby was crying.

After everyone had eaten, the father of the family and his father left the table, went into the study and closed the door.

And now it was nighttime and Andreas was lying down, sharing his bed with the Armenian boy. His name was Hayk and he was twelve years old.

"I'm only twelve even though I look older. My father said I mustn't forget to say I'm only twelve."

"Why? It must be fun to say you are older. I'm small. So everyone thinks I'm younger and I hate it."

"You don't have to worry. You're lucky."

"Lucky?" Andreas peered out into the darkness of his room. The windows had been shuttered even though it was so hot.

"They are taking men and boys between fourteen and forty-five years old."

"Taking? Who is taking men and boys?"

"The Turks. They are rounding up the men and boys and taking them away to the desert. The cavalry galloped down our streets and killed people. Everyone tried to lock their doors, but some of the soldiers broke down the doors. They threw everything out of the stores into the street," the boy spoke without taking a breath.

Andreas wished the boy would stop talking. He felt sorry for the poor Armenians. They must have done something really terrible for the Turks to be punishing them. He was glad his family was Greek and not Armenian..

"My father made my sisters hide in the cellar."

"You said they were taking away men and boys. Why did your sisters have to hide?"

"They were taking girls to defile them!"

"Defile them?"

"You're still a boy, so you probably don't understand."

"I understand." At least, he thought he did. His friend Stathis told him some things about men and women and what you could do if your father took you to a house where bad women lived. "Well, your family is safe with us. We're Greek and the Turks don't hate us. My father does business with the Turks."

"They are going after Greeks too. While we were running through the streets, we saw the Turks point their guns at a Greek man. They made him give them his clothes and shoes."

"He gave them his clothes and shoes?" Andreas felt his heart begin to pound.

"Yes, he did, and then they shot him in the head! There was blood all over!"

Stop! Andreas wanted to shout. Stop! I don't want to hear anymore. "I think we should go to sleep," Andreas murmured, closing his eyes.

The boy kept silent, but Andreas thought he heard him crying into his pillow.

I am safe, Andreas told himself, over and over. My family is safe. Patéra has his red fez hat and his medals. We are safe, he repeated to himself over and over again. But he couldn't erase the image of the man taking off his clothes and being shot in the head. Yesterday, he was so unhappy that his school was closed and he had to stay indoors. It was brutally hot and he longed to at least go outside into the garden. But tonight he didn't care if he had to stay inside. He was safe inside. His family was safe. His father had his fez and his medals and his gun.

And then the Armenian boy started talking again. Please stop! Andreas put his hands over his ears, but the image of the naked man being shot was still playing in his mind.

The next morning, Andreas pretended to be asleep when the boy stirred and dressed. Andreas heard the door close and he sat up in bed. There were sounds outside in the street coming through the shuttered windows.

Andreas dressed and made his way to the dining room as his father's voice echoed down the hallway.

"Andreas." His mother smiled at him. "You're a late sleeper this morning."

"Yes, Mamá." He kissed her cheek and took his seat at the table, which was now shared with the Armenian family: the grandparents, the baby, the parents, the boy who shared his bed and the three girls who had slept in Maria's room.

Andreas sat quietly, barely touching the food on his plate. Sophia had cleared away the dishes when his father pushed back from the table and cleared his throat. "Armen, you and your family are welcome to stay as long as you want, until it is safe for you to leave."

"Elias, no one is safe. We saw many Greeks being slaughtered on the streets. The soldiers started in the Armenian quarter, but that is just the beginning. My people fled to the churches for sanctuary. But the grounds could only hold so many. No place is safe in Smyrna. We are going to get on one of those ships in the harbor."

"But," his father began.

"I know, I know. I heard the same thing. They want to maintain their neutrality. But that was before the slaughter by the *cerrete* began."

"*Cerrete?*" his mother spoke up.

"Irregulars. They were actually prisoners, low lifes who were released from the prisons and encouraged to create mayhem in our streets. The Great Powers won't sit idly by while we are being brutalized by the Turks."

Patéra was silent.

"We will gather up our things and be gone. Thank you, Kìrios Elias. My family thanks you. Please, you all must go. No one is safe. You have always been such a dreamer, Elias. Even our Turkish brethren, who lived side by side with us, took to the streets looting and worse. We saw many Greeks and Armenians accused of collaborating with the government being executed. The members of the Asia Minor Refuge League are being hunted down like animals."

"Our city has always been a jewel of toleration," his father sighed. "Turks, Jews, Armenians, Greek Orthodox. We've always lived together as brothers in harmony. Everyone will come to their senses, you'll see."

"You always believe in the goodness of others. But this is no time for such grandiose ideas."

"I understand you've made up your mind." Patéra took a swallow of his coffee. "I will tell Sophia to make up food bundles for you and your family to take with you."

Andreas took a spoonful of his yogurt. He knew his father understood everything. He was so smart. How lucky to have a father so brave, so smart. Andreas's appetite had returned. He was sure that soon he'd be permitted to go outside. Maybe today. Otherwise, he'd have to convince Maria to pay a game of *pentóvola* with him. When they were younger, he'd agreed to play with her dolls, but he was too old for that now. After all, he was eight years old.

September 13, 1922

Maria was the first to see it. Andreas was in the parlor, gathering up the small stones from their game of *pentóvola*.

She had opened the shutters, hoping for a breath of fresh air. She pointed her finger at the distant horizon. "Look at the sky. It's all black and smoky over there."

"Where is that? Is that smoke? Is there a fire?" Andreas wondered. "Let's go ask Patéra." Andreas and Maria ran into the dining room where his parents and Baby Lina were finishing their lunch. Sophia was standing before their father and shaking her head as she frowned and spewed forth a rush of words. Maria and Andreas waited patiently. It would be impolite to interrupt her. They both loved Sophia, who had worked for their family since before they were born. Not only did she run the household and kitchen, she'd helped take care of them when they were young.

"Kìrios Sefaris, I can bake bread and make one more batch of cookies for dinner," Sophia was saying. "But then I have no more flour. I just came back from shopping and learned all the bakeries are closed, every single one of them. And this morning, the water has stopped coming out of the faucets. I ran next door and they told me for sure it was the Turks who turned off the water supply and closed the bakeries."

"We will manage, Sophia," his mother said in a reassuring voice.

"I'm sure it's just temporarily," his father told her. "Soon the Turkish army will restore order. You'll see."

"Please, take the baby." His mother handed her sleeping daughter to Sophia.

Sophia smiled at the sleeping child with a handful of soft curls, as she cradled her in her arms. "I'll put her down." Sophia left the room.

"Elias, I'm worried," Mamá said in a calm voice.

"Patéra," Andreas burst out with his news. "Mamá! Look at the sky!"

His father pushed away from the table and walked to the window, opening the shutters. "That's the Armenian Quarter and that's smoke. It must be a terrible fire to produce so much smoke. I'm going out to find out what's going on."

"Elias, please be careful," his mother beseeched him.

"I will wear my fez hat and my medals. I speak impeccable Turkish. There's no need for worry."

Andreas noticed a bulge under his father's vest. Was that his gun, he wondered?

The day grew hotter and hotter and the wind shifted. "It's now blowing all that hot air from the desert," Sophia told him and Maria as they sat in the kitchen eating some fruit.

"I wish it would stop," Maria complained. "It's too hot and we can't go outside and I can't see my friends and there's no water from the faucet. Patéra keeps saying that soon this terrible time will be over. When? When? I'm really not happy."

"No one is happy, Maria. We all must have patience." Sophia wiped off the kitchen counter.

⋘⋙

September 14, 1922

Maria and Andreas spent the morning entertaining their baby sister, making her laugh and giggle with delight.

Patéra had gone out again, against Mamá's protests. When he returned, he pulled his fez off his head and threw it on the floor. "I need a drink, Daphne. Have one of the servants go down to the wine cellar and bring up our finest wine."

"The servants are all gone, except for Sophia. They left this morning to go back to their families."

"Just as well," he sighed. "The smaller our household, the easier it will be to protect."

"I'll have Sophia bring up our wine. Our finest wine that we save for special occasions?"

"If we have to evacuate, we shall have to leave our wine behind, won't we? Daphne, Daphne, what a day I have had. The people and their priests went to the American Consulate, begging for protection. They were sent away! Can you imagine? The Americans sent them away. There were some women who had cut strips of white, red, and blue cloths for their children to wear, hoping, praying their children would receive pity and sanctuary. But no. I could see the faces of the Marines guarding the Consulate. They weren't without compassion, but they had no choice than to follow orders.

"I saw every business and personal connection I've had for years: Italians, Brits, French, Americans, the tobacco corporations, the rug merchants. Our friendship got me in the door, past the mobs. I had an audience. I was told how fortunate I was to have an audience. But the answer was no, always no. Only their American citizens would have safe passage. No passage out of the country for our family and Sophia. It wasn't a matter of price. Orders had come down from above. Neutrality must be maintained for the sake of world order. Only their citizens will have passage out of the city. They are afraid, Daphne. Afraid of the Young Turk, Kemal Mustafa."

Andreas looked down at the fez on the floor. Did it have magical powers that kept his father safe each time he went out into the crowds of people who filled their streets?

"Did you learn more about the fire, Elias?" his mother asked as she poured the wine into a glass for his father.

"Yes, the fire started somewhere in the Armenian quarter and then the Turkish soldiers helped it along by splashing gasoline and kerosene on the buildings and pouring it down the streets. Many claim it was the Turks who started the fire in the beginning."

"Why would they do such a thing?" His mother gasped. "And with the water turned off, how can the fire be stopped?"

"Yes, indeed. How can the fire be stopped?" his father spat out his words.

After dinner, Andreas stood beside his father, the telescope pointed toward the fire that filled the horizon with thick black smoke. His sisters and mother had gone to their rooms and Patéra had promised Andreas another game on the backgammon board. "I think it is getting worse, Patéra." Andreas watched the orange glow in the black smoke.

"It is, Andreas. It is. My little *pitsirikas*, you are a smart boy and a boy of courage. You have always made me proud. I fear there will be trying times ahead for the Greeks of Smyrna. But you and I will not waiver in our courage, will we? You must remember to always be brave and have courage."

"Patéra. I am very brave."

"Of course you are. After all, you are my son." His father enveloped him in a huge hug.

"How long will the fire burn in the Armenian quarter?"

"I don't know. But I think there will be nothing left of it. Those poor Armenians will have no homes or businesses to return to."

September 15, 1922

The fire that started in the Armenian quarter had now spread, engulfing street after street. It was now in portions of the Greek quarter, burning house after house, causing more and more desperate people to flee towards the harbor. The residents of Smyrna joined the refugees from the countryside on the quay.

Andreas and Maria had played another game of *pentóvola* in the parlor. It was so oppressive and hot with the shutters closed, They could still hear the retreating Greek soldiers straggling down the street, being forced by the Turkish cavalry to chant "Long Live Kemal."

This morning, Andreas had seen his father gathering drachmas and gold to give the Turkish soldiers in case they came to their door. Patéra explained that the fire was spreading through the Armenian and Greek quarters, but shouldn't enter their area on the northern end of the quay where their house stood. He told them the drachmas he would pay to the soldiers would keep them safe until order was restored.

There was a pounding on the door and when their father hurried to the front door, Andreas and Maria ran into the shadows of the hall to watch.

"I'm coming. I'm coming." Patéra threw open the door to the giant of a man in a Turkish uniform.

"This house is mine!" The soldier roughly pushed his father out of the way. "You need to get out!"

"Please sir. Be reasonable. I have gold to give you. I'll go to the bank and get you more. This is my house. The house of Sefaris for generations. I'm not leaving."

"We have already taken over your banks, ignorant infidel." The soldier raised his fist and smashed it into his father's face.

Maria gasped and let go of Andreas's hand. She ran across the hall. He knew she was off to find Mamá. The soldier looked up as Maria sprinted out the doorway.

"A pretty one, isn't she?" He grinned.

"Please sir." His father caught his breath. "I have gold, drachmas…"

Andreas watched his father's fingers start to move up toward his vest. He's going to get his gun, thought Andreas. Yes, Patéra, get your gun and shoot this horrible man.

"Your gold, your drachmas and your house and that pretty little infidel. It all belongs to me and the Turkish cavalry."

"Please!" his father begged.

"Enough of you!" the soldier thundered. He suddenly drew his sword and thrust it deep into Patéra's chest. He pulled it out and wiped it on his pant leg. Andreas saw the horror and look of shock in his father's dark eyes as he crumbled to the floor.

"Baba!" Andreas cried out the childhood name for his father as he ran to his side. "Baba!" The tears filled his eyes.

"Where did that girl run off to?" the soldier yelled and then stepped over his father's body.

"Elias!" Andreas heard the sound of his mother's scream as she and Maria ran into the room.

There was blood seeping out of his father's chest as his father's eyes fixed on Andreas's face. "Be brave, my son," he whispered and then his eyes turned sightless.

"Elias!" his mother shrieked from the opposite end of the hallway while sheltering Maria behind her.

"Well, aren't I a man of good fortune," the soldier laughed. "First, I'll take the little girl and I'll make her mother watch. When I'm done with her, I'll do the mother and kill you both, slitting your throats from ear to ear!" He ran his finger across his neck.

The soldier grabbed Maria from behind Mamá. His fingers ripped open Maria's dress.

"No, please!" his mother cried out. "She is but a child!" she sobbed.

Andreas continued to crouch beside his father's body. His hand moved up his father's blood sodden chest to his vest. Andreas's fingers reached beneath the vest until he felt the steel of the gun.

"Shut up!" The soldier struck his mother across her face.

Andreas grabbed the gun and put his fingers around it like Patéra had shown him. The soldier was unbuttoning his pants, his eyes fastened on Maria, who was screaming in terror.

Quietly Andreas got to his feet and crept behind the soldier. He took a deep breath, aiming the gun high towards the soldier's upper back. He took another deep breath, willing his hands to stop shaking and he squeezed the trigger. It was so loud. The soldier whirled around, a look of surprise on his face. Andreas pulled the trigger again and again, pointing it up toward the soldier's chest until all the bullets were gone.

CHAPTER 3

"BUT," MARIA SOBBED. "Why are we going? What will we do without Patéra?"

"We shall be fine." Their mother took a deep breath as she tied the tablecloth together into a bundle that she hoisted onto her shoulder. "I'll take care of us."

"Mamá, you are a woman," Andreas said in a quiet voice…. the images of his father on the floor and the soldier covered with blood swirling through his mind.

"Yes, Andreas, I am a woman." Mamá gave him a weak smile. "But a woman can be strong if she needs to be. And now, without your Patéra, I will make the decisions, and you will all listen."

"Of course, Kiría Daphne," Sophia demurred, holding her small bundle with one hand and Baby Lina in the other.

"Why do we have to go?" Maria's voice quivered as they opened the front door.

"Another soldier will come to our door. The Turkish army will take over our house. Someone will find the dead Turk. We can't stay here." Mamá closed the door behind them and turned the key in the lock.

"Patéra…. He is still in the house." Andreas fought back tears as he held onto his small bundle of possessions.

"We must go. Each of you hold tight to your things. Maria, Andreas, hold my hands so we aren't separated." His mother ignored his words. Averting her gaze from the lifeless bodies that littered the streets, Mamá pushed them to join the throngs of fleeing refugees.

"What's that noise?" Maria asked as they all fought to stay together in the surging crowd.

Andreas heard it too, loud horrible squeaking, or was it shrieking?

"Rats," Sophia told them. "Look down at the street. The rats are running from the fire."

"Rats!" Maria exclaimed.

"Maria, Andreas, pay attention and hold on to my hands," his mother said sternly.

Andreas did as his mother told them. Masses of women and children pushed at them. The crowd carried them along, pressing in from all sides. There was a sudden scream of terror. "Get out of the way! Run! Hurry! A horse!" Everyone tried to flee out of the way of a riderless horse that was galloping full speed down the street, trampling young children and the elderly who couldn't flee fast enough.

"Keep going!" Mamá pulled them back into the street after the horse had passed.

"Where are we going?" Maria gripped Andreas's hand.

"To the quay," Andreas repeated what his mother had told them. "The quay where everyone else is going." Andreas was forced to step over the body of a small child that had been trampled by the horse. He couldn't stop to help. No one stopped to help. As Andreas looked down at the cobblestone street, anxious to avoid any other trampled bodies, he noticed for the first time, his shoes and pants were stained with blood. Patéra, Patéra, the voice screamed inside his hand. My Patéra, my Baba…. No, no, he told himself, banishing the vision of his father's lifeless body and the sounds of the gun he had fired, pulling the trigger over and over again. He must do as his mother said. Hold on to each other; follow the crowd to the quay. Be brave, his father had said. Have courage.

Andreas was anxious to reach the quay where the ships were anchored. His Mamá was right. They must hurry to where the boats would take them to safety until the Turkish army left. Then they could go back to their house and their life. But again, he saw his father's body on the floor. Would his Patéra still be laying there when they returned? Andreas knew once they reached the quay, they would be able to get on one of those warships that he had watched through his telescope. The Armenian family was already on one of those ships. Soon they, too, would be safe and away from these crowds.

Suddenly, the crowd in front of them came to a stop and rushed to the right. "Fire!" someone yelled. "The fire is coming down this street!"

Mamá held tightly to their hands and pulled them down another street. Sophia ran beside them, clutching Baby Lina against her chest.

They continued to fight to stay together through the pushing and shoving crowd. They finally reached the area of the quay nearest the ships anchored in the harbor. He heard his mother gasp as they all looked up. As far as the eye could see were women, children, old men sprawled next to their bundles... bundles just like the ones they carried.

"How many people are here?" Andreas asked. Were they all going to get on the boats, just like we were, he wondered? Were there enough ships?

"Thousands." His mother caught her breath. "Come, we must find a good place for ourselves," Mamá said with a firm determination in her voice. Andreas had never heard that tone before from his soft-spoken mother. Perhaps a woman could be strong. Mamá would know what to do. She would find out how to get to those ships.

"When will we board a ship, Mamá?" he asked.

"Soon. I will find out how we board," she answered.

"I don't know how to swim," Maria said with a catch in her voice. "How will I get to a ship if I can't swim?"

"Small boats will come to pick us up, Maria. Don't worry." Andreas had seen small boats going back and forth to the ships in the harbor when he peered through the telescope.

But after they squeezed into a place for themselves and Mamá spoke to those around them, they heard the awful truth. No boats were coming to take anyone to the ships.

"What if someone swims out to a ship?" Andreas asked an old man leaning on a cane, who sat beside them. Andreas was a good swimmer. He knew he could swim that far easily. He'd get to a ship and ask them to send a small boat for his family.

"Many men have tried and drowned," the old man said impatiently.

"But I'm a good swimmer," Andreas protested.

"You are a stupid boy. Don't bother me anymore. Those men who make it to the boats aren't permitted to board. They throw hot water on them. They push them back into the sea. Other men who try to swim to the boats are shot by the Turks. Go sit by your mother, boy. You're not going anywhere." The old man turned his back to him.

◦◦◦◦◦

On the quay Smyrna: September 18, 1922

They used to promenade on this very quay after dinner, everyone in their best clothes, the taste of the lemon sherbet dessert still on their tongues, the smell of jasmine heavy in the air… But the smell of jasmine was gone. All the trees were burned down and the horrible stench of the crowd was overpowering. Andreas watched the horizon. How many days and nights since they fled from their house?

"Hurry! Hurry! As fast as you can!" His mother had shouted at them that terrible night. "Take what you might need: shoes, clothes in a small bundle you can carry. Maria, change your dress. We must leave right now, so hurry."

After they had assembled before the door, Mamá had distributed everything of value: jewels, gold, and drachmas between the four of them. "Here." His mother had placed two nuggets of gold into his hands. "Keep it safe. Don't show it to anyone," she instructed as they had picked up their small bundles.

How many days had gone by since then? Andreas didn't remember. The sun was beginning to set through the billowing clouds of smoke, yellow, crimson and orange flames. Night, soon it would be night. His heart began to pound with fear. Maria, who huddled next to their mother, was also looking at the setting sun, and she started to quietly whimper into Mamá's skirts.

Night. Why did the darkness have to come so quickly? When they had lived in their wonderful house, when Patéra was alive before the soldiers, before the fire, did night come as quickly? Did it last as long? Surely it didn't.

Baby Lina had finally fallen asleep in Sophia's arms. She cried so much, day and night. Mamá said she was sick. There weren't enough doctors. There wasn't enough medicine. "She'll get better," Mamá had told them. "You'll see, soon she'll get better."

Andreas's gaze turned from the setting sun to the throngs of people squeezed next to his family, as far as the eye could see. The Dalakoglo family next to them, all six of them… They had a sick baby yesterday. The baby boy died, and despite the older children trying to pry the baby from her arms, his mother refused to let anyone take him away.

Andreas pulled a small crust of bread out of his left pocket. His right pocket held the pieces of gold his mother gave to him

He hated it here, pressed beside so many people, barely a space to sit down beside their possessions. On one side of them, ships were anchored in the harbor; on the other side, flames and smoke billowed up to the sky. Ashes, ashes everywhere in their mouths and noses, in the air they breathed. And all the dead bodies that had been thrown into the sea... The terrible, terrible, stench of so much death was all around them. The suffocating heat from the fire that burned on the other side of the quay seemed to get worse every day.

The food Sophia had packed for them was rapidly diminishing. Andreas was sent out each morning in search of water and bread supplied by relief agencies. But there was never enough: too little food, too many desperate people. At first, he had tried to push his way forward. But because he was small, he was elbowed aside. He quickly learned to use his small size as an asset, as he ducked beneath arms and skirts while making his way to the front of the line.

One morning, he had tightly held on to the skein filled with water and the loaf of bread he was to share with his family. He was jostled one way and then another before he got back to his family in the midst of the crowded quay.

Andreas reached fingers inside his pocket, where he had put the gold nuggets his mother had given him. He liked to hold the gold in his hands, knowing how the shiny metal would give them passage on one of those boats and ensure a new life for them. His pocket was empty! The gold couldn't have fallen out! The pocket was too deep! He reached inside to the bottom of his pocket, searching for a hole. There was no hole. With horror, he realized that because of the all the pushing and shoving when he stood in line for the food, some horrible person had stuck their hand in his pocket and stolen the gold. *Christe mou!*

He'd failed her. He couldn't tell his mother. They needed all the gold. Mamá had told them the gold would buy them passage and help them make a new life away from Smyrna. What would his mother say when she found out? He'd ruined their chance for a new life. He was just a stupid boy, he told himself. Stupid and bad! When they were ready to pay for their passage, he would have to stay behind. They would go on without him. It was only fair. What would he do all by himself? Would he have to stay on the quay with all these crowds, or would a Turkish soldier come to kill him since he would be all alone?

"Andreas, you must eat," his mother chided him.

"I'm not hungry," Andreas told her. "Give my portion to Baby Lina."

"I've already tried to give Baby Lina my portion. She doesn't seem hungry. She's not eating at all." His mother patted Baby Lina's back as she cradled her daughter against her shoulder.

And now it was almost night. Maria took her place between Sophia and Mamá, crouching down between them as her mother instructed after that first night when they saw the soldiers coming through on horseback, grabbing young girls and taking them away. The girls screamed in terror. Their mothers cried and begged for mercy, all to no avail. The next day, some girls, bleeding and horribly injured, made their way back to their families, and some girls never returned at all.

Darkness had fallen. Andreas watched as Giorgos, a man who was with the family beside them, bid good-bye. "Where are you going?" Giorgos's mother cried.

"Out to the sea."

"You can't swim."

"We shall never be allowed on those ships. Every night the soldiers come through, grabbing men of my age. I will not be force marched into the desert to die a slow death, Mamá. This is my decision. I love you. I must go." He walked away as his mother tried to cling to his shirt.

Andreas looked away from the sobbing woman and turned to his own mother. She was making the sign of the cross and had begun to silently pray.

"Mamá, why are the Turks taking men away? Why did they want to take over our home? Did the Greek people do something bad?" He waited for his mother to answer. But she was silent.

"Why did they kill Patéra? Do they hate us? We aren't bad people, are we?" Andreas struggled to understand what was happening.

"It's because we are Christians," his mother said with sadness in her voice. "We've always lived together in peace, both Muslims and Christians. I can't give you an answer, Andreas. I don't know the answer."

As darkness descended, the horrible sounds began, the crying, the wailing, the moaning, the praying. He hated the wailing and the crying, the moaning all night long, broken by shrieks as soldiers grabbed up young women, or at the point of a sword, roughed up and robbed any family that looked prosperous. Tonight there was a new sound out on the water, the sound of music and singing was wafting over the sea.

"What is that?' Andreas asked.

"It's coming from the warships, I think." Sophia looked puzzled.

"It's Enrico Caruso singing Pagliacci," his mother told them. "Pagliacci is an Italian opera. It's the story of a clown. Your father took me to see that opera. I loved it. Such beautiful music."

"Why are they playing opera music?" Andreas asked.

"Maybe they are entertaining the sailors on the boats. I don't know. Let me tell you about that opera," his mother began. "Yes, let us all talk about good things. You children are good at pretending. Let's pretend we are far away from here. I will tell you about that night at the opera. Your father," she paused, and for the first time Andreas saw tears begin to slip down her cheeks. "Your father was such a good man," she began and then her shoulders began to heave and terrible sobs wracked her frame.

"Mamá," Andreas got to his feet and went to his mother. She buried her head into his shoulder and wrapped her arms around his waist as she wept.

Mamá's weeping grew louder and Sophia and Maria began to cry. Andreas had often wondered, when he saw so many other women praying and sobbing, why his own mother had shed no tears. And now, somehow, he understood that Mamá was being strong for all of them. If she broke down, she knew that the rest of the family would lose themselves into sadness for Patéra and for having to live in this crowd of people and for the ships that wouldn't let them on board.

"Mamá," Andreas tried to soothe his mother as he patted her head. He was the only man in the family now and he must be strong. He must do as his Patéra had told him.

"I'm sorry." Mamá gave him a hug and looked down at his face. She kissed his cheeks. "Enough crying. Enough." She dried her tears with her sleeve. "My son, my son, you are a wonderful boy."

I'm not, he thought. When Mamá finds out I lost the gold, she will realize what a bad son I am.

"Let me tell you of the night Patéra took me to the opera to see Pagliacci." She dried her tears with the back of her hands. And so his mother told them all about the grand opera house decorated in gold leaf and the beautiful dresses the women wore. "I had such a lovely blue gown, with roses sewn down to the sleeves. Patéra said I was the most beautiful woman in all Smyrna." And his mother continued to talk as the moaning and sobbing went on all around them.

Try as he might, he couldn't focus his attention on what his mother was saying. He knew she was trying to take their attention away from the mournful sounds of the crowd. But Andreas only heard the prayers to God, praying to the warships, pleading for help. When the searchlights from the ships swept over the quay, the horrible moaning stopped. The robbers and soldiers who preyed on the helpless Greeks and Armenians, stopped their evil deeds and slipped back into the shadows until the lights were turned off.

Each day Andreas watched the fires consume the houses, the restaurants, and hotels along the other side of the quay. At times there was a large crash, as the skeletons of destruction collapsed. The heat of the fire permeated the air, the crowds. It was scorching hot, day and night, night and day. And there was the terrible smell from so many people and from the dead bodies swelling in the heat. The seas turned red with the bodies of those who had tried to swim to the boats, the bodies of those who decided to drown rather than face the wrath of the Turkish soldiers, and those slaughtered and thrown in by the Turkish soldiers.

The next day Andreas watched as a small boat entered the harbor. People rushed towards it.

"Mamá, Mamá, let's go!" Maria jumped to her feet.

"I don't think we'll get there in time. We're too far away," Mamá surmised.

"Look!" Sophia gasped and made the sign of the cross as they watched swarms of people scrambling to get inside the boat. The boat tossed around in the water and then turned over, trapping the people inside as the boat sunk in the sea.

Maria bit her lip and looked away.

"Sister." Andreas took her hand. "Let's pretend we are home and getting ready for school."

Maria shook her head. "I can't pretend Andreas. I don't know how to do that anymore. What if we try to get on a boat and it tips over? I'm afraid, Mamá. I don't want to get on one of those boats. Mamá?"

Maria watched her mother who wasn't paying any attention to her. "Mamá, you aren't listening to me."

"Let me hold Baby Lina." Mamá put out her arms to Sophia.

"Kiría Daphne." Sophia, who was holding baby Lina in her arms, continued rocking her back and forth. "Kiría Daphne," she began again.

"What is it, Sophia? Baby Lina does seem better now, doesn't she? She's sleeping so peacefully. Maybe when she wakes up she'll have more of an appetite. I saved her some cookies. It's the last of them, but she loves them so much. Remember how she found a plate of them in the parlor and when no one noticed, she ate all of them and got so sick all over the carpet." His mother was talking too quickly, rushing one word past the other. Something was wrong. Why was Mamá talking so fast?

"Kiría Daphne." Sophia handed Baby Lina to her mother. Baby Lina's arms fell at her sides. "She's gone," Sophia said softly.

Mamá gathered his baby sister close and kissed her forehead, her cheeks.

Gone? Gone? Andreas turned the word over and over in his head. Baby Lina wasn't gone, Mamá was holding her. Gone! Gone! His baby sister was dead.

Maria began to scream, "No, no, Baby Lina! No! No!"

Andreas turned away and focused on the warships. Why wouldn't they let the people on the ships? Baby Lina, my sweet baby sister, such a good girl, such a big smile and giggle when he tickled her. She wasn't coming with them to the new life. She wouldn't be with them when they returned to Smyrna. He forced himself not to turn around. He willed himself not to hear the wailing of his sister Maria, his mother, and Sophia.

Later in the afternoon, when Sophia had distributed the last of the food they had brought with them, she tapped him on the shoulder. "Eat something," the maid told him.

"I'm not hungry." Andreas didn't want to turn around.

"You must eat," she insisted.

Andreas turned around to find his baby sister was gone and his mother and Maria softly praying to Christ to speed her soul into his arms.

The next day, it seemed the heat was more searing, as he watched the flames light up the sky. Soon it would be night again and the terrible sounds would begin. Why did those ships, the same ships he and Patéra had watched through the telescope laying in the harbor, not help anyone, not let anyone onto the ships? Wandering around through the crowds, he'd heard the word neutrality whispered over and over again. "What is neutrality?" he'd asked Sophia.

"I don't know," she said. "It must be a bad word if it means no one wants to help us. Ask your mother, she may know that word."

"What is neutrality, Mamá?"

"Neutrality? That is the word that means the ships aren't helping us. But you'll see, they will help us. How can they see our suffering and not help? I heard there was a Japanese ship that saw the horror of our people. They threw their cargo into the sea to make room for our people. Those few lucky Greeks and Armenians were taken to safety. There are good people in the world, Andreas. Don't forget that. We've seen so much evil and bad people. But remember, your father believed in the good of mankind. You must remember that in honor of your father, may his memory be eternal." She made the sign of the cross.

"So neutrality means don't help?"

"Neutrality means those ships that have come from all the Great Powers, the French, the Americans, the Italians, the British… they don't want the Turks to get mad at them. Especially the man called Kemal Mustafa. He is the leader of the Turks. And helping Greeks could make him mad."

"Why?"

"I'm not sure I understand it myself. But Patéra told me about it. He said that as a woman I shouldn't concern myself with politics. But then he laughed and shared much about what was going on in the world. He mentioned oil. Yes, he said, there were oil fields in a place called Mosul. The Turks have this place and if the Turks get angry, they won't let the Great Powers have the oil."

"I don't understand why no one wants to help us." Andreas shook his head.

"It's hard to understand, Andreas. But you'll see. Help will come for us."

Andreas looked down at his shoes, still covered in blood, Patéra's blood. "If help doesn't come, what shall we do?"

"Andreas," his mother lifted his chin. "I told you, it will come."

"What... what if all of us don't get on the boat together?"

"I would insist we all stay together."

"But what if there wasn't enough gold to pay for everyone's passage?" He couldn't meet his mother's gaze.

"Of course, there's enough. I also have jewelry that is worth a great deal."

"I'm not coming with you and Sophia and Maria. I have to stay here. I'll go back to our house. I'll take the key and go back home."

"Andreas, the heat is affecting you. You aren't eating enough. You're talking nonsense."

"I lost the gold you gave me. I'm a stupid bad boy," he said fighting back tears.

"You lost it!" Maria yelled.

"You were robbed, weren't you?" Sophia interjected. "It must have happened when you were out getting us bread and water."

"Yes, I think that's what happened," Andreas said in a whisper as he hung his head in shame, afraid to look up at his mother's face. "Everyone was pushing at me and when I got back here and put my hand in my pocket, it was empty."

"Oh, Andreas." His mother enveloped him in her arms. "Of course we aren't going to leave you behind. There is enough gold, more than enough for our passage."

"But what about the gold we need for our new life?"

"We shall be okay. All of us." His mother sighed and pulled out her jeweled crucifix from inside her blouse. "If need be, I will part with this. It is a very fine piece your father gave me at our marriage, and it is worth a great deal."

CRDO

September 24, 1922

Andreas was watching the harbor, as he did each day, hoping to see small boats being launched to take people on board. But all he ever saw were people throwing themselves in the water, people who couldn't swim and the families left behind crying. And then there were those who swam for the boats. It was too far away for him to see what happened, but he heard from the crowd around him that no one was allowed on board. They were thrown back into the sea where they drowned.

But today there was something new on the horizon. Were more ships coming? Andreas saw other people pointing towards a dark line that had appeared. A line of ships were sailing into the harbor. Would those ships take all the people away? The crowd began to cheer. They were still too far away to see their flags. "I wonder where those ships are from?" Andreas pondered.

"The people on those ships have to let us on board," Mamá said to herself.

"Let me go out into the crowd and learn what I can," Sophia said as she wearily got to her feet.

"Be careful!" Mamá cautioned.

"Of course." Sophia managed a weary smile.

Andreas continued watching the new ships. If he were home with Patéra's telescope, they would see the flags flying on the ship, and Patéra would tell him what country the ship had sailed from. Patéra. Andreas closed his eyes and saw him, as they sat across from each other over the backgammon board. He remembered the sound of the door closing when Patéra came home from work, the smile on his face when he greeted his family, and then the memory of Patéra lying on the floor with blood all over his chest. The blood all over Andreas's shoes and pants was now dried, brown and crusty. His father's words "be brave, have courage," played over and over again in his mind.

Sophia returned with good news. "Those are Greek ships. They aren't allowed to fly a Greek flag, but they've come to rescue us!"

The crowd all around them was caught up in desperate agitation. Andreas and his family got to their feet and, clutching their bundles, were swept along toward the edge of the quay. "Stay together! Stay together!" his mother shouted at them.

There were Turkish soldiers all along the quay, funneling the crowd on the dock. Makeshift fences had been constructed to keep the crowd under control. The soldiers were grabbing able-bodied men, pulling them away from their families, while their wives, mothers, sisters and daughters fell to their knees crying for mercy. But the soldiers laughed at them as they dragged the men away.

"*Christós!*" his mother moaned as they watched people being searched for valuables, the soldiers beating people over the head with batons. "Stay close to me, beneath my arms," his mother told him. "I will keep you safe. If a soldier comes near, you must keep going."

"Mamá, if the soldiers rob us of our gold, how will we board with no money to pay for passage?"

"We've heard that the Greek ships aren't demanding payment for passage. But when we arrive in Greece, if our valuables are taken away we will be paupers," his mother said through pursed lips.

The crowd pushed and shoved. Mamá, Sophia, Maria and Andreas desperately clutched at each other, fighting not to be separated.

The heat was even more brutal as the crowd pressed in around them. People collapsed, but the crowd moved forward, trampling the poor souls who had fallen. People lost shoes in their haste and children were separated from their parents as the crowd surged forward.

"Just go!" Mamá yelled at them as they tried to avoid the body of an old man sprawled on the ground. And then the huge crowd stopped moving.

"Stop!" yelled a soldier. "No more filthy infidels on this boat. You'll have to wait until tomorrow."

In the distance, the sun was setting through the clouds of smoke. The boat was filled. Everyone would have to wait until morning. Another night of fear before tomorrow.

There would be another night of the moaning and shrieking and the floodlights from the boats causing the terrible sounds to stop for a brief while. And the opera singing…. No food. Would they get on the next boat tomorrow? Of course they would.

"Will there be food on the boat?" Maria asked, her face burned from the sun, her hair askew. Mamá and Sophia arranged their hair with hairpins every morning, but Maria seemed not to care if her hair tumbled down to her shoulders.

"Sure, there will be food." Andreas tried to smile at her. "Those peaches that you like and fabulous *baklava*."

"Andreas." Her face brightened with a smile. "How could you know that? You are making it up."

"Maybe," Andreas teased her. "But you won't know until we get on the boat."

Mamá gave Maria a hug. "I know you're hungry. We are all hungry. Tomorrow we will be on the boat. I'm sure they will feed us."

"Where do you think they will take us?" asked Sophia.

"It could be anywhere. Perhaps a nearby island."

"My late husband, may his memory be eternal, had a brother, Erasmus Nopoulos, in Kavala," Sophia told them. "Did you or Kìrios Elias have any family in Greece?"

"No, we have been in Asia Minor for generations. But I'm sure if those are Greek ships taking us to Greece, they must have prepared a welcome for us no matter where we land."

Andreas was wondering what it would be like in Greece. "Are there Turkish soldiers in Greece?" he asked, hoping his mother would say no.

"No Turkish soldiers in Greece, I promise."

Andreas sighed in relief. That was good to hear. Was Greece like Smyrna? "Will we have a nice house in Greece like our house in Smyrna?"

"We will be safe from the Turkish army. That's all that's important."

The sun had set. The sounds of the crowds, wailing and moaning, were broken by the crash of collapsing buildings, reduced to burnt-out shells by the raging fire. Another day went by and there were no new ships on the horizon. Were no other ships ever going to come? Andreas was afraid to say it aloud.

Night descended with the wailing and the praying. Andreas was dozing as the floodlights swept over the crowd. The moaning, crying and praying had stopped. But then the floodlights were gone, and it all started again.

At the sound of an approaching horse, Andreas's heart leaped in his throat. It was a Turkish soldier on horseback coming toward them.

"Maria," his mother's voice was filled with dread and terror as she tried to hide her daughter with her skirts.

Rob someone else, Andreas began to pray. Please, *Theós,* don't let him take our gold.

The horse pulled up sharply beside them. "Now, who do we have hiding here!" Andreas was filled with terror as he looked up into the dark eyes and thick lips that seemed to snarl at them. The cavalryman shoved Mamá to the ground to reveal Maria cowering on her knees.

With one fell swoop, he lifted Maria off the ground onto his horse. Maria kicked and screamed. "Help! No! No! Mamá, help me!"

"Stop! No!" Mamá shrieked. "Please!" Mamá grabbed at the soldier's boot in the stirrup.

Maria kept kicking and screaming, straddled across his saddle.

"Please, have mercy!" Mamá pleaded, continuing to grab at his boot.

"Get away, you infidel whore!" He thundered and tried to kick at Mamá's face, but she held on for dear life. He raised his baton and started beating Mamá on her hands and head. He hit her over and over as the blood started to flow down her hair. But Mamá wouldn't let go. There was a loud crack. And then Mamá's head burst into a spray of crimson and white matter as she finally let go, crumbling down to the ground.

Andreas looked away, crouching down, trying to make himself as small as possible. His sister was screaming in terror.

Don't take me! Don't kill me! Please don't take me, he prayed silently.

He heard the sounds of the horse galloping away. He heard Sophia crying, "Kiría Daphne! Kiría Daphne!" Andreas squeezed his eyes tight, his breath in gasps. No! No! Mamá! Maria! But he couldn't look up. He couldn't. He rocked back and forth on his heels, wanting to drown out the sounds of Sophia crying as he heard her moving around and shifting the bundles. Mamá! Mamá! His chest tightened. He couldn't breathe. Mamá! He lost track of time as he crouched low on the cobblestones.

"Andreas." He heard Sophia's voice and he jumped when she touched his shoulder. He kept his head down, his arms tight across his chest, waves of icy cold sweeping over him in spite of the brutal heat of the night air.

"Andreas, you and I will board the boat tomorrow. I told you I have family. We will find them."

He looked up into her face, lined with fine wrinkles. "We can't go, Sophia. We can't." He had to make her understand. "We can't get on the boat tomorrow and leave Maria behind. When the soldiers take the girls, sometimes the girls come back in the morning and they are hurt. When Maria comes back and we are gone, she'll be all alone. We must stay to take care of her."

"Andreas, we must get on the boat," Sophia said firmly.

Andreas looked at where Mamá and Maria had been before the soldier came. There were nothing but bundles there. Had Mamá's body been thrown out to sea? Would he see her body in the morning if he looked out into the water?

"I must find my sister." He got to his feet. "I'm going to find the soldier and my sister."

"No, you are not!" Sophia grabbed hold of him.

"You can't stop me!" Andreas started to hit at her.

"Andreas." She grabbed him and held him against her. "You must stay here with me. Your Mamá wouldn't have permitted you to wander around at night. It is too dangerous. The girls who are taken away come back in the morning. You said so yourself."

"I wish we brought Patéra's gun with us. I would have killed that soldier, too."

"There were no more bullets for the gun. You know that," Sophia said gently. "Here, I have your Mamá's *stavrós* for you." She placed the golden-jeweled crucifix in his hand.

Andreas clutched his mother's cross as his legs gave way beneath him and he collapsed against Sophia's soft body. Mamá! He screamed silently. Sophia rocked him in her arms as he sobbed uncontrollably. And then he moved away from Sophia and rolled up into a tight ball waiting for morning. He didn't want to listen to the soothing tones of Sophia's voice, telling him they would be fine. No, nothing was going to be fine. If Maria didn't come back in the morning, he would search for her. He would find her and together they would board the boat with Sophia.

❧❧❧

September 27, 1922

The moaning and praying had stopped. It must be daylight. As the sun rose on the horizon, he saw more ships without flags making their way into the harbor. The crowd began to yell with excitement. Sophia and Andreas staggered to their feet and the crowd started to push. "I want to find Maria!" Andreas yelled to Sophia, but he couldn't get away from the crowd that was pushing toward the debarkation point where the Turkish soldiers stood guard. I want to kill them, he thought. I wish I had the gun.

He wasn't tall enough to see over the heads of the crowd. "They're beating people to slow them down. They're robbing people, pulling away more men!" Sophia gasped.

He was trying to push away from the crowd. He was small. He'd go underneath the crowd. He had to find Maria. But the crowd was pressing around him, and Sophia was holding tight to his hand.

All around them was pushing, pressing into a funnel of people as they drew closer to the edge of the quay. There were so many ahead of them. No, he was sure there wouldn't be room on this boat and he could break away and find Maria. They could all get on the boat tomorrow.

They were almost at the entry point and the pushing and shoving grew stronger. The Turkish solider in front of them raised his baton to beat people coming through the line. "Slow down!" he thundered at them.

Andreas ducked down beneath the person's arms in front of him to evade the swing of the baton. He felt Sophia's hand loosen from his fingers. He was being pushed ahead. "Stop!" a soldier yelled at the crowd behind him. "No more room. Another boat will come later."

"No!" He heard Sophia screaming. "That little boy is mine!"

"Too bad." Andreas saw the soldier roughly shove Sophia backwards.

"Andreas! Andreas!" Her voice was growing fainter as the crowd pushed him up the gangplank.

CHAPTER 4

THE CROWD SHOVED him up the gangplank. Holding onto his bundle with one hand, clutching his mother's crucifix in his pocket with the other hand, Andreas reached the deck of the ship. He found himself surrounded by women who were prostrate before the sailors, kissing their feet, thanking them. They were safe, he heard over and over. *"Efharistó Thée,* thank you, God of Mine," they prayed.

His dark eyes scanned the crowd left on the quay. Was Maria there? Was she hurt? She'd be on the next boat and he'd find her after they landed. Where was Sophia? In the crowds of people still left across the quay, their arms outstretched toward the ship, he could hear them crying. "Help me! Save me! Save my baby!" He couldn't see Sophia.

A lady in a white uniform handed him a tin of milk. He gulped it down, looking for a place to sit among the crowds of women, children and old people. The smell was still so bad, almost as bad as on the quay. The ship started to move.

He was safe now. Everyone around him said they were safe, thanks to God. Did that mean there were no more Turkish soldiers who wanted to kill him or use their bayonets to slice into his body? What if a soldier had come on the ship hidden in the crowds? Maybe they weren't safe. Surely in all these crowds, a Turkish soldier could have come aboard to kill them... to kill him. He closed his eyes and took a deep breath.

Maria, maybe she was already on the ship. He needed to look for her.

He put down the tin, shouldered his small bundle and began to squeeze through the crowds of women, children and old people. "Have you seen my sister Maria Sefaris? Have you seen her?" he asked over and over again.

He was met by blank stares. "Who is Maria Sefaris?" he was asked.

"My sister. She was taken away by a Turk, but by now she would be back. I need to find her."

Some people just hung their heads and ignored him. Others smiled weakly and shook their heads.

A lady in a white uniform smiled down at him. "Where are your parents, little boy? Your mother?"

"My parents?" Andreas swallowed hard. He didn't want to tell her what happened to his parents, to his Mamá and Baba. "They are on the ship over there." He pointed in the distance. Lying was bad. Surely the woman would know he was lying. "They told me to look for my sister."

"I hope you find her." The woman patted his head. "Here, have some bread."

She didn't know he was lying... It was so easy to lie. He grabbed the bread. "Thank you," he mumbled. He still must have manners, shouldn't he? But maybe it didn't matter. If he could lie, manners didn't matter. All the things that he learned and had been taught to him... Maybe nothing mattered in this world of people crying and praying, where everything and everyone he had ever known was gone, crumbled into dust.

The bread wasn't enough to fill his stomach. He needed to search for Maria. He shouldered his small pack and began to push through the crowds again. He kept pushing his way through. He paused before a young girl who could be Maria, dark hair, slight build. Her face was all swollen, but she could be Maria. "Maria?" he whispered.

"She is not Maria," an older woman told him and the young girl, whose blood-covered clothes were torn to shreds, began to sob.

The young girl looked at Andreas. "No! No!" she whispered as the woman beside her tried to give comfort by wrapping the young girl in her arms.

Andreas backed away from the wild, desperate look in the young girl's eyes. He was going to ask her if she'd seen his sister, but the look on her face scared him.

And when he was too tired to push his way through the crowds any longer, he collapsed in a small corner, his fingers reaching inside his pocket, holding his mother's crucifix. He hung his head and tried to make his mind blank. But the image of his father laying on the floor, blood all over his shirt, kept repeating over and over in his head.

"Young man." A woman in a white uniform was standing in front of him. "Where are your parents?" This woman was older than the other one. She had gray hair and a kind face. "All the orphans are assembling over near that railing," she told him.

"Orphans?" His stomach turned over. "I'm not an orphan. My parents got on a boat before me. We got separated." Yes, it was easy to lie. But he realized his lies could fall over each other and catch him, if he wasn't careful.

"Young man." The woman shook her head at him and gave him a kindly smile. "All the orphans are being taken to an orphanage on Mytilene, and then you'll be sent to Athens or Salonika where you will be taken care of in an orphanage. Don't you worry. You'll be taken care of."

"I'm not an orphan," Andreas repeated. How could he be an orphan? He had a family!

"See right over there, that group of boys? Why don't you go over there? They are all orphans."

"I'm not an orphan," Andreas announced emphatically. "Can I get some more to eat? I'm hungry." Go away, he wanted to scream. Go away! I'm not an orphan! He couldn't be taken to an orphanage. He'd never find Maria if he was taken away to an orphanage.

"When we disembark, if you aren't with a family, you'll have to go to an orphanage. You will be well taken care of."

He turned his back to her. She touched his shoulder and he flinched. "Don't touch me," he muttered. Go away, go away.

When she brought him back a tin with some bread and cheese, he didn't say thank you. He just grabbed it and started to eat. The woman walked away. He finished the food and clutched his bundle to his chest.

"Hey."

Andreas was startled to find a tall boy standing over him.

"Where you from? Smyrna or one of the villages?" the boy asked.

"Smyrna. What about you?"

"I'm from an orphanage in Smyrna."

"Well, I have a family."

"They take pretty good care of you in an orphanage. Food, a place to sleep."

Andreas turned away.

"Look, that lady Miss Johnson asked me to come over and talk to you. She said she doesn't think you have a family."

"Well, she doesn't know. She doesn't know. I have a father and a mother and a sister; actually I have two sisters. And our maid was coming with us, but she didn't get on the ship."

"Where are they?"

"We got separated in the crowd."

"Once all the ships have docked, if you can't find them, you'll be sent to the orphanage."

"Well, I'll find them."

"I was told there will be lists so families can be reunited."

"That's good."

"If you can't find them, an orphanage really isn't so bad."

"Look, thanks for talking to me, but I have a family. I'm tired."

"You have blood on your clothes. Don't you have another shirt in your bundle?"

Andreas clutched his bundle closer and closed his eyes, ignoring the older boy until he heard him walk away.

I am not going to an orphanage, he vowed to himself. I'm going to find my sister Maria.

⊂⚬⚭⚬⊃

On the island called Lesbos, a place called Mytilene, where everyone got off the ship... There was a line to give your name to see if the rest of your family was found. Should he give his name? They would learn he was alone. They would put him in an orphanage and he would never find Maria. But Sophia would be here soon and he wouldn't be alone. Together, they would look for Maria. So he decided he must give his name and that way he could find his sister and Sophia. She'd also give her name, like he did, and they'd be reunited.

Andreas again began his search for Maria just as he'd done on the ship. "Have you seen a girl named Maria Sefaris? She's twelve years old."

He'd searched all day and now he was so tired. But he'd keep trying. He saw a mother with three young daughters who had found a small area for themselves.

"I'm looking for my sister," he began wearily.

"Where is your mother? Your family?"

"They are on another boat. My mother and father and I got separated while we were boarding." How easily the lies now fell off his tongue.

"Is your father an old man?"

"No, of course not," Andreas protested and then realized how his lie could catch him.

"Separated? If your father wasn't an old man, he would have been pulled away by the Turks, just like my Nasos. We put my husband in one of my dresses, hoping to fool the Turks, hoping they'd think he was a woman. But it didn't work! They pulled him out of the line before we could even say good-bye. They beat him and kicked him and took him away. They say 'to a work detail.' But we all know the truth. He will be marched out into the desert with the others. My girls will never see their father and I will never see my husband again." She began to sob.

Andreas stood there looking at the woman and her daughters. Her story was sad, but somehow Andreas couldn't bring himself to say he was sorry to her. All around him, as he walked through the crowds, were people with terrible stories, crying, sobbing or just staring into space, their eyes unseeing. He would never share the story of his family with anyone. It was his story and he needed to guard it, holding its horror close to himself.

The woman wiped her eyes and straightened her shoulders. "I am Kiría Fotiadis. How old are you, child?"

"Eight," he answered.

"Your name?"

"Andreas Sefaris from Smyrna."

"So you're not from the countryside," she paused. "Too bad you aren't older. You could be of help on a farm. Even if you are a city child, I could teach you. Well, I'll have to do the labor myself. My girls are too young. If you like, you can share our space until your mother turns up or until we are transferred to our new home."

Andreas studied the woman's face. She looked kind. Could he trust her? He was so tired. "Thank you, *efharistó*," Andreas hurried toward the empty space on the dirt floor next to the Fotiadis family. He sat down and promptly fell asleep with his bundle held tightly in his arms.

⌘

At day break the next day, he was first in the line at the registration desk, asking for Maria, asking for Sophia. Hadn't Sophia gotten on the next boat? He asked for his mother and father, although he knew it was a mere ruse. Their names would never be there.

He returned to Kiría Fotiadis and her daughters, who were eating some cheese, olives and bread. He sat on the dirt floor beside them. She offered him some food, which he gladly accepted. The woman was helping her daughters, urging them to eat to keep up their strength. He didn't talk to the woman. She didn't talk to him. He was grateful for the space next to this family. Those women in the white uniforms would think he was part of the Fotiadis family and not bother him.

They kept telling him there was an orphanage waiting for him in Salonika. He'd heard of Salonika. It was a big city. But he wasn't going there. He wasn't going to an orphanage. He wasn't an orphan! Orphans don't have a family. He had a family. He clutched his mother's crucifix tightly in his fingers. Mamá, he thought with so much sadness in his heart that surely his chest would burst. No tears, he'd told himself over and over. He was brave. He was strong. And what good would tears do for him? Tears could not change what had happened to his Patéra, his Mamá, his sister Baby Lina. And now something had surely happened to Sophia or she would be here. He would find his sister Maria. He would.

"Child, so you are looking for your sister?" Kiría Fotiadis spoke up.

Andreas looked at her, as she cradled her youngest daughter at her breast. "Yes. I'm sure I'll find her."

"Did she get separated from you when you boarded the boat?"

"No, she was taken away by a Turk in the middle of the night when we were on the quay."

The woman shook her head, sadness etched across her face. "You think she is here on this island?"

"Many girls were taken away and then they came back the next day. I saw it with my own eyes," Andreas told her emphatically. "They were hurt, but they came back. I'll take care of her when I find her."

"Child, I'm sorry to say most of the girls didn't come back."

"Were they killed?" Andreas took a deep swallow and held his breath waiting for her answer.

"Some were killed; but many were just taken away."

"Where? Where were they taken to? I will go there and find her."

"Many were taken as wives or brought to harems."

"What is a harem?"

"A Turk may have many wives if he so desires. That is called a harem."

"No, I'm sure that didn't happen to Maria. If she was taken as a wife or into a harem, that means she wasn't killed. So maybe that isn't so bad," Andreas paused. "But she's only twelve years old and she doesn't know how to take care of a household. She wouldn't make a good wife. I'm sure she must have been brought back."

The woman held her child closer to her breast and said nothing.

"If she was brought back to Smyrna after all the rescue ships were gone, what would she do?" he wondered out loud.

"There will be no more Christians in Smyrna," she told him.

"Well, I'll find her."

"You should eat a little more," the woman told him, pointing to a small hunk of bread.

"You need that for you and your girls. I'm fine, thank you." He found his manners had returned. The woman had been kind to him.

"Hello." A woman whom Andreas recognized from the Near East Relief Fund walked up to him. She looked down at a piece of paper and then smiled at him. "You are Andreas Sefaris?"

"Yes," his voice was tentative. Had they found Maria? Of course they had. That's why this woman was here.

"Kiría Fotiadis came to see us this morning and she told us all about you. She said you are a nice little boy with no family. You need to come with me, Andreas."

"Come with you?" He looked at Kiría Fotiadis who was looking away, not meeting his gaze.

"The boys for the orphanage are assembling at the dock. We have a place for you in Salonika with the other orphans."

"I'm not an orphan! I have a mother and a father and two sisters!" He jumped to his feet and clutched his bundle.

"Now, now." The woman reached out her hand towards him.

"Don't touch me!" he yelled and pushed past her. He ran and ran through the crowds. He wasn't going to an orphanage! He wasn't an orphan!

"Get out of my way!" he shouted at the crowds that wouldn't part for him.

Someone tried to grab him and he bit down hard on that person's arm. "*Mikrós bastardos*! Little bastard!"

He ran and he ran, his lungs bursting from the effort. And then he saw the waterfront lined with boats He needed to hide where no one could find him... where no one could take him to an orphanage with other boys who had no parents. He decided to walk slowly, trying not to call attention to himself. He looked at the fishermen milling about who were engaged in animated conversations. They didn't pay any attention to Andreas as he made his way along the dock next to the boats.

He could hide on a boat, under the sails, until he could figure something out, until those people stopped looking for him.

And then he saw one of those women again, the ones in the uniforms. She was coming straight towards him. He bolted across the dock and jumped into the closest boat. He ducked down and covered himself with the tobacco leaves that lay across the bottom of the boat.

He intended to stay hidden and then peak out to make sure the woman was gone. As he laid in the bottom of the boat, he inhaled the smell of tobacco. The smell reminded him of Patéra and his smell on those evenings when he returned home after spending the day in his tobacco warehouse. "The finest tobacco!" his father would announce with pride. "That is why the American Tobacco company pays such a high price for Sefaris tobacco."

Then he remembered his father embracing Mamá and whispering something into her ear that made his mother blush. He and Maria would giggle at those frequent displays of affection between their parents.

He tried to wrap himself in those wonderful memories, the warmth of his family, the smell of Patéra's tobacco. Andreas fell into a deep sleep, the first one in so many days and nights. He woke up to the gentle rocking of the boat. It was moving. Andreas didn't care where it was going. It was taking him away from the ladies in the white uniforms who wanted to imprison him in an orphanage. He fell back to sleep.

"Boy!" Someone grabbed his ear and yanked him to his feet. At first it was too dark to see, but then a lantern lit up the face of a man with a scar across his cheek.

"Put me down! You're hurting me," Andreas complained at the pain in his ear.

"What are you doing on my boat? How did you sneak on here?"

"I didn't sneak," Andreas answered rubbing his ear. "I just got on the boat."

"You filthy, *mikrós bastardos,* little bastard." The man held up the lantern to shine on Andreas's face. "You're one of those *tourkosporoi,* seeds of Turkey, refugee trash, aren't you?"

"No, I'm not. I'm Andreas Sefaris."

"Where are you from? You're not from Lesbos."

"I'm from Smyrna and I want to go back to Smyrna. My sister might still be there and I need to find her," he paused and looked up at the man.

"Are you a Christian?" the man asked.

"Yes," Andreas hesitated. "You aren't a Turk, are you?" His eyes widened with fear. *Thee mou,* had he gotten on to the boat of a Turk, who was going to kill him? "Please don't kill me!" he started to beg. "I'm sorry I got on your boat. I'll jump into the water. I'm a good swimmer."

The glare on the face of the man softened. "So you are a refugee from Smyrna? A Christian."

"I'm not a refugee. I saw lots of refugees going past my house. They came from the villages. I'm from Smyrna. I am a Christian. Are you a Turk, sir?"

"No boy, I'm not a Turk." The man pulled out his crucifix from inside his shirt. "But I still don't want you on my boat. I'm not a nursemaid. Today I have no fish to sell. But I have several stops to drop off my tobacco and then I'll take you back to Mytilene."

I'm not going back there, Andreas said silently to himself.

The rest of the night was spent in silence between them. Andreas looked up at black velvet heavens with stars twinkling like diamonds. The same stars, the same constellations he learned from his mother. It was when he was younger, maybe four or five years old. Patéra often traveled for days at a time and Andreas was alone with Mamá after the rest of the household had gone to bed. "I will teach you about the stars. Come here Andreas." She would pull him on her lap. "And you know, the constellations are named for the Greeks. All over the world people tell stories of our ancestors and the Greek Gods. Look over there, a shooting star!" She would point up at the night sky as he leaned back against her soft body.

Mamá, Mamá, he thought. I was a good boy, wasn't I? I listened to you and Patéra. Then why have I been left alone? What did I do that was so bad? He bit his lip to keep from crying. He didn't want the fisherman to hear him. But his heart ached for his mother, the touch of her hands, the comfort she gave him when he was upset. Be brave, he told himself, be brave.

The next morning, he looked out at a sea that was blue, not red with dead bodies and blood. They sailed into a small port. It was too close to Lesbos. Andreas was determined to get off the boat, as far away from the island of Lesbos as he could.

"How long until we arrive back in Mytilene?" he asked the fisherman.

"Three days and I'll have you back. You realize how stupid it was for you to get on my boat? Running away from your family because you did something bad, heh? I bet you're already missing your family. I'm sure you'll get a good beating for what you did. Making your family worry about you. Or are you such a bad boy that your family won't even miss you and they'll think, good riddance?"

Andreas clutched his bundle more tightly, looked away from the man and closed his lips in a tight line. The boat reached a small harbor where the man unloaded some of his tobacco leaves.

"I heard there was lots of trouble in Smyrna," the man said as he set sail again.

Andreas watched the waves lapping against the side of the boat and didn't answer.

"You don't have much to say, do you?" The man took out a cigarette from his pocket and lit a match. "Well, I'll tell you boy. Your people come to my island, filthy with disease, and you think the Greeks are going to take care of all of you. Feed you, clothe you too, I suppose. I work hard for a living. I don't get handouts. Why do you people think we're going to take care of all of you? The nerve of you people! So was it really that bad, Turks slicing people up, chopping off heads? You see any of that?"

Andreas tried to make himself smaller. He wanted to disappear and not hear the words of this man. How soon would they reach the next port? As soon as the boat touched the next harbor, he was jumping off, away from this man and his mean words, away from this man who wanted to take him back to Mytilene, back to the people who wanted to put him in an orphanage.

Another night passed with few words between Andreas and the fisherman. He offered Andreas a small chunk of bread and a tiny slice of feta. "*Efharistó*," Andreas thanked him as he watched the man gorging on olives and large pieces of bread. Andreas's stomach gnawed with hunger and he closed his eyes and tried to sleep.

The sun had risen high in the sky as they approached the shore. The man bent over to hoist the tobacco onto the dock. Andreas, tightly clutching his bundle, jumped down to the dock and started to run.

"Good riddance!" yelled the man.

Andreas ran faster and faster up the winding street. He was out of breath when at last he turned to make sure the man hadn't followed him.

It was small town and no one seemed to notice him as he wandered the streets. He saw a mosque high up on a hill and he ran in the opposite direction. Turks, there were Turks here. People weren't running through the streets. There were no fires burning. But Smyrna was once like that, no burning, Turks were kind neighbors, until it all changed. He was about to run away from the town with the mosque when he smelled food cooking. He'd had nothing but a slice of bread and some cheese the man on the boat had grudgingly shared with him. Andreas followed the smell of food. He spied a garbage can and when he was sure no one was looking, he routed through the rubbish and pulled out a chicken bone. He ate the shreds of meat and crunched down on the bone.

He heard the sounds of a family gathering around a table, laughing, talking, the scraping of a spoon against a pot. A family... he had a family once. He would never have a family again with a mother and a father. It would only be Maria. When he found her, they would be a family. He made his way down another street and followed the sounds of a marketplace.

There were stands with beautiful displays of fruit and vegetables, fish packed in ice. He made his way close to a display of beautiful peaches. Stealing? He asked himself, a Sefaris boy stealing? But did he have any other choice? You always have a choice to do the right thing; he heard the voice of his father. But the choice of right and wrong belonged to another world, where there *was* a right and wrong. In this new world, where his stomach cramped with hunger, and his baby sister died because there wasn't enough medicine, and his brave, kind father was stabbed by a Turk's sword and his mother only wanted to save Maria... The world made no sense. Everything he had been taught, to be good, to be honorable... Not in this world of evil.

He reached out to a large peach on a display. But before he could slip it into his pocket, a broom came crashing down on his head. *"Kléfti!* Thief!" He ducked and dropped the peach. He ran up the street and hurried down a small lane. He stood in a doorway, waiting. But no one was in pursuit.

He spied another garbage can. No chicken bones, just potato peels and rotten fruit. As night began to fall, he made his way toward the hills surrounding the town. He slid to the ground next to a stout tree.

The wind brought an evening chill and Andreas opened his bundle for the first time. He pulled out his fine linen shirt and pulled it over his blood-covered shirt. It didn't provide him much protection from the cold, but that was the only piece of clothing he'd brought with him when Mamá said to grab what he needed and "hurry, we must get out of the house." Before he buttoned the new shirt, he placed his hand over the blood stains on his other shirt. Was it Patéra's blood or was it the blood of the Turkish soldier? He heard the sound of the gun as he pulled the trigger over and over again. The surprise in the eyes of the Turk, the stain of bright red all over his neck and chest. Andreas had been so afraid. But he'd saved his mother and his sister. He was only an eight-year-old boy, but he'd done as his father would have instructed.

He'd been brave. He had courage. And now. He tried so hard to erase the image of the soldier on the quay grabbing his screaming sister and his mother fighting against the Turkish soldier with her last breath of life. He found himself trembling at the terrible images. At night, those images came back and grabbed him, and pulled him down into silent screams that tortured his dreams.

He took out the other items inside the bed sheet he'd used to form his bundle. There was his most prized possession, a small pouch of beautiful marbles his father had brought back from one of his travels. He had never played with the beautiful small balls. At night before bed, he would take them out and his fingers would smooth over the balls, imagining the day he would be playing with his friends. He would take them out and the other boys would gasp in astonishment at the bright striations of color. He picked up the book, *Don Quixote,* that had been given to him at last year's Name Day celebration. He had promised Patéra he would read it and they would discuss it, but Andreas never seemed to find the time. The week before the refugees started to stream past their house, his father had come to his room one night at bed time, and they had begun to read together. It was in French, a language that came easily to Andreas; but some of the words were difficult and Patéra had to help him. They hadn't read many pages before the refugees entered their town, and Patéra had stopped coming to his room for reading.

Andreas looked at the blue ribbon given to him in recognition of being the best student at his school. He held tightly onto his mother's beautiful *stavrós*, and closed his eyes in sadness.

It must be October by now and the evenings would begin to chill. He hadn't thought to bring a coat, as he was sure they would be coming back to their house in a few days. He saw Mamá locking the front door with her key and slipping it into her pocket. Mamá must have thought they would be coming back soon and she would unlock the door for them. He didn't want to think about that anymore. He didn't want to remember anything. He wanted emptiness, nothingness.

At first light, he put all his belongings back in his bundle and looking up he realized he was sitting beneath a plum tree. He climbed up the trunk and helped himself to as many plums as he could eat, savoring the sweetness and the moisture in his mouth. Then his stomach started to ache and he vomited all that wonderful fruit. He sat on the ground fighting against the miserable feeling that threatened to overwhelm him.

He couldn't just sit here feeling sorry for himself. He wiped his mouth with the back of his hand. He placed more plums in his bundle and made his way back to the road.

He passed the windows of families seated around their breakfast tables. And then later, he passed groups of boys with books, making their way to school.

Andreas saw a woman bending over, drawing water from the central fountain. She was an older woman with wide hips and gray hair just like Sophia. He suddenly remembered the maid telling him about her family in Kavala. He didn't know where Kavala was. He'd ask someone to point him in the right direction. Maybe somehow Sophia had found a way to get back to her own family. At first he thought he must make his way back to Smyrna. But if there were no Christians there anymore… only brutal horrible Turks, it made no sense to return. And surely Maria would have left as well. She was a Christian. Surely, she was also now on the Greek mainland just like he was and he would find her. They would be a family, brother and sister. He'd find some kind of work. He was small, but he was strong.

He asked for the directions to Kavala. "It's far away. It's to the east of here. Follow the main road," he was told by a woman hanging up her wash on a clothesline. "Do you have family there?"

"Yes," he lied. Lying was becoming fun. He could make up whatever story he wanted and if he seemed convincing, people would believe him.

And so he had walked during the daylight hours. Sometimes a boy would look askance at him when Andreas looked longingly at candy in his hand. One boy offered to share. But later that afternoon, several boys chased him, throwing stones to make him get out of their way.

Occasionally, a woman would notice him as he walked by and offer him a hunk of cheese and a slice of bread. But more often, he had to hunt through garbage cans, competing with the dogs that ran in packs through the streets. He'd learned not to eat everything he found, after he'd gotten sick from eating spoiled meat. He'd learned to be more adept at stealing fruit off artfully arranged displays. He had learned that lesson after he'd grabbed a fig to slide into his pocket and the entire display slid to the ground. Andreas had started to run, and someone tripped him sending him sprawling on the ground. "Thief!" The word followed him. Someone had kicked him in the ribs. Andreas caught his breath at the pain of the assault, scrambled to his feet and ran away as fast as he could from the market place. "Thief! *Kléfti!*"

The leaves on the trees were beginning to turn colors. As he walked down the roads, leaves began to litter his way. He enjoyed watching the sun dapple through the orange and yellow leaves. There was still beauty in the world, wasn't there? Nights were the most difficult, as they grew colder and colder. He shivered and took the sheet that held his possessions and placed it around his shoulders. But it barely made any difference. He slept in empty doorways, trying to shield himself from the wind. When there was enough light after the moon rose in the sky, he opened his book with the beautiful cover and the gold leaf. He labored over many of the words, but reading the pages summoned up the images of his father and what it was like to be seated next to him, the smell of his tobacco and his soap. The days had lost much of their warmth. In each town he passed, he asked for directions to Kavala. The soles of his bloodied leather shoes began to fray and now they flapped as he walked. He had grabbed a vine from an arbor and tried to use it to fasten the soles more firmly onto his shoes.

He made no attempt to keep track of time. One day after another, another shivering night, one step, another step as he followed the directions to Kavala. He needed to pull his pants more tightly around his waist. Had his pants somehow gotten bigger because of all his walking?

Finally, there was Kavala stretching out before him. It was a town with a harbor and mountains in the distance. The sea was aqua blue under the turquoise sky. The sea was not red with blood and bodies. From the distance, he could see a giant aqueduct. He'd seen pictures in books of aqueducts left from the times of the Romans. And what was that large structure? Was it an old castle? Yes, it seemed to be an old castle perched on a hill.

He needed to find Sophia's family. He needed some food. Even if Sophia hadn't yet arrived, he'd tell her family who he was and they would help him. They would give him some food and perhaps a place to live.

On the outskirts of town, he began to ask for Sophia Nupoulos's family. He was met with empty stares.

He finally met an old farmer shoveling hay who said he remembered them. "All died from the influenza, poor souls." The man made the sign of the cross across his chest. "Good people. It's been a long time, a very long time. It was after the Great War. So many were struck down, even the young and healthy."

"All of them died?"

"Every last one of them."

Andreas turned on his heel. Every last one of them. *Maybe* Sophia would make her way back here, just as he had. It was only a matter of time. But he didn't believe it. He had walked all this way for nothing. He was alone, a thief, a bad person.

He wandered the streets that wound up and down the hills and around the harbor where the boats small and large were anchored on the water. He passed large warehouses for tobacco storage. Not as big as the ones Patéra owned, but very large. He was hungry but he was used to that emptiness in his stomach. It was a prosperous town. There would be many garbage cans for him. Is this what his life would be? Wandering streets, stealing, being called *kléfti*, having stones thrown at him? Would he be caught someday and put in jail? Andreas Sefaris, a common thief, bringing shame to his family name. A family that no longer existed.

But that isn't what he wanted. He smoothed out his rumpled shirt and started to knock on the doors of stores and shops. "Please, I'm a hard worker. I would do anything. Sweeping, cleaning. Please I'm reliable. I need a job."

"Sorry, I don't need anyone… How old are you?"

"I'm eight years old."

"You don't look eight years old. Go away."

"I'm strong. I'll work for nothing until you see what a good worker I am," he pleaded.

"Go away." He heard over and over again, though sometimes he only received a scowl. Occasionally someone handed him a piece of bread and some cheese before telling him to go away. He occasionally recognized the sound of the Ladino language, which he knew from his days strolling the Jewish quarter in Smyrna with his friends.

He walked down one alleyway after another, knocking on one store after another. He was going to prison for being a thief. If not today then tomorrow, unless he wanted to keep wandering from town to town where no one knew him. But he was tired to the point of exhaustion. He wanted to stay in this town of Kavala, if there was only a small chance that Sophia would eventually come here looking for her family. There was a small chance perhaps, but the only chance of something good, the only chance.

It was growing dark. Over on the horizon he saw billowing clouds. His heart began to pound. Was that a cloud of smoke like those that had filled the skies of Smyrna? Was it a fire? And then he heard the rumble of thunder. Andreas let out a deep breath. There was no fire. Those were rain clouds. He needed to take cover or he'd be soaked and even colder. As he walked down the lane, he saw an open door to a storage shed. The rain began to pelt from the gray sky and he hurried inside. It was warmer in here. There was a bowl of milk on the floor. Andreas bent and smelled it. It wasn't spoiled. He gulped it down. How long had it been since he had any milk? He also saw a bowl with a lamb bone still covered with meat. He wolfed down the meat on the bone. How lucky he was to have found this place. If it was a storage shed, no one would be coming inside during the night. It was so much warmer than outside. He clutched his bundle as he found a space between two large sacks and promptly fell asleep.

What was that? He heard a sound. Was it an animal?

And then someone turned on a light in the shed. Someone was coming toward him.

CHAPTER 5

Kavala, Greece: October, 1922
AT THE SOUND of the birds chirping outside the window, the little girl opened her eyes, hoping it was finally first light. The armoire in the bedroom was lit with the streaks of sunlight that crept in through the slats of the shutters. Rebecca bent down and kissed the head of the puppy, who was snuggled in her arms. She couldn't risk getting up in the dark, waking the household and in particular, her five older sisters who shared the bedroom.

As she peeled back the quilt, she heard the voice of her sister Liza. "I know you slept all night long with that puppy in our bed. Really, Rebecca, don't you have any sense? When Papá finds out what you did, he is going to be really angry. He's told you over and over again, no dogs in the house. And besides, dogs are filthy."

"He isn't filthy. I gave him a bath yesterday. And I know, I know Papá will be angry if he finds out." Rebecca braided her hair and hurriedly put on her clothes as she watched the puppy make a puddle on their floor.

"And now, just look at what he did!" Liza wrinkled her nose with disgust.

"Go back to sleep. I'll take care of it. He hurt his foot and I needed to keep him inside with me 'til he was better." Rebecca grabbed a rag and wiped up the puddle.

"You're going to get into trouble again," her sister warned.

"I'm not, if you don't tell." Rebecca grabbed up the puppy in her arms and giggled as he licked her face. "I think his foot is better today and I won't bring him back into bed tonight. I promise. *Por favor*, please don't tell, Liza."

"What will you give me if I don't tell Papá?"

"Shhh! You'll wake everyone up."

"How about that pretty handkerchief you embroidered with Kiría Matsakis?"

"No! I'm saving that for my dowry. I have another one." Rebecca searched through her drawer. "See, this one is nice. Don't you think so?" She held out one of her earlier attempts at embroidery.

"I want the other one."

"Well, you can't have it. Tell Papá. I don't care." Rebecca turned her back on her older sister and quietly walked out the door.

Rebecca held the puppy in her arms, and stealthily made her way down the hallway, past her parents' bedroom, where her father's snores told her that Mamá and Papá were still asleep. Next, she hurried past her brothers' bedroom and then quietly crept down the stairs. She avoided the third step because that was the one that always creaked.

Rebecca found some scraps from last night's dinner and put them down for the dog. The puppy wasn't limping anymore! The little dog wolfed down the food. She opened the door and the puppy scampered away. "Bye puppy!" she called after him. "Come back tonight!"

Rebecca quietly closed the kitchen door and wiped her hands on a cloth towel. She opened a drawer and withdrew a small paring knife. She took the basket of apples and deftly began to peel them for today's baking. She needed to peel all of the apples in the basket because there would be a lot of baking today. Bright light was now streaming through the windows. The sun had fully risen. She needed to work quickly, so that when her mother came downstairs to the kitchen, the apples would all be peeled. Otherwise, when her mother saw Rebecca reading one of her brothers' school books, she would surely chastise her for wasting time.

She loved the book, *Great Expectations,* and hoped her brother Leon would let her have it to read again when he was finished. Leon read so slowly, laboring over each word. He was so unlike her, who read like the wind. Leon particularly had trouble reading in French. The Alliance Israelite School he attended gave all instructions in French, and Leon had such a hard time with any language other than Ladino.

Rebecca loved the sounds of the French language. Every day, after school, her brothers shared with her what they had learned. French was absolutely her favorite language and she so enjoyed this translation of Dickens. She was forced to read quickly, since in their household, there was no time allotted for an eight-year-old girl to read books, especially an eight-year-old girl who wasn't going to school.

She remembered standing on the other side of the door, listening to her parents as her mother urged her father to let her attend school. "Issac, let her go for just a year or two."

"That's foolish, Esther and a total waste of my hard-earned money. Why does a girl need to learn how to read? Well, Esther, tell me one good reason why Rebecca, the eighth daughter, needs to learn how to read?"

"She's very smart, Issac. You've often said she's the smartest one, even smarter than our two boys. When she was only three years old, the boys taught her how to read."

"Smart means nothing for a girl. Why does a girl need to be smart? I allowed you to talk me into sending our eldest two girls to school. Even you agreed with me it was a waste of our hard-earned money. Esther, you are such a good mother. Our girls will make wonderful wives to some lucky husbands. And I assure you, men are not looking for girls who have book learning. Is that why, when I saw you that day twenty years ago, I was smitten and knew I must marry you?"

"No." Rebecca heard her mother laugh. She knew the story of her parents' meeting was about to be shared again between them. It was such a romantic story that she had heard over and over again. Her father was a Romaniote Jew from Ioannina. His people had been in Greece for over a thousand years. They only spoke Greek. When he had journeyed to Kavala to do business and walked into her grandfather's store, he was thunderstruck with love. He saw Mamá and knew she was the one he must marry. But there were many obstacles to fulfilling his heart's desire. Nono, Mamá's father, only grudgingly accepted the fact her father was really Jewish. Papá didn't speak Ladino, the language of the Sephardic Jews who had been expelled from Spain in 1492. But Papá wouldn't give up. And he could tell the way Esther shyly met his gaze, that she felt the same way. "If you want to marry my daughter, you will leave your home in Ioannina and settle here," Nono told him.

"Yes," her father had agreed.

"But the first condition is that you learn Ladino. The Jews of Kavala speak Ladino."

"I will. I will learn it," her father had vowed.

"Go away and don't come back until you've learned our language."

"You won't have her married before then, will you?"

"I make no promises to a man I expect isn't even a Jew. You'd best learn quickly."

And so Papá had learned quickly and returned to Kavala. Mamá had waited for him. She'd had other suitors, but she had refused them. "My heart belonged to Papá," she told her children.

Mamá had a wonderful dowry as she was the only child of her parents. And because Mamá had no brothers, Nono had taken Papá into his dry goods store. The name of the store could never be changed, Nono told him. And so it was called Rouso Dry Goods. Papá had agreed to all conditions and they were married. Two boys and eight girls were the blessings of their marriage, one child coming quickly after another. Rebecca was the youngest. "Another girl, another girl," her father sometimes would call her instead of "Rebecca." Rebecca knew that being the eighth daughter was not a favored position in a family, particularly in a family that only owned a dry goods store.

"If only you were a boy," Papá often said. "You are so smart, learning to read and write from your brothers. But you waste your time, Rebecca. You waste your time with your nose in a book and a pencil in your hand."

"I get all my work done in the house. I do everything that Mamá tells me to do," Rebecca told had him as she sat on the stool in his dry goods store.

Papá had just shook his head and continued to stack the shelves.

"I want to have a wonderful love story like you and Mamá had. Do you think reading will make a husband not want me?" Rebecca had been concerned.

Her father had turned around and affectionately patted her head. "Little Rebecca, reading and writing won't make any difference to a man who would seek a match with you as his bride. However, you're wasting your time with all this learning you get from your brothers. I know you are the best at learning Greek, the language of my family. Your sisters are hopeless, even though I have spoken to them in Greek since they were babies. I'm depending upon you, Rebecca, to teach my grandchildren Greek."

"I'll teach Greek to all my children."

"Well, I want you to be able to teach your sisters' children Greek, and perhaps your brothers' children, if they are too lazy to do that."

"How many children do you think I will have Papá? I want ten just like you and Mamá have."

"Only God knows the future," her father told her.

❧❧❧

Breakfast was displayed on the long dining room table. Cheese, olives, yogurt, and bread were arrayed on big platters.

Before they all sat down, her brother Leon pulled her into the hallway. "Did you finish looking over my paper? I have to hand it in tomorrow."

"It's getting better," She said with a smile to her brother. "I made some corrections and I put it inside your notebook."

"*Graysas*, thanks!" He gave her a kiss on the cheek. "You're the best! Too bad you aren't a boy. You'd be at the top of our class. If you were the oldest girl, like Miriam, they would have sent you to school and you would have excelled. But after she and Roza did so poorly, almost to the point of being a family embarrassment... "

"I know. Papá realized it was a waste of money to send a girl to school," Rebecca echoed the words she'd heard. "And Papá is right, you know. A husband isn't looking for a girl with book learning."

"Remember, boys," their mother told them as they sat around the table eating their breakfast. "This afternoon, your sisters Miriam and Roza are coming over with their mother-in-law. Your cousins are also coming. Don't take any detours on your way home from school and don't dirty your clothes. You'll just have to say hello to everyone and then you can go up to your room and do your school work."

Rebecca smiled as she helped herself to some cheese from the serving platter. There would be all kinds of cakes and cookies this afternoon, including *spentzopountza*, the raisin and nut pastries that reminded Papá of his home. She couldn't wait to visit with her twin sisters. Rebecca always marveled that her parents had arranged such a wonderful marriage match for them with two brothers. And now, both Miriam and Roza were expecting their first children within two months of each other. She was going to be an aunt, a *tia!* She couldn't wait to hold the babies.

"Rebecca," her mother spoke to her while pouring coffee for Papá. "I know you're going over to Kiría Matsakis this afternoon, but don't forget the time. You need to be back when your sisters arrive."

"I will. I will. Cousin Vida isn't coming, is she?" Rebecca asked. "She's so mean."

"She's your cousin, and so, of course, she is invited."

"She is mean to Rebecca," Liza agreed. "The last time we were all together, she told Rebecca that because she was the eighth girl, our Papá wouldn't have any money for her dowry and so she was never getting married. I told her to stop saying bad things to my baby sister."

"Rebecca will be well taken care of." Her father took another swallow of his coffee. "It's almost time for the store to open and I need to say good-bye to my family." He got to his feet and gave Mamá a kiss on her cheek.

Rebecca took her last bite of breakfast. "I peeled the apples this morning, so they'll be ready for us to make apple cake. I'm so excited. Kiría Matsakis said her new Singer sewing machine arrived and she'd show it to me. She's expecting me after lunch. I'll be back before everyone arrives."

"Does a *makina de cuzir*, sewing machine, do all the sewing for you and you don't need to pick up a needle?" asked Allegra.

"I don't think so. I think a woman needs to do something for it to work," Rebecca replied.

"Why can't we get one?" asked Bella.

"Because they are expensive and Kiría Matsakis is a seamstress. She needs one to do her work," Mamá told them.

"Well, when I get married I'm going to ask my husband to get me one," announced Klara.

"You're the fifth girl. I don't think you're going to have a grand enough dowry to get yourself a rich husband." Hannah wiped her chin with a napkin.

"Enough talk of dowries and husbands. Only Allegra is close to the age for marriage. Girls, get up from the table and off to the kitchen with you.

There's work to be done. We need to start the baking," Mamá commanded and everyone was silent. Mamá always sounded stern before company was coming.

The morning was spent clearing the breakfast dishes and then washing and drying them. Hannah, Klara and Allegra began helping Mamá with the apple cake. Yesterday, they had baked *kourabiedes,* cookies, and *pan despanya*, almond sponge cake. Before everyone arrived, Mamá would fry the *loukoumades* so they would be hot and fresh when their company arrived.

"Rebecca." Her mother turned towards her. "You don't have to stay in the kitchen with us this morning. You already peeled all the apples. Your sisters will help me with the baking. You can work on your embroidery and go visit with Papá. But remind me before you go to Kiría Matsakis this afternoon, that I would like to talk to you."

"About what, Mamá? Can't you just tell me now?"

"No, you and I will talk alone."

Rebecca ran upstairs, grabbed her embroidery box and dashed back downstairs. "*Adyo,* bye!" she called out as she hurried outside and into Papá's store. It was called Rouso's Dry Goods. That was Mamá's last name before she married Papá. How Rebecca loved the store with shelves and shelves of canned goods, ribbons, and fabrics of every description. She had a favorite stool in the corner where she would sit, working on her latest embroidery project, watching all of Papá's customers and listening to them talk to Papá about what was happening in their lives. Some of his customers were Christians who spoke Greek and others were Jews who spoke Ladino. And of course, her Papá was fluent in both languages.

"Hi Papá," Rebecca called out as she walked inside the store. "Mamá says I could come over. My sisters are helping in the kitchen."

"I'm not very busy this morning." He smiled at her. "I received a new shipment of ribbons. Go take a look at them and pick something out for yourself. I'll cut you two pieces for your braids."

"Yes, *graysas,* Papá!" She ran over to the ribbon display. She stood there pondering her choices. Which color would look best tied to her braids? She couldn't decide. Should she select the blue or the red? "I can't decide," she told her father.

"Well, you think about it. Let me know before lunchtime."

"I will." Rebecca looked again at the pretty ribbons before she sat down on the stool behind the counter. She picked up her embroidery and began to make tiny stitches with her needle.

"Isaac!" A young man walked inside.

"Botsis, I haven't seen you in quite a while." Her father grasped the young man's hand in greeting.

"I've been off with the Greek Navy for the last few months. Let me tell you, it seemed like forever. I've come to purchase a present for my wife. She wants me to leave the Navy, stay in Kavala and not sail all over the world."

"And will you listen to your wife?"

"After this last voyage, I think I might be finished with being a sailor. Hi there." He noticed Rebecca and smiled at her.

"Hello." Rebecca looked up at him and returned his greeting. Her attention was then focused on her embroidery and the beautiful colors and small stitches she had worked on to achieve a pattern of birds and flowers.

"So which girl is this one?" the man asked.

"She is number eight," her father explained.

"I know you have eight girls and you're not a rich man… But you do have two sons, don't you?"

"Yes, two fine sons," he answered with pride.

"My wife is having our first. I'm sure it will be a boy. Maybe I'll have eight sons," he mused.

"Where did you sail off to this time?" asked her father.

"We were sent over to Smyrna, in Asia Minor. It was so horrible, horrible."

"We've heard rumors. There has been a wave of refugees who came to us after they stopped off in Lesbos. They came from Asia Minor and particularly the areas around the Black Sea."

"I don't know what you've heard about Smyrna. But it was worse than anything you could imagine." The young man settled into a chair and accepted the cup of coffee her father offered him.

"Rebecca, why don't you go into the back room and count up the large boxes of nails that came in yesterday. And don't forget to close the door behind you," her father told her.

"Yes, Papá." Rebecca jumped off her stool and headed toward the backroom. She knew she wasn't supposed to hear what this Greek Orthodox man was going to tell Papá. But if she pressed her ear against the door, she could hear. She wanted to hear everything, to learn about everything there was in the world. Papá often asked her to leave and go to the backroom, but she always listened through the door. Sometimes she didn't understand everything that was discussed, but she liked listening anyway.

"Tell me, Botsis. Do you know if the Jews from Smyrna were hurt?"

"No, your people were safe Isaac. But the Christians. Oh my God. The Greek Orthodox and Armenian areas were burned to the ground. Those who could escape ran down to the quay. Did you know, Isaac, that the harbor was filled with over twenty war ships from all the Great Powers?"

"How fortunate they were there to rescue those fleeing the fire."

"They didn't. Neutrality, they said. They had to maintain neutrality. The Turks, in particular their new leader, a fellow called Kemal Mustafah, would exact a price, if the English and Americans helped those poor people. The story we heard was that an American minister, a *sotíra*, took it upon himself to demand help for those on the dock. He arranged for the Greek navy to come. We weren't able to fly our flag. We couldn't offend the Turks."

"And you were able to rescue everyone?"

"Those poor people were left on the quay for two weeks before there were any rescue attempts. Every night, the Turkish soldiers rode through the crowd and took many of the women. There was rape and murder everywhere. People who tried to leave the docks were shot by the cavalry. When the refugees got on the boats, there were only old men, women and children. The younger men had all been taken away by the Turks.

"The sailors said that on the other warships at night, there was so much wailing and crying from the dock that they played music to drown out the horrible sounds. The sailors couldn't bear to hear the crying and moaning. And let me tell you, the people who got on our boat were pitiful, just pitiful.

"I never want to witness such horrors again in my life. I'm glad to have done *Toú Theoú to thélima*, the Lord's work, that day. But I am ready to leave the Navy and take up a settled life. Just thinking about what I saw… I can't get the images out of my mind. They will haunt me forever. Those poor people were burned out of their homes. Some houses were burned with the people inside. What had they done wrong but be Christians?

"Do you have some of that fine *retsina* under your counter?" Botsis asked. "I need a drink."

"Of course."

"*Yassas*," her father toasted.

"*Yassas*," the Greek Orthodox man answered.

Rebecca walked away from the door. She picked up the inventory notebook. Would bad people come after the Jews like they had come after the Christians, burning down their homes? She was sorry that she had listened. She willed the horrible images out of her mind and looked down at the inventory book.

⚜

Rebecca hurried through her lunch. She picked up her plate and put it in the kitchen sink. "I'm leaving!" Rebecca called as she walked toward the door.

"Remember to be home before our afternoon gathering."

"I will. I will. And I'll tell you all about the sewing machine!" Rebecca grabbed her embroidery and an apple.

"Rebecca, I wanted to talk to you. I forgot, with all the baking and preparing this morning," her mother called to her as she ran out the door.

"Don't worry Mamá. We can talk later."

"But… "

Rebecca skipped down the street. She couldn't wait to see the new sewing machine. She could always talk to her mother.

Rebecca walked inside the Matsakis cobbler shop. The sweet smell of leather enveloped her as she waved at Kìrios Matsakis, who was pounding nails into the boots he was crafting.

"Go on, Rebecca. My wife is waiting for you. The new sewing machine has arrived."

"I'm so excited." She ran to the back of the cobbler shop and entered the Matsakis sewing area.

Kiría Matsakis was a tall woman with very straight posture and smiling hazel eyes. She always wore her hair in an old-fashioned bun at the base of her neck. Her soft, soothing voice, seemed like warm honey to Rebecca. And there she was, sitting next to the sewing machine. The Singer... all shiny and black and beautiful. It wasn't even a used machine, but totally brand new. Kiría Matsakis was bent over a dress pattern, but she looked up when she heard Rebecca's footsteps.

"Oh," Rebecca breathed, as she approached the machine. "How wonderful!"

"Come, come, my little one." Kiría Matsakis got up from the pattern and took Rebecca by the hand. "Here it is!"

"Can I touch it?"

"Of course." The woman smiled as Rebecca ran her hand over the shiny black machine.

"Have you tried it yet? Oh, of course, you must have tried it. Does it sew? Does it really sew? Can I watch? Someday, someday, if I promise to be careful, will you let me try it?" Rebecca gushed as her eyes fixated on the machine, and she ran her small hand over the shiny black body, decorated with golden scrolls.

"Yes, of course, I tried it as soon as it was delivered. It sews beautifully, beautifully. And yes, little Rebecca, I will show you how it sews and you can try it."

Rebecca hugged herself with excitement.

"Especially now that you will be spending all day with me, we'll have so much time for you to learn everything."

Rebecca wrinkled her brow. "I'll be spending all day with you? I don't understand. I love sewing with you but I need to be at home most of the time to help Mamá and my sisters."

"Didn't your mother tell you?" Kiría Matsakis sighed.

"Tell me? She said she wanted to talk to me before I came over to see the Singer, but we got too busy. The women in the family are coming over to visit later this afternoon, and there was so much preparation to do."

"Well, your parents and I had a long talk. I told them what a wonderful seamstress you could become someday. That you had talent I had never seen before in one so young. And we all agreed, you should be my seamstress apprentice. In a few years, you could accompany me when I travel out of town. The wedding dress I delivered last week… everyone was overcome with the beauty of the embroidery that you had sewn on the sleeves."

"As much as I love sewing... a woman with children can't be a seamstress, traveling away from home. You told me how sad it was that you and Kìrios Matsakis never had any children. A woman with children needs to stay at home. I don't understand," Rebecca shook her head and smiled down at the gray cat that rubbed against her shins.

Whiskers wasn't an outdoor cat, like the ones at her house who left every night. Whiskers stayed inside all the time with Kiría Matsakis, meowing and rubbing up against her legs, wanting to be picked up. Rebecca reached down and pulled the cat onto her lap. "Well, when I go home, I'll ask Mamá. Maybe I could spend more time here, but certainly not all day."

"Yes, Rebecca. Ask your Mamá. Now, come close and I'll show you how the Singer works. See this?" She pointed toward the metal plate under her foot. "This is the treadle. It makes the machine sew. You're still too little for your feet to reach it, but soon you'll be big enough." Kiría Matsakis pressed down on the treadle and the noise made the cat jump off Rebecca's lap. Rebecca watched with fascination as the needle went up and down on the piece of cloth.

"Look how fast it goes!"

The seamstress smiled at the sewing machine.

Rebecca was helping her sisters dry dishes from the afternoon get-together with the ladies and girls in her family. She wondered if she had eaten too many sweets because her stomach felt near to bursting. But all of her favorites were displayed on Mamá's special entertaining china and

Rebecca couldn't stop herself. It was always so much fun to visit with the Rouso cousins and it was wonderful seeing her sisters who were about to become mothers and make her *Tia* Rebecca, an aunt. She couldn't wait to see their babies. Tia Rebecca. And someday, Rebecca mused, it would be her sitting in Mamá's parlor and everyone would be so excited about her becoming a mother for the first time.

"Mamá," Rebecca called to her mother when she brought in the last of the dishes from the table. "I saw the sewing machine at Kiría Matsakis's today. It sews so fast. My legs are a little too short to reach the treadle. A treadle is what makes the machine sew. But soon I'll be able to use it and she'll teach me."

Her mother smiled at her.

"I want to go over to see it too," said Bella.

"I'm sure that would be alright. I'll ask Kiría Matsakis when you can all come over to see the Singer. Mamá, she said something about me spending more time with her that I didn't understand."

"Come." Mamá beckoned to her. "Come with me into the parlor, Rebecca. Girls, finish up in the kitchen and start preparing for dinner."

"Yes, Mamá," the girls chorused, as they continued washing and drying the dishes.

Mamá closed the door between the kitchen and the parlor. She sank down into the chair. "I think everything went well, didn't it? But I'm exhausted. I worry so much if everything will be just right. I hope my Rouso cousins will praise my baking. I've always been known as the best baker in the family and I don't want to disappoint them."

"Oh, Mamá, you are the best baker," Rebecca assured her.

"Well, let us talk now. I wanted to talk to you before you went over to the Matsakis place, but I was distracted by the ladies coming over. What did Kiría Matsakis tell you?"

"She said you and Papá had talked to her about me spending my days with her, learning to be a seamstress. And when I got older, I could travel with her to do fittings. I love to sew, Mamá. But a woman with a family, with children, doesn't do such things. It would be nice to make beautiful clothes for my children. Poor Kiría Matsakis doesn't have any children, so she has the time to sew for other people."

"And you know, of course, that people pay her money for her beautiful work?"

"Yes," Rebecca replied with a frown. She didn't understand something. But she was only eight years old and her mother would explain to her what wasn't making any sense.

"Your Papá and I only want what is best for you and for all of our children, who we love with all our hearts. Papá is not a rich man. But we have a roof over our heads and food on our table.

"Our little Rebecca, with a heart of gold and such a pretty little face, who is the eighth daughter... Papá is barely able to provide a dowry for Hannah, our seventh daughter. Who knows what man would be content with such a small dowry? But we will hope for the best. Rebecca, try as we might, there isn't enough left for a dowry for you. Without a dowry, there will be no husband. I'm sorry."

Rebecca felt a tightness across her chest. No dowry, not even a small one?

"Papá and I will always have a place for you in our house. But we won't live forever and we want to make sure you are well cared for. We don't want you to have to depend on the charity of your brothers and sisters. Of course, they would take you in. But you have such a talent for sewing and Kiría Matsakis is so fond of you. You'll learn how to be a seamstress and you'll be able to earn money, so not having a husband to take care of you won't be so bad."

Rebecca wanted to say something, but words failed her. She tried to blink back tears, but they began to slip down her cheeks.

"Here." Her mother handed her a handkerchief.

"I wanted to be a mother," she whispered.

"I know. But you'll be a wonderful aunt. I'm sorry Rebecca. Papá has already taken out loans to provide for your sisters' dowries. If there was any way we could think of to accumulate a dowry for you... But it's just impossible." Her mother gathered Rebecca into her arms and held her.

CQ∂D

Kavala: November, 1922

Rebecca hurried into Kiría Matsakis' workroom.

"The *bris* just ended and I needed to change my clothes before I came over."

"That's alright," the woman assured her as she looked up from cutting out a pattern. "Come sit beside me and you must tell me all about the circumcision of your nephew."

"Look, I brought you some sweets." Rebecca sat down and unwrapped the napkin she withdrew from her pocket. "You must taste the *spentzopountza*. They are Papá's favorite and Mamá has to make them whenever there is a celebration. They are from his family, the Romaniote Jews and it reminds him of home in Ioannina. Everyone was celebrating and so happy. Have you been to a *bris*?"

"Only Jews and Muslims circumcise their boys. Christians don't do that," she explained.

"Really? Papá said the *bris* is done to honor the covenant between God and the Jewish people. But the *bris* is also to give a name to the boys. What do Christians do to give a name to their boys?"

"We have a Baptism in church." Kiría Matsakis placed pins on the pattern over the cloth. "Well, Tia Rebecca, what is the name of your nephew?"

"Samuel. I think I like that name. Don't you? A *bris* is done on the eighth day after a baby is born. It has to be the eighth day. And it wasn't just a usual *bris*, because it was a first born son. It's really important to have a son, you know."

"Yes, I do know. Among the Orthodox Christians, it's the same."

"So anyway, the house was packed, all the Rouso family and friends and other cousins. We'd baked for days and days. That's why I didn't come over on Monday and Tuesday."

"So what does this nephew of yours look like?"

"He's really, really small. His hands and feet are so tiny. I have to tell you a secret. I'm not sure if I think he is so cute. Do you think he will look better when he gets older?"

"I'm sure. Babies look better as they grow."

"Oh, that's good. Because I had to say how cute he was when I didn't think so at all."

"Your Mamá must be so happy to have her first grandchild."

"Oh, she is," Rebecca said. "Any day now, Roza will have her child. If it's a boy there will be another *bris.*" She noticed Kiría Matsakis pursing her lips into a tight knot.

"Kiría Matsakis, does it make you sad when I talk about children? I know you told me that it was God's will that you and Kìrios Matsakis didn't have any children. But I think that makes you sad. I don't want to make you sad. I'm sorry I talked about it."

"Don't fret about me, Rebecca. I have my successful business. I give everyone pleasure with my sewing and I have a good husband. I am also aunt to many nieces and nephews."

"I will be Tia to many nieces and nephews, too."

"Of course you will. Now tell me, what did your sister Miriam say when she saw the beautiful baby clothes you had embroidered for her little boy?"

"Not just Miriam, but all the ladies said they had never seen such beautiful baby clothes and asked if I could sew some for their children."

"You see, Rebecca? You have such talent. Now pin the pattern to the cloth while I get more fabric to work on."

"Kiría Matsakis, could I get some more of that lamb dish you made? Just a little bit for the puppy I'm feeding? I want to put some out in the shed, now that it's getting cold. Papá was really mad when he heard I kept the puppy in my bed. He said cats are okay because they kill mice, but puppies don't do anything useful. But I think the puppy can stay in the storage shed out back, at least at night when it gets cold... Until Papá finds out. You won't tell, will you?"

"That is between you and your father."

"When I found puppy he was so little and he'd hurt his foot. He couldn't walk very well. After I took care of him for a little while, he could run."

"Come." Kiría Matsakis held out her arms and gave her a hug. "Rebecca Solomon, you are the most wonderful little girl, with such a big heart. If I had a daughter, I'd want her to be just like you."

"But I couldn't be your daughter because I'm Jewish and you are Christian," Rebecca said seriously.

"That is true. But we can be dear friends, can't we?"

"Yes, we are friends. I love coming here and spending time with you and learning to sew." Rebecca began to pin a pattern to the fabric. "I think I should give the puppy a name. How about Zeus?"

"Zeus is a wonderful name for a dog.

"And I think you shouldn't call me Kiría Matsakis, but Kiría Eleni."

⊱⊰

Dinner was over in the Solomon home. Rebecca and her sisters had finished cleaning up.

"Leon, you left the door to the back shed open, so I had to close it," Papá admonished her brother as his son looked up from his book.

"I don't think I did," Leon said with a puzzled look.

"Well, you were the last one in there, when you got the sugar from storage."

"Alright, I guess it was me. But I'm really careful about that."

Rebecca put down her embroidery. "I have to go out to the Matsakises."

"Now? It can't wait until tomorrow?" Her father frowned.

"No, it can't. I promised her something and I forgot." Rebecca pulled her coat over her dress and tossed her braids over her shoulders. She'd left the door open to the storage shed so the puppy could get in, spend the night and eat the food she'd provided for him. If the door was closed to the storage shed, Zeus would be locked out and have to spend the night with no food, in the cold.

"Everyone in this family is forgetting today." Papá shook his head as he inhaled on his cigarette. "Well, hurry back."

"I will." Rebecca ran out the front door and then continued down the lane behind the house until she stood at the storage shed with the closed door. How was puppy going to get the food she had left for him if the door was closed? As Rebecca reached for the door handle, puppy came running up to her, wagging his tail.

"Did you get any food, Zeus?" she asked, as she picked up the dog and opened the door. She pulled on the chain for the overhead light bulb and dropped the dog to the floor. The bowl was empty. So, he had gotten fed tonight even though the door was closed?

Suddenly the small dog started barking and jumping up and down. "What's the matter?" she asked him. Zeus snarled and growled. Rebecca took a step backward. Was there a wild animal hidden behind the sacks of flour? Something moved. Rebecca picked up a nearby shovel as she walked toward where the puppy was growling.

"Don't hurt me!" She heard a voice speaking Greek. And then she saw two dark brown eyes peering out at her.

CHAPTER 6

REBECCA TOOK A deep breath as she saw the large dark eyes looking up at her. Who was hiding in their storage shed? She continued to grip the shovel in her hands tightly.

"Why are you in our storage shed?" she tried to sound grown up.

There was no answer.

"Come out of there. Come out. You can't stay here," she said in Greek. She watched as the flour sacks parted and a boy dressed in ragged clothing, clutching a bundle, stood before her. "You have to leave. Go on!"

"It's cold outside," the boy with the large dark eyes told her in a soft voice.

"Yes, it is cold." She put her shovel down as the puppy walked over to the boy and wagged his tail. "So you need to go back to your own home."

"I can't," he told her.

"It's dark... your family must be worried about you."

He didn't answer.

"What part of town do you live in? I could ask my Papá to bring you home."

"I'm from far away." He clutched his bundle more tightly.

"Where?"

"Smyrna, far away from here."

"Where is your family?"

"Please, let me stay until morning. It will be warmer then and I'll leave."

"Don't you have a coat? It's too cold to be outside without a coat."

The boy sat down on the floor. "I don't have a coat and it's cold outside."

Rebecca stooped to pick up the dog and walked closer to the boy. The puppy licked her face and she giggled. No, she told herself. I have to be serious and talk to this strange boy as if I were a grown up. She noticed the boy was wearing shoes held together with vines. He must come from a very poor family. Maybe Kìrios Matsakis would have an old pair of shoes to give to this boy. With winter coming, his feet would get cold. She must think of what Mamá would say if she found a strange boy in their storage shed.

"Then you need to go home where it's warm and get your coat. Your family is going to wonder what happened to you."

"Just let me stay until morning, please."

"Well, I guess since it's dark and cold," Rebecca paused and sensed the overwhelming sadness in this boy. It wouldn't do any harm to let him stay until morning. Would it? "What's your name? My name is Rebecca."

"Andreas Sefaris, from Smyrna. Are you a Turk?" he asked.

"A Turk? Heavens no. I'm Jewish."

"I saw mosques in your town. There must be Turks living here. Don't tell them I'm here. Please don't tell them."

Rebecca heard the desperation in his voice. Something was very wrong. As she sat down next to him, she remembered the Greek Orthodox sailor who told that terrible story to her father of the Turks burning down the city of Smyrna and the people being killed. Was this boy from that place?

"The mosques are for the Muslims. They aren't Turks. They are Greeks."

"Are you sure?

"Of course, I'm sure. The churches are for the Greek Orthodox, the synagogues are for the Jews and the mosques are for the Muslims. We are all Greek. There are no Turks here."

"They could come here. The soldiers could come here and kill all the Christians. Maybe they would kill the Jews, too. They killed the Armenians. Does your Patéra have a gun?"

"Why would my father have a gun?"

"He needs to have a gun to protect your family from the Turks."

"I told you, there are no Turks in Kavala. I have to go back to my house. You must be gone by morning or my father might find you, and I'm sure he won't let you stay in our storage shed." Rebecca needed to get back before her father sent one of her brothers to find her. But she hesitated. The boy was so sad. Why wasn't he home with his own family? "If you're from Smyrna, which is far away from here, where is your family living now?" she asked him as she got to her feet.

"Do you have any food you could let me have?" he asked, ignoring her question.

Rebecca stopped in midstep as she held the dog against herself. He was hungry. This poor sad boy was hungry. "I can bring you something."

"Thank you. Anything, please, just anything."

Rebecca looked at him again. His pants were covered with a brown stain. Was that blood? Was he hurt?

"Are you bleeding?" she asked him with concern. She was going to have to get her mother. She hoped Mamá hadn't already gone to sleep. "I'll get my mother. She'll take care of you."

"No, no. Please don't tell anyone I'm here. I'm not bleeding."

"Are you sure? My father can take you back home tomorrow morning."

"I don't have a home."

"Everyone has a home," Rebecca told him. "Where are your parents? You need to go home to your parents."

"I have no parents."

Everyone has parents, she thought. Everyone has a home.

"Stay here and I'll bring you some food." She looked down at the empty bowl where she had left food for the dog and the stray cats.

"I ate it," he said in a soft voice as if he could read her mind. "I'm sorry if I ate the food for your dog. I was hungry."

If this boy had eaten the table scraps she'd left for the dog, he must really be very hungry.

"I'll be back soon," she told him.

"Promise me you won't tell anyone I'm here. Promise me," he beseeched her.

"I told you there are no Turks here. No one will hurt you."

"But if people from the orphanage find out I am here, they will take me away and I won't be able to find my sister. Just promise me, please."

"Alright, I promise," Rebecca told him and ran out of the shed and up the lane back into her house, trying to be as quiet as possible.

"You were out with your puppy again?" Her mother was sitting in the kitchen.

"His foot, there is something wrong with it, and I was holding him and feeding him."

"Rebecca, you want to take care of the whole world of stray cats and dogs, and you can't. Now off to bed with you. We'll go together."

Rebecca and her mother went up the stairs to their bedrooms.

"Good night, Mamá." She watched Mamá close her door.

Rebecca hurried into her own bedroom. All of her sisters were asleep, save for Liza who was peering out over the quilt she had pulled up to her chin.

"Where were you?" her sister asked. "Taking care of another dog or cat?"

"Liza," Rebecca whispered. "I have to go back outside."

"You aren't supposed to be going out at night. I'm going to tell on you."

"Look." Rebecca reached into her drawer. "See, you can have the pretty embroidered handkerchief you wanted." She pulled it out and waved it in front of her older sister. "But you can't tell on me."

"I won't." Liza grabbed the handkerchief out of her hands. "I'll save this for my dowry. It's so beautiful."

"If you tell, I'll take it back."

"Go on. Go take care of that disgusting dog."

Rebecca crept downstairs, not making a sound. She walked past the closet where the linens were stored and searched for a heavy blanket. Then she made her way inside the kitchen. She opened the cupboards, looking for the leftovers from dinner and the *bris*. First, she filled a plate with food and then she gathered some apples into a napkin. She saw the face of that poor ragged boy and his plea for something to eat. She shuddered. She had to help him. If only she could tell Mamá, Mamá would be happy to give him food and something warm. Maybe even some old clothes from Ephraim and Leon. But she had promised not to tell and she always kept a promise.

She unlocked the kitchen door and closed it quietly behind her, her hands clutching the blanket and all the food she had gotten from the kitchen.

She ran to the storage shed, for a moment afraid the boy, Andreas, would be gone before she had a chance to give him the food. Imagine, the boy was so hungry he'd eaten the scraps of food she'd left for the dog.

He was there, crouched on the floor, blowing into his hands to keep them warm.

"You came back!" He gave her a small smile, the first smile she'd seen on that sad face. He stood up and she noticed that those pants, that were covered with blood, were much too big for him.

"Are those your pants?" she asked as she handed him the blanket. He wrapped it around his shoulders. At the sight of all the food, his eyes widened with surprise. He reached for the plate of food with dirty hands. She wanted to tell him to wash his hands before he ate, but there was no running water in the shed.

"Thank you, thank you," he whispered as he took a hunk of bread and cheese. "This is so good!" Rebecca had never seen anyone eat so fast. "Thank you! *Efharistó*! Thank you!" he kept repeating.

"You said you don't have a home. Then where are you getting food to eat? Where do you live?" she asked as she sat down beside him.

"I don't live anywhere," he said in between swallows. "I eat from garbage cans. This food is the best I have ever had."

Garbage cans! She wanted to shout. You eat from garbage cans?

"How old are you?"

"I'm eight, but I'll be nine soon."

"I'm eight too," Rebecca told him. How could he be eight years old and have no parents? No wonder he was eating from garbage cans. She felt so sad for him. She imagined herself without Papá and Mamá. What would she do? She heard the wind blowing outside the shed and then the sound of heavy rain on the roof. The boy pulled the blanket more closely around his shoulders.

"Why are you wearing pants that are too big for you? Are they your pants?" Maybe he found them in one of the garbage cans when he was searching for food to eat.

"I've been doing so much walking it must have made the pants too big. They are my pants." And for a moment, he stopped eating and ran his fingers over the stains she had thought were blood.

"*Efharistó*. Thank you so much. Thank you. I'll be gone in the morning. I'll leave the blanket right here. It will just be so good to be warm tonight. I don't have much to give you to pay for all that you have given me tonight. Someday, when I have a job, I'll come back and give you some drachmas."

The boy ate every last crumb and wiped his grimy hands on his dirty pants.

"You don't have to pay me," she told him.

"Wait, I have something maybe you would like to see." He reached down to the floor, to the small bundle and opened it. Rebecca saw a book, a jeweled crucifix, a piece of blue paper and a pouch. He reached inside the pouch and withdrew beautifully-colored marbles. He looked down at them and then closed them up in his fingers.

"You said you came from Smyrna?"

"Do you know Smyrna?"

"I… I heard some bad things had happened there."

Rebecca tried to remember what the man had said that day in Papá's store about the burning and killing. But she'd tried to put it out of her mind because it was awful, very awful. She needed to get back to her house and the warmth of her bed, under the covers beside her sisters. But it seemed wrong to leave the boy alone in the shed.

"I might be able to get you some different pants," she offered. "I have older brothers and they have old clothes that we haven't given away yet."

"I don't want different pants," his voice was hoarse and his face contorted with sorrow. "This is blood on my pants and I need to keep it." He opened his fingers and looked down at the marbles. "Aren't they beautiful? My Patéra, gave them to me."

Rebecca watched as the tears began to slip down his cheeks, making streaks on his dirty face.

"Yes, they are beautiful," she told him, thinking don't cry, don't cry. Don't be so sad. I'll find food for you. I'll find clothes for you and you can keep the blanket.

"Does your Patéra have a gun in your house to protect you?" Andreas asked in a whisper.

"Protect me from who?"

"From the Turks. When they come, he must try to protect you. My Patéra had a gun and he let me see it. My pants are covered in his blood."

He started to cry. "There was a knock on the door, a terrible loud banging and a Turkish soldier came into our house. He was going to take our house away and Baba said no and the soldier stabbed him with a big sword. There was so much blood on Baba's shirt," he continued, one word rushing past the other. "And then the soldier was going to hurt my Mamá and my sister Maria and so I shot the evil man with Patéra's gun." Andreas started sobbing, his shoulders heaving.

Rebecca reached out her hand to him tentatively. Sobbing and crying, he put his head in her lap. "And then we went down to the quay because the town was burning and people were running, and my baby sister died because we didn't have any medicine. And then a Turk came and grabbed my sister and Mamá tried to save her and the soldier banged his baton on Mamá's head and kicked her and Mamá was dead and my sister was gone…" He sobbed and sobbed and Rebecca placed her hand on his thick head of dark curls, trying to soothe him. Her own eyes welled with tears that slipped down her cheeks. He grabbed her waist and buried his head in her lap, lost in tears and terrible sobs that shook his body as he clung to her. Rebecca felt his pain deep in her own heart.

"It's alright," Rebecca whispered, as she smoothed her fingers through his hair. Alright, she thought, how could it be alright? This poor sad little boy with no family... But she knew nothing else to say as he sobbed in her lap. Rebecca continued to sit on the floor beside the crying boy. She should be getting back home. She wasn't sure her sister Liza could be depended upon to keep her secret for very long. But she couldn't leave Andreas; she just couldn't, as his pain seeped deep inside her.

Andreas straightened up and wiped his dirty cheeks. "I'm sorry."

"Don't be sorry. I need to go back home before I'm missed and get into trouble."

"I don't want you to get into trouble. Will you be my friend?"

"Of course," Rebecca answered with a smile, trying not to break down into tears at the sadness in this boy.

"I'll bring you more food in the morning." She reached over to the blanket and wrapped it more securely around his shoulders. "You'll have to leave in the morning after I bring you some food because my family goes in and out of this shed during the day. They won't want anyone living here."

"In the daytime, I'll be gone. I'm looking for my sister Maria and our maid Sophia. I'm trying to find a job."

A job, Rebecca thought. You're too young and too little. This boy was no bigger than she was and she was a small girl. "I'll see you tomorrow morning."

"You'll come back in the morning with more food, won't you?" he asked with so much hope on his face that Rebecca had to bite her lip to keep from crying.

"Do you want puppy to stay with you tonight?" she offered. "Go on, puppy."

The puppy scampered into the boy's open arms. "I'll turn off the light," Rebecca explained, as she pulled down on the light bulb chain. For a moment she stood in the darkness. She didn't want to leave him all alone in the shed but she couldn't stay. She walked slowly toward the door.

"Bye, Rebecca, my friend. *Efharistó*, thank you."

"I'll be back early in the morning, as soon as the sun has risen."

⊂⧼⧽⊃

Rebecca spent a restless night in the bed she shared with Liza. She'd close her eyes, hoping for sleep, but all she could see was the sad boy crying and sobbing with his head in her lap. She couldn't just feed him in the shed each day. He couldn't live there like one of the dogs and cats living on the streets that she liked to feed. He needed a Mamá and a Papá. Could he live with them? Would Mamá and Papá take him in? Because he spoke Greek she thought he must be a Christian and they were Jewish. Rebecca didn't know if it was possible for a Christian to live in a Jewish home. And Papá was always complaining about having enough money. Surely he wouldn't want another mouth to feed. She needed to talk to her parents. They would know what to do.

At first light the next morning she entered the shed, laden with food and some water to drink. Andreas was still asleep on the floor. His arms were curled around the puppy, who looked up at her and wagged his tail.

Rebecca cleared her throat.

"You came back!" The boy smiled.

She put down the food for him and a small bowl for the dog. "I can't stay," she told him. "I have to get back to my family."

"You'll be here again tonight?"

"Yes, I will. Take care, Andreas." She smiled at him. She wanted to tell him she was going to tell her parents about him. Surely they would help him.

"Rebecca, you aren't going to tell anyone about me. You promised. There are people who want to put me away in an orphanage and I'll never be able to find my sister."

"I promise I won't tell anyone about what happened to you and your family in Smyrna. I must go."

Rebecca hurried away, hoping he wouldn't realize she hadn't promised not to tell anyone he was in their shed. She had to tell. She was too young to know what to do. She had to help him.

Everyone was gathered around the breakfast table. "Mamá," Rebecca began, "I need to talk to you this morning before I go to the Matsakis shop."

"Of course," her mother answered as she speared an olive off her plate.

A young boy burst into the dining room. "Señor Rouso told me to run as fast as I could. Señora Roza is having her baby and you need to come quick!"

"Yes, of course!" Her mother threw her napkin onto the table. "Tell her I'm coming! Goodbye, everyone. Maybe by tonight there will be another little one in the family!" She grabbed her coat and started out the kitchen door.

"A boy!" her father shouted after Mamá.

"I'll see what I can do." Her mother laughed.

"Papá," Rebecca began. "I have something important that I need to talk about to you."

"Not this morning, my little one. Kìrios Samaras will be here in another minute. He's placing a really big order with me. The first one he's ever placed."

"But…" Rebecca protested.

"Tonight. It can wait until tonight, unless we will be celebrating my new grandchild." Papá pushed away from the table.

"It's important, Papá."

"And what could be so important that it can't wait? You're a child. What you think is important is really not so important that it can't wait." Papá left the room.

Rebecca put down her fork.

"Tell us, Rebecca," her brother Ephraim offered.

"I need to talk to a grown up."

"I'm sixteen." Ephraim took a hunk of bread.

Rebecca got to her feet. "Never mind," she muttered.

She needed to decide what she was going to do about that poor boy sleeping in their shed. And she couldn't wait until tonight. Tonight, with the new baby coming, no one would have the time or interest in talking to her. Everyone would soon be consumed with the new baby. They wouldn't care about Andreas Sefaris. No one would care.

Rebecca knew she was expected to help clear the breakfast dishes but she didn't want to stay in the kitchen with her sisters, who were talking about future husbands, how many children they would have, and what new clothes they wanted to buy. Most days her sisters tolerated her musings about a future rich, handsome husband although everyone knew a marriage would never be arranged for her. But this morning, she didn't want to listen to her sisters' hopes and dreams. She grabbed her embroidery work box and put on her coat.

"Rebecca, just because you work with Kiría Matsakis doesn't mean you don't have to help in the kitchen," Klara complained.

Rebecca didn't answer as she walked out the door, pushing her braids behind her shoulders. Because she was the youngest one, no one took her seriously. She couldn't have anything important to say. But she did. She needed to help Andreas and she didn't know how to do it. She heard a rumble of thunder. What would Andreas do if it rained? He'd get soaked and he was already so cold. He'd get sick. Maybe he'd die. Rebecca hurried into the Matsakis house as raindrops began to pelt from the gray sky.

Rebecca took her place on the stool and pulled out her embroidery.

"Not even a good morning to me?" Kiría Eleni chided Rebecca as she looked up from the sewing machine.

"I'm sorry. *Kalimera,* good morning," Rebecca looked back down at the embroidery she was supposed to be stitching. Her fingers seemed to lack any talent this morning, as she envisioned Andreas in the cold rain, searching through garbage cans.

"Rebecca! Rebecca!" Kiría Eleni was standing over her. "What's the matter? I've been calling your name. You aren't sewing this morning. You're just looking off into thin air. Are you not feeling well? Do you want to go home?"

"Kiría Eleni, may I ask you a question?"

"Of course. But why don't you put down your sewing."

Rebecca put it in her lap. "What... what would a child of eight, a child as old as me, do if that child didn't have a mother or a father or sisters or any family?"

"What a curious question. Is everything alright in your home?"

"Yes, everything is fine. My sister Roza is having her baby today." Rebecca gave a small smile as the cat jumped into her lap and began to purr.

"How wonderful. But why are you asking about a child without parents?"

"I just want to know. Please, what happens to a child without parents, without a house to live in? Do they have to live on the street?" Rebecca bit her lip to keep from crying.

Kiría Eleni put her hands on Rebecca's shoulders and lifted her face until Rebecca's eyes met her gaze. "What is this all about? Children don't live on the streets. That's why there are orphanages, to take care of children who are orphans."

"But what if the child doesn't want to go to an orphanage? Do they have to live on the streets eating from garbage cans?" Rebecca tried to stifle her tears, but she saw Andreas with his ragged clothes. "I don't know what to do. I'm only a child."

"Shh, shh. What is this all about?"

Rebecca wiped her eyes with the back of her hands and took a deep breath. "There is a poor, sad boy that I found last night in our storage shed. He has no home and no parents. He was so hungry and cold. I brought him a blanket and food. He told me he eats from garbage cans. Like an animal,

Kiría Eleni. He has to live like an animal because he has no one to take care of him. He's only eight years old, like I am."

"Did he run away from an orphanage?"

"No, he did have a family. He's from that place, Smyrna, where everything got burned down. He said he can't go to an orphanage because he wants to find his sister. He is afraid that Turks are coming to get him. I told him that we have no Turks here in Kavala, but I don't think he believed me. I wanted to tell my parents about him and ask them what I should do, but everyone was too busy to listen to me. Please, Kiría Eleni, tell me how to help him. He's so sad and his clothes are rags and winter is coming and he doesn't have a coat. He needs shoes. His shoes are held together with vines. Do you think Kìrios Vassilis might have an extra pair of old shoes for him? He really needs them."

"You have such a good heart, little Rebecca. Don't worry. Together we will find a way to help this boy."

The house was bustling with news about Roza. The baby wasn't born yet, but it would be coming soon. If it were a boy, they would start their baking for another *bris*. If it were a girl, there would be no special celebration. Maybe next time Roza would have a boy. Mamá had returned for a brief time before dinner to make sure the girls had prepared the evening meal for the family. And then she was gone again. The sisters were all busy in the kitchen, arguing about the best way to prepare *burekas*. After dinner, the boys were busy with their school work.

"I have to go to Kiría Eleni for a while tonight. I need to do some more work at her house," she told her sisters. Rebecca put some dishes in the sink, grabbed her coat and left. No one seemed to notice.

It was starting to get dark as Rebecca walked towards the shed, hoping Andreas would still be there. She smiled when she saw Zeus running toward her, jumping up, wanting to be petted and wagging his tail.

Yes, Andreas was still there in the same spot, between the burlap bags of flour.

"Hello, Rebecca. I hoped you'd be back tonight." Andreas gave her a broad smile. "Your puppy stayed with me all day. He followed me when I walked around town after the rain stopped. I went exploring at that beautiful old castle. Since you said you'd bring me some food tonight, I didn't have to hunt through garbage cans today. I'd always wanted to explore that old castle."

"I used to play with my friends there, but my parents told me I was getting too old to do that."

"Too old?"

"Well, I'm a girl and there are more important things for me to do," she said wistfully. She did miss climbing on the old castle with her friends.

"I hope you didn't mind that your puppy followed me around today."

"He's not allowed in my house. He really isn't mine. I just feed him," Rebecca told him.

"He's a really nice dog," he paused and his face fell with disappointment as he looked at her empty hands. "You didn't bring me anything to eat tonight. I thought... "

"There is a place where you can get a real meal, with as much as you want to eat and drink," she repeated what Kiría Eleni had told her to say.

"You didn't tell any orphanage people about me, did you? I trusted you, Rebecca." His voice was filled with anguish.

"I didn't tell any orphanage people about you. I don't know any orphanage people." Rebecca tried to sound stern, but even to her own ears it didn't sound like a stern tone of voice.

"Where is this place where I can get a meal?" Andreas sounded skeptical.

"It is just a few doors down from here."

"Is it a restaurant? I don't have any drachmas to pay for food."

"It is the cobbler shop and a seamstress shop."

"And they have a meal for me?"

"Yes, I told you so. Now, come on." What was she going to do if he refused to go?

"Do you think I could do some work there like sweeping the floor to pay for food?"

"You'd have to ask."

"Come." Rebecca put out her hand to him. "Let's go."

He took her hand in his own. "Wait." He stopped her and reached inside his bundle. He drew out his small pouch. "I need to give you a gift. I want you to choose one of the marbles. Pick out the one you like best. You are my friend and the kindest girl I've ever met. I don't know when I'll have money to repay you. So please take one. My Patéra gave them to me."

"You don't need to repay me. The marbles are beautiful. I don't want to take one from you."

"Please, I want you to have one."

⟨⟨⟨⟩⟩⟩

Kìrios Matsakis had a broad smile on his face when he opened the door. "Welcome!" the man said as he greeted them.

Andreas stood still. Rebecca could tell he was afraid. He didn't want to come inside. Rebecca pulled on his hand. "Come on, Andreas. They have dinner on the table. I told you they would."

"Come, child," Kiría Eleni hurried to the door. "Come inside, it's getting cold."

"Aren't you hungry?" Rebecca urged him. "Come eat."

Andreas took a step inside, his eyes darting wearily in all directions. "You aren't Turks, are you?"

"We are Greek Orthodox Christians. May I take your bundle?" Kìrios Matsakis asked him.

"No." Andreas clutched it closer as he followed Rebecca to the living quarters. His eyes widened at all the food on the table.

"Sit down and eat." Kiría Eleni smiled at him.

Andreas hesitated as he looked at all the food displayed before him. He looked down at his hands. "Is there some place for me to wash my hands. I'm sorry, but they aren't clean."

"I'll take you to the sink. Come with me," Kiría Eleni offered.

Andreas didn't move.

"Rebecca, why don't you take him to wash his hands," Kiría Eleni suggested.

As Andreas ate the food on his plate, Rebecca nibbled on some olives. He didn't eat as much as she thought he would. She watched as he ate with a fork and knife and used his napkin expertly. She'd been afraid he would wolf down the food like he did when she had fed him in the shed.

"That's all that you want to eat?" Kiría Eleni asked him.

"If I eat too much, it can make me sick. May I take some food with me when I go?"

"If you like," Kiría Eleni said as she began to clear the table.

Rebecca stood up to help with the dishes and started toward the kitchen.

"Where are you going?" Andreas asked anxiously. "You're not leaving, are you?"

"I'm just going help Kiría Eleni in the kitchen."

"I think I need to go." Rebecca could hear the fear in his voice.

"No, no. You need to stay a little longer." Kiría Eleni smiled at him and reached out to touch his shoulder. She frowned when he backed away from her hand.

"Please don't touch me," he murmured.

"I'm sorry. I won't touch you. But you can't leave before the best part of our meal. Dessert! Don't you like dessert? Rebecca, no need to help me in the kitchen. Stay here with your friend while I bring out dessert.

"I… I do like dessert. I haven't had any since... since..." He bit back his tears.

"Baklava? Kourabiedes? Which is your favorite?"

"I like all of them."

"Andreas, I'd like to help Kiría Eleni get all the desserts ready to bring out. I will be right back," Rebecca told him, eager to have a few minutes alone with Kiría Eleni.

"You are in for a treat, Andreas. My Eleni makes the best baklava in all of Kavala." Kìrios Matsakis beamed with pride.

"Rebecca, you'll be right back?"

"Yes, of course. I'm just going into the kitchen for a few minutes. "

Rebecca stood next to the older woman, who was assembling the desserts on a plate and putting away the food left over from dinner. "He is a nice boy, don't you think, Kiría Eleni?"

"I think he must have come from a well-to-do family. He has quite good manners. He does seem like a nice boy who has been through a very difficult time. We will let him stay with us for a while and we will see."

"I'm sure you will like him," Rebecca tried to sound enthusiastic. "Just give him a chance."

"Do you know what happened to his family?"

"They all died except for a sister who he is searching for."

"Kìrios Vassilis and I will let him stay with us for a while. We bought him some clothes today."

"Thank you. You won't be sorry," Rebecca told her.

"Rebecca." She heard him calling out to her.

"Yes?" She went back into the dining room.

"I think it's time for me to go. Can I take the dessert with me? Thank you so much, Kìrios Matsakis and Kiría Matsakis. I am very grateful. When I get a job, I'll repay you for your kindness," he said politely.

"It's quite cold out there." Kìrios Matsakis cleared his throat. "Would you like to stay here tonight?"

"Stay here?" He looked at Rebecca uncertainly.

"Yes, Andreas, why don't you do that," Rebecca tried to reassure him.

"Well," he hesitated. "It is cold outside." He clutched his bundle tightly in his arms.

Say yes, Rebecca tried to urge him in her thoughts. Say yes, Andreas.

"It is warm in here. I'll just lay down by the door on the floor," he said.

"No, no, we have a bed you can sleep on," Kìrios Matsakis told him.

"Do you have a gun?"

"A gun?"

"In case the Turks come, you need a gun. I will sleep by the door with a gun," Andreas said with determination.

CHAPTER 7

Kavala: February, 1923

REBECCA SAT IN front of the sewing machine and dangled her legs down towards the treadle. She knew she had grown taller because her dresses had gotten shorter. But her legs still hadn't grown enough so she could reach the treadle. Someday it would happen, she told herself, as she ran her hands over the shiny black machine. Then she would be able to sit in front of the machine and sew like the wind, just like Kiría Eleni. She'd make beautiful clothes quickly and expertly. It would happen. Everyone grew. Her older sisters all got bigger, she reassured herself. Someday it would happen to her.

She got up from the Singer and sat down in her usual chair. She could hear Kiría Eleni busy in the kitchen, the sounds of banging pots and pans coming through the door. Rebecca had offered to help, but the older woman said no. It was her pleasure to do all the Name Day baking for her husband, Vassilis. Early next week, on February 11, all the Matsakis family and friends would come over, have some refreshment and leave small gifts for him. Rebecca was learning more and more about Greek Orthodox traditions during the time she spent in the Matsakis household. The Greek Orthodox didn't celebrate birthdays the way her family did. Instead, they celebrated the Name Day, which was the day of the saint for whom the person had been named. So, next week, everyone with the name Vassilis would visit with each other and celebrate. Rebecca wondered how many men also named Vassilis would come to visit.

After listening to Kiría Eleni explain Greek Orthodox traditions and customs, Rebecca would share the customs and traditions of her Greek Jewish family. She delighted in explaining all about her favorite holiday, Purim, which was fast approaching. Rebecca, her sisters and her brother Leon would all dress up in costumes, celebrating the story of Esther, the Jewish woman who married a King and saved all the Jewish people from death. Kiría Eleni had helped her sew a wonderful costume of beautiful colors so that she could dress up as Queen Esther. Rebecca couldn't wait to wear it. She was certain her sisters would wish they had a costume as wonderful as the one she had made. She also loved the holiday of Purim because it was the only holiday that celebrated a woman, a woman who had saved her people.

Rebecca looked up at the clock on the wall. It was almost sundown, and because it was Friday, she needed to be finished with her sewing before the Sabbath began. Jewish people didn't work on the Sabbath. But Papá had to keep his store open.

"What choice do I have, a man with eight daughters who need dowries?" Papá would grumble, when he was about to leave their home and open the store on Saturday morning. "I'm not allowed to keep the store open on Sunday. Two days closed and I couldn't compete with the other stores. We should move to Salonika." And with those final words, Papá would be gone.

"Why would we move to Salonika, Mamá?" Rebecca had asked when she was younger.

"Because, in Salonika there are so many Jews that even the docks of the port are closed on Saturday," her mother explained.

"Are we going to move there?"

"No, your Papá just says that. But we aren't going anywhere." Her mother would smile.

By now, Rebecca was used to her father's threats to move to Salonika. She was sure he would say that again tomorrow morning.

Rebecca glanced up at the clock. She probably had enough time to finish cutting the small pattern before she had to go home.

"Kiría Eleni, I'm ready to start cutting!" she called out.

"Just a minute and I'll be there to watch you." The sound of Kiría Eleni's voice came through the kitchen door. Rebecca heard the water running, as Kiría Eleni washed the flour which must have been coating her hands after a day of baking.

Kiría Eleni hurried into the workroom to watch Rebecca. "Alright, let's see how you do. Now take your time, Rebecca."

Rebecca grasped the scissors and began to cut. She'd never been allowed to do that before, but Kiría Eleni told her she was ready to cut fabrics. Rebecca was pleased with herself as she cut along the pattern. It really wasn't hard and she could see she was doing very well.

"Wonderful, Rebecca," the woman told her. "I knew you were ready to start cutting fabric. You did that very well."

"Thank you." Rebecca beamed under the woman's praise. "I'll have to leave soon. It's almost sundown."

"You'll miss Andreas unless he and Kìrios Vassilis get home soon. He'll be sad if he arrives home after you're gone."

"He could come over to visit tomorrow and have lunch with us. Mamá won't mind. Andreas has taken quite a fancy to Mamá's cooking. Though I think there isn't any food that he wouldn't like." Rebecca laughed.

"I'll tell him to go to your family for lunch tomorrow. But Rebecca, the moment he walks in the door expecting to see you and you aren't here, his face just falls. He asks if you are alright even if it is Friday and he knows you must leave early before sunset."

"I like him a lot. I miss seeing him on Fridays. School's been out for a long time. Why is he late today?"

"Kìrios Vassilis took Andreas on his search today. He promised the boy that once each month, they would go to the areas where the refugees from Asia Minor have gathered and see if his sister or his maid are there. They look at what has been compiled to see if their names are on any lists. And, of course, they will tell those in charge to let us know if the two names appear. They also visit churches, to make the priests aware of Maria Sefaris. More and more refugees are flooding into town every day, so maybe, soon, he'll find his sister."

"I hope he finds her," Rebecca mused. "It would make him so happy. And don't you think he isn't so skinny anymore? He looks so much better."

"All he needed was enough to eat. He still isn't sure that there will always be enough and I find food inside his pants pockets every night. But I hope someday he will understand there will always be food for him and he will never go hungry again. And he doesn't seem very sad much of the time. It's mostly the nights that are so bad for him."

"He told me he isn't sleeping on the floor by the door anymore."

"Yes, two weeks ago he agreed to sleep on the bed in our spare room. But he has terrible dreams in his sleep. He calls out and cries and when I wake him up, he doesn't even remember his nightmares. Tomorrow is the Saturday of the Souls. We'll all go to church to pray for those who are no longer with us. I don't know if that will give him any comfort, but we will take him with us when we pray for our departed family members. He said his parents are dead. He says he can't remember how it happened. Vassilis told me that after the fighting in the Great War, many soldiers who saw terrible things couldn't remember them."

"Do you think because it was so terrible that Andreas can't remember? I think the night I found him he told me what happened. But all I remember is that it was awful and Andreas was so sad and crying."

"Kìrios Vassilis believes it is the mind's way of protecting us from terrible memories. Andreas is a good boy, Rebecca. We thank God that you brought him to us."

Kiría Eleni had told her that although Andreas rarely talked about his life in Smyrna, she could tell he came from a very well-to-do family from the things he occasionally said, .

Kiría Eleni also said that after spending the first night with the Matsakis family, Andreas had been eager to help in the shop. He offered to sweep the floor in return for the food they had given him.

"That boy had never used a broom before in his life," Kiría Eleni related. "He said the servants in his house did all the sweeping and cleaning. But he learned quickly when Kìrios Vassilis showed him. It's so important for him to feel he is doing something to repay us for taking him in."

"When we talk, he doesn't keep asking me anymore how soon you and Kìrios Vassilis will ask him to leave. I think he's not afraid anymore that if he does something you don't like, you'll throw him back out into the streets," Rebecca told her.

"It's only been a few months. Little by little, he is accepting that his place is secure with us."

Andreas had been welcomed by Rebecca's family as the new member of the Matsakis household who lived down the street. It was only her brother Leon who seemed to harbor bad feelings towards him. Rebecca knew why. It was because of school, where Leon always seemed to struggle. He resented this new boy, who was much younger but was moved up to his grade because he was so smart.

"It's probably because the schools were better where he came from," Rebecca tried to console him when he complained about Andreas, a younger boy suddenly entering his classroom.

"I just don't like him. He always has the answer to every question the teacher asks. And he speaks all those languages: Greek, Italian, Turkish, French."

"But he doesn't speak Ladino very well." Rebecca tried to make Leon feel better as she handed him the paper she had corrected the night before.

"Hmpph." Leon made a face.

Andreas had made a few friends at school. Because the Israelite Alliance School was the best in town, all the Jewish, Christian and Muslim families who could afford to pay sent their children there. Andreas told her that sometimes, boys who were bullies would call him *tourkosporo,* the seed of Turkey. He didn't answer them back. "I don't care what they call me," he told her. He had even overcome his fear of Muslims and had a Muslim friend, Iskendar. Iskendar was definitely his best friend and Andreas often spoke of him. Rebecca's cousin, Joseph Rouso, had also become a good friend.

Rebecca heard that when the Matsakises first broached the subject of going to school, Andreas had refused. "Why should I go to school? If you let me, I can be an apprentice to you, Kìrios Vassilis. I could learn to be a cobbler. Or, when I'm a little bigger, I could work in the tobacco warehouses."

"You'd want to work in the warehouses?" Kìrios Vassilis looked up from his cobbler's bench and knitted his brow.

"I see them all over town. Maybe it would be easy for me to get a job there."

"We do have many tobacco warehouses in Kavala. You are still young and I would welcome you as an apprentice in my cobbler craft. But first, you must attend school for a few years before you decide what you want to do."

Andreas had gone to school grudgingly the next day.

"It was as if a light was turned on inside of him," Kiría Eleni told Rebecca the following morning. "He enjoys learning and the teachers say he is a very smart boy."

"Why aren't you going to school?" Andreas asked Rebecca when he returned from school that first week and she was sitting on a stool embroidering a blouse with a floral decoration.

"I don't go to school. I'm a girl."

"Of course, I can see you are a girl. But there were girls in my class."

"Well, it costs money to attend school," Rebecca tried to explain.

"Who is paying money for me to go to school?" He frowned.

"Kìrios Matsakis must be paying for you," Rebecca surmised.

"He is? He is a nice man. So, Rebecca, your father can't afford to send you to school? My sister went to school. She didn't like it very much. Maybe you wouldn't like it either." Andreas sat beside her with an apple in his hand as he watched her making small stitches on the fine silk cloth. "But does that mean you can't read anything or write anything? I guess because you're a girl it doesn't make any difference since you're good at sewing. You'll be able to make clothes for your children."

"I do know how to read," Rebecca said indignantly. "My brothers taught me."

"That's good," Andreas said.

"I'm reading *Great Expectations,* by Charles Dickens, right now," Rebecca announced. She liked Andreas. It didn't feel good for him to think she was illiterate. She didn't care if many other girls could not read or write. She could read and write and she was proud of her abilities.

"You are? I've heard about that book. Would you let me borrow your copy when you're finished?"

"It doesn't belong to me... it's my brother's. But I'll ask him if, when I'm done, you can borrow it. Do you like to read books?"

"I love to read. My Patéra and I used to read together," he said wistfully.

"Do you like school?" Rebecca asked.

"It's okay, I guess. Some of the kids asked if I was a Turk when I said I came from Smyrna. I like it here in this house. Kìrios and Kiría Matsakis are kind and there is so much food to eat. I like sitting next to Kìrios Matsakis when he works and makes things. He has such big strong arms. He said his arms are so big because of all the work he does with a hammer. I wonder, if I became a cobbler would my arms get that big?" he paused. "Do you think they'll let me stay for a while?"

"Yes, I think they will." She smiled at him.

"Rebecca, you're so nice. I like you a lot. I think when we grow up, I'll marry you."

"Oh, no, Andreas." Rebecca laughed. "We can't get married. You are a Christian and I am a Jew."

"So what?"

"You will marry a nice Greek Orthodox lady," she told him. There was no point in telling him that because she had no dowry, she would never marry a nice Jewish man.

"Oh." Andreas wrinkled his brow. "Are you sure?"

"Yes, I am sure," she told him and looked back down at her sewing.

❧

Kavala: May, 1923

Andreas and his best friend Iskender lay on their backs near the old castle and looked up at the stars in the sky. It had been cloudy all week, but tonight it was totally clear. The boys took turns identifying all the constellations.

"My mother taught me all the constellations," Andreas said, his voice filled with melancholy. "I miss her. I miss my whole family. I often wonder why I am here and they are all gone."

Iskender turned toward him. "It's really sad that you don't have your parents any more. Did you decide if you could call Theo Vassilis and Thea Eleni, Patéra and Mamá? instead of aunt and uncle? They asked you that last week, didn't they?"

"Yes, they did. But they said it was alright if I just wanted to keep calling them *Thea* and *Theo*, aunt and uncle. What do you think, Iskender?"

"They have been very good to you."

"But I already have a mother and father." Andreas looked back up at the star-studded sky. "I do think it would make them happy if I called them Mamá and Patéra. I'm not sure what I should do."

"You're probably right that it would make them happy, since they have no children of their own. That must make them sad, don't you think?"

"Yes," Andreas sighed and looked back at his friend. "They have been so good to me. They don't even scold me when I forget to do my chores in the shop."

"I think, one day soon, it will seem right to you to call them *Mamá* and *Patéra*. There's no hurry. I think it's almost time for us to get back home. Tomorrow there's no school. Let's meet again back here at the castle. I like to jump off the rocks, even if my parents tell me not to. I love to think of all the times the castle was destroyed and then built up again. I like to pretend I am one of the soldiers standing on the ramparts, fighting off the invaders." Iskender got to his feet.

"I'll meet you here tomorrow. But I don't want to pretend I'm a soldier. I like to pretend I'm flying when I jump off the high places. I don't want to be a soldier or even pretend to be one."

The Government of the Grand National Assembly of Turkey and the Greek Government have agreed upon the following provisions:

As of May 1, 1923, there shall take place a compulsory exchange of Turkish nationals of the Greek Orthodox religion established in Turkish territory and the Greek nationals of the Moslem religion established in Greek territory. These people shall not return to live in Turkey or Greece respectively without the authorization of the Turkish Government or the Greek government.

Kavala: November, 1923

This morning, when Andreas left his house for school, he found himself in the midst of crowds of Muslims who were streaming past the house. Andreas held his books in his arms as he walked along the waterfront. He was on his way to school and if he didn't hurry, he was going to be late. But he couldn't force his steps toward school. He stood still and looked off towards the harbor where so many boats were anchored. Were these boats going to help the Muslim people or would the people have to sit on the dock, hoping, wailing, praying for help?

At least there weren't any Turkish soldiers shooting people. But maybe they came at night, like they did in Smyrna. The crowds of people, all pushing toward the quay, mothers clutching babies... Memories came flooding back to him in a great rush: his family fleeing down the streets with all the pushing and shoving and stepping on old people and children. On the Kavala quay, there were so many people with their meager possessions He remembered when he was on the ship to Lesbos and women were sobbing about their husbands who had been taken away.

He felt a tightness in his chest. A young boy passed by with a pinched look on his face. Andreas knew the child was hungry and he dug out the lunch Kiría Eleni had prepared for him. "Here," he said as he thrust his hand to the child.

"*Efharistó!*" the boy thanked him and shoved the food into his mouth.

Other Muslim children, seeing what Andreas had done, hurried over to him. "Me, please," they called out to him. "I am hungry. Food please!"

"I don't have any more," Andreas said and then ran away when more and more desperate children, women and men started to surround him.

Why was this happening again? Why, oh why? Were the ships going to let the people crowd onto the docks and not let them board? He looked up at the sky wearily. There were no billowing clouds of smoke and flames.

The image of the quay in Smyrna appeared before him. Andreas leaned against a building as he tried to catch his breath. He felt the heat and saw the flames in the sky. He saw the corpses he had to walk on top of in order to get to where ladies were handing out bread and he remembered reaching into his pocket and finding it empty. The sorrow of knowing he would be left behind because there wasn't enough gold washed over him. Andreas sank down to the cobblestone street and put his head in his hands. He felt as if he couldn't breathe. It was happening all over again. Today it was the Muslims, but later it could be the Greek Orthodox, just like last year, when his family was thrown out of their house. Then, would it be the Jews? Would Rebecca's family be forced out of their home? He felt his stomach heaving.

What had these Muslims done? Why were they were being forced out of their homes just like his family had been? They weren't bad people.

Only bad people should be thrown out of their homes and forced to leave. But his family weren't bad people. This made no sense and Andreas felt sick to his stomach. He leaned over and vomited into the street.

He sat there on the cobblestone street, sweat beading on his forehead. He needed to go to school. There was an important exam today and he was supposed to present a report on Greek Independence. He couldn't. He couldn't go to school. He turned back to the Matsakis home.

He burst into the cobbler shop and started to run past Patéra Vassilis as he made his way up to his room.

"Where are you going in such a hurry, Andreas? What's the matter child?" Patéra Vassilis grabbed his arm.

"I don't feel good," Andreas would say anything just to be left alone.

"What is it? I can tell that you're upset. You must tell me," Vassilis said as he put down his hammer and the leather strap he was working on.

"You told me about that Treaty of Lausanne. You said that more Greek Orthodox people like me would be leaving Asia Minor. But why are the Muslims who live here going away? I don't understand it. My good friend Iskender is going to be sent away, isn't he? He's my best friend. Why does he have to go?"

"Sit down beside me and we will talk about this. I told you that this Treaty from last January said everyone who was Greek Orthodox who lived in Asia Minor had to leave and come to Greece."

"Are their houses going to be set on fire, like Smyrna?"

"I don't think so. But the Greek Orthodox from Asia Minor are coming here to Greece and will have to start new lives. You've seen the people who get off the boats. Most are very poor and many of them are sick. You've seen the people in the refugee camps where we go to search for your sister."

"But why are the Muslims leaving? I was afraid of them at first. I thought they were Turks who wanted to kill me, but they aren't. Iskender is my best friend. I like to go to his house and his whole family is nice to me. He was the first boy at school who didn't make fun of me and call me names. Where are the Muslims going to go? What are they going to eat?" Andreas started to cry. It was as if this was happening to him all over again. Having nowhere to live, nothing to eat...

"Iskender is my friend. I have to help him. Could he come to live here? Would you take him in like you took me in? He could share my bed."

"Andreas, he has a family. The Muslims living in Greece must go back to Turkey."

"Go back? Iskender told me he doesn't speak Turkish and his family hasn't lived there in hundreds of years. If he doesn't speak Turkish, no one will understand him." Andreas wiped away his tears as Kìrios Vassilis put his arm around him.

"Indeed, Andreas, this is terrible. It is an awful affliction put upon our people and our Muslim neighbors as well. These people who made this treaty are called the Great Powers: England, France, Italy and America. They decided to have what they are calling a "population exchange." Doesn't that sound like such a nice term? But it is a forced expulsion of people against their will. It is people leaving where they have lived for countless generations. Many Orthodox Christians were killed, massacred before this so-called exchange. The Christians and the Muslims have to abandon the graves of their ancestors. Who will visit the cemeteries where they are buried? It is horrible beyond description what happened to your family, the Greek Orthodox in Asia Minor and now the innocent Muslims who have lived in harmony with us."

"It's not fair. It's not fair."

"No, it's not. But I think those Great Powers, the men making such decisions, care little about the people they are forcing out of their homes. Here in Greece, it has been a terrible burden to feed and house those who have come to us and continue to come to us from Asia Minor. I have heard more than one million people will be arriving here. People without heart, and there are many of them. Now they say that the Muslims are leaving, the Asia Minor Greeks can take over their houses, and that will be for the greater good."

"You mean some strange family will live in Iskender's house?"

"Yes, indeed."

"Do you think maybe his family will be sent to Smyrna and maybe Iskender and his family could live in my house? It was a very fine house."

"I'm sure it was."

"And what about the farm with their almond and olive trees?"

"Someone will take that as well."

"That's wrong. I don't want him to go." He couldn't lose this dear friend. He couldn't lose someone else.

"I'm sorry, Andreas. The ways of the world can be harsh as you well know."

"Look, look out the window. More and more people, where are they all coming from? I don't think they all live in Kavala. Many of them look so tired and I think they are hungry. I gave a boy my lunch today and he was so hungry. And then all these other people came after me, wanting some more food. I got scared and ran away. But I had nothing else to give them. "

"This afternoon, I will close up the shop for a few hours and you and I can bring food down to the quay. We always have extra food. You don't have to give up your lunch."

"Do you think the Solomon family might have some extra food? I can ask Rebecca."

"I'm sure the Solomons will give us food for the poor, unfortunate Muslims. And no, the Muslims you see aren't only from Kavala. They are coming from all over our area of Greece. That's why they are hungry. Some of them have walked a long distance to get here. They will be sailing to Asia Minor from our port."

Later that afternoon, Andreas and Vassilis distributed food to the people who congregated on the quay. After the food was all given out, they returned home. Patéra Vassilis was working on a horse's harness and Andreas was watching intently. He needed to erase the terrible memories of being crowded on the quay in Smyrna, which, once resurrected, kept clouding his mind.

"Are you feeling better now?" Patéra Vassilis asked, "We'll hand out more food tomorrow. Unfortunately, it will make only a small difference. We can't feed everyone."

"It's terrible to be so hungry. This morning, when I saw all those people on the quay, I started remembering some bad things that I don't want to remember," Andreas told him.

"I know this is hard for you," Patéra Vassilis enveloped Andreas with a giant hug. "That book you brought with you. Tell me about it." He turned to his bench and started pounding nails into the leather.

"It's called *Don Quixote*. My Patéra gave it to me. We used to read it together at night."

"Is it a good book? Would you like to read it to me? I could do some sewing and gluing of the leather so I won't make much noise and I can hear what you're reading."

"You'd really like me to read to you?"

"My reading is not as good as yours. I didn't go to school very long since I went to work with my Patéra in the leather shop at a young age. That book you brought with you, *Don Quixote*, what is it about?"

"It's about a man who thinks he is a knight. He has adventures and a good friend named Sancho Panza. The book is in French, but I can translate for you."

"I'd like that, Andreas."

There was a knock on the door and Iskender burst into the cobbler shop. He was out of breath as he grabbed Andreas's hands. "I have to go, Andreas. There isn't much time. We're leaving. I ran out of my house, but I have to get back right away. The boat has come to take us away."

"Iskender!" Andreas let go of his hands and gave him a big hug. "I shall miss you. I shall miss you so much. Here." He reached inside of his pocket. "I was going to give you this in school today, but I didn't go. On this paper is the address of my house in Smyrna. If the boat takes you to Smyrna, go to my house. It's a really nice house for you and your family to live in. I also wrote down the name of my sister. If she hasn't left and doesn't know where I am, please give her my address. Tell her I'm waiting for her. Patéra Vassilis said all the Greek Orthodox must leave Asia Minor so that means if my sister Maria is still there, they will make her leave."

"Okay. Andreas, I don't want to go," his friend said with sadness as tears welled in his eyes. "This is our home. I don't want to go to some other place. You have been such a good friend to me. I will miss you. I gave my dog Blackie to the Christians who live next door to us. I can't bring him with us. Please stop by sometime to see him and make sure they are taking good care of him. I have to go. Goodbye."

The two boys gave each other a last hug. Andreas stood still, looking at the closed door.

"Do you want to read to me?" Patéra Vassilis was asking him.

"No, no, I can't," Andreas whispered and turned away. He ran up the stairs to his room and slammed the door shut. He opened his drawer where he kept his mother's jeweled crucifix as well as his old pants that were still covered with dried blood. He grabbed them close and collapsed in tears on his bed. "Baba, Mamá," he cried for his parents.

Everyone, everyone he ever cared about... All of them had something terrible happen to them or were taken away from him. His family and now Iskender. It hurt so much to say goodbye to his friend, his friend who had defended him from the slurs of his classmates when they called him the seed of Turkey. He was glad that Rebecca said he couldn't marry her when they were grown up. Something bad would happen to her just like everyone else he had ever cared about. And the pain of losing his father and his mother and his sister Maria washed over him again. He put his head under his pillow and sobbed. He didn't want Mamá Eleni to hear him. For he knew she would come in to comfort him as she always did when he had his nightmares. The pain overwhelmed his heart as he cried himself to sleep.

CHAPTER 8

Kavala, Greece: September, 1936

IT WAS A gloomy day. It had begun at breakfast that morning with Papá folding the newspaper and scowling. "That Metaxas government. Ugh! They call a state of emergency because of a so-called communist danger. And then they adjourn our parliament! Greece is the cradle of democracy and now, to have such a government... I read about the rest of Europe... the whole world is upside down."

"Don't get yourself worked up over politics, Isaac," her mother said in a soothing voice. "Why do you read the paper if it upsets you? Our life here in Kavala is untouched by what goes on in other places. We have a good life. We have almost twenty grandchildren. The years have been good to us. Our family has thrived."

Papá just shook his head.

"The newspaper, please?" Rebecca held out her hand.

"You shouldn't read the paper. Girls don't need to concern themselves with such things."

"Papá," Rebecca sighed and took the paper. She would read it later this afternoon.

And so this gloomy day began. After helping Mamá with the breakfast dishes, Rebecca walked down the lane to the Matsakis shops. So little light was coming through the windows in the workroom, Rebecca had to turn on the lamps.

Kiría Eleni took off the eyeglasses that helped her with small stitching and smiled up at Rebecca. "I received a letter from Andreas yesterday."

"You did? I haven't received any word from him all month." Rebecca sat in front of the Singer, pressed her foot on the treadle, and began to guide the fabric under the needle expertly.

"He just returned from the Olympics in Berlin. I'm sure you'll receive a letter any day now. He never fails to send us letters at least once each month."

"Did he tell you about the Olympics? He wrote that he was going with some of his friends from Athens."

"Yes, he had a wonderful time. When our work is done for today, I'll give you his letter and you can read it for yourself. But I have good news. He will be coming home for a visit in two weeks. He's bringing friends with him," Kiría Eleni said as she continued basting the stitches on a silk blouse.

It had been over five months since Andreas had been home for a visit. He usually came at least three times a year, but this year, he'd only be home twice. Completing his training as a physician at the hospital in Athens kept him very busy. On the weekends, he had devoted his time to the refugee slums around the city. And, of course, he never stopped looking for his sister, Maria. She knew he would never give up searching for his sister. He didn't put it into words, but his heart couldn't stop aching for her.

In his letters to Rebecca, he had described the terrible conditions people were forced to live in those refugee slums. These were the same people who had been expelled from Asia Minor to Greece thirteen years ago, the year after Andreas had been forced to flee from Smyrna. Many of these people who lacked skills still lived in makeshift conditions. Sadly, they were looked down upon by the mainland Greeks. Some of the refugees who had come from places around the Black Sea and were called Pontic Greeks, spoke an old-fashioned dialect or didn't speak Greek. The language barriers made it even more difficult for them to assimilate with the mainland Greeks. Kavala had also become the home to countless Asia Minor refugees. Many of them had been able to find jobs in the tobacco industry and were slowly becoming integrated into the fabric of the Kavala community.

The hours flew by as the two women worked together on their sewing.

"You'll need to leave by four-thirty." Kiría Eleni looked up at the clock on the wall. "You don't want a scolding again, like you received last week."

"Yes, I know. I'm almost finished with this skirt." Rebecca turned the balance wheel of the Singer as she guided the fabric under the needle. "It was almost the Sabbath when I walked through the door and Papá wasn't pleased. Tonight, we are having a guest for the Sabbath meal and I don't know who it is. I was instructed to put on a very nice dress. It must be someone important. Maybe it's someone who wants to invest in Papá's store. I suppose we should all look very prosperous to impress this investor."

"You look wonderful with your new hairstyle."

"Do you really like it?" Rebecca looked at herself in the mirror, admiring the soft chestnut curls that framed her face. It was such a fashionable style, just like the ones she'd seen in the magazines.

"It's most becoming."

"I wish I had dark hair like everyone else. My Mamá said we probably have ancestors who were Ashkenazi Jews from Hungary, and that is where I get my lighter hair and gray eyes. The color of my hair is so, so…," she said, searching for the right words.

"Your hair is beautiful and so stylish," Kiría Eleni said with reassurance. "Remember, on Monday next week, we are going to Miss Ethel in Drama to do the last fitting for her bridal gown. We'll be leaving early in the morning. Don't forget, you promised her some of the rose petal perfume that you craft from the roses in your family's garden."

"I have a vial ready to take with us. Her gown is the most beautiful we've ever sewn. Do you think she'll ever learn to speak Greek? I've tried to learn some English so we can communicate with her."

"After Kìrios Syrimis was smitten by this foreign woman, he didn't care if any person in his family could speak to her," Kiría Eleni sighed. "I'm sure his family is not happy about this marriage. I think how I would feel if Andreas brought home a bride who couldn't speak to us. Kìrios Syrimis, the bridegroom, is paying us so handsomely for our work. After I am paid, I'll have a substantial amount for you. Do you ever spend your earnings on anything besides charcoal, drawing tablets and books?"

"My parents remind me I must save for the time when they are no longer here. I will probably be living with one of my brothers or sisters and I must try not to be a burden on them."

"Of course," Kiría Eleni agreed.

"In this letter," Kiría Eleni continued, "Andreas wrote that he's bringing friends with him. Do you think maybe one of them is a prospective bride? He spends so much of his time with foreigners and he hasn't shown any interest in the good Greek girls we invite over whenever he comes home for a visit. Maybe he will choose a foreign woman."

"Kiría Eleni, you mustn't keep worrying about that. I'm sure whoever he brings home will be a wonderful girl, even if she might be foreign.

He hasn't written anything to me about a special girl. But maybe he met someone in Berlin?"

"A German girl? I hope not. But Vlassis and I are so eager for him to marry and have children. We're not that young and we want to see grandchildren."

"You are not that old. You have many years to see grandchildren. I'm certain that someday Andreas will bring home a wonderful daughter-in-law for you, and you and I will sew her the most splendid bridal gown."

"Well, I'll find some Greek girls to invite when he comes home. If he married a local Greek girl, maybe he could be persuaded to come back here to live."

"I'd like it if he moved back here."

"Do you know *Despinis* Veta? Do you think Andreas might like her? She has a fine dowry and Andreas, as a physician, is quite a desirable man."

"Despinis Veta? She's very pretty. We did some sewing for her mother last year. How old is she?"

"She's already eighteen, ready for marriage."

"Then why don't you invite her? But first, wait to see if one of these friends he is bringing home is a woman he has already found for himself."

"Yes, you're right, Rebecca."

"I finished the drawing of this dress and I put it in the book this morning. Last night, I sketched some new designs for bridal gowns and some modern frocks that have become so popular with our clients. I'll leave them for you to look at and see what you think"

"I'll look at them later this afternoon. You have such talent, Rebecca. Remember to take the leftovers for the dogs on your way out the door. What would those poor dogs in the streets do without you?"

Rebecca looked up at the clock. "Bye," she called as she flew out the door and down the narrow cobblestone street toward her house.

She put down the bowl of food for the dogs who gathered around her. She hurried inside and was greeted by her mother, who was stirring a pot of soup. "The family isn't coming over tonight," her mother told her. "We'll all be together tomorrow at lunch time. We're having a special guest tonight. You need to change into a nice dress."

"The family isn't coming tonight?" Rebecca was disappointed. She loved seeing her nieces and nephews. "Has Papá left for the synagogue?"

"Yes, he has and he wasn't pleased that you weren't home yet."

"Kiría Eleni and I had a lot of work to do today."

"You know, that is not a good excuse. But you're home now. So go upstairs and change your clothes."

"Who is this special guest?"

"Change into your nice dress and come back to the kitchen. We'll discuss our special guest then. Oh, you have a letter from Andreas. But you'll have to read it later. Hurry."

"Yes, Mamá." Rebecca pocketed the letter lying on the table. She so looked forward to letters from Andreas. She expected this one would be filled with his experiences at the Berlin Olympics. She envied his travels and lived vicariously through his experiences in foreign countries. Would she ever travel outside this part of Greece? Just going to Athens and seeing the Acropolis would be thrilling. But it looked like she would never leave the area around Kavala. Dreams were just dreams, not reality for an unmarried woman.

Kìrios and Kiría Matsakis had insisted on sending Andreas to the best schools. That first summer he spent with them, he asked if they could travel to Athens. They had gone to the capital of Greece, and Andreas sent Rebecca postcards with the wonderful image of the Parthenon. There was a very large settlement of refugees from Asia Minor that they visited where they inquired about his sister. When they returned home, he told her all about the Acropolis that she had dreamed of seeing for herself one day.

But what Andreas could not forget from that trip were the slums where many Asia Minor refugees were living. The families had no men to support them. All men, except for old men and young boys, were taken away to forced labor camps by the Turks, where they survived for a few brief months before succumbing to disease and starvation. After he returned home, he confided to Rebecca that he wanted to become a doctor. "They need medical care. There is so much sickness and disease. If I became a doctor, I could help them."

She agreed with him, although she knew that meant schooling somewhere away from Kavala. She would miss her good friend.

Rebecca hurried upstairs and put on the new pink dress with white flowers. She had finished sewing it only last week. She had created it to look just like the frock she had seen in the latest fashion magazine. She placed the letter from Andreas in the large box which held all his letters. She buttoned up her new dress, checked the seams in her nylon stockings, and put on some lipstick. A special guest? Mamá always had a flare for the dramatic.

"You look very nice," Mamá complimented her and untied the apron around her waist.

"So who is our special guest?" Rebecca tried to appear sufficiently interested, although it was annoying that she would have to sit through a boring conversation with someone after dinner. It would be especially hard, because all she wanted to do was go upstairs and read Andreas's letter.

"Señor Kapeta. He owns that large house up on the hill."

"I know who he is. He has four sons who went to school with Leon and Ephraim. Is he going to invest in Papá's store?" Rebecca took a spoon and tasted the *fasolada* soup. "Very good, Mamá. It's delicious."

"Enough salt?" her mother asked.

"Maybe a pinch more," Rebecca suggested. "Is Señor Kapeta going to invest in Papá's store? I've heard he is a very rich man. How exciting that would be for Papá."

"He is coming about a marriage."

"Marriage? A marriage to whom?" Rebecca asked as she sprinkled some salt into the pot.

"To you, Rebecca."

"But I don't have a dowry." Rebecca took a deep breath. She knew that man was old enough to be her grandfather.

"We have been blessed, because he says he doesn't care if you have a dowry. He is very wealthy and you would lack for nothing. This is the first offer you have ever had, and it is a miracle someone so well-to-do would consider you for marriage."

Mamá was right, of course. This might be her only chance to become a mother. The realization that she would never have children had always filled her with sadness.

"We would never force you, Rebecca. But we do think this marriage would be in your best interest."

"I'll meet with him, of course," she agreed.

"I know he is old and not the best looking. But you needn't worry about sharing his bed."

"What do you mean?"

"One night at the taverna, after having too much *raki*, he told Papá he no longer could do such things. You are not to say I told you anything about such a delicate matter. But I thought you should know, since his appearance is not very appealing."

Marriage to Señor Kapeta wouldn't give her children. "He can't give me children?"

"He's a very wealthy man and you would lack for nothing."

Her father and Señor Kapeta would be arriving from the synagogue at any moment and she would meet him. If her parents thought it was a good match, they knew best. She was a dutiful daughter and didn't want to disappoint her parents….

She heard the sound of voices at the front door. Mamá took off her apron and Rebecca straightened her shoulders as they walked into the parlor. Papá was helping Señor Kapeta take off his coat. The older man looked intensely at Rebecca. He was as she remembered: stout with wispy white hair and coarse features. His clothes were of expensive material, impeccably tailored.

All through dinner, Rebecca remained silent, looking across the table at this man who would be her husband. Her mother and father chatted with him, offering him condolences for the recent loss of his wife, asking about the welfare of his four sons.

"It has been a difficult time since my Sultana passed away, may her memory be eternal. The household doesn't function like it used to. Servants aren't adequate for the smooth running of a household."

He wants someone to run his household, thought Rebecca. Well, she certainly could run a household. Mamá had taught her and her sisters well.

"Our Rebecca is quite adept at such things. Since all the other girls are gone, she is a tremendous help to Esther," said her father.

"She is a pretty little thing. I hear you spend time with Kiría Matsakis, sewing things."

"Yes, I do," Rebecca said with pride. "I enjoy sewing."

"Well, it is premature to speak of such subjects, Señorita Rebecca. But if you would consent to be my bride, you would have no need to work with that Christian woman. You could sew for my boys. I must say, I'm very impressed with your daughter, Señor Isaac. She says very little. Her clothes are a bit too stylish for me. And that lipstick," he sighed and shook his head at her. "I'm an old-fashioned man."

Rebecca took a deep breath. Of course, as a married woman, there would be no need to work and it would be unseemly to do so. She would have to resign herself to that.

"I also hear you spend time with your nose stuck in a book. What a waste of time reading is for a woman. Learning new ideas is not good for a wife. As my wife, there would be no time for such frivolous pursuits. The smooth running of a household requires all the attention of a good wife. You would lack for nothing. You'd have the finest clothes and furs. My wife, Sultana, was a woman who commanded much respect in our community."

Rebecca sat back in her chair. No, no, this was not right. This wasn't possible. She couldn't say yes. No sewing, no reading, so she could live comfortably with this ugly old man. And he was ugly in both appearance and his antiquated ideas. She kept silent for fear she would say something that would embarrass her parents.

"So, Señor Isaac. Do we have an agreement?" Señor Kapeta wiped his mouth with a napkin. "We'd have the wedding as soon as possible. I have some relatives visiting from Salonika and it would be wonderful to have them here for the celebration."

"I will give you an answer after Shabbat," her father said. "We should not conduct such a transaction on the day of rest."

"I'm sure it will be yes. You have a very lucky daughter to have found favor in my eyes. My son Avraam told me to consider her. What a smart boy I have."

Rebecca managed a small polite smile. "*Shabbat Shalom*," she wished him goodbye as he got up from the table and made a bow to her.

Rebecca walked into the kitchen and stood beside her mother. She started to dry the dishes. Her father came in to join them. "Well?" he asked expectantly.

"Well? The answer is no," Rebecca replied in a soft voice.

"Rebecca, I understand he is not the perfect bridegroom. But he has made you the only offer you have ever had. You are a girl without a dowry. He is quite wealthy. Your future welfare would be assured."

"He is looking for a servant to take care of his household and his sons. I know you are looking out for me, but I say no, and I will never, never, change my mind!" She tried not to raise her voice.

"But, Rebecca," her father protested.

"Isaac, no more," her mother told Papá. "Rebecca, put down the dishrag and go up to your room."

Rebecca did as she was told and hurried out of the kitchen up to her room. She closed the door and took a deep breath. Give up her reading? The walls of her room were lined with all the books Andreas had given her and those she bought with her earnings from Kiría Eleni.

She unbuttoned her dress and slipped her nightgown over her head. She opened Andreas's letter and then folded over the sheets of paper without reading them. She'd read them tomorrow when she could concentrate on his words, when her mind wasn't clouded by the awful thought of being Señora Kapeta, of sharing life with that unpleasant, narrow-minded man.

She pulled out her box of treasures. It held all that was dear to her... Andreas's letters and her sketches. And at the bottom of the box were her savings.

When she was no more than ten years old, she had displayed a talent for drawing. At first, she'd helped Kiría Eleni sketch dresses for her clients, but it soon became apparent that Rebecca's skill at sketching dresses far exceeded Kiría Eleni's drawing abilities. One afternoon, Rebecca had brought home a tablet to work on a sketch and she suddenly was seized with the idea of capturing her room on the drawing tablet. Later that evening, as she watched her sisters getting ready for bed, she began to sketch them. Many evenings before bed, she had enjoyed capturing the images all around her until her sisters insisted she turn down the lights.

That awful man would probably have forbidden her to do any sketching. She wanted to forget what happened tonight with Señor Kapeta. She knew she had disappointed her parents. They would be relieved if she had a husband to care for her. But she couldn't do it. She'd always longed to be a mother, but with Señor Kapeta that wouldn't happen. She closed her eyes at the revolting image of sharing that man's bed.

For so long, she had never thought of marriage. When she was young and still in her teens, in that time before sleep, she had dwelt in a fantasy world. She'd imagine that she was courted by a young man who looked just like Andreas, but he was Jewish and he professed his love for her. She envisioned their wedding in the synagogue.

Sometimes she'd imagine them sitting at the table, surrounded by their children. But as she grew older, she had put those fantasies away. Some evenings, she might lose herself in a great romance novel, but she knew it was imaginary. Marriage was not her fate. She would be Tia Rebecca to her nieces and nephews. And as her sewing improved and her talent as a seamstress spread throughout northern Greece, she knew that was to be her life. She was Señorita Rebecca Solomon, designing wonderful dresses for both the well-to-do and those of more modest incomes.

She envisioned Señor Kapeta again, as he leaned across the table towards her, and her body shuddered with revulsion. She turned off the light. And then for the first time in many years, fantasy intruded on her thoughts and she was walking down the aisle in their synagogue with a Jewish man who looked like Andreas... A man who enjoyed reading and a man who would admire her talent for sewing and sketching. A man who loved her like Papá loved her Mamá. She closed her eyes and warmed to the picture in her mind. Of course, it could never be, for she had no dowry. But for a little while tonight, in an effort to forget her marriage proposal from Señor Kapeta, she could imagine she was a bride to a husband she had chosen.

Andreas stood by the ship's railing, looking out over the turquoise water of Kavala's harbor, the town where he had grown up and become a man. This was where he learned to accept and love the good people who were his adopted parents. "Look." He pointed across the water. "Do you see the castle and the aqueduct?" he asked his English friends.

"This is your home? Looks like a fine place," Nigel told him.

"Come, Barbara," he pulled his wife up from her chair. "Look at that aqueduct and that castle. Will we be able to see them up close? Are they easy to get to?"

"Very easy. The aqueduct goes through the middle of town. My family lives close by. Of course, I'll take you there. I promise it will be the highlight of your trip."

"Do your parents speak English?"

"No, but your Greek is good enough after living in Athens. I'll translate if there's a problem."

"How do we say hello Mr. and Mrs. Sefaris?" Barbara asked. "First impressions are so important. We want to be polite."

"My parents are Kìrios and Kiría Matsakis. They are my adopted parents. I never gave up the name of my birth parents."

"Oh." Barbara looked over at him. "You never mentioned that to me before."

"No, I didn't. Subject closed," he said in what he hoped was a congenial manner, but in a way she would understand that the discussion of this was over.

"Andreas," Nigel redirected the conversation. "Tell us about Kavala. Look at those clouds so white and the sea so blue. You know, as long as we live in this country, I continue to be amazed at its beauty. The colors are so vibrant. There is a special quality to the light. I wish I was an artist instead of a doctor. What beautiful work an artist could capture here."

"And we would both starve if you were an artist. I do prefer eating," his wife teased.

"What is on the schedule for us? Lots of sightseeing, I presume?"

"Well, first of all, my mother will ply you with wonderful food. You must not refuse anything, even if you have just a small taste. Otherwise, she will be insulted. And I have a friend, a neighbor, who will also bring over her family's specialties. They are Greek Jews and have their own delicacies. She's an old friend of mine and I hope I can convince her to join us on some of our excursions. She works with my mother as a seamstress. Now, back to food... We will have many meals with my parents where there will be an unexpected guest... a young Greek woman who my parents think will make a wonderful wife for me. They'd like me to move back here. I'm loathe to give up my work for the Red Cross, helping out the refugee community. There are refugees here as well, but the need for help is greater in a city like Athens, where there are so many slums."

"Here, in Kavala, do they have any of those places where they play that *rebetiko* music, the music of the refugees? It sounds just like the American blues. I'm quite fond of those places," Nigel commented.

"And I assume I'm not allowed to come with you fellows, just like I wasn't allowed to go in Athens?" Barbara pouted as she looked up at Andreas and shielded her eyes from the sun.

"Those dens are no places for a respectable woman. And the music is filled with sadness. You wouldn't like it."

"But the hashish offered in those places is quite lovely." Nigel laughed.

"There are many places to see in Kavala," Andreas told them. "And I have a surprise for you, Barbara. My friend does wonderful lifelike sketches and portraits. Would you like me to arrange that for you?"

"Did he study at a Greek art school?"

"It is not a he but a she; it's my friend Rebecca. She didn't study art in school. She was just blessed with talent. She lives down the street from us and, as I mentioned, she'll be there for dinner tonight."

"This is where you were born and grew up?" Barbara asked Andreas. "And you left to attend the University in Athens?"

"I was not born here. I was born in Asia Minor."

"Come on, Barbara." Nigel grabbed her arm. "Let's go to the other side of the deck."

"But I want to ask Andreas about Asia Minor. That sounds so exotic."

"Andreas doesn't talk about that."

"But why not?"

"Barbara, I said we are going over to the other side of the boat." He grabbed his wife's elbow and led her away.

Andreas was grateful to his friend who never questioned why he didn't speak about his past before Kavala. Nigel also knew he often inquired about the whereabouts of his sister Maria. He told Nigel that many years ago, when they were fleeing their home, he and Maria got separated. Nigel was astute and never asked him anything else.

Andreas held onto the railing as a big swell lifted up the boat. He noticed a buildup of clouds on the far horizon, huge dark clouds. He shivered as the dock they were approaching changed to the quay in Smyrna. The clouds that only a minute ago were just dark and brooding, suddenly turned crimson with flames. Why did these horrific memories continue to haunt him? He closed his eyes and willed the memories to go away, to retreat back into the dark recesses of his mind. He was going home to Kavala and he forced his thoughts to the small house, the cobbler shop, his adopted Mamá, Patéra, and his dear friend Rebecca.

❧❧❧

The door of the cobbler shop was open and Andreas ushered his friends inside. "Patéra!" he called out to the man with thick gray hair who was bent over his cobbler's bench.

"Andreas! My Andreas!" Patéra moved away from the bench and enveloped Andreas in his arms, kissing his cheeks.

"Come in, come in," his father welcomed Nigel and Barbara.

He turned around and called out to his wife. "Mamá! It's Andreas!"

Mamá hurried into the room from her work quarters and hugged him, her eyes wet with tears.

"It's so good to see you!" he told his parents. "So good. And here are my friends, Nigel and Barbara Cameron. Nigel and I both volunteer for the Red Cross in the refugee areas." His eyes scanned the room. Rebecca was standing near the window with a big smile that lit up her face. How he had looked forward to seeing her again. Each time he came to visit, he had to remind himself this beautiful woman was the tiny little girl with the long braids and the big heart who had found him shivering in the storage shed.

"Rebecca, come meet my friends." He held out his hand and she grabbed it tightly.

"Welcome, welcome," she told everyone.

"This is the girl who could sketch a charcoal portrait of you."

Barbara whispered something to her husband who seemed to nod in agreement. Andreas frowned at his English friends. How rude for them to be whispering like that.

"Mamá, why don't you take the Camerons up to their room?" Andreas asked.

"Of course, come with me," she beckoned to them.

"I need to go back to sewing. It's so good to see you, Andreas," said Rebecca.

"I'll ask Mamá to prepare a picnic basket for us to go up to the castle tomorrow. You must come with us."

"I don't know. There is a lot of work to do. We have a wedding coming up."

"I'm sure Mamá will let you go with us. Remember when we used to climb up to the castle when we were little?"

"Of course, I remember. We did have a lot of fun up there."

◌৩৯০

The next day was all Andreas could have asked for to introduce his friends to the beauty of Kavala. The sun was shining, white clouds drifted in the azure sky, and a slight breeze blew in from the sea. The two women walked ahead; Andreas and Nigel followed behind with the basket of food, Rebecca's tablet and a blanket.

"Well, old chap, now I understand," Nigel said.

"Now you understand what?"

"Your type, of course."

"My type of what?"

"Woman, my good man. You have a type of woman that you prefer, from the secretaries for the legations to the nurses on the hospital wards."

"I've told you, Nigel. I can only go out on the town with foreign women. Greek women aren't allowed to be with a man until they are married. It's a very different culture here. And I am delighted to be living in Athens, where I can enjoy the company of many women."

"Well, that's obvious. You do have that Greek charm that few women can resist. When will you decide to settle down with one of the girls your parents find for you?"

"Me, settle down? First of all, Greek men usually don't marry until they are older. And I have no intention of ever marrying anyone, foreign or Greek. Never. But you have me curious what you said about my type. I don't think I have a type. I've spent time with English, French, German women. I love them all."

"Yes, you have a type. Barbara and I found it quite amazing when we were introduced to your friend Rebecca. Light brown hair, light eyes, small boned, fine features. Your type, my friend, is all about replicating your childhood friend Rebecca."

"That's ridiculous, Nigel. She is like a sister to me."

"Both Barbara and I agree. She is not like a sister to you. And the look on your face when you introduced her to us... "

"Well, the two of you can think whatever you want." Andreas felt his face grow hot and he walked ahead. It was true. Rebecca, his Rebecca. Every time he came home and saw her, it became more difficult and more uncomfortable for him to deny his feelings. Was it that noticeable to his friends? He thought he was so good at masking his feelings. But apparently, he was wrong.

The four of them walked beneath the aqueduct. Andreas related its history as a Roman structure with sixty arches of different sizes, as they made their way up to the castle. He relayed that the castle was reconstructed in 1220 by Suleiman the Magnificent.

The women spread out the variety of dishes from the basket and everyone quite enjoyed the different sweets and savories prepared by Kiría Eleni.

"I love it up here, especially at night," Andreas told them. "Rebecca, remember when we used to sneak out at night and come up here?"

"Of course, I remember. The stars were so beautiful and you taught me all the constellations. When my parents discovered I was sneaking out

at night, my sisters kept guard to make sure I didn't leave my bed until morning."

"Yes, I was punished as well. When I was even younger, I used to sneak out with my friend Iskender. That was before he and his family were forced to leave. How old were you and I when we got caught? Ten?"

"Certainly no more than ten," Rebecca laughed as she gathered up the remains of their lunch.

"Let's go up to the ramparts again," Andreas suggested.

"Barbara and I are exhausted from all this climbing. We're going to stay here to digest all the wonderful food. You two go off and do some more climbing." Nigel stretched out on the blanket and closed his eyes.

"And you, Rebecca? Are you too tired?" Andreas asked.

"Of course not," she answered. "I want to take my tablet with me to do some sketching."

"I'll grab it for you." He reached down and picked up her tablet and then extended his hand to help her up. She ignored it and got to her feet by herself. "Remember when I used to race you up to the ramparts?" he asked.

"Yes, and I was so foolish to think I could ever win a race against you." She walked beside him.

"Sometimes I used to let you win." He smiled at her.

"I know."

They walked the rest of the way up to the ramparts in comfortable silence, with Rebecca leading the way.

Thee mou, but she was beautiful, he thought. My little Rebecca. Whenever he made his visits to Kavala, he saw her in the midst of family. Today was the first time in so long that they were actually alone. Feelings stirred inside of him. Emotions that were wrong, that were futile.

"Let's stop for a few minutes so I can catch my breath." Rebecca leaned against a pillar.

"I used to call you a mountain goat," he teased.

"Well, these days I spend all my time sitting while I sew or read or sketch. I'm not used to so much climbing. Just give me a moment." She took a deep breath and looked up at him.

Those lovely gray eyes, so different than dark Greek eyes. That smile. Indeed, Nigel was right. He was always searching for Rebecca when he was in Athens, when he talked those foreign women into his bed. Rebecca dwelled in a place within his heart that no one else could ever occupy.

"In your last letter you told me about your marriage proposal. Were your parents angry when you refused the offer of marriage from that old man? You wrote that it wasn't hard for you to say no."

"No, it wasn't hard to refuse his offer. He wanted me to give up my sewing and my reading. I've known, since I was little, that marriage was not in my future. I'm content with how things are."

"Do you think your parents might find you another suitor?"

"For a girl without a dowry, what are my prospects? I'm already twenty-three years old. There is one thing that does make me sad. When Mamá told me I would never marry, I wasn't unhappy that I wouldn't have a husband. I was disappointed that I would never have children. But I'm a good aunt to all my nieces and nephews and that is enough. When I refused the proposal, I think my parents were not pleased, especially Papá. My marriage would have lifted a burden from his shoulders. But my mother told me, in some ways, she was relieved. My sister Hannah is always complaining to her about her husband and she didn't want to listen to complaints from another daughter."

"He is the one who is a bit simple minded?" Andreas remembered what Rebecca had written about him.

"Yes. He is nice enough and from a well-to-do family. But because of his intellectual deficits, what other girl would say yes to him but a girl like Hannah, the seventh daughter with a paltry dowry?"

"Are you going to do some sketching while we are up here?"

"May I have my tablet?" she asked him.

They sat upon a huge boulder. As Rebecca sketched quickly, the sound of charcoal was loud against the paper. How good it felt to sit beside her like this.

"What are you sketching?"

"You and the castle." She smiled at him. "Well, I'm done."

He looked down at the sketch. "May I have it?"

"Of course." She handed it to him. "But it's not all that good."

"I'll keep it as a reminder of this lovely day." Andreas folded it and put it into his vest pocket.

She got to her feet and looked out at the town and the sea harbor sprawled beneath them. "Andreas, isn't this the most beautiful place on earth?"

"Yes, it is," he agreed. "Well, we better get back to Nigel and Barbara. Mamá has a big dinner planned for tonight and I'm going to be meeting a wonderful Greek girl with a big dowry."

"Your mother told me all about her. She's quite pretty."

"It upsets my parents when I tell them I will never marry, so I don't say that any more. I just smile when they bring new girls to meet me whenever I come home."

"Oh, Andreas, I think some day you will change your mind. Maybe even one of those foreign women will capture your heart. So, let me hear all about Berlin."

"We had an amazing time." He loved talking to her. It had always been like this between them, so easy. "I wrote to you about the Negro runner from America, Jesse Owens. That Hitler fellow got his comeuppance. You know he is always claiming the racial superiority of the German Aryans. It was wonderful to see this Negro man be the fastest runner. Everything looked so normal and festive in Berlin. But, as I wrote you, we were told all the anti-Jewish signs had been removed from the city before the games. Did you ask your father about that?"

"I did mention it to him. He said it was unfortunate that the Jews in Germany were having a hard time. But he said not to worry. The trouble will blow over and soon there will be a better, different government in Germany. The German Jews will be fine. "

"That makes a lot of sense. Your father is a wise man."

"Before we leave, I just want to stand here for another moment looking at the sea."

Andreas walked over to her as she gazed down at the water on the horizon. He couldn't help himself from leaning down and breathing in the smell of her rose water perfume. "Rebecca," he whispered into her ear. His arms encircled her waist.

She turned around and looked up at him, a quizzical expression on her face. Her eyes widened as she met his gaze. She swallowed as he tenderly placed his hands around her face.

"Rebecca, my Rebecca," he whispered. He shouldn't, but he couldn't help himself, even though he knew it was wrong. He bent down and gently kissed her lips and pulled her close.

He felt her begin to pull away and then she stopped resisting. He kissed her again. What was he doing? This was madness, he told himself as he drew her into his arms and she returned his kisses. It was so good to hold her and her kisses were all he had ever imagined them to be.

"I'm sorry. I'm sorry," he whispered as she melted into his embrace. He felt his body respond to her leaning against him. He should release her, but he couldn't.

Rebecca said nothing as he continued to hold her. He put his fingers under her chin so that her gaze met his own. "I love you, Rebecca Solomon. I've always loved you and I will love you for the rest of my life." The words came from deep in his heart.

"And I love you," she whispered as a tear slipped down her cheek.

He brushed it aside with his fingertips. She looked up at him. He held her tightly in his arms' embrace, never wanting to let her go, never wanting this moment between them to end.

After awhile, she pushed away. Andreas sighed when she bent over to retrieve her tablet. "Rebecca, I meant no disrespect."

"I know you didn't. But this can never happen again," she cautioned him.

"I promise, it won't," he vowed.

Andreas stood beside the cobbler bench as Patéra examined the shoe he was repairing, checking the soles for wear. "Why did this man wait until the soles of his shoes were so worn before bringing them to me?"

"Because he knows you will work your special magic on his old shoes." Andreas marveled, as he always did, at his father's bulging arm muscles.

"Come sit beside me like when you were a little boy. The first time we saw you, you were such a little skinny fellow."

"I used to complain to my Baba that I would never grow. He assured me he had also been little before he grew into a tall man. Of course, he seemed tall to me. I never knew how tall he actually was," Andreas said wistfully.

"Well, you are over six feet, a very tall man. Stay here with me while Mamá is busy in the kitchen preparing the food. Joseph Rouso stopped by last week and we invited him to come tonight for dinner."

"Thank you. I had planned to stop by to see him tomorrow. And I assume tonight you are also inviting a nice Greek girl."

"Why of course."

"It's a waste of everyone's time."

"Look, my son. I know you are still a young man. But Mamá insists. She never was blessed with her own child to hold in her arms and she wants a grandchild so much."

"I know," Andreas sighed. "I'm sorry. I told you I will never marry."

"You do like women, don't you? My brother Roilos didn't fancy women, but he married anyway. He had two sons and kept his inclinations private. We wouldn't judge you."

"No, no, Patéra," Andreas tried to reassure him. "I like women very much. These foreign women in Athens are quite exceptional."

"Mamá would prefer a good Greek girl of course. But she will love and accept anyone you bring home like a daughter."

"Foreign or Greek. It doesn't matter Patéra. I will never marry."

"Perhaps there is another reason for you not to marry. Perhaps you love a woman who you cannot marry."

"What are you talking about?"

"Rebecca Solomon. I can see it on your face when you look at her."

"Patéra that is preposterous. She is a Jewess."

"Yes, of course, Andreas. That is preposterous. In Greece, a Jew and a Christian are not allowed to marry. But, of course, you know that." The older man put down his needle and placed his calloused palm over Andreas's hand. "Then perhaps there is another reason. When you were a child, you told me you would never marry because anyone who you cared for, you would lose. Something bad would happen to her."

Andreas didn't answer him.

"You never told us what happened to your family."

"Everyone is gone. I still have those terrible nightmares and when I wake up, I remember almost nothing except for my sister screaming as she is carried off by a Turkish soldier."

"Maybe if you talked about whatever it is you do remember…."

"Stop," Andreas interrupted him. "It wouldn't change what happened, would it? I will never lose anyone again. Why *Hári Theoù,* by the grace of God, you and Mamá are still unharmed is a miracle. No marriage, no family, not ever. I'm sorry if that makes you and Mamá unhappy." He didn't need to tell this man, who was so good to him, who loved him like a son, that at first he had tried so hard not to love him and Mamá as a son loved his parents. He was so afraid he would lose them. But he did love them. How could he not give them the honor, the love and respect they deserved? As a devoted son, he sent them drachmas each month to make their lives easier.

"Alright," Patéra sighed. "I don't want to upset you. Why don't you tell me about your trip to Salonika last May, when you visited with my brother Constantine."

"Theo Constantine." Andreas frowned with distaste. "You have taken me to see him and his family since I was a boy. But I have to tell you that it never ceases to amaze me that you two are brothers and you came from the same home with the same parents."

"Well, we each went our separate ways, which often happens."

"Separate ways? He is a mean-spirited man. I was polite, of course, because he is family. But when he invited me for dinner with his friends, he cautioned me not to mention I came from Asia Minor. He told me how lowly those refugees were, almost as bad as the Jews. During dinner he went on a rant about the Jews and how the Nazis in Germany had the right idea about them."

"He just likes to talk."

"Well, I find it offensive and because he is your brother, I said nothing. But I'm not going back there. I will not deny who I am and that my family was from Asia Minor. And the Jewish people in our town have done nothing to deserve ill treatment. Theo Constantine is an ignoramus."

CHAPTER 9

Kavala, Greece: October 28, 1940

THE TAVERNA WAS filled with the haze of blue smoke as the men sat at small tables, drinking glasses of *ouzo*, listening to *bouzouki* music, and debating about the news.

Andreas, seated beside his Patéra, tried to block out the sound of their arguments. He didn't want to hear about war. He didn't want to think about war. "What's the matter with everyone?" Andreas sighed with exasperation. "Why are they so eager to fight and be soldiers? War is not a game."

"Of course, I know it is not a game as these young men will soon learn. I fought in the Great War and it was horrible beyond imagining. Mamá and I had just married and I feared I would leave her a young widow. But, my son, the Italians have been provoking us for months and now they are amassing at our borders with their armies. It was just a matter of time. And now that time has come."

"Can you imagine the nerve of the Italians and that clown Mussolini?" Joseph Rouso, his good friend, who sat beside them, interjected into the conversation. "Telling Prime Minister Metaxas, the head of Greece, that they were coming into our country and we should put down our arms and accept their occupation. Of course he said *oxi*, no. We will fight. We will all fight for our honor, for our country!" Joseph pounded his fist on the table.

Andreas said nothing as he crushed a cigarette on the floor with the heel of his shoe.

The tempo of music changed and his fingers began to drum on the tabletop. Two men rose and started to dance, their arms entwined around each other's shoulders. They beckoned to him, but he shook his head no. He watched the men. One was Ephraim Solomon, Rebecca's oldest brother. The other was a stranger to him.

"Who is that younger man?" Andreas asked Joseph.

"Don't you recognize him? It's been a long time, but he went to school with us. David Tiano. Do you remember him?" He nodded towards the young man in the finely tailored clothes.

"Yes, of course. He moved away with his family to Salonika. His father was in the silk business, wasn't he? There was better opportunity in a bigger city. I never cared for him very much. Wasn't he pretty much a braggart as a kid? But it would be a terrible world if, as grown men, we were held accountable for every bad deed we did as children," Andreas acknowledged.

When the music stopped and the two men gave their final stomp on the floor, Andreas beckoned to them to pull up chairs and join them at their table.

"Hello!" Andreas greeted them. After introductions between the men who had not seen David Tiano for many years, Andreas poured glasses of *ouzo* for everyone.

"*Yassas!*" They raised their glasses in salute.

"To our victory over the Italians!" David toasted.

"*Neh*! Yes," they all replied in unison.

"David, what have you been up to all these years and what brings you back to Kavala?" asked Ephraim.

"Kavala has always been home to me and I wanted to come back here again. It's been too long. I've been working in my father's silk business. Salonika has the charms of a big city, but Kavala called to my heart for a visit."

"Where are you staying?"

"That little hotel by the waterfront."

"No, no. You must come and stay with us," Ephraim offered.

"No, thank you. I'll stay at the hotel. However, I have no family left here and a home cooked meal would be greatly appreciated. I would love to see your big family again."

"Then tomorrow night you must come for dinner. My sisters and my brother are no longer in the house. They all have families of their own. But because I am to inherit my father's store, I decided it would be best for my wife and I to live with my parents. That way my wife Sara can be a help to Mamá and when the little ones come, Mamá can help with her grandchildren. Oh, and of course, Rebecca still lives at home."

"Which sister is she?" David inquired as he swallowed another glass of *ouzo*.

"The youngest, the eighth sister, so of course, she has no dowry and she'll never marry."

"Andreas, didn't she work with your mother? I remember going over to your mother's shop to collect a dress she had sewn for my mother."

"Yes, she did. Actually she still does," said Andreas.

"She's really done the best a spinster can do," commented Ephraim. "Kiría Matsakis gives her drachmas for her labor and Rebecca is saving them so that she won't be such a burden on the family in the future. Of course, the family will take care of her."

Andreas lit another cigarette and blew out a cloud of smoke. The family will take care of her? Rebecca had written to him about the new living arrangements with Ephraim and his wife Sara. They had only recently married. Ephraim hadn't been in a hurry for marriage. But Rebecca had written that once her brother reached forty-three years, the pestering of his family forced him to ask for the hand of Sara Yohai, a girl with a large dowry. It had been a struggle for Rebecca ever since Sara joined their family. Sara always seemed to have an unkind word for her, no matter how hard Rebecca tried to be pleasant. And so, Rebecca spent more and more time in the evenings either up in her room or visiting with her sisters and her nieces and nephews, who didn't live very far away.

"Ephraim and Joseph, you're so fortunate to have wives who will write letters to you when you are on the front. Those letters will help keep up your fighting spirit," David told them.

"I'm sure we'll also get letters from our sister. Rebecca is a great letter writer," Ephraim smiled. "She corresponds with Andreas at least once each month."

"Your sister writes letters to a man?" David frowned.

"Andreas and Rebecca have been friends since childhood," interjected Patéra.

"Yes, they are like brother and sister. It's harmless. I think if we told Rebecca not to write to him, she wouldn't listen. She is very strong willed. We love her dearly, even though she is a bit odd. Can you imagine a girl spending almost every evening reading a book, closed up in her bedroom?

You know she had a proposal of marriage from a wealthy man who didn't care if she had a dowry. And she turned it down." Ephraim inhaled on his cigarette.

"Really?" David took another swallow of his *ouzo*.

"Being so independently minded is not a good trait for a woman. A strong-willed woman like her probably isn't suited for marriage anyway. It would have lifted a burden from the family if she had married. Well, enough about my spinster sister. Do you see those fellows over there?" Ephraim pointed across the room. "They were all supposed to be married in the spring, but they are moving up the time for their weddings. Who knows what a man will face on the battlefield? And these men are eager to experience the joys of their wedding nights. There will be a group wedding tomorrow before they go off to fight with the Greek Army."

"Andreas, will you be signing up for the army with us?" Joseph asked. "We could all go off and fight together, side by side."

"Have you read the newspapers? The Greeks are far outnumbered by the Italians." Andreas shook his head.

"You think we should just give up and let the Italians come in and take over our country?" Joseph frowned at him.

"No, I'm not saying that," Andreas sighed. "But I have work to do here in Greece. Doctors are still needed to help deliver babies, which is how I spend much of my time in Athens. And the poor refugees still suffer so much from disease. They need my care."

"I'm sure the war won't last very long," commented David. "We'll rout those Italians in no time."

"I saw enough killing when I was a boy to last a lifetime. Being a soldier has no attraction for me." Andreas lit another cigarette.

"Mamá and I are glad to hear you aren't going off to fight." Patéra put his arm around him.

Andreas smiled at his adopted father. He was such a good man and Mamá was a wonderful loving mother. He realized how fortunate he had been to be taken in by this couple who loved him as a son. For so long he had tried, in vain, to tell himself to keep his distance from them. And now, as he spent so much time away from them, he felt even closer to them. He enjoyed coming home to Kavala and basking in their love. No, he hadn't been born to them and his own parents would always have a place in his heart. But Eleni and Vlassis Matsakis were his parents as well and he loved them dearly. Fate had not hurt them as it had hurt everyone else in his life. But deep inside he worried. He always worried. And this situation with the Germans and the Italians was not an imaginary worry. It was real, very real.

The nightmares he had suffered since he was a boy had diminished. A month could go by before he had a dream that caused him to awaken with his heart pounding, but no memory of what was dreamt. The newspapers were filled with reports of Italians amassing on the border and Germans invading Norway, Denmark, France, Belgium, Luxembourg, Romania and the Netherlands. Each country fell to the Nazis like so many dominos. Britain was valiantly fighting on, with nightly bombings. The world was turning upside down and now Andreas's nightmares had returned to haunt him almost every night. He still couldn't remember them when he woke up in bed. He could only remember the sounds of Maria screaming when the Turk took her away. And, of course, he remembered the terrible conditions on the quay and all the death and misery.

Until the news of war filled the air and was on everyone's lips, life had been good. He enjoyed his work at the hospital in Athens. He had a talent for diagnosis and his calm and soothing manner made him a favorite of the patients. He had recently undergone additional training in obstetrics. Delivering babies, bringing new life into the world, was a special joy for him.

On weekends, he volunteered his time with the Red Cross in Nea Smyrni, outside of Athens, fighting against disease, trying to offer hope to a second generation of the refugees. These people still struggled for their rightful place among the mainland Greeks as they mourned the loss of their homeland. Their wonderful *bouzouki rebetika* music filled the tavernas with soulful songs of sadness and longing.

In addition, he had developed an understanding with Margaret Finch, an older divorcee who had no interest in marriage. She had come to Greece to work for the British legation. They had a vibrant social life.

But that life he had carefully constructed for himself, no attachments, lots of hard work... that cocoon could not withstand the onslaught of the world events that threatened Greece and everyone he held dear.

"Don't you worry you might be called a coward if you don't sign up and fight for Mother Greece?" David asked him.

"It doesn't worry me in the least." Andreas exhaled the smoke from his cigarette.

"But, as I remember, you aren't really Greek, are you?"

"Excuse me?" Andreas felt the hair bristle on the back of his neck. Here it comes. How dare this man insinuate that he was not a patriotic Greek, that he was different? He remembered keenly the taunts of his childhood, calling him *tourkosporo*.

"Well, you weren't born here were you? You are one of those Turkish immigrants from wherever."

"I am as loyal a Greek citizen as you are. I am not Turkish. No, I wasn't born here. And if I were you, I'd shut up!" Andreas knocked the glass of *ouzo* out of David's hand.

David's eyes widened in fear. "Look, Andreas, I didn't mean any harm."

Patéra put his hand on Andreas's arm. "Enough," he cautioned in a low voice.

"I'm sorry." David put out his hand to Andreas. "I'm often accused of speaking without thinking. I apologize."

Andreas didn't want to take his hand after he had been so vilely insulted, but his father was squeezing his shoulder. And so he took David's hand, and then took a large swallow of his *ouzo*.

"Anyone up for a game of *bareeta*?" David looked over towards some men walking out the door. "Yiannis has invited everyone up to his place. I'm feeling lucky tonight."

A few men nodded in agreement as they took their drinks with them and started to walk next door to Yiannis's apartment. An older man requested another bottle of *ouzo* to take with them as they left the taverna.

"Joseph," Andreas called out to his friend. "Stay here with me for a moment. I'd like to talk. We can join the others later."

"Of course," Joseph agreed.

"Joseph." Andreas moved his chair closer to his friend. "We haven't had much time to talk on this visit. I'm going back to Athens in a few days and soon you'll be off to fight the Italians. I'm sure you will fight bravely and be a credit to your community and to Mother Greece. Before you leave, I wanted to tell you how dear you are to me. Many years ago, after Iskander was forced to leave, I was so distraught. And you were there for me. You were there when the other boys taunted me, calling me a seed of Turkey. I have never forgotten that."

"You were such a skinny little runt in those days." Joseph laughed. "Someone needed to come to your aid. Oh, Andreas, you are my dearest friend. I was so bereft when you went away to Athens to attend the university. I do miss you. Maybe someday, you'll come back to Kavala. Every night we'll carouse in the tavernas and dance in celebration of the goodness of our lives."

"That is something to look forward to." Andreas got to his feet and the two men embraced. "Stay safe. May God bless you."

They picked up their glasses and joined the others next door for games of chance. All the men were in such high spirits as they boasted of their predicted prowess on the battlefield. As Andreas threw the dice and started to refill his glass, his spirits were not high. He wanted to drink until he stopped feeling anything, especially this impending doom that nagged at him. His father covered his glass with his large calloused hand. "Enough, Andreas," he told him.

This talk tonight of battles and fighting brought up long-buried visions of soldiers on horseback, their swords dripping with the blood of Orthodox Christians. After he had read the newspapers today, his sense of dread increased. The German army was unstoppable. Everyone in Greece believed that the German army was too far away to be a threat…. and all they had to worry about was Mussolini and the Italians. But if their boasts came true and they could hold off the Italians, for how long could they keep them out of Greece? Would that madman, Hitler, allow his ally, Mussolini, to be beaten by a small country like Greece? Andreas remembered what he learned in Berlin about the targeting of Jews and he felt the bile rise in his throat. When a group is targeted because of religion, like his family had been, what recourse did the civilians have against an army? He hated the thought of bloodshed in Greece, with some people thinking they were better than others. Trying to block out the feeling of an approaching catastrophe that had enveloped him ever since war had been declared today between the Italians and the Greeks, he threw the dice with a vengeance.

⊂≈∞⊃

Rebecca hurried inside her house. Kiría Eleni hadn't minded when she left early today, especially since she promised to finish sewing the final bead work on that last order at her home tonight. Rebecca had told Mamá and Sara she would arrive early to help with the baking. She wanted to impress upon her sister-in-law that she wasn't trying to shirk the responsibilities in the kitchen. Rebecca kept trying to get into Sara's good graces, if that was even possible. The celebration for Papá's birthday was quickly approaching and there were hours and hours of baking ahead of them.

"You're late. And what is that on your arm?" Sara frowned.

"I had to bring the dress home with me to do the finishing touches. That's why Kiría Eleni said I could leave early. We've had so many orders for ball gowns from the tobacco families. They're having a grand ball next weekend, and this is the last dress to be completed. This lady and I are the same size and I'm aching to try it on."

"Are you allowed do that?" Sara asked.

"No one will know. I just want to try it on for a few minutes." And pretend, she thought. Pretend I am going to a ball and I will dance and have a good time.

"Go on, Rebecca." Her mother smiled at her. "Hurry, there is much to do in the kitchen."

"She's always trying to find ways not to help us," Sara complained.

"Sara, she won't take very long. And she works hard all day with Kiría Eleni."

"She only makes a pittance, which she doesn't contribute to the household. My Ephraim works hard for this family and she is just a burden to us all."

"Sara, your tongue is sharp. You need to be quiet," Mamá said.

Rebecca was not upset by the stinging words of her sister-in-law. She was used to them.

Up in her bedroom, she laid down the aquamarine ball gown with utmost care, and then placed it over her head. It was a bit difficult to manage all the fastenings by herself. And then it was done and she slipped her feet into her shoes and stood before the mirror. What a gorgeous gown! It was a bit snug across her waist, but the décolletage she had created fell perfectly across her breasts. She whirled around in front of the mirror, caught up in the moment, humming to herself, and pretending she was at the tobacco ball, dancing with a handsome stranger.

"Rebecca, come downstairs!" She heard her mother calling. "Let us see the dress before you take it off."

Rebecca lifted the dress off her ankles as she hurried down the stairs and into the kitchen.

"Beautiful! So beautiful!" her mother said with admiration of the ball gown. "What exquisite work you've done. I don't want to touch it. My fingers are coated with flour, but I can see what expert work you did."

"And Mamá, it didn't come from a fashion magazine. I designed it all by myself," Rebecca said with pride.

"Well, I guess you need something to occupy your time," said Sara.

Rebecca was about to turn away to go upstairs when she heard her brother's voice.

"Come in," Ephraim's deep voice boomed as he walked into the kitchen with a well- dressed young man. "Mamá, Sara, Rebecca this is David Tiano. Do you remember him? He used to live in Kavala. He went to school with us."

"Welcome," said her mother.

"Hello, I guess this means another plate at the table for dinner." Sara continued rolling out the dough.

"There is always room for another at our table," Mamá assured him.

"Welcome," said Rebecca to the good-looking man who was staring at her.

"I didn't realize I should have worn my formal attire for dinner at the Solomons." He gave her a big smile which brought a twinkle to his dark blue eyes.

"I... I excuse me." Rebecca's cheeks scalded red. She turned and ran up the stairs to her room. She slid out of the dress, carefully laying it across the bed. She needed to finish the last of the bead work before tomorrow morning when it was due at the Matsakis shop. She put on one of her own stylish dresses with quarter length sleeves, padded shoulders, and a cinched waist. It was a light blue color that she knew looked best on her. She told herself she was being foolish. But that man Ephraim had brought home was so handsome and it never hurt to look one's best. It made her feel better about herself, to look fashionable and pretty.

She tried to remember David Tiano from her childhood, but she couldn't even recall his name. He must not have been close friends with her brothers. She slipped into her favorite shoes with the small heels, looked into the mirror and gave her hair a few quick strokes with a brush. She applied a fresh coat of scarlet lipstick.

Rebecca hurried into the kitchen and grabbed an apron from a nearby hook to cover her dress in preparation for her tasks in the kitchen. The three women worked side by side in silence. What a good-looking man, thought Rebecca, as she was about to assemble the filling for the *bourekas*. "What kind of filling is this?" Rebecca didn't recognize the ingredients.

"They are the specialty of my mother's kitchen," replied her sister-in-law. "Ephraim says he prefers my mother's *bourekas* to the kind you make here."

"I'm sure they will be very good," said Mamá with what Rebecca knew was a forced smile upon her face.

Rebecca began filling the *bourekas* with the ingredients suggested by Sara. Why did her sister-in-law seem to take such delight in saying that Ephraim preferred her mother's cooking to Mamá's? But Mamá always smiled and tried to never disagree with her new daughter-in-law. How hard it must be for Mamá to live in the house with Sara… to share her kitchen.

Sara had been given a beautiful house from her parents as part of her dowry. But sensible Ephraim realized because he would be working side by side with Papá, that it was foolish to be on the other side of town when he needed to spend so much time at the store. The house he loved and grew up in was next door to the dry goods store. Because all his siblings except for Rebecca were gone, there was lots of room for what he hoped would be his growing family. He had rented out the other house, much to Sara's annoyance.

Sara was much younger than Ephraim's forty-three years. She was even younger than Rebecca. She needed time to adjust to her new role of wife and daughter-in-law. Mamá had explained this to Rebecca after another long week of Sara's complaining about having to prepare luncheon for the large Solomon family on *Shabbat*. But Rebecca felt strongly it wasn't Sara's youth or adjusting to new roles that was responsible for her sharp tongue. Sara just had a sour disposition and Rebecca felt sorry for her brother to have wed a girl with such an unpleasant temperament.

Rebecca enjoyed the simple pleasures of her life, playing with her younger nieces and nephews. She loved sewing and creating wonderful clothing, traveling with Kiría Eleni to towns where their fashionable artistry was requested. And, of course, she could lose herself in wonderful books and the travelogues that frequently accompanied Andreas's letters. Life was good, but when she thought about her future... Someday Mamá would be gone and it would just be her and her unpleasant sister-in-law sharing the kitchen and the house. Hopefully there would be children. But what other choice did she have than to live with them? Ephraim, as the eldest, had promised her father that he would take care of his spinster sister and she would always have a place in his home.

Everyone tried to get along with Sara. Rebecca was gone much of the day and only had to contend with her complaints after she returned from sewing. Once the women cleaned up after dinner each night, Rebecca hurried up to her room and closed the door. Sara liked to blare the music of the phonograph. Rebecca enjoyed popular music. But why did it have to be so loud?

"I'm eager to taste your family's version of *bourekas*. I'm sure they will be delicious." Rebecca tried to give Sara a compliment as her thoughts drifted back to the man in the parlor. Was he married, she wondered? Well, that didn't matter. After all, no man would be interested in a girl without a dowry. She had accumulated a nice amount of savings from the earnings that Kiría Eleni paid her. But it was a pittance in comparison to what a girl needed for a dowry.

Rebecca was delighted at the sound of her sister Miriam's daughters entering the house. "Tia Rebecca! Tia Rebecca!" The little girls ran into the kitchen. Rebecca wiped her hands on her apron and gathered them up for a kiss.

"Do you have time to draw a picture for us before dinner?" Five-year old little Rachel asked her after giving her grandmother a kiss.

"Not tonight. Maybe tomorrow. You're spending the night with us, aren't you?" Rebecca asked.

"Yes, Papá and Mamá have a celebration to go to and Nona said we could spend the night with you."

"Go on now. Wash up for dinner. It's almost ready," Sara told them.

The women removed their aprons and placed all the wonderful dishes they had prepared on the dining room table.

Rebecca found herself seated across the table from David Tiano. She would glance up from her meal and see him looking at her, smiling. She smiled back, a feeling of butterflies in her stomach. As he ate his meal, complimenting every course, he regaled them with stories of life in Salonika.

"It sounds like your father is doing quite well in the silk business," Papá commented as he reached for a slice of bread.

"Yes, our move to Salonika was a very good opportunity for my father. He has a brother there and their business ventures have prospered."

"You've just come back for a brief visit?" Her mother offered him another piece of lamb.

"Well, I had intended to come for a brief visit and then our Prime Minister declared war on the Italians. So of course, I need to do my patriotic duty as a Greek man and go to fight beside my fellow Greeks."

"War," Papá sighed. "I thought we were finished with that after the Great War. But I guess we never learn. My sons and sons-in-law will all take up arms in the next few days. I hope my grandsons don't want to go off to war."

"To Greece and victory, may it come soon!" Ephraim raised his glass in a toast.

Everyone raised their glasses and repeated Ephraim's toast.

Rebecca caught David looking at her again. "Señorita Rebecca, where do you get all your ideas for fashion? I must say that dress you are wearing is quite becoming. Even in a city like Salonika, we don't see such beautiful frocks."

"Why thank you." Rebecca smiled at him. "I study fashion magazines and I designed this dress from my own ideas."

"You have such talent."

"But she doesn't do much cooking," Sara said and everyone at the table looked her way.

"Well, she doesn't," Sara muttered in embarrassment, after becoming the unwanted center of attention.

"With such talent, she doesn't need to cook." David gave Rebecca a wink. "Ephraim, what do you say about going out after dessert? What about the cinema?"

"Let's do that, Ephraim." Sara got to her feet and started clearing the table. "We haven't gone in ages."

"Sure, that's a fine idea. Won't see any movies when we're on the front lines."

"And you must come as well, Señorita Rebecca," David Tiano invited her.

"Me? I…. I must help Mamá in the kitchen."

"If all four of you are going together, it is alright for you to go with them, Rebecca. Let's hurry and clear the table. With the three of us, it won't take long to finish in the kitchen." Mamá stacked the dishes in her hands and hurried out to the kitchen.

The dishes were washed and put away. Rebecca made her way to the front door and David helped her with her coat. She didn't go to the cinema often. The friends she had socialized with when she was younger were all married women now.

The four of them walked down the cobblestone streets toward the cinema. Ephraim and Sara walked ahead, engaged in what seemed to be an argument. "Your brother Ephraim mentioned that you spend much of your time reading books," David said to Rebecca.

"Yes I do. I love to read," Rebecca told him, looking up at his face. He sported a fashionable mustache like all the men in her family. Even Andreas had grown a mustache the last time she had seen him. David had blue eyes and wavy dark hair; truly a good-looking man.

"I didn't go to school. I'm the eighth daughter and there was no money for something so unnecessary," Rebecca explained. "But my brothers taught me what they learned in school. I had a knack for reading and now I buy books as often as my funds from sewing allow. My good friend Andreas Sefaris also sends me books he thinks I might find interesting."

"Well, I think it is most admirable that you read without having an education and you have been able to accumulate some drachmas on your own by working as a seamstress."

They walked the rest of the way in comfortable silence. He was being so nice and paying attention to her. But what could come of it? She had no dowry.

Rebecca sat beside him in the movie theatre, watching the moving images on the screen, feeling so aware of the attractive man seated next to her. Her brother and his wife sat on her other side. She felt David's hand reach out to hers with a gentle squeeze. She looked up and noticed he was staring at her with intensity. She should move her hand away, but she enjoyed the warmth of his hand holding hers. He leaned over, his lips close to her ear. "Rebecca Solomon, you are a beautiful woman," he whispered.

⋘⋙

When they returned home, David approached her parents who were sitting in the parlor. "Sir," he addressed her father. "If I may speak with you privately," he said with solemnity.

"Not tonight. You may come to see me tomorrow."

"I will do that," David told him.

"*Nochada buena*, Rebecca," David called to her in Ladino.

"*Nochada buena*," Rebecca answered and walked up the stairs to her bedroom

She pulled out the dress and the beads she needed to finish sewing. Could she dare and think, even hope? Her thoughts raced wildly. As she sewed on the beading, she could think of nothing but David Tiano holding her hand, telling her she was beautiful. He was going off to war. He'd be gone in a few days. She wondered why he wanted to speak to her father.

The next day when Rebecca returned from sewing, she was met by her mother in the kitchen. "Rebecca, come into the parlor." She was instructed.

Her father was seated in his usual comfortable chair and Mamá stood at his side.

"Rebecca." Her father cleared his throat. "This man, Señor Tiano, wants to spend time with you so that you might get to know him. He intends to ask for your hand in marriage before he leaves for the front."

Rebecca took a deep breath. Could this really be happening!

"These are not normal times, my daughter. There is war at our doorstep. Men are rushing off to fight. David Tiano said he wishes to marry you now, before he goes off to the front. He appealed to me, saying he knew the story of my love for your Mamá. The moment I saw your Mamá, I knew I loved her and must marry her. He said it was the same for him. He said he is a very prosperous business man and that he doesn't need a wife with a dowry."

Rebecca, who had been standing, sank down into a nearby chair.

"Oh, Papá" she breathed and could think of nothing else to say.

"My girl, we know nothing, absolutely nothing about this man. Yes, his family used to live here in Kavala. But since that time we've heard not a word about them. In normal times we would make inquiries in Salonika. You would have an engagement. But these are not normal times. I will make inquiries, but we will not learn anything until the men have gone to the front. Do not give me an answer tonight. He will come tomorrow and spend the day with you and then he will come to my birthday celebration. You must decide quickly."

Rebecca went up to her room. Her mind was racing, filled with thoughts of David Tiano telling her she was beautiful, holding her hand, making her feel special. Was fortune smiling on her after all these years? Was David's proposal a sign that God had heard the prayers she had sent to him when she was younger, before she accepted her fate as a spinster?

"What do you mean Rebecca isn't going to help us in the kitchen! She promised she wasn't going to the sewing shop today so she could help with the baking!" Sara's voice was a high-pitched whine.

"Rebecca has company today." Mamá's eyes narrowed with annoyance at her daughter-in-law. "Hannah and Allegra will be coming over to help us prepare for Papá's birthday celebration."

"Company? What kind of company?" Sara asked with exasperation.

The doorbell rang and Rebecca hurried into the parlor where her father was opening the door to David. Her handsome suitor walked over to Rebecca with a huge bouquet of flowers. He gave her a big smile. "It's so good to see you, Señorita Rebecca."

"Thank you." She took the flowers.

She led him to a small table across the room from where Papá sat with the newspaper. Rebecca started to pour David a cup of coffee. Don't be nervous, she told herself. What if her hand shook when she tried to hold the pitcher? Would he think she didn't have the skills to be a good wife, that she was just a foolish girl?

"Rebecca, I apologize. There is so little time before I must go off to fight for our country. Ever since we parted the other night, I couldn't stop thinking of you. I have so much I want to say to you. Your father told you that I want to propose marriage?" he asked as he looked intensely at her with his dark blue eyes.

'Yes, he told me and he said I must make my decision quickly."

"Today we must talk so you will get to know me and realize you must say yes. I'll be leaving soon, and Rebecca, I knew when I saw you that first moment that you were the girl for me. I want to fight for you. I want to have your picture with me that I will carry close to my heart, knowing you are home waiting for my return."

Rebecca sat at a respectable distance beside this attractive man while he told her all about his life in Salonika. How he and his family had done so well in the silk business. They had prospered and had a good life. David had been hoping someday to find a girl to share his life. There had been no urgency. But now that he was about to go off to war, perhaps never to return, he realized how alone he was. If he had a wife, he'd have someone to return to, someone to fight for, and someone to live for. How he envied all the men in her family with wives and children. How sad it would be to not have a good wife at home writing him letters, waiting for him. And the moment he saw her, he knew she was the one with whom he wanted to share his life.

He asked her about the books she read and which were her favorites. He asked about the towns she traveled to with Kiría Eleni and the people for whom she fashioned her dresses in the latest styles. She talked and talked to him. And he was so interested in everything she had to say. He made her feel as if every word she uttered was the most interesting he had ever heard. When he spoke to her, she was mesmerized by the fascinating life he led. He was a wonderful man. How had she become so fortunate, so blessed! He actually wanted her to be his wife. She'd never dared hope she would be a wife and mother. If she said yes, she would become Señora Tiano. She would have a husband. It was so rushed. But she could feel herself beginning to care for him. How could she not?

"My whole family is in Salonika and they will certainly love you. But while I am at the front, you should stay here with your family and continue to work for Kiría Eleni."

"You don't mind if I work while you're gone?"

"You are such an artist, Rebecca. Once I come back from the front, we will return to Salonika and I will set you up in your own shop. You will employ women to work for you."

"Really. You wouldn't mind me working?"

"Once the children come, of course, we would have to decide. But I can see how much your sewing means to you."

"Yes, it does. Thank you for understanding."

"As your husband, it will be my duty to always keep you happy and content Rebecca."

Of course, her answer was yes. Papá had his birthday celebration, and the next day they appeared before the Rabbi.

She was a married woman... married to a wonderful, kind man. The whole family came together for a hastily-prepared wedding feast.

The day was a blur as she thanked everyone for their congratulations, *Bueno mazels*. She saw David gazing at her with love and that twinkle in his blue eyes that she found so attractive. She forced herself not to think about him going off to war, fighting against the Italians. For the next two days, her husband David would be with her and she would get to know him, what kinds of foods he preferred, his moods, what made him smile, what made him frown. She wanted to be a good wife.

Kiría and Kírios Matsakis had come to the celebration. Kiría Eleni presented Rebecca with a beautiful embroidered silk nightgown. They expressed Andreas's regret that he had to return to Athens and could not attend the celebration.

David and Rebecca would be sharing her bedroom until it was time for him to go. When he returned, they would move to Salonika where he had a fine house in the best neighborhood, filled with shops, cafes, and cinemas. He assured her that although she would miss her family, she would love Salonika. This was her chance for a new life as a married woman.

On their wedding night, he closed the door of her bedroom and looked around the room. "All those books, impressive! What else do you have besides books? Any clothes?"

"Of course, I do." She laughed at him. "See this is my armoire." She opened the door to reveal her dresses and shoes.

"And what treasures lay inside that box?" He pointed to her special keepsake box.

"That's where I keep my savings, some special sketches that I cherish and letters from Andreas Sefaris. You know Andreas, don't you?"

"Yes, I do. But my dear little wife," he gathered her in his arms. "You know it is unseemly for you to be corresponding with a man, especially since now that you are a married woman?"

"I suppose so." She caught her breath as his hand caressed the bodice of her dress.

"You will get rid of all those letters. You are my wife now. Do you understand?"

"Yes," she whispered. Wonderful new sensations of pleasure coursed through her body, as he unfastened the front buttons of her dress and his fingers slid inside to touch her.

⚮

Rebecca lay in his arms, drowsy with sleep and feeling so content. She had a husband. Maybe she would conceive a child before he left. The act of marriage had been uncomfortable, but not as much as she feared and he was tender and loving with her.

Suddenly there was a thunderous pounding on the door downstairs. Rebecca's thoughts raced with fear. Had something terrible happened at one of her sisters' houses?

They were startled by a loud knocking on their bedroom door.

"David!" It was the sound of her father's voice. "David come out here!"

"I'm coming, just a moment." He got out of bed and pulled on his pants. "What is it?" He opened the door.

"There are two men who have come to see you in the middle of the night." Her father's tone was harsh and disapproving. "They are most insistent that you see them right now."

"Alright, alright." David quickly threw on his shirt and slipped into his shoes.

Her father stood in the doorway as David rushed past him. "Rebecca," Papá muttered, shaking his head with disapproval and then turned and went downstairs.

Rebecca could hear voices outside, loud and arguing. She put on her robe and went out onto the balcony, which looked down upon the street. David was standing there with two men who were shoving him. Rebecca's heart pounded in her chest, as she saw one man punch him.

"David, oh David," she whispered. Who were these men? Wasn't Papá going to help him? David was his son-in-law now.

Rebecca watched as David came back inside the house. The two men stood in the street pacing back and forth. She heard the sound of Papá's voice and David's voice. But she couldn't discern their words.

David opened the door of her bedroom and hurried inside.

"David, are you hurt?" She touched the red mark on his cheek tenderly. "Who are these men? We should call the police!"

"I'm taking care of it. Don't worry." He rubbed his hand over his cheek. "I need your money."

Rebecca's eyes widened in shock.

"Don't just stand there. I said I need your money. That box with your earnings. I need it. You're my wife and what you have belongs to me. Now get it for me."

"But...."

"Those men. There has been a misunderstanding. They say I owe them money. But they cheated me at cards. If I don't give them some money to pay them off, they are going to hurt me, maybe kill me. Do you want to become a widow on your wedding night? Now get me the money right now. Those men don't have a lot of patience."

With a shiver coursing through her body, Rebecca went to her armoire and withdrew her box filled with drachmas. She handed it to him.

He opened it up and counted the money. "This is all you have?"

"I have some gold. Papá gave it to all of us in case of an emergency."

"Well, where is it?" he asked impatiently. He watched as she retrieved the gold from her drawer. "Hurry up. Don't look so worried. When I get back to Salonika I'll have access to my own funds and we won't need your money." He grabbed the money and the golden nuggets and ran out the door.

Rebecca stood in the middle of the room, her stomach turning over. What was happening? Why had those men cheated David? How had they found him here in Kavala?

A few minutes later, David returned. "Well, that is all taken care of. Now, come back to bed." He stripped off his clothes and climbed back into bed "Don't just stand there. I said get back into bed, Rebecca. I told you everything is taken care of now."

"Are you sure you're alright?" She leaned over and gingerly touched his cheek that sported a red mark.

"I'm fine." He kissed her fingertips. "Now come to bed my lovely bride," he said with a softened tone. "There is nothing to worry about. It's all taken care of. Don't worry your pretty little head about it."

Rebecca took off her robe and laid down next to her husband. He was her husband. She was his wife. Rebecca fought against a nagging sense of unease as David took her in his arms.

CHAPTER 10

Kavala, Greece: November, 1940

SINCE THE MEN had left for the Greek army mobilization, Rebecca's sisters and their children spent more and more time at the home of their parents. It often seemed like the old days when they were all together, before everyone had married. Only now, there were younger and older children seated at the table. Some days, they had to eat at different times, because the table couldn't accommodate the whole family.

Sara had gone back to live with her own parents. Mamá had told her it was perfectly fine for her to stay there until Ephraim returned. Sara was in the early stages of her first pregnancy. Mamá told Sara that her mother would enjoy having her back home. Rebecca was glad to have her sister-in-law gone. After Rebecca's marriage to David, Sara no longer disparaged her as a spinster. Instead she grilled her about David, asking questions Rebecca couldn't answer. All she knew about him was that David was a kind and charming man from Salonika. He was going to set her up in her own dressmaking shop in Salonika or perhaps Athens. He was a man of means, who didn't care if she had a dowry because he was so taken with her the first moment he saw her.

She tried very hard not to dwell on the men who stood below her balcony on her wedding night. The men who had threatened David... And most of all, she tried to forget that her box, which contained her drachmas, and the gold nuggets Papá had given her, her savings for her future... That box was now empty. She didn't need it anymore because she had a husband. She tried to forget David demanding her savings and her gold nuggets. But sometimes, that memory bubbled to the surface, especially when she went to her armoire to retrieve her sketching tablet and saw the box, now empty. She forced her thoughts to return to her husband and his kind and charming nature. She needed to worry about him on the front.

She needed to pray for his safe return. But if she was truly honest with herself, what she prayed for more than anything else was that she would soon be a mother. They only had two nights together, but it was possible.

Rebecca, who loved her books as if they were dear friends, started to visit the library, looking for those books she would have bought if she were able... if she had the money. Before David left, he told Rebecca she should ask Kiría Eleni to increase her wages. He said that Kiría Eleni was taking advantage of her talents. But though Rebecca knew, as a dutiful wife, she must obey her husband, she was too embarrassed to ask the older woman to increase her salary.

Kiría Eleni was more than her employer. She was a dear friend, like a second mother. In actuality, Rebecca spent more time with her than with her own mother. Because of their combined efforts, Kiría Eleni was able to purchase a second Singer. And as they sewed, they talked about everything and anything. When the seamstress asked why she was going to the library, Rebecca told her she thought it the prudent thing to do, to be more cautious about spending since now she was a married woman. Rebecca never told anyone that her savings box was empty. It was her husband's right to ask for her money, but the memory of those men under the balcony continued to haunt her.

She didn't throw away Andreas's letters as David had instructed. She worried that she was not going to be a good wife after all. Obedience was a virtue for a married woman, and Rebecca wondered if she was sorely lacking in that aspect of her character. In time, she told herself, in time she would learn to be more obedient, especially once her husband returned and they had lived together for more than two days and nights. She no longer wrote to Andreas. She hadn't received a letter from him this month. Andreas was not a fool. He must realize that because she was a married woman, it was not appropriate for him to write to her anymore. She tried not to dwell on the loss of her dearest friend. But on days when she returned home and realized there would never be a letter from him waiting for her, she couldn't help but feel a deep sadness in her heart.

She dutifully wrote to her husband and looked forward to receiving his letters from the front. She had received a letter shortly after David departed, sent before he had arrived at the front. He filled it with words of love and affection. How happy he was to have her as his wife. How he looked forward to having sons. Rebecca wrote back to him. But it seemed unreal to be writing to this man who was her husband. Sometimes it seemed like a dream that she was actually married. Maybe if she knew more about him. Was there something elusive about this man or was that just her imagination? She often thought about those two days and nights they spent together. But that time seemed veiled in a mist. She tried to recall anything of substance they talked about. However, she could only remember stories he told her of his business prowess and how he was so well regarded in Salonika. She was fortunate, she told herself. Fortunate, to have a loving husband. She now had a future she had once thought impossible. Papá never mentioned that night when the men came to their door and she could almost convince herself that it never happened.

After her recent marriage, Rebecca had a rightful place among all the married women at the table. She had a husband. She was no longer the spinster sister, a woman to be pitied. But as she sat at the table with her niece Gracia on her lap, Rebecca felt she really didn't belong among the married women, that she was only pretending to be one of them. Yes, she was a woman whose marriage had been consecrated by the Rabbi. But she'd spent only two days and nights as a married woman.

Her sisters and sisters-in-law spoke of the bravery they knew their husbands possessed and how they believed their spouses would return triumphant over the Italians in Albania. Would David be brave? She didn't know. There was so much she didn't know about him. Indeed, when she tried to think about him, what she knew about him, the realization that she was married to a stranger loomed over her... Well, of course, he would be brave, she told herself.

At the mid-day meal on Sunday, the family sat together at the table, eating the food all the women had prepared. "Do you think the men will return soon, Papá?" Liza asked. "I worry so about Eliezer. Eliezer said they would whip the Italians in no time. Do you think that's true?"

"Daughter, I don't know. Our men are valiant but the Italians have superior forces in every way. They have many more soldiers and planes. But our men will fight as only Greeks can fight."

Rebecca passed the plate of *batsaria*, a cheese and spinach pie, and then felt a crush of disappointment when cramping in her stomach indicated that she was going to begin her flow. There would be no baby. "Excuse me." She got up from the table to attend to her needs.

She had really wanted to be a mother. When David returned with the other men, it would happen. She would be a mother sometime in the future and she would give him the sons he wanted.

The first day after their marriage, as they had laid next to each other in bed, David had told her of his wishes to have a large family. Yes, that is what she also wanted fervently. He had asked for paper so that he could write a letter to his parents, telling them all about her and their marriage. He had also suggested she write a letter to his parents, telling them about herself and her family. After all, he told her, she was going to be the mother of their grandchildren. And as an obedient wife and daughter-in-law, she had composed the first letter she would write to his parents. David had told her they would love her just as much as he did.

She had hoped to be the mother to their grandchildren. Someday... after he returned. He would be safe and return, she told herself. So many nagging worries that she tried to put out of her mind. Would he be safe? Would he be injured? And those men who had threatened him… She must be positive about her future. She would move with him to Salonika. She would miss her family, but his family would become her family. David would return with her brothers and brothers-in-laws. They would start their family. She would truly feel like a married woman then.

It was the end of November and Rebecca was ready to leave for Kiría Eleni's shop when she noticed a letter for her on a table in the parlor. Was it from David? The return address showed it was from David's parents. She slipped the letter inside her pocket to read later when she had a spare moment, perhaps during lunch. There was a large amount of sewing waiting for her. She needed to be on her way.

The two women sewed all morning and then discussed adding some new designs to the sketchbook. Rebecca had seen some new dresses in a fashion magazine that she thought their customers might be keen on.

Kiría Eleni was seated behind the Singer and Rebecca had just finished pinning a pattern over beautiful silk fabric. Rebecca walked into the kitchen and took out her lunch of cheese, bread, and olives. She brought it into the sewing room and sat at a small table away from the fabrics to eat lunch hurriedly. When David returned, she would be leaving Kavala. She'd have to say goodbye to her family. That would be sad. But a wife always follows her husband. And Salonika wasn't that far away. She could come home for visits. Saying goodbye to Kiría Eleni would be difficult. All the days she'd spent with the seamstress, learning her craft, sharing so much between them... Rebecca tried to put those painful thoughts out of her mind.

She took a bite of the bread and reached inside her pocket to withdraw the letter. How exciting to have her first contact with David's parents. When she moved with him to Salonika, they would become her family. "A letter from David?" Kiría Eleni asked her.

"It's from his parents. I wrote to them before he left and now they've answered me," Rebecca answered.

Rebecca skimmed the letter and her heart started thundering in her chest as she reread it more slowly.

> *"Dear Rebecca,*
>
> *We wish we could say it was a pleasure to hear from the wife of our youngest son. But unfortunately, we have disowned the man who is your husband. We loved him dearly and perhaps we spoiled him, but he grew into a man with no ambition, save to win at cards and dice. He owes us, his brothers, and his cousins an enormous amount of drachmas because of his gambling debts. We finally said, "no more," and told him not to return to us until he could pay back all that he borrowed. I urge your family to guard against loaning him any money, no matter how compelling his tale of woe or his grandiose opportunities for investments.*
>
> *It is our fervent hope that marriage to a good woman will change his ways. If that day should arrive when he*

has an honorable, decent job and a means to repay us,
we will welcome you and David with open arms.
  We are sorry to be the bearer of bad news. Be assured
we do pray for his safe return from the Italian front.

~ Malka and Shimon Tiano

Rebecca crumbled the letter and shoved it into her pocket.
"Rebecca, what's the matter? Your face is white!" Kiría Eleni pushed her chair away from the Singer and hurried over to Rebecca.
"I don't feel well. I have to go home. I'm sorry." Rebecca ignored the woman's outstretched hand. "I'm sorry."
Rebecca ran out the door.
"Your coat!" Rebecca heard Kiría Eleni's voice trailing after her.
The chill November wind whipped around her, but Rebecca didn't feel the cold as she ran blindly through the narrow street to her home. Her mother was in the kitchen, stirring a pot with a heavy spoon.
"What's wrong?" Mamá asked with concern.
"I received the most terrible letter from David's parents. It says horrible things about him!"
"Come into the parlor, Rebecca. I will go to get your father at the store. We must talk. Papá has received letters from his contacts in Salonika about David."
"Why would they say such things?" Rebecca bit her lip to keep from crying.
Mamá hurried out the door as Rebecca sank into a chair in the parlor, pulling the letter out of her pocket and rereading it several times. Her lunch rose in her stomach and she swallowed hard. Papá would look at the letter and explain why these people said such terrible things about her husband, about their son. His parents must be awful people.
Papá and Mamá walked into the parlor, Papá sat down across the room and Mamá sat next to Rebecca on the settee.
"Oh, Papá!" Rebecca exclaimed. "I received the most terrible letter from David's parents! They said they disowned him and that he was a gambler who owed everyone money."

"Rebecca, my child. I take full responsibility for what has happened." Her father shook his head sadly. "I've received letters in response to my inquiries into your husband. I am told he is not of sterling moral character. If it wasn't for the war coming, we would have had time to learn more about him. But Rebecca, we must hope that with the influence of a woman like yourself, he will turn himself around. You will have children and he will learn to shoulder the responsibility of a father. He can stay here in Kavala with us and work in the store."

Rebecca said nothing. Her father wasn't saying what she wanted him to say. She'd been sure he would tell her not to pay attention to the letter from the Tianos, that they weren't to be believed.

"David borrowed money from me to pay off those men who came to the door in the middle of the night," Papá said in a hoarse voice. "He is your husband Rebecca, but make sure to safeguard your savings before his return. Perhaps you should keep your drachmas in the bank instead of in your room."

It's too late, she wanted to scream.

"Rebecca." Her mother gave her a hug. "We are here for you. We will always be your family. I'm sure when David returns from the front, you will help him to reform and be a good husband. The experiences of war can change a man for the better, teach him what is important in life."

"I want to lie down," Rebecca told her mother and got to her feet stiffly. She walked up the stairs to her room, closed the door and laid down on her bed. This was the bed she shared with David, where he beguiled her with stories of the shop he would open for her, the fun they would have in Salonika. Exhaustion and sadness crushed her and she fell asleep.

She woke up with a pounding headache. She straightened her clothing and drew a brush through her hair. It was going to be alright. She knew it was. She hadn't waited so long for a husband to have her hopes and dreams vanish into thin air. David Tiano was a good man, she knew it. He had been a bachelor with no responsibility. But now, that was all different. When he returned, it was going to be good between them. He would work with Papá and give up gambling. She would keep her earnings in the bank so he couldn't access them until she was certain he had changed his ways. They would have children. They would have a fine life together.

Rebecca wrote him a long letter, expressing how much she cared for him and how she prayed for his safety. She told him she and her family had learned that he had accumulated many debts because of gambling. She assured him that he could begin a new life with her. They would both work hard and pay back his debts and go forward into the future. She re-read the letter. Yes, that is what she wanted to say; what she had to say.

When she came downstairs and joined her parents for their evening meal, there was an awkward silence between them.

"Are you well?" her mother asked as she passed a platter of fish to her.

"I'm alright. Everything is going to work out. When David returns, he will have a new beginning with our family. He just needs everyone to give him another opportunity to right himself," Rebecca announced with determination.

"You are strong, Rebecca," her father told her. "You will be a good wife for him. That's what he needs."

⋘⋙

The news from the front was sporadic. The Greeks had to march at night because during the day, Italian bombs fell from the skies. The weather was getting colder as November passed into December. The Greek army suffered from a lack of food and ammunition. But still, the brave Greek patriots persevered. In the month of December, the cold grew more intense. There was freezing rain and the soldiers didn't have winter clothing. All the women in the family spent their afternoons knitting socks for the soldiers. Winter was coming soon and in the mountainous areas where they would be fighting, it would be bitter cold.

The British were now helping them and Greeks were winning, in spite of all the back and forth, with territories being captured and recaptured. The Greeks now had gained control of almost all their national territories They had captured Sarande and Gjirokaster, among many other places. Then they destroyed the 9th Italian army and took many prisoners. Fighting in the mountains had been an advantage to them. The Italian vehicles couldn't get through the mountain roads. Everyone was confident the Greek patriots would triumph.

Ephraim and Leon, Rebecca's brothers, wrote about the terrible conditions that they faced. Soldiers were suffering frozen toes and fingers. David had received her letter and promised life would be different when he returned. He vowed to give up gambling and be a good husband to her. He accepted her father's offer to work in the store. He told her how much he loved her and how fortunate he was to have such a good wife. He said he could think of nothing but the joyous day of his return and how it would be to hold her in his arms.

One day they received a letter from Ephraim, telling them that he and David had been wounded. Not gravely wounded, he explained. But they were being sent to a Salonikan hospital to recover. As soon as he knew more, he would write again. David had injured his hand and could not grasp a pencil, but he told Ephraim to give Rebecca his love. Once they were recovered sufficiently, they would be coming home.

Coming home. How wonderful that sounded to Rebecca. She would be a loving wife to him no matter what kind of wounds her husband suffered, She had drawn a picture of him from memory and pinned it to her wall. If only her brother Leon and her brothers-in-law would return safely, as well.

She was grateful when Kiría Eleni gave her a raise in earnings. Although there was war with the Italians and so many men had gone to serve their country, women, especially well-to-do women, continued to request beautiful dresses, skirts and blouses. And the work of the Matsakis sewing shop was so well regarded that they considered taking on another woman to help with the orders. But after the seamstress had interviewed several women, she could not make a decision about hiring another helper.

Every morning Rebecca hurried off to the sewing shop, hoping this was the day that David and Ephraim would knock on the door. Ephraim wrote that he had lost two toes to frostbite and now had a limp. He had suffered a wound to his hip, but the doctors reassured him he would make a full recovery. He said that David was recovering well from his chest wound, but still did not have the use of his hand for letter writing. He said David sent her all his love.

By the end of January, the Greeks had secured the line along the locations of Trebessina-Boubessi-Mali Spandarit. There had been fierce fighting and now the two armies were waiting out the harsh conditions of an unusually freezing winter in the mountains of Albania before again engaging in combat.

The longer the men were gone, the more the women's anxiety grew. For Jewish women, the threat of becoming an *agunda,* a chained woman, loomed over them, day after day when their husbands hadn't returned. Jewish women must be given a *ghet*, a Jewish divorce decree by their husbands or they are unable to ever marry again. If a man was killed in battle, with no witnesses, the rabbis would not grant the woman permission to ever remarry. Two witnesses were necessary to officially declare the man dead.

Her sisters spoke among themselves of this worry until Mamá told them to be silent. God would take care of them and their husbands. Speaking of such things could bring the evil eye down upon them, cautioned her mother.

The evening meal was finished and the women were washing the dishes, putting away the leftover food to be eaten another day.

The young children were begging Tia Rebecca for another story. Her mother told her to go into the parlor and tell them a story so they wouldn't be underfoot in the kitchen. The flames roared in the fireplace as the wind blew outside the windows, shaking the window frames. Little Gracia sat on her lap and the five other children sat on the floor in rapt attention as she told them the story she created. She also showed them the pictures she had sketched of the story's characters. They never seemed to tire of hearing the story. A story of good and evil and of course the triumph of good at the conclusion of the tale. They giggled as her voice modulated between the good and bad characters. Gracia began to doze off, laying her head against Rebecca's shoulder.

"Tia Rebecca, are dragons real? Have you seen one in Kavala?" her nephew Aaron asked. "Do they live inside the castle?"

"Dragons and monsters aren't real. They are made up for the story to scare little boys like you," Rebecca teased the six year old.

"Are you sure? Sometimes I get scared at night in the dark."

"There's nothing to be frightened of in Kavala. You know your Mamá and Papá will always keep you safe. The Rouso family is so big, they would all protect you from any monsters if they were real. But I promise you, they aren't."

"Are you sure?"

"I'm very sure. Now I think it's time for everyone to go home and go to sleep."

"Just one more story, Tia Rebecca. Just one more!" they chorused.

"Tomorrow. More stories tomorrow."

"Good night, Tia Rebecca," they said as one by one they kissed and hugged her good night.

"Julie, you left your dolly," Rebecca said to her five year old niece.

"Oh, oh. I can't sleep without her." The little girl scooped up the doll in her arms and ran out of the parlor with her cousins.

Rebecca carried Gracia into the kitchen and placed the little girl gently into her mother's arms.

After everyone put on their winter coats and left, her parents went up to bed. Rebecca settled in front of the fireplace with the book she had been reading. She enjoyed reading the *Good Earth* by Pearl Buck. China... how exotic, how foreign. She lost herself in the heroine's struggles with life. The house was quiet, save for the ticking of the large clock on the wall.

There was a knock on the door. Rebecca hurried across the room. She didn't want the knocking to disturb everyone in the house, who had already gone to sleep.

She opened the door to find a man in full beard, dressed in ragged clothing. A soldier from the Albanian front, she thought. Did he need food?

"Rebecca," the man said in a voice that seemed familiar, but she couldn't quite place it.

"Sir, can I help you?' she offered.

"Don't you recognize me?" he smiled.

"*A Dio,* oh God, David!" she gasped.

"Aren't you going to let me in?"

Rebecca moved aside as he entered the front hall. I should be running into his arms, she thought. My husband has returned. She closed the door behind him, shutting out the winter wind.

David held out his arms to her and Rebecca fell into his embrace. A stranger, why did he seem a stranger to her?

He held her tight against himself. "How I've dreamed of this moment," he whispered, and bent down to kiss her.

Rebecca dutifully returned his kiss as a wife should. "Are you alright? Your wounds have healed? Where is Ephraim?"

"He is spending the night with Sara at her parents' home. I'm weary and starving," he told her.

"I'll go to the kitchen and find you some food. Come, sit down in front of the fireplace and warm yourself, David. I'm so glad you're home and you're safe," she said and hurried into the kitchen. What was the matter with her? Her husband had returned to her. He was alive and well. Why wasn't her heart filled with joy? It was because they only had two days of marriage. Of course... that explained her lack of proper feeling.

She returned to find David sunk into a chair in front of the fireplace. He had dropped his knapsack on the floor. His eyes were closed, but he stirred at the sound of her footsteps. He opened his eyes and watched Rebecca putting bread, cheese, olives, and a spinach feta pie on a small table next to him. She also put a heavy blanket around his shoulders to help warm him.

"You really didn't recognize me?" He chuckled and took a hunk of bread.

"You didn't have a beard when you left," she explained.

"It seems you don't care for it?" He grabbed the spinach pie and ate as a famished man.

Rebecca didn't answer.

"Well, would you like me to shave it off?" He took a large swallow of the glass of raki she had poured.

"I would like that," she answered and sat down across the table from him. It would help, she thought, to at least have the stranger she married look the way she remembered. This stranger who borrowed money from her father. This man who was disowned by his own parents... who demanded her savings, a man who owed so much money that men came looking for him, wanting to do him harm in the middle of the night. Try as she might, she couldn't banish those terrible memories. No, she told herself. My husband has returned. He's alive. He deserves a warm, loving welcome.

"Then, of course, I will, my little wife. I'm exhausted," he sighed as he finished off the food in front of him.

"Come up to bed." She offered her hand as she knew she should.

He's your husband, she screamed silently. He's come home. He's alive. He wrote and said he'd mend his ways; he'd work for Papá... he'd be a good husband.

But their reunion didn't bring her the joy she'd imagined.

She helped him strip out of his dirty clothes and slipped one of his nightshirts over his head. He muttered a soft "thank you," as he sprawled out on their bed. His eyes closed instantly.

The days and nights of February were bitter cold. News of the suffering troops was on everyone's lips. Fighting had not yet resumed. But everyone was confident that when the weather moderated and the fighting resumed, the Greek men would be triumphant.

David went dutifully to the store every morning with Papá. He told Papá he was grateful for the opportunity to work for him and learn the business of the dry goods shop. But at night, in the darkness of their room, he spoke of his plans to return to Salonika to make his fortune. He was going back into the silk business. But if he had to pay off his debt to Papá, how could he accumulate enough funds to embark on what Rebecca considered outlandish schemes? He assured her he'd find a way.

One night, shortly after his return, they were getting ready for bed. "I was wondering," David mused as he undressed and slid beside her under the covers. "Do you still keep your sewing earnings in that little box?"

"No. Papá opened a bank account for me."

"As your husband, the account should be in my name." He started to unbutton her nightgown.

"You were away fighting," she reminded him as he pulled her against himself and she felt him probing hard between her inner thighs.

CRD

Rebecca tried to be a good wife. She listened patiently as he told her his plans for the future. She shared his bed each night. Those first nights after their marriage, she had been eager to learn the ways between husband and wife and had enjoyed his touch and the sensual delights between them. She thought, in time, her feelings would deepen into love. And she so wanted a child. But the closeness she had experienced with him immediately after their marriage was gone. The pleasure she had experienced from his touch was different now. There was still sensual pleasure, but the sense of joy, of connection, was gone. No matter how much she willed herself to feel otherwise, she couldn't forget how he had taken her savings and how he never mentioned it. As if her savings didn't matter, weren't important at all. And after he asked again about her savings, it brought a chill to her frame that she couldn't forget.

She was good at pretending, pretending to care for him, pretending to enjoy his company. What was wrong with her? Would she never be a good wife? Perhaps she was asking too much of David. He'd been wounded. He'd been fighting the Italians. She needed to give him more time. She needed to try harder. In truth, she yearned to be by herself and escape into her novels.

He had been home for a month now. The light of dawn flooded their room. She had learned her husband enjoyed lovemaking early in the morning. Love, the word he had used so often during their two nights together after their marriage. He never used that word anymore. She actually was pleased that the word "love," which had so easily slipped off his lips, was no longer uttered. It freed her from responding, "I love you," in return. That was the phrase she knew, as a good wife, she was obligated to say. She no longer had to pretend to have feelings that weren't real.

And now he was lying on his back under the covers, watching as she dressed. "How I enjoy watching you dress." He gave her that wicked smile she had once thought so alluring. "Can't you come back to bed?"

"I have to help with breakfast and then I have to go to work," she said.

Rebecca opened the door to leave their room but stopped when he called out to her. "Rebecca, I wanted to talk to you about something."

Rebecca turned around. "Yes?"

"All those books you have. You've already read them. Why don't I sell them? I'm sure I could get a good price for them."

She took a deep breath, trying to calm herself before she responded. "David, I'm not going to sell my books."

"What good do they do sitting on a shelf? I'll make arrangements and have them sold."

"They aren't going to be sold," she raised her voice to him for the first time and felt the color rise in her cheeks.

"Don't you speak to me in that tone!" he shouted at her.

"Do not even think about touching my books!" She whirled around and slammed out the door.

She would never be a good wife to him; it just wasn't possible.

She should help with breakfast. But she grabbed her coat and flew down the cobblestone street to the Matsakis shop. If he dared to touch her books... If he dared...

"You are early," the seamstress commented as Rebecca sat down in front of the sewing machine and spun the balance wheel of the Singer.

Rebecca didn't answer.

At lunchtime, she returned home for a brief moment. She told her parents about David's scheme to sell her books and made them promise they wouldn't allow her books to leave the house under any circumstances.

It was almost March when Ephraim and Sara returned to live with them. Ephraim's gait had never recovered from the loss of his two toes from frostbite and now he had a permanent limp. Sara was at the end of her pregnancy and told the household she had to stay most of the day in her room because her condition was very delicate. No one complained that they didn't see her except at meal times. David and Ephraim ate heartily at every meal. Everyone was pleased to see them putting back the weight they had lost at the front. Mamá made Ephraim his favorite dishes, as Sara never appeared in the kitchen. Rebecca learned David's favorite dishes were *soupa de lentejas,* lentil soup and *yaprakites de sardela,* sardines in grape leaves. She made them often for him as a good wife should.

"What a wonderful cook you are," David praised the special dishes she prepared for him. Rebecca smiled and gave him a second helping. It was if they were both actors in a play: she the dutiful wife, David the appreciative husband, with her family as the audience. He never mentioned selling her books again.

Rebecca accepted how things were between them, for what other choice did she have? He was her husband. She was keenly disappointed she hadn't conceived. Maybe she wouldn't. Some women, like Kiría Eleni, never did.

David kept pleading with Papá for some spending money until Papá relented and gave him a small amount.

"I work at that store all day long. It's monotonous work, stacking, counting inventory," he complained to Rebecca one evening.

"David, there are such interesting people who come to make purchases. They like to tell Papá all about their lives. When I was young and I had time, I used to love listening to the people who came into the store," Rebecca told him.

"It's boring, deadly boring. You were just a child who knew nothing. Don't wait up for me. I'm going to the taverna tonight. Now that I have a few drachmas on me, I can pay for some *ouzo* and sit with men. I need to get away from this stifling life, if for only an evening."

David left and Rebecca sat up in bed, relishing the time alone with her new novel, *Rebecca,* by Daphne du Maurier. Once she started reading it, she couldn't bear to put it down. When David returned, he was surprised to find her still awake.

"Waiting up for me?" He smiled that charming smile she once found so attractive. But she had learned it was merely a mask, a fake smile. Beneath it was nothingness, emptiness.

"I'm reading," she paused and then said what she knew he wanted to hear. "And, of course, I wanted to be awake when you returned."

Kavala, Greece: March 10, 1941

It was the middle of the night and Rebecca was startled awake by the sound of voices downstairs. She reached out for David beside her but his side of the bed was cold. She grabbed her robe, hoping against hope that men had not come looking for David because of bad debts again. He swore to her that his life of gambling was over. Was he telling her the truth? She hurried down the stairs to see what the commotion was all about. The light was on in the downstairs parlor. Mamá stood at the bottom of the stairs.

"Go back to your room," her mother instructed.

"What's happening?" Rebecca asked with concern.

"Go back to bed," her mother repeated in a soft voice.

She heard the sound of David's voice. She walked past her mother to find Papá, his face beet red, holding David by the throat.

"Please," David was pleading. "Rebecca, please help me. Tell your father to let me go!"

Rebecca noticed the suitcase at his feet... David's suitcase.

Papá released his grasp and threw David against the wall. "Open up your suitcase!" Papá demanded.

"There's been a misunderstanding, sir." Rebecca heard that affable tone returning to her husband's voice.

"A misunderstanding? You are sneaking out of our house in the middle of the night. What is it that I do not understand?"

"It just isn't working out for me here. I wasn't meant to be a shopkeeper."

"So, you were going to have your wife wake up in the morning and find you gone?"

"I didn't want a scene. I thought it was better this way. You understand that, don't you, Rebecca?"

Rebecca crossed her arms against her chest. She watched in disbelief as this man, her husband, was abandoning her after a mere few months of marriage.

"Esther!" her father shouted to his wife. "Go wake up Ephraim and get him down here. Go quickly!"

Rebecca stood immobile, watching her father, her husband and the suitcase.

"Empty your pockets!" her father shouted at David. "Turn them inside out!"

Rebecca swallowed hard.

David turned his pockets out. "See, there is nothing there. What is it that you are looking for?"

Ephraim came hurrying down the stairs in his pajamas. "Papá, what is it?"

"Open his suitcase and dump it on the floor! Tomorrow is the day I make the deposit at the bank and my money pouch is gone. Then I hear this bastard sneaking out of the house in the middle of the night... "

Ephraim opened David's suitcase and there, among his clothes, was the Rouso store money pouch.

"Call the police, Papá!" Ephraim shouted, taking a lunge toward David.

"Stop!" David held up his hands defensively, warding off the blows from Ephraim's fists.

Ephraim backed away and looked at him with scorn.

"Please don't hurt me. You have to understand. I'm going back to Salonika, to a real city. I'm going back to the silk trade and I needed an investment to get started. I promise I'll pay you back. I just can't stay here any longer. I feel like a prisoner. You can't expect me to leave with nothing. I've worked hard and what do I have to show for it? I finished working off my debt to you. Just let me go. No hard feelings, ok?"

"I won't call the police on you," Papá said calmly. "Under one condition."

"What condition?"

"You intended to sneak out of the house, leaving my daughter as an *agunda*, a chained woman. She would never be able to marry again without a *ghet*, a divorce decree from you. "

"She doesn't need one. No one is going to want a woman without a dowry, especially a woman who is barren. If I just leave, it should make no difference to her future. She doesn't have one anyway."

Rebecca's hands fisted at her sides. She wanted to spit in his face.

"We've caught you red-handed David Tiano! If you want to avoid arrest, then tomorrow you will go with me before the rabbinical tribunal, the *Beth Din*, and start proceedings for a *ghet* so that Rebecca is officially divorced from you, you low-life bastard. And once the divorce decree is given, I never want to see your face in Kavala ever again."

Athens: April 15, 1941

Andreas squeezed the hand of Emily, the young woman from the American legation, who sat beside him in the café. He reminded himself that he needed to pay attention to her after he had brought her to the café this evening with his British friends Nigel and Barbara. Margaret, the woman with whom he had worked out a comfortable arrangement, had returned to England. Now Andreas was spending time with sweet Emily Jackson.

But he couldn't concentrate on Emily. Two weeks ago, the Germans had lost patience with their Italian allies and had launched an attack on Greece. Their tanks and troops had faced almost no resistance in Salonika, the major port city in the north. The Greek troops were still on the Albanian border. And so the Germans had taken over that thriving city of Salonika. Now, there was little to stop the Nazis from continuing down to Athens and then all of Greece. Soldiers, the thought of soldiers occupying his city of Athens made him feel sick. Every day there was such tension in the air, as everyone waited for the Germans, who were surely on their way.

Andreas couldn't help but remember Smyrna, now called Izmir by its Turkish rulers. His home had been filled with cafes and shops, just like Athens. The Nazis didn't seem interested in burning down cities. But now that the Germans were in Greece, the nightmares of his childhood rose up to haunt him when he slept. He still couldn't remember what had happened to his parents. But when the terror of his dreams subsided, he was left with an overwhelming sense of guilt. His parents were dead and somehow he knew he was responsible. He remembered the screams of his sister, but that was all he could summon from his memory. The guilt was always with him because he hadn't been able to save his family... He still looked for Maria all these years later. In his heart, he knew he most likely would never see her again. At times he dreamed of being hungry, so hungry and walking from place to place, without a home, without a family. And then, like a beacon of light, he would hear the voice of a little girl with long braids of chestnut hair calling his name, smiling at him, her arms reaching out to him. Then he would see Rebecca holding a shovel. "Don't hurt me," he had said.

"Well, Andreas." Nigel sliced into his veal cutlet. "I'm afraid to say it. But I think our days in your wonderful country will be coming to an end very soon."

"No, Nigel. I want to stay here," Barbara sighed. "I've so enjoyed our time in Greece. Why do we have to go?"

"Because the Germans are our declared enemy my dear."

"Maybe they'll stop at Salonika?" she offered hopefully.

"They are already on their way. Nothing can stop the German army. Haven't you seen the maps, where they gobbled up one country after another? They have swept through the Netherlands, Belgium, Luxembourg, France, Denmark, Norway and Poland. The Greek army is no match for them. Herr Hitler is not going to be stopped. Surely you think I am right, Andreas?"

"Sadly, I have to agree," Andreas said quietly. "Those Nazis will soon be marching through the streets of Athens. There's no way of stopping them."

"Will I have to leave too? I've only just gotten here," Emily asked.

"Yes, you will, I'm afraid. I don't think Americans would feel safe being here after the Nazis take over. So let's enjoy the evening while we have it," Andreas tried to sound more hopeful then he felt.

"I was thinking about your friend in Kavala. That Jewish family you were so fond of," Nigel said.

"I've been thinking of them as well. When we were in Berlin, we heard the stories of how the Jews were treated so poorly. I hope that doesn't happen here. You know the father of the Solomon family comes from Ioannina. His family goes back for more than two thousand years in Greece."

"I believe the Jews have been in Germany for a long time, as well. That hasn't stopped the Nazis from mistreating them. When we were up in Germany for that conference, remember when we realized that all the

Jewish doctors had disappeared... They weren't allowed in the universities anymore. They couldn't treat non-Jewish patients. There is something called the Nuremberg laws that regulate what Jews can do. Do you think they would institute such laws here in Greece against the Jews?"

"I don't know. But I hope not." Andreas crushed his cigarette in an ashtray.

"Come, Emily," Andreas smiled at his young companion for the evening. "Let's order that ice cream called the Chicago. It's enough for all four of us and then some."

"Be careful, Emily. Sharing food with Andreas can be an eye-opening experience. At times he eats like there is no more food to be found in this world than what is in front of him."

"I love ice cream sundaes. Let's not talk about war anymore tonight," Emily smiled at Andreas as she leaned her cleavage across the table.

Andreas had had second thoughts about taking her up to his room tonight. But maybe, he needed the distraction to help forget about the approaching Nazis, at least for a few hours.

CHAPTER 11

Kavala, Greece: April 17, 1941

TODAY REBECCA WAS given the day off from her sewing duties and had arranged for a visit with her sister Klara. Klara had married a very wealthy man. She didn't have the biggest dowry, like their oldest sisters Miriam and Roza. But her charm, grace and a dowry of respectable size had won the heart of Carlo Mizrahi. As always, Rebecca enjoyed seeing the elegant furniture and rugs in her sister's beautiful home. But most of all, she loved visiting with her two young nieces. Klara's older two girls were attending school and they wouldn't be home until later in the afternoon.

Little Gracia wrapped her chubby arms around Rebecca's neck and giggled. "Do I have to take a nap now?" she whispered. "Tell Mamá, I don't need a nap today."

Rebecca laughed and placed the little girl on the bed next to her older sister. Dark-haired Julie was clutching Dolly in her arms, her chest gently rising and falling in a deep sleep.

"When you wake up, I'll draw some sketches for you and Julie. Would you like a dog and a cat?"

"*Si, si,*" Gracia answered yes as her eyes closed with sleep.

"Have a good nap," Rebecca whispered and pulled the quilt over her two little nieces.

She turned to find her sister Klara standing in the doorway. Klara looked so much like Mamá, the shape of her face, the way she smiled, even the way she carried herself. And her oldest daughter Esther, named after Mamá, looked just like her namesake. When Rebecca was younger, she had fantasized about a daughter of her own who would resemble her, with gray eyes and chestnut hair. But that would never happen. She would never have children of her own.

"You're so good with the girls." Her sister put her arm around Rebecca's waist as they walked into the parlor.

"Sit down," Klara urged her as she placed a spoon sweet on Rebecca's plate. "We haven't had a chance to really talk since... " she paused.

"Since my divorce," Rebecca supplied the word she knew her sister was loathe to say.

"I'm so sorry," said Klara as they sat down across the table.

"Don't be sorry, Klara. It was for the best." Rebecca swallowed the sugared spoonful of fruit. "Let's not talk about it." She knew her sister was trying to be kind.

"Alright. I just thought... you might want..." Klara's voice hesitated with discomfort.

"How is Carlo doing?" Rebecca changed the subject to Klara's husband, who had recently returned from the front.

"Carlo was so lucky that he wasn't hurt. When I see so many of the men coming back with such terrible injuries or I hear of men who never came back," she paused. "I know how fortunate we are. Carlo has returned to his family's tobacco warehouse already. He is a fabulous accountant, you know. I'm so glad to have him home. He's sure our next one will be a boy." Klara placed her hand over her swollen belly. "I'm so happy he returned before this baby was born.

"If only all our sisters were as blessed as I have been. Poor Roza and Liza, to have been widowed so young and left with fatherless children. They kissed their husbands goodbye just like I did and they'll never see them again."

"Let's hope the rest of our men will be home soon." Yes, Rebecca thought, I also kissed a husband goodbye...

"At least our widowed sisters' husband's families have been so welcoming to them and their children," Klara commented. "What do you think of Roza's new husband Iakov?"

"He laughs a lot, doesn't he?" Rebecca smiled, thinking of her jovial new brother-in-law.

"Roza was a lucky widow, getting a marriage proposal so quickly. It's true she was a very prosperous widow. But she had four children to raise. To have caught the eye of Iakov, who had just lost his wife in childbirth, was truly a blessing. Of course, having four children of his own, he was in desperate need of a wife. I know Roza wasn't sure if she should accept his proposal. But he is from Ioannina and Papá knew his family. Roza didn't want to move to Ioannina, but Papá and Mamá assured her it was for the best," Klara related what Rebecca already knew.

"I wouldn't want to leave Kavala either," Rebecca acknowledged. "When I thought I was going to leave, it made me really sad. But a woman must always follow her husband..., " her voice trailed off. Yes, the dissolution of her marriage was all for the best. Rebecca tried to imagine what it would be like not to see her family every day; to visit her family and her parents only for special occasions like weddings; for her children to grow up without the warmth of her family's love. But she would never have any children. So why think of such things?

"Well, we're not going anywhere. Carlo's family has such a prosperous tobacco business. And we're hoping to have many sons who will take over the family businesses someday."

Rebecca smiled politely. She wished the best for her sister and hoped her next baby would be a boy. But it had only been two brief months since her own hopes of ever being a mother had been dashed. She tried so hard to not think about David at all. But she found it impossible to erase all the memories, both the good and the bad, from her mind. She'd been so full of hope for her marriage and motherhood on the day of her wedding. But those hopes had turned to ashes, leaving her with the shame of a divorce after only four months of marriage. If she had done something to keep David happier and more content in their marriage, maybe he wouldn't have left, maybe he wouldn't have tried to steal Papá's money. If David hadn't been a gambler, if he'd been able to accept Papá's offer of a respectable means of earning a living. If he'd taken the second chance her family had given him to walk on a path of righteousness. Then she might have had a chance to be a mother, to have a new life growing inside of her, to hold her own baby in her arms. She had to rid herself of all those ifs. She needed to accept what was. She would only be Tia Rebecca, aunt to her sisters' and brothers' children. Surely that was enough. That would have to be enough.

"Rebecca, can you figure out why Papá told my husband to take his money out of the bank and buy more jewelry and gold? I already brought so much beautiful jewelry with me as part of my dowry. Why do I need more?"

"You know what just happened in Salonika, don't you?" Rebecca asked patiently. Most women, including her sisters, had no interest in what was happening in the world. Husbands were confident that their women gave no thought to anything save for the children and running their households. And so they shared little of worldly concerns with them. But times were different now.

"Yes, I know. Carlo told me the Germans came into Salonika. His family is worried about their businesses there. But what does that have to do with gold and jewelry?"

"The Germans have no reason to stop in Salonika. Our army is still coming back from Albania and can't defend us."

"Will the Germans come here? Why would they do that?"

"Papá said there is a rumor that our part of Greece might be given to the Bulgarians."

"Carlo's parents said the Bulgarians took over Kavala years ago... and they were very bad people." Klara frowned.

"I've heard the same stories. But perhaps since it was so long ago, people exaggerate or don't remember so well. Anyway, no matter which army comes to Kavala, Papá and the other men in our family are afraid the banks could be taken over. We might lose all our drachmas. That's why Papá has been buying jewelry and gold."

"I still don't understand," Klara sighed. "Carlo has the pistol he brought home from the front. I guess it is a good thing he has it. If an army comes into town, he'll be able to protect me and the girls."

Rebecca took a bite of the *loukoumades,* dripping with honey. Klara was the best baker of all her sisters. She claimed to have a secret ingredient in her *loukoumades* that she refused to share.

After a pleasant afternoon, Rebecca decided to stop off at Kiría Eleni's. Tomorrow's trip to Doxato needed to be finalized for the delivery of the ball gowns and she needed to learn how early they were leaving in the morning.

It was a lovely spring day, with wildflowers bursting into bloom, reds, yellows, purples all along the hillsides. Rebecca breathed in the scent of the blossoms as she walked down the narrow cobblestone streets. Her Kavala was so beautiful. Puffy white clouds scuttled across the brilliant blue sky. Surely nothing bad could happen in such a place of beauty.

And then she remembered what Andreas said about his home in Smyrna. He had told her of the people taking nightly promenades on the waterfront, strolling besides the cafes and shops... The operas his parents had enjoyed. His family had been wealthy and educated and even his sister had gone to school. But a brutal army had invaded his town and destroyed all he had known. Andreas told her it was a cosmopolitan place where Christians, Muslims and Jews lived beside each other in harmony before it was burnt to the ground and the people were massacred. She knew his parents were both murdered, although Andreas had never told her how it had happened. He had said he couldn't remember. He'd tried to remember, but he couldn't.

Rebecca's recalled that first night she met him and how he cried in her lap and told her about their deaths. She couldn't remember what he said about how they died. She only remembered it was bad. Could something like that happen here in Kavala?

Papá talked about the banks being taken over. He never talked about people being killed. But Andreas told her his family had no idea of the mayhem that would be descending upon them. He told her some people had left, but his father was confident their family wouldn't be harmed. Rebecca wished she could talk to Andreas about what was happening in Greece. Their correspondence, once stopped, had never resumed.

As soon as Rebecca entered the Matsakis shop, she could sense something was wrong. Kiría Eleni, with her glasses perched on the bridge of her nose, was staring at her accounting book, a frown on her face.

"Kiría Eleni?" Rebecca slipped her shawl from her shoulders and sat down next to the woman.

"We are not delivering the dresses tomorrow," Kiría Eleni announced.

"When are we going then? We need to deliver them by the end of the week, before the ball."

"These dresses, these beautiful gowns." The older woman lifted her arm and pointed toward the rack of high couture dresses styled in the latest fashion. "These dresses aren't going to be delivered today or tomorrow."

"I don't understand."

"I kept calling Kiría Movropoulas and there was no answer, which is so unlike her. And then this morning, someone finally answered the telephone. I was told the Movropoulas, Skordyles and Panagiotis families have all gone. They have left for Salonika."

"They all left?" Rebecca took a large swallow, looking at the beautiful gowns they had spent countless hours sewing and stitching. "And the money they owe?" Rebecca asked, although she already knew the answer.

Kiría Eleni sadly shook her head.

"I've heard of some people leaving, afraid of a Bulgarian takeover. Papá said they are fleeing to the area controlled by the Germans."

"All of our best customers." The older woman sighed and closed her accounting books. "Vassilis and I are going nowhere. This is our home. We aren't going to leave our shops and start all over in a new place. Andreas writes that we should leave. That we should go to our family in America. He doesn't understand. We aren't young anymore. We aren't going to start all over again in a new place. And your family Rebecca? Are they going to leave?"

"Oh, no. Papá said he isn't leaving his store. He promised Nono, Mamá's father, the Rouso name would always be on the front of the store. And Papá said our family and Mamá's family are too big for everyone to leave. If everyone doesn't go, no one will go. Kavala is our home no matter what army comes here." Rebecca repeated her father's words from last night over the dinner table.

⊛

Kavala, Greece: April 20, 1941
Rebecca didn't go to Kiría Matsakis this morning. The Bulgarian troops were already entering their town and it was unwise to be walking along the streets, even for the short distance to the sewing shop. Instead, she accompanied her father and her brother Ephraim next door to the dry goods shop. Although the army was many streets away, Rebecca could hear the terrible thunder of troops entering their city.

"Can you imagine?" Papá sighed as he straightened some items in the glass showcase. "There are foolish, foolish people who are lining the boulevards to welcome a conquering army. Who would want to watch the Bulgarian barbarians strut through our streets? Not a shot was fired and there they are. Have our people no spines, no principles? Here Rebecca." He handed her a package. "When you go back to Kiría Matsakis, you can bring her the buttons and ribbon she ordered."

"I'll take it to her. I'm sure it won't be a problem for such a small package. But her cash flow might be in trouble."

"Her credit is always good. What's the difficulty?"

"We sewed several dresses for the tobacco matrons. We just heard that they left and fled to Salonika without paying for all the work we did."

"To flee like frightened rabbits and not settle their debts." Papá shook his head in dismay. "You both do such fine work. I'm sure you will have no problem finding business during this occupation. Women always want beautiful dresses."

Rebecca was about to enter the stock room and help Ephraim with his inventory when they heard sounds outside of the door to the store. Papá walked outside, leaving the door open.

"What are you doing?" he shouted to someone up on a ladder in front of the store.

"Your store is now Bulgarian. We are putting up the new sign," the faceless voice announced and then there was a resounding crash as the Rouso sign fell to the ground and broke into pieces.

Papá turned around and came inside, slamming the door behind him. She heard him mutter a curse word and saw him reach for his bottle of *raki* in the cabinet beneath the counter.

Ephraim fisted his hands at his sides. "Papá! How can they do that!"

"Well, they can and they just did. Welcome to the Bulgarian occupation." Her father tossed back a large swallow of raki.

The door swung open suddenly and a uniformed Bulgarian officer with a Bulgarian flag in his fist, stomped into the store.

"I am Pulkovodets Akulov. I have been assigned to take charge here.

"Our flag will be raised outside and all of the signs within the store must now be written in Bulgarian," the short man with a double chin announced to them.

"Yes, of course," Papá smiled. "Please sir, sit down. Have a seat. May I offer you some refreshment? I have some very fine *raki*." Papá began to pour a glass.

Rebecca watched with amazement as her father completely altered his manner. His charm offensive, her mother called it. When he wanted something from someone, no one could resist the honeyed words of Isaac Solomon.

"Ephraim." Papá turned to her brother. "Take down all the signs in the store and replace them with Bulgarian words. You know Bulgarian, don't you?"

"Enough to make the signs," her brother muttered.

"And put up the Bulgarian flag." Papá put his arm around his son who stood immobile with a scowl on his face. "Now, do as we have been told by this fine officer. The Bulgarians have begun their occupation of Macedonia and for now, we must raise their flag."

"Your name is?" the Bulgarian officer asked.

"Solomon. Isaac Solomon."

"Solomon, I'm afraid you are mistaken. We have not come to occupy your city. This area of Thrace is now part of Bulgaria. It has always been part of our country, unjustly taken away by the Greeks. They stole it from us and now it is rightfully back as part of Bulgaria. Solomon? You are a Jew?"

"Yes." Rebecca heard the hesitation in her father's voice.

"You and your people owe the Greeks nothing. You should be grateful we will be instituting measures that will make life hard for the Greek scum. They need to make room for colonists from my homeland. Our settlers from Bulgaria will soon be here and we will take over the businesses and the houses and the land. It is all rightfully ours. If you and your people collaborate with us against the Greeks, it will be much better for you."

Papá chose not to answer. "Another glass?" He offered the Bulgarian.

As the officer finished it off, he noticed Rebecca standing against a display case, a tablet in her hand. "A customer? Come in. Come into this fine Bulgarian store."

"This is my daughter, sir. Rebecca Solomon."

"Were you out with the crowds welcoming our troops?" He smiled at her.

"No sir. I've been helping my father in the store."

"What is that tablet for?" he asked her.

"It's for sketching."

"Do you sketch the likenesses of people?"

"Yes."

"Are you good?"

"Yes, I am."

"Well, we shall see. Sketch my likeness and I will be the judge of your talent."

Rebecca locked eyes with her father and then picked up her charcoal.

"Hurry, hurry. I don't have all day. I have much to do to Bulgarize this pathetic, Hellenized country of yours."

Rebecca sketched quickly, tore a sheet of paper off the tablet, and handed it to him.

He broke into a broad smile at his likeness. "Such a good artist." He beamed. "What do you think?" He showed the sketch to Papá and Ephraim.

"A wonderful likeness," Ephraim agreed as they all looked at the sketch of a man minus his double chins, with a smaller nose and lips, looking ten years younger.

"Let me see your tablet." He grabbed it from her. "What other people have you drawn?"

He frowned as he paged through her sketches of women in dresses. "Where are the other portraits?"

"I'm a seamstress. These are sketches for our customers."

"Mm. My wife will be arriving in a few days. She will look at your sketches and if she likes them, you will be appointed her personal seamstress."

"It will be my honor." Rebecca gave a perfunctory smile as she felt the bile rise in her throat.

"Well, Solomon. You are indeed fortunate that I was sent to your store this morning. My orders were to take over your store and your house. We need all these stores and houses for our Bulgarian colonists. But I like you." He raised another glass of *raki* in salute. "So, for now, you will only have your store renamed. You will fly the Bulgarian flag and all signage in Greek will be changed to Bulgarian. You will be working for the Bulgarian government. I will allow you to remain in your house and to work in this store. You have the best *raki*. A taste of heaven. I shall take your bottle."

Papá handed it to him.

"*Doburot*," the officer wished them goodbye.

"Close the door," her father instructed Ephraim after the Bulgarian walked out of the store.

Ephraim made his way across the floor with a noticeable limp, an unfortunate reminder of his time in Albania. "How could they do that!" He burst out after he closed the door. "Our store just taken from us. They have no right!"

"They have every right." Papá sank down on a stool behind the counter.

"Sara's father said they came in as occupiers before, when he was a young man," Ephraim told him. "They were cruel and heartless. Her family has decided to leave, to go to the German areas where things will be better."

"Yes, their occupation after the Great War was brutal, but we survived then and we will survive now. However, this time, the Bulgarian pigs don't see themselves as occupiers. They say Macedonia has always belonged to them and it will be un-hellenized. Our area was given to them by the Germans as a reward for joining the Axis. Can you imagine asking me to collaborate against the Greek Orthodox because we are Jews?" Papá muttered as he wiped off the counter where the Bulgarian had been drinking.

Rebecca was silent. How was it possible that a foreign army could descend on her homeland and take over, tossing people out of their houses and businesses? Well, it was better than what happened in Smyrna. But how much money would her father earn now that the store was taken over by the Bulgarians?

❦

Kavala, Greece: May 30, 1941

The Bulgarians were determined to rid Kavala of every last vestige of what was Greek and to replace it with Bulgarian. The street signs were changed. All stores needed to display signs in Bulgarian. The Greek Orthodox priests were replaced with Bulgarian priests. The teachers in the schools were replaced with Bulgarians teachers. Her nieces and nephews now attended Bulgarian schools. Scientists, mayors, landowners, industrialists, judges, lawyers and intellectuals were deported. The Greek press was taken over, and listening to foreign radio stations was forbidden. Speaking Greek in public spaces was also prohibited.

As Papá had predicted, the banks were taken over. It was indeed a blessing that Rebecca's father had the foresight to convert the family's wealth into gold and jewelry.

People with professions needed to obtain a license, at an exorbitant fee, in order to practice. At first it seemed that Vassilis and Eleni Matsakis would be thrown out of their shops. But when the authorities saw the fine work done by the couple, they allowed them to continue. However, their shops were now owned by Bulgarians and the Bulgarian masters would also decided how much to pay the couple for their labors. Rebecca continued to work in the shop when it was determined she was an accomplished seamstress. Of course, now she only received a fraction of her former earnings. And the Bulgarian officer had appointed her as his wife's personal dressmaker. For those labors, she earned a bit more, which she contributed to her family's meager earnings from the dry goods store.

Rebecca's family, like the Matsakises, earned little from their Bulgarian-owned store, but at least they could still work there and they hadn't been thrown out of their home. One never knew when the Bulgarian officer would change his mind and his generosity toward them would end. Every day they woke up to this possibility.

Andreas had written letters continuing to plead with his parents to leave, to relocate to Athens with him or in Salonika with Vassilis's brother. He had given up trying to convince them to consider going to America, because Greece had closed its doors to all immigration. His parents continued to refuse to leave. Kavala was their home. Andreas was expected home any day now, and Rebecca was sure he would continue to urge his parents to leave.

At the sewing shop, Kiría Eleni and Rebecca rarely had a visit during the week from their Bulgarian masters. On Friday, the Bulgarian officer made his rounds to their shop, checking their account book, distributing their small salaries and confiscating their remaining Bulgarian *levs*, the new currency of Kavala. After completing the monetary transactions, he would look over the completed dresses and select at least two for his wife. The next week, she would appear and demand the frocks her husband had chosen for her be altered immediately.

This Tuesday morning, all was quiet as they went about their work in silence. Aphrodite, a young woman, came into the shop to pick up a dress for her mother. Rebecca was attending to the transaction when the young woman leaned close to her. She looked over toward Kiría Eleni at the opposite end of the room, whose head was bent over her sewing. "Rebecca," Aphrodite said in a soft whisper. "Are you outraged by the terrible things that the Bulgarians have inflicted upon us?"

"Of course," Rebecca answered. "They're heartless barbarians."

"Some of my friends are trying to make a difference, to resist them. Do you want to join our group ?"

"Me? A woman?" Rebecca was confused.

"I promise there is a place for someone like you. We are meeting tonight. If you come you mustn't tell anyone where you are going. We are calling our gathering "a celebration" for my engagement. If you agree to come, I'll send someone to escort you," she continued quietly, so that Kiría Matsakis couldn't overhear their conversation.

"Yes, yes." Rebecca whispered. "I will come."

"We all use fictitious names. Yours will be Phaedra."

Rebecca bid the girl goodbye and sat down at the sewing machine. She tried to focus her thoughts as she sewed a straight seam. If there was anything Rebecca could do to help, she certainly wouldn't hesitate to do it. Those hateful Bulgarians... If she could play even a small role in ridding them from her country, she was eager to do her part.

⌘

As instructed, Rebecca told her parents she was going out to a social gathering.

The wine flowed freely and the music blared from the phonograph player. It was the latest music, Benny Goodman and Guy Lombardo. Many couples were swing dancing, which had become the rage among young people. A man asked Rebecca to dance and she happily accepted. Everyone was having a good time and there was no mention of the true purpose of this get-together. She had received several compliments on her floral dress, with fashionable broad shoulder pads and a cinched waist. The hour was growing late when the door to the outside was closed and a young man with thinning hair stood up in front of the group. "Please, may I have your attention."

Rebecca sat down in a nearby chair and prepared to listen.

"We have gathered here tonight for a special purpose. Something must be done about these brutal Bulgarians who have taken over our country. Our communist movement believes in equal rights for everyone. There will be no masters, no slaves. We will show the Bulgarians they will not enslave us. Be aware that whoever joins us will be given new names, a *nom de guerre*. If you are ever questioned, you will not be able to give up the names of your fellow resistors." Rebecca sat up in her seat, mesmerized by the speaker who spoke with so much passion and conviction. She'd heard rumors about a nascent resistance among the young people. She didn't know what she could possibly do. However, she was eager to help. She knew it might involve risk, but she had no children to care for, no husband to forbid her participation.

Suddenly there was a hand on her shoulder. She looked up to find Andreas standing behind her. "Hello." He gave her a broad smile. "I just arrived and was invited to come to this meeting tonight."

"Hello!" she returned his greeting. How glad she was to see him.

The man continued to speak about a communist resistance that could shake the brutal yoke of the Bulgarians. "How dare they come into our country and take over!"

"How dare they!" The crowd answered back.

"We will break into small groups. Someone will approach each of you and tell you which group to join. Everyone who was invited here tonight was invited for a purpose. If you have reconsidered and do not want to join our movement, please leave now. You will not be judged."

There was silence as everyone looked around. But no one moved towards the door.

"First, I ask if there is anyone who wants to join our movement of partisan *andartes* up in the mountains. We will live together in the mountains where the Bulgarians can't find us. This, of course, means leaving your families. We will wage guerrilla war until we win back our dear country. Both women and men are accepted into our movement."

Several people stepped up to the front of the room and they were ushered up to the second floor.

An older woman approached Rebecca and took her aside. Rebecca had hoped Andreas would be part of her group. But he was standing on the other side of the room among several men.

The older woman smiled at her. "Phaedra, you would be willing to help us?"

"I'm not sure how I could help."

"You are the seamstress who works with Kiría Matsakis?"

"Yes."

"And you make deliveries of your goods up to Drama?"

"Yes, we do. We don't go as often anymore because most of the wealthy Greek women are gone. But little by little, the Bulgarian women are asking for our dresses. How can that help the cause?"

"We will have messages that you can take to Drama for us. You must tell absolutely no one what you are doing. Do you understand? Working with us is not without risk... it could be very dangerous for you, if you are discovered."

Rebecca was determined to help. "I understand. I want to do what I can to help."

"Good, Phaedra. We will work out a method for you to let us know when you will be going to Drama and we will give you messages to deliver."

☙❧

Andreas was waiting for her across the room.

"Come on," he said. "I'll walk you home."

Rebecca looked up at him and smiled. "It's been so long since you came home. I started to wonder when I'd see you again." She went outside and fell into step beside him.

"Did you miss me? I missed you, Rebecca."

"Yes, of course I missed you, Andreas."

"Rebecca," he spoke softly as they continued along the moonlit cobblestone streets. "You aren't going to get involved with these communist partisans are you? Tell me you aren't going to put yourself in danger. Promise me that you won't join this movement. I couldn't bear it if something were to happen to you."

"I was invited to this meeting just as you were, to help the cause. How would your parents feel, how would I feel, if something happened to you? Just as you are making your choice, I'm making mine. It is not up to you to decide what I will do, Andreas." She looked down the street into the shadows. She hoped they wouldn't be confronted by any Bulgarian soldiers who would ask for their identity papers. They could be so nasty, their chests puffed with power. She turned back to him. "Andreas, you can't expect me not to help our country. If there is something I am asked to do, I won't refuse."

"Stubborn as always," he sighed. "I can see you have made up your mind and nothing I can say will change it."

"Yes, I will not change my mind. So let's not discuss this anymore," she said. "I missed your letters."

"And I missed yours, but after you married... " His voice trailed off and he stopped walking. "When I heard you married David Tiano… Did you love him?"

"I barely knew him the few days before we married, and then he went off to war."

"He didn't deserve a fine, wonderful woman like you."

"I guess no one deserves me," she said wryly, and they resumed walking.

"Oh!" The toe of her shoe caught in a loose cobblestone and she started to stumble.

"Be careful!" He grabbed her elbow. Instead of letting go, he pulled her into an alleyway.

Rebecca looked up at him

"Oh, Rebecca Solomon, how I've missed you," he whispered and pulled her close.

She wanted him to kiss her. And then he bent down and his mouth was upon her own. A rush of feeling coursed through her body. She opened her lips and folded into his arms, her body pressed against him. It was wrong, but she didn't care. How wonderful it was to be held in his arms, his kisses tender and then more demanding. She wrapped her arms around his neck, pulling him closer.

"Rebecca, why can't we be together?" He breathed against her hair.

"Oh, Andreas, you know why." She leaned her head against his chest, listening to the thunder of his heart. "And besides, haven't you always told me that you were never going to marry?"

"Yes, I did say that." He released her. "I love you, Rebecca."

She reached up to his mustachioed lips with her fingers, feeling their softness. She closed her eyes as he kissed her fingertips.

"Rebecca" he murmured and kissed her again long and hard. "I should take you home." But still he held her in his embrace.

She looked up at him, and she saw love in his eyes, the love she had never seen in the eyes of her husband.

They kissed harder, deeper, over and over again. Rebecca felt the pleasure of his hands cupping her breasts. "Andreas," she whispered as desire began pulling her down into a forbidden place. "We can't. We can't," she whispered, blinking back tears.

"No, we can't," he repeated, his lips buried in her hair. And then he cleared his throat and released her.

They walked out from the shadows and continued down the road. "Rebecca, I wish you and my parents would leave."

"Kavala is our home."

"But I worry for you and your family most of all. I worry about the Jewish community. In Salonika, the Jewish community leaders have all been arrested by the Nazis. All the radios have been confiscated. Jews are no longer allowed into cafes or the cinema. They can't use public transportation. I know these are the Germans and your masters are the Bulgarians. But I don't trust them either.

"Rebecca, I want you to give me a photograph of yourself. I'm going to have false identity papers created for you when I am back in Athens. I have friends with contacts who produce forgeries. The next time I return to Kavala, I will bring the papers to you."

"I don't need false papers," she scoffed.

"Just get me a photograph before I leave. Please."

"Alright," she agreed and looked up at him again.

It seemed like forever that she had loved Andreas... since that night when they were children and she'd found him in the shed, his big brown eyes filled with fear. But they couldn't act on these feelings between them. No good could come of it.

Rebecca told her parents she had enjoyed the engagement party. Then she said good night, and walked upstairs to her bedroom. She closed the bedroom door and reached into a far corner of her dresser drawer. She pulled out a cloth and opened it. There was the marble Andreas had given her all those many years ago. She looked at it and smiled, remembering when he asked her to select one marble among those his father had given him. That sad young boy had given it to her as a thank you for her friendship. She had kept it on the bottom of a drawer for all these years.

Friendship... her dear childhood friend who had climbed the hill near the castle with her, who had helped her find scraps to feed the dogs and cats that wandered the streets. She watched him grow from a small boy haunted by tragedy into a confident, caring man. And now she was in love with a man she could never have. She held the marble tightly in her fingers as she felt his arms around her, his kiss and the pleasure of his touch.

CHAPTER 12

Nea Karvali, outside of Kavala, Greece: September 1, 1941
ANDREAS HAD BEEN home for a week. He spent most of his time
in nearby Nea Karvali, a town in Greece established by the refugees
from Cappadocia in Asia Minor during the population exchange between
Greece and Turkey. He brought medicines with him that he had obtained
with great difficulty in Athens. Medicine and medical supplies in Athens
were tightly controlled by the Nazis. But Andreas had learned the art of
bribery and using the black market, since the Nazis had marched through
the streets of Athens and raised their swastika flag over the Acropolis. He
knew that Greek physicians in the Bulgarian Zone had been prevented
from attending to the sick unless they received a license from the Bulgarian
authorities. In addition, anyone with expertise in any field was encouraged
to leave or was deported from the Bulgarian Zone of Occupation. The
increasing lack of professionals: doctors, lawyers, teachers was having
the desired effect. More and more Greeks were leaving the Bulgarian
zone, fleeing to other areas of Greece.

It broke Andreas's heart to listen to the desperation of people in Nea
Karvali, who, twenty years ago, had been forced out of their homelands and
were again finding themselves as "undesirables." The Bulgarians wanted
these Greek Orthodox people, who had made a place for themselves in
a new land, to be gone, to be refugees once again. Many of them had
decided to go to Salonika in search of employment in the tobacco industry.
He often thought about his sister Maria. She would be a wife and mother
by now. He hoped that she wasn't in the Bulgarian Zone. He hoped she
was somewhere else in Greece, where she wouldn't be forced to flee again
and find a new home.

Andreas was washing his hands after delivering a new grandchild for
Kiría Melidis. He had known this family for years. When he was a boy, he
had visited Nea Karvali with Kìrios Vassilis, looking for his sister Maria.

The Melidis family always had a smile for him and a piece of candy. As he grew older, they hoped he might accept a marriage match with one of their daughters. Andreas would thank them, assuring the family their daughters were lovely, but he was not ready to take a wife.

The grandchild had been in a breach position and the birth required more expertise than a midwife could provide. Andreas felt fortunate to have been in town when the young mother went into labor.

The Melidis household was in disarray today as they tried to pack up the minimal belongings the Bulgarian government allowed them to take with them. They could bring only the most necessary of belongings, including livestock, and they had to obtain a certificate from the local authorities certifying they had no outstanding debts.

Kiría Melidis, her gray hair tied back in a bun, was sitting on a stool, her head in her hands.

"You have a new grandson," Andreas tried to cheer her. "A healthy boy!"

"A new grandson who will never know Nea Karvali. Who will never know Cappadocia. Almost twenty years ago, we had to flee our homes or risk death from the Turks. We had to start all over again. When we arrived here, there was so much misery, malaria, that struck all the young ones. It was terrible. But you know our story Doctor. When we were forced out of Cappadocia, my husband Staithis fortunately was fifty years old and so the Turks didn't take him away. Our family, with our young sons and daughters, fled for our lives. One daughter was not well and she died along the way. It was hard, so hard.

First they sent us to Piraeus, where we were tormented for speaking Turkish. Then we were sent somewhere else, where we were forced to live in a Turkish cemetery. Eventually we came here to Kavala where we lived in tents. But we worked to establish our new life here in Nea Karvali. And now, because we are Greek Orthodox, again because we are Greek Orthodox, we are being forced out of our homes. What have we done, Dr. Sefaris? What have we done that we must leave behind all we worked for and start all over again?"

"You've done nothing wrong. You know that, Kiría Melidis." Andreas placed a hand on her shoulder in an attempt to comfort the woman, whose tears streamed down her face.

"You know, Dr. Sefaris, that we had to change our name from Baloglou to Melidis? With the name Baloglou, everyone knew we came from Asia Minor and my Staithis couldn't get a job. He wasn't young, but he was strong and a hard worker. So he changed his name to Melidis. The man who hired him knew he was a refugee. But he told his boss Staithis's name was Melidis and he got a position in the warehouse. All that we've saved over the years will be gone. We can take only 300 *levs* of the Bulgarian currency with us and few of our belongings. Thank the Lord our daughters have already married. We'd have no dowries for them in a new place. Where will we live when we get to Salonika? Will we again have to live like nomads in a tent? There are thousands who are being forced to leave."

"I'm sure the government will take care of you and the others who are immigrating to Salonika," Andreas tried to assure her that her family wouldn't suffer in this flight from Kavala. What else could he say? How could Greece, now occupied by foreign powers, possibly have the resources to take care of the thousands descending on the areas administered by the Italians and the Nazis?

Andreas bid a heartfelt farewell to the Melidis family. He probably would never see them again unless he listened to his father. Whenever he came home, his father would remind him about the offer from his uncle Constantine to relocate to Salonika. His connection with the high-ranking Nazis would provide Andreas a good position in one of the best hospitals. There was a desperate need for physicians, since all the Jewish doctors had been dismissed. His father had urged him to go. "And you know there are a vast number of refugees from Asia Minor living there. You could be a help to them." Andreas had considered the offer. He knew that so many refugees had come from Asia Minor in the 1920s that the majority of the Salonika population was no longer Jewish. But he wasn't ready to relocate. Maybe someday he'd change his mind.

The days he spent in the refugee towns made him more determined than ever to help his people anyway he could. He was a man who had to stand up for what was right. He was a man who must fight against injustice. The terrible tragedy befalling the refugees, being forced out of their homes, reinforced his decision to join the resistance here in Kavala. There was an uprising planned in the very near future and he was going to be a part of it. He might only administer to the wounded. But he would do whatever he was asked to do without hesitation.

At the end of the day, Andreas walked into the cobbler shop and gave a hearty hug to his father. He offered a perfunctory hello to the young, bored-looking Bulgarian man, who was sitting next to his father. This man had been assigned to the shop to learn the cobbler craft. His father told Andreas that the Bulgarian was lazy and hadn't a shred of talent for working with leather. The administrators dismissed Vassilis's assessment. So the young man continued to show up most mornings, only to disappear at lunch time and return right before the shop closed its doors.

After greeting his mother, Andreas went to his room to change clothes and wash up before going to the gathering this evening at the Rouso house. In the week since Andreas came home, he hadn't been able to find even a moment to be alone with Rebecca when they weren't under the watchful eyes of her family or his parents. He had the papers that had been created with a new identity for her. Tonight there was a farewell gathering of her family and friends that he had been asked to attend. Several of her cousins had decided to leave Kavala and go elsewhere.

Greece had been divided up between the members of the Axis. Macedonia, where Kavala was located, was given to the Bulgarians. The rest of Greece, including its islands, were divided between the Germans and the Italians. Many people were taking their families to Salonika, others had decided on Athens, and there were those families who had decided to immigrate to the island of Rhodes. Any place seemed better than living under the yoke of the Bulgarian oppression. Andreas had offered to help find lodgings and positions for those who had chosen Athens. He knew how difficult it was for them to leave most of their possessions and wealth behind. But once a draft of young men into the Bulgarian army was instituted, these families felt they had no choice but to start all over in a new place.

Tonight, Andreas vowed he would talk to Rebecca, away from anyone who could overhear their conversation. He knew she wouldn't be receptive to these forged identification papers and he would have to convince her to take them just for the possibility that she might need them sometime in the future. After what he had witnessed in Berlin, he thought it best for Rebecca to have papers identifying her as a Christian.

During the week he had been home, he realized it was better for him to stay away from her. It was too difficult to see her work beside his mother, not being able to touch her, to tell her that he thought about her all the time, that he loved her and would never stop loving her. The world was turning upside down with the Axis occupation of Greece. But one thing didn't change. A Jew and an Orthodox Christian could not marry. He had always vowed he would never marry, as he was certain anyone he made his "family" would have something terrible happen to her like his parents in Smyrna. So that made it easy, he told himself. He shouldn't marry Rebecca even if it were possible. That would keep her safe. But was anyone truly safe now?

The Rouso house was filled with people saying goodbye, *sano i rezio,* wishing them a journey of milk and honey to new homes, *kaminos de leche i miel,* bringing small gifts of remembrance, and shedding tears of farewell.

Andreas smoked one cigarette after another as he waited for Rebecca to appear. What if she didn't come? He had to give her the papers tonight. He was leaving in a few days, going back to Athens to perform his duties at the hospital, taking care of Nazi patients.

Why didn't Rebecca's father want to flee from these oppressive Bulgarians? Andreas didn't think the Germans were any less brutal, but the Italians seemed to have a lackadaisical attitude toward the occupation. The Solomons should consider going to the Italian Zone, to a place like Ioannina. Andreas had also learned of Jews who decided not to wait and see if the Nazis were going to institute the harsh measures they had imposed against Jews in other European countries. They were fleeing by boat to Turkey and then to Egypt or other places. It involved bribery, but he was certain Isaac Solomon could manage the bribery fare for himself, his wife and Rebecca. But Andreas knew he would never leave his other daughters and their families. Only one of the girls had left Kavala with her husband. And of course there was the Rouso family that numbered over thirty individuals who remained. Isaac Solomon, like his parents, believed nothing terrible could happen to his family and Kavala would remain their home.

Rebecca entered the room with her brothers Ephraim and Leon and their wives as well as her parents. Rebecca was wearing a fashionable polka dot navy blue dress, which Andreas knew was an advertisement for the sewing shop. She saw him from across the room and waved casually in greeting before she turned away to speak to a young couple who was going to be leaving. People had gathered around the piano and were singing. Andreas looked at the very expensive piano and understood that once the family vacated the premises, Bulgarians would confiscate the house and all its possessions. Perhaps they would be people who couldn't play a note, but would enjoy the prestige of owning such a fine piece of furniture.

As everyone was singing and laughing, Andreas saw an opportunity to escort Rebecca away from the crowd without being noticed.

"Come with me into the garden," he said in a soft voice as he stood beside her.

"Someone might see us," Rebecca cautioned him.

"They are too busy eating and drinking and I need to talk to you alone. I'll go first. Wait a few minutes and then come outside."

"You know my family would be upset if I was seen alone with you,"

"No one is paying attention. Now, please, Rebecca. It's important or I wouldn't ask you."

"Alright," she acquiesced.

He waited in the garden, holding the package he had brought with him. The perfume of roses in the air reminded him of Rebecca. A full moon shone overhead. What a beautiful evening. How he yearned to be able to enjoy this lovely night and hold her in his arms instead of having a furtive meeting. He was lighting another cigarette when he saw her movement in the shadows.

"I'm here," she announced with a small smile.

"I'll only keep you for a moment. No one will notice," he said quietly. "I have something for you... a gift." He gave her the small package.

Rebecca pulled off the paper and looked at the book with delight. "It's in Greek! No one is allowed to speak Greek or they have to pay a fine.

They aren't selling books in Greek anymore and even the library doesn't have books in Greek. Everything is in Bulgarian. Thank you!"

"I wish I could give you something more, Rebecca. I wish I could give you jewelry and flowers. I wish I could give you a gift to show how I feel about you and you could keep it with you. But I know I can't."

"I do have something with me. Look." She withdrew the marble carefully wrapped in a soft cloth from her pocket.

"You still have that?"

"Of course I do. I was your friend, remember? I keep it with me and I think of you, all the time."

"As I think of you, my love," he paused. "But I brought you out here to give you something else." He withdrew the papers from his vest.

She peered down at the paper with her photograph. "What is this? Who is Katerina Kostakos?"

"It is you. I had it made up with your picture."

"And this Katerina? It says she is a Greek Orthodox Christian. Oh no, Andreas. No." She tried to hand the papers back to him.

"It's just in case, Rebecca. Just in case the Bulgarians come after the Jews. There has been some persecution of the Jews, even in Athens where the Italians are ruling with the Germans. Every morning I encounter executed bodies hanging from the lampposts. And even though there are not that many Jews in Athens, there are always Jewish men among the dead."

"I'm not a Jewish man. I'm a mere woman. What harm could I do? I don't want these papers. What if my parents found them? A document that has my photo and says I am a Greek Orthodox Christian? No!" she said emphatically. "I know what happened to your parents in Smyrna was terrible. But the Bulgarians, as bad as they are, aren't killing men, women and children like the Turks did. I will never renounce my identity as a Jewish woman, never. It's not who I am. I am proud to be Rebecca Solomon, a Greek Jewish woman." She pushed the papers at Andreas.

"Be stubborn, Rebecca. Who would you be if you were not stubborn Rebecca Solomon?" He put the papers back inside his vest. "I'm going to give these papers to my parents for safe keeping."

"Do whatever you want with those papers. Thank you for the book," she said tersely and turned around to leave the garden.

"Wait." He grabbed her elbow. "There is something else I need to tell you."

"What is it? I'm sorry I sounded cross with you," her voice had softened. "I know you are trying to help. But really, you needn't be concerned."

"You and my mother are going to Drama this week for a delivery, aren't you? And you are only staying overnight, correct?"

"Yes... Why do you ask?"

"After this week, you are not to return to Drama. You must promise me that you won't go back there until October at the earliest."

"But what if we have more orders to deliver?"

"Rebecca, I am demanding that you not go back to Drama. I can't say anymore, do you understand? And you must not tell anyone, not even my mother. If you get another order, you must find some way of delaying."

"But, but..." Rebecca frowned.

"I don't care how many orders you might have to deliver or what you are being told to do by others." He didn't mention the word "resistance," but he knew she was well aware of whom he spoke. "You can't go back there for a while. You must promise me this." His voice was emphatic.

Rebecca looked away. He knew she was thinking, deciding what to say, what to do. He suspected her work as a courier these last few months. She must realize his request had something to do with the resistance and she was weighing what could she do if the resistance gave her another message to take to Drama.

"I promised to do whatever they told me," Rebecca said quietly, trying to make him understand.

"Tell them you are sick. You will think of something and you must not allow my mother to go by herself."

"She won't go if I'm not with her. She can't speak Bulgarian very well. But why shouldn't we go?"

"You must stay here in Kavala until I tell you otherwise. You trust me, don't you?"

"Of course, I do. Can't you tell me... "

"I shouldn't even have said this much. Now promise me you will stay in Kavala." He needed her to promise. The resistance was planning an uprising and he had to make sure Rebecca and his mother would be far away from the fighting. "Now, you better go back inside before someone starts looking for you."

Rebecca reached up to his cheek tenderly. "Andreas, I miss you so much when you're gone."

And then she turned and left him alone in the garden.

Mountainside near Drama: September 29, 1941

Sounds of moaning and cries of pain filled the air. Andreas looked at the man who had been clutching his hand. The man's hand was now lax, his eyes sightless. Andreas made the sign of the cross and gently closed the partisan's eyes. There was nothing more to be done for that poor man, even if Andreas had the proper medical supplies. Most of the men who were brought to him were close to death. His medicine and supplies had run out early this afternoon. He'd have been of more use if he was ordained to give last rites to the dying, than a mere mortal without medicine to relieve pain or to heal. This resistance, this uprising, was doomed from its inception. Poor planning, not enough rifles or ammunition, going up against far superior forces....

"Doctor!" Three men came running up the path. "Hurry! The Bulgarians are coming! You have to go! Now!"

"But the wounded?"

"The Bulgarians will kill them for sure and if we don't hurry, they will kill us. Now hurry! This way!"

Andreas looked at the moaning men spread across the ground, who were far from death. He should stay with them. But what could he do? He had taken the Hippocratic oath to heal, but...

"Doctor, move!" Two men grabbed his arms. Another man picked up his rifle from the ground and shoved it at him. "Now! The Bulgarians are going to kill us all!" they yelled at him.

He grabbed his rifle reluctantly and followed them up the trail.

"We've been overrun! They are close on our heels," Kountoura, a young man with a slight build, told him as they scrambled further up the hillside. Andreas heard the report of the rifles. He knew they were killing the wounded soldiers he had been forced to leave behind.

"The uprising was a shambles." The partisan leader stopped them at the crest of the hill. "I don't know if the Bulgarians had an informer. But the KKE Communist Party was outmatched in every way. We didn't have enough rifles. We didn't have enough men. It's been a suicide mission. We need to split up! You two go to the left. Papálas you come with me!"

Andreas and Kountoura scrambled up the trail as fast as they could. And then they heard footsteps behind them, getting closer and closer. "Get down," Andreas cautioned the young man to crouch next to him beside a huge boulder.

Two Bulgarian soldiers came into view, out of breath and huffing from their exertions. "Where are you, you Greek dogs? We will find you and string you up!"

Andreas prayed the soldiers would continue up the path. But they weren't going away. They were searching behind every boulder. Kountoura lifted his rifle and aimed. He motioned for Andreas to do the same.

Andreas swallowed hard, his heart pounding in his chest as he picked up the rifle he had been trained to use by the partisans. He wasn't good at this. During his training, he had begun to sweat and hesitated. "What's the matter with you?" The man giving instruction had admonished him. "You're a doctor who is going to help our wounded, but you still need to know how to protect yourself. Now, pick up the rifle and fire the way I've taught you! If you freeze, you'll be dead. Others will be depending on you. Be a man, damn you, fire your rifle."

Now that feeling again that he fought against, a terror deep in his heart that was threatening to overwhelm him. Kountoura aimed and fired. The soldier fell over. The other Bulgarian roared and started toward their boulder. Andreas fired and watched as the soldier stood still and the blood began to ooze from his chest before he fell to his knees. And then it wasn't the Bulgarian, but a visage from long ago appearing in front of his eyes. Not a blonde soldier with blue eyes, but a man in the Turkish cavalry with darker skin, standing before him, and Andreas pulled the trigger until he had no bullets left.

"Come on!" Kountoura was yelling at him. "Damn. Stay here then and get killed. I'm getting out of here."

Andreas couldn't move as he crouched behind the boulder. He was seeing the nightmare that he knew haunted his dreams all these years. The nightmare he never remembered when he woke up. He closed his eyes, and saw his father covered with blood, lying on the rug. "Baba," he whispered and the tears rolled down his cheeks. He remembered. He remembered.

From within his dream he heard the sound of Bulgarian boots on the rock formation before him. Was he meant to end his life here, murdered by a soldier, the way his father's life had ended? How terrible it must have been for his father, knowing he couldn't protect his family, the sacred duty of a husband and father. But for Andreas Sefaris, there was no wife, no children to protect.

Rebecca, he felt her presence. She wanted him to fight, to live.

He cleared his mind and gripped his rifle.

Kavala, Greece: October 2, 1941
Kiría Eleni had told Rebecca not to come into the shop until the afternoon. They had both been working hard to complete new orders for their Bulgarian customers, who were extremely rude and demanding. "Take some time off, Rebecca. We can both do our sewing this afternoon. If our Bulgarian bosses have any complaints, I will take full responsibility."

Rebecca didn't mind having the morning away from their sewing. She wasn't sleeping well at night and she woke up so tired every morning. She thought, perhaps, she could sleep later this morning, but her eyes opened at first light and her mind was filled with the rumors that had spread like wildfire through the community, both Greek Orthodox and Jewish. There had been an uprising in Drama and the surrounding towns. It had not gone well. But the gruesome details, more rumors... The men were taken prisoner, the men were being executed. Women and children were killed indiscriminately. Whole villages were massacred by the Bulgarians to teach the Greeks a lesson. She remembered Andreas insisting that she and his mother not go up there last month. Rebecca couldn't help but think that Andreas was somehow involved and she feared for his safety. His parents hadn't received a letter from him in quite a while. They excused his missing letters, explaining that he must be too busy.

She had offered all kinds of reasons to Kiría Eleni as to why they couldn't go to Drama. Rebecca didn't feel well. She needed to help a sister who had just given birth.

Her contact in the resistance who visited her at the shop had looked down at her with scorn. "We thought we could count on you, Phaedra. But you keep giving us excuses. We don't care if you feel sick. You should put our cause above your own needs. We had to find someone else to help us. Let me tell you, there is no lack of patriots who are happy to help."

"I really was too sick to go. I'm sorry. I will help next time," Rebecca had offered.

Rebecca arose from bed and went down to the kitchen to help lay out breakfast on the table. She had begun a new novel last night, but it was hard to concentrate on the words. She needed to find something to do to occupy her time this morning. She didn't want to talk to her mother, who complained incessantly about the diminished amount of food that was available at the market. There no longer were leftover scraps of food to feed the dogs and cats that wandered the streets. And now there were fewer and fewer homeless animals to be seen in the lanes and the back alleyways. With people in dire need of food, it wasn't hard to image what was happening to the stray animals.

Rebecca didn't want to hear her sister-in-law Sara asking over and over again why they couldn't go to Salonika with the rest of her family. Rebecca needed something that would take her mind away from the nagging worries about Andreas.

She walked over to the dry goods store. There were no customers yet. She started to help her father arrange items in the display case. Papá had an abundant supply of goods from the Bulgarian general. The store did a brisk business, but, of course, it wasn't his store anymore. He was merely a poorly paid employee, as was her brother Ephraim.

"Greetings!" Rebecca cringed at the sound of the Bulgarian officer's voice and his boots echoing across the wooden floor. "My refreshment." He smiled at her and winked.

Her father drew out his bottle and placed it on the counter. "To your health!" Her father poured the *raki* into his glass.

"You've heard the news?" The Bulgarian gushed with excitement as he swallowed the *raki*.

"What news?"

"About the so-called resistance in Drama, Dovato and Choristi?" He wiped his mouth with the back of his hand.

"A resistance?"

"They are called the Communist Party of Greece. What a laugh! They thought they could rise up against us and we would hand back their country. What fools!"

"So what happened? Were they all put in jail?"

"Jail? Really! Solomon, don't be such a simple-minded imbecile. Once our Bulgarian troops moved in, all the men between the ages of eighteen and forty-five were rounded up. And then they were executed. At least 3000 were killed in Drama alone. Our troops needed to teach the Greeks a lesson, a lesson they will never forget. The women and children were forced to watch as their men were massacred in front of their eyes. You know, we tried to get the Greeks to leave our country. Now, maybe, they will reconsider their stubborn decision to stay put where they don't belong."

Rebecca felt light-headed as she sank down on a nearby stool. No, it couldn't be. It couldn't be. Andreas had gone there with the resistance. She was positive of it. If all the men had been executed, Andreas was dead.

Days stretched into weeks and there was no word from Andreas. Kiría Eleni would speculate every morning that perhaps the Bulgarians were confiscating their mail. In the past year, since the occupation began, Andreas always wrote to his parents every week, and now it had been over a month and they hadn't a letter, nothing.

Rebecca fought against revealing her suspicions. She couldn't mention why she thought Andreas hadn't written to his parents. He wasn't in Athens where he was too busy to write to his parents. The Bulgarians hadn't confiscated his correspondence. The man she loved with all her heart was no more. Why had he volunteered to put his life in danger? She knew the answer. He often quoted the words of Edmund Burke who said, "The only thing necessary for the triumph of evil is for good men to do nothing." And so he had done what he felt compelled to do.

When she saw the photos from the uprising in the newspapers, of men hanging from lampposts, she studied every lifeless body. Was that man Andreas? No, was that man Andreas? She couldn't share her thoughts, her grief, even with his parents. She couldn't sleep. She lost interest in eating. Her mother thought she was trying to save the diminished food portions for her parents out of respect for them. "You must eat more than that," her mother had admonished her.

"I'm just not hungry," Rebecca murmured and pushed away from the table.

"Are you ill?" Papá asked with concern.

"No, I... I. Maybe the brutality of this Bulgarian occupation is finally affecting me."

"Are you talking about what happened in Drama? It was a blessing you and Kiría Eleni weren't up there making a delivery when the fighting broke out," her father said.

Rebecca didn't answer. She couldn't answer. She hurried up to her room and closed the door. She sank to her knees on the floor, pulling out the marble from her pocket. She clutched it in her hand. Andreas knew trouble was coming to Drama and that was why he was so adamant that neither she nor his mother travel up there. Andreas.... The tears slipped down her cheeks.

⳼

Early in the morning, Rebecca walked over to the dressmaking shop, holding the key in her hand. Before the Bulgarians had come, no one ever locked their doors. But now it was different. Your things could be stolen or squatters could move in and take over your house.

Kiría Eleni had told Rebecca she was going to spend the morning with her sister, whose husband had recently suffered a heart attack. Kìrios Vassilis needed to accompany a Bulgarian to a tannery for the purchase of leather and he wouldn't be back until the afternoon. Rebecca would have the shops and the house to herself. She unlocked the door and took off her coat. She sat in front of the Singer, but she had no wish to begin sewing. At least she was alone here and didn't have to pretend that her heart wasn't aching for the man she would never see again, never feel his arms around her, never see the look of love in his eyes. The world was gray, without color, without joy, now that Andreas was gone. She felt so alone.

She put her head down in her arms and closed her eyes, remembering the first time she had seen him, so frightened, so sad.

Thump! What was that? She raised her head. Had she heard a sound from the living quarters above the store? Thump! There it was again. The Matsakises were gone, weren't they? What was that?

Rebecca grabbed the large sharp scissors next to the sewing machine and got to her feet. Had someone gotten into the house, someone who thought, with no one home, they could take over the house from the Matsakis family? Well, they couldn't do that! She wouldn't let them. Those horrible Bulgarians! She hated every last one of them.

Rebecca walked to the staircase and quietly climbed up the stairs. Scrape! Yes, she heard a noise again. It was coming from the bedroom at the top of the stairs, the bedroom that belonged to Kiría Eleni and her husband Vassilis. Rebecca gripped the scissors in her hand like a dagger and pushed open the door. She clutched the scissors high above her head, ready to defend herself. "Get out!" she yelled as the door swung open.

A Dio!! My God! It was Andreas, standing before a bowl, shaving his face, wearing only a tee shirt and pants.

"Are you going to stab me with that, Rebecca Solomon?" He broke into a broad smile and wiped off his face with a nearby towel. "Didn't have time to find a shovel?"

"You're alive!" She breathed with relief. "Oh, Andreas, I'm so glad you're alive!"

He held out his arms to her and she ran to him, tightly squeezing her arms around his chest. "I thought you were dead. I thought you'd been massacred in Drama. Andreas!" She looked up at him with wonder. He was here! He was alive!

He gathered her close and kissed her over and over again. "My Rebecca. I thought I'd never see you again, never hold you again. How I love you!" He crushed her in his arms.

"Andreas," she whispered as her heart beat wildly in her chest and she gloried in the warmth and closeness of him pressed against her. "Are you alright? Are you hurt? What happened? I was sure you were dead!" And then she couldn't help herself as she broke down into tears.

"Shh," he tried to soothe her and held her more tightly in his arms. "Don't cry. I'm fine, especially now that I'm with you. Perhaps someday I'll tell you about what happened. But now I'm just glad I'm alive. I arrived last night and I was totally exhausted. I didn't even clean up. My parents insisted I take their bed and I just collapsed here."

"Your parents told me they were leaving early today." She fought to compose herself and wiped the tears from her face. "Didn't they want to stay with you this morning after you came home?"

"Yes, they did. But it was important for them to go on about their lives, not arouse suspicion that I am here, that I escaped from the Bulgarians. I need to leave this evening to go back Athens. But they will be back early this afternoon and we will have time for a proper reunion."

Time for us to be alone, she thought. A few brief hours, but hours they had never had before. She never wanted him to stop holding her. She never wanted to let him go.

Suddenly there was no right or wrong. There were only the two of them, alive, so glad to be alive and in each other's arms. She felt as if she was melting into him. His nearness flooded her senses with desire.

""I want you," she breathed. "I love you so much. Please, please."

She took a deep breath as he unbuttoned her blouse and slid it off her shoulders. Rebecca shivered as his lips touched her bare skin.

He held her hand as he guided her down to the bed beside him and pulled her against the length of his body. He began to caress her, to kiss her. Rebecca knew he wanted to please her, to take his time with her. But she wanted him so badly. She wanted him now.

"Andreas, *te amo,* I love you."

Their joys, their pleasures as they entwined, their lips, their bodies, their limbs. Breathless pleasure...They were alive and their joy in each other, their pleasure, made the world stand still...

Rebecca lay spent against his chest as his arms held her tight.

"I need to leave," she sighed. "Your parents will be back soon."

"How can I let you go?"

"Maybe I can stay for just a few more minutes." She snuggled closer, reveling in the male smell of his body. She didn't want to leave the warmth of his embrace. "If only I could wake up beside you in the morning."

"I assure you it isn't something you would enjoy. My sleep is haunted by nightmares, ever since I was a boy when I first came here…. I never sleep beside someone until dawn, for fear I would frighten them."

"You wouldn't frighten me," she told him.

"Rebecca." He nuzzled her shoulder and held her closer. "When I had a rifle in my hands and I was supposed to kill the enemy as he approached, it suddenly all came back to me... how my father thought he could reason with the soldier who had barged into our house. I saw the soldier's sword slicing into my father. He killed my father and then the Turk was going after my mother and my sister. Rebecca, I grabbed my Baba's gun and I shot the Turk. I pulled the trigger over and over. The noise was so loud. The blood," his voice faded to a tortured whisper. "I should have shot the soldier before he killed my father. It was my fault. I should have saved my father."

She reached up to his face and held it between her palms. "You were only a child. You couldn't have saved everyone."

"If I had shot the Turk before he killed my father, my father would have been alive. He would have saved everyone. It's all my fault," he said his voice filled with desperation.

"It's not your fault. You were such a brave little boy. It's alright, it's alright," she whispered, her heart aching for him. "It's not your fault."

"It was my fault. I know it was my fault. That's why I couldn't remember all these years. It was too painful."

"You are wrong," she told him, looking into his dark eyes. "It was too painful to remember, but not because it was your fault. Seeing your father murdered in front of your eyes. The horror of that memory made it too painful. You need to stop blaming yourself."

He took her hands and pressed his lips against them. "Rebecca, *te amo*. I will always love you."

They kissed again, their hunger for each other made them forget the time, the impending arrival of his parents.

And then she wearily eyed the clock. "I do need to go now. Your parents will be back soon."

They both rose from the bed, each reaching down for their clothes that lay strewn around the floor

"I was very careful this morning." His expression grew serious. "But if something happened, you are to let me know. Promise?"

A baby, she thought. A baby with the man she loved, but couldn't have. "Yes, I know that isn't a possibility for us." She turned her back to him. She didn't want Andreas to see the mist of tears in her eyes.

"Rebecca?" He asked as he pulled up his pants.

She took a deep breath and turned around smiling at him. She needed to forget any sadness she felt about a baby they could never have. She needed to focus on the joy of this moment. Would there ever be moments again like this between them, when the world stopped and it was just the two of them? "Yes," she responded.

"You remember that my parents have your new identity papers."

"Andreas, of course, I know they have the papers. You're not to worry. I will never need them."

CHAPTER 13

Kavala, Greece: November, 1942

ANDREAS HAD BEEN home visiting his parents for two weeks.

"Andreas." His father beckoned to him. "Why don't you and I go out for a stroll this afternoon? I'd like to discuss something with you. That Bulgarian in charge of my shop is so grateful to you for having saved his son that he won't complain if I'm gone for a while. And remember, you are not to tell anyone you aided his wife with the delivery. Greek physicians are prohibited from practicing here without a special license."

"I know," said Andreas as he put down the book he was reading. "The stupidity of their laws is incomprehensible. There aren't enough Bulgarian doctors who have settled here and those I've met don't have the expertise of the Greek physicians. If we are going out, we need to be back in time to attend the gathering at Joseph Rouso's house."

"Yes, I know we are all going there tonight. It's such an outrage that his pharmacy was taken away by the Bulgarians because he is a Jew. The Bulgarians are such brutes. Now, come with me. Let's walk down toward the harbor." His father grabbed his jacket and tossed Andreas a coat.

After they bid goodbye to Kiría Eleni and Rebecca, who were bent over their sewing, Andreas and his father made their way down the cobblestone streets toward the harbor. Winter had not yet descended upon their town and there was only a slight chill in the air as they walked down the streets. The sun was shining in a brilliant blue sky.

"I worry about our neighbors," his father confided, as they passed by what used to be the Rouso shop which now had a Bulgarian name on its storefront.

"I worry as well," Andreas agreed. "It's bad enough what those Bulgarian barbarians have imposed on us Greek Orthodox, but they've been even more harsh toward our Jewish neighbors. Imposing a 20% tax on all Jewish real estate, coupled with confiscating their pharmacies, their commercial warehouses, mines, insurance agencies... Didn't you also tell me that all the Jews working for the government were fired?"

"Yes, but in the midst of all these outrages, I believe the most concerning is the insistence here in Eastern Macedonia that everyone must obtain Bulgarian citizenship. What Greek would want such a thing? But without it, we have no rights. And as for the Jews, like Isaac Solomon and his family, they are denied Bulgarian citizenship. They have no rights. I'm afraid this eventually could lead to some terrible calamity."

"Jews cannot be citizens?" Andreas was incredulous.

"They have no citizenship anywhere. These are dreadful times, my son." His father sat on a boulder and looked down at the aquamarine blue water of the port.

"I think I should be living here, to help take care of you and Mamá in these uncertain times."

"Don't worry about us." Vassilis put his hand on his son's arm. "You are doing good work with the refugees in Athens. You wouldn't be able to practice medicine here because you are Greek. But I'll remind you again, there are so many refugees in Salonika and now, with the refugees fleeing the Bulgarian occupation, thousands more will join them. We have family in Salonika.

"The Bulgarians have made life more and more restrictive for the Greek Christians, hoping that more will leave. They have taken away the obstacle of having a debt as a legitimate reason to keep them from leaving. But for the Jews, it is different. They need special visas for traveling and they aren't permitted to leave."

"I offered to have fake identification papers created for my friend Joseph and his family. He has a large family, including many children, his parents and his wife's parents. But he told me, no. He said there were too many of them to try to escape with false papers that would identify them as Christians. I don't know what else I can do to help them." Andreas looked out at the water.

"You tried. There is nothing more that you or any of us can do to shield our Jewish neighbors from these harsh restrictions. I brought you away from the house to speak with you about other matters."

"Yes, I know you well, Patéra. You didn't ask me out here to just talk about the terrible times that have befallen Kavala."

"That is true," his father sighed. "Today, we are attending the gathering at the Rouso house to celebrate a birthday, I believe? Your friend Joseph?"

"Yes." Andreas looked out at the waves and the boats with Bulgarian flags bobbing up and down in the water. This had been one of his favorite places. But would it ever be again? Could there be beauty in the intense aquamarine water, the white foam, the blue sky, when the world had turned into such an ugly place?

"The Solomons will be there and Rebecca?"

"I would think so."

"Andreas, I was thinking that perhaps you shouldn't come with us tonight."

"Why shouldn't I come? Joseph has been such a good friend to me since we were boys. His spirits are so low since his pharmacy was taken away. I need to be there to show him my support."

"Last year, when you came home looking so terrible and fell into our bed, I surmised you'd been involved in the resistance movement. You were lucky to have gotten away with your life, so I gave thanks to God. I never asked you, but I was able to put the pieces together. After that horrible tragedy in Drama, I hope you are no longer risking your life with the *andartes*."

"You needn't worry," Andreas told him. This was all about what happened in Drama? "I now focus all my attention on my medical practice in Athens. I'm not taking part in any resistance movements. I'm not well-suited for them."

"That afternoon," his father continued, "when I returned from being dragged around by the Bulgarian pig from tannery to tannery, I was exhausted from smiling at the imbecile and his conversations at the tanneries. You and Rebecca were sitting at the table eating lunch, not a word between you, which is rare. I didn't think much of it until I went upstairs to lie down."

Andreas's smile froze on his lips. He knew. Somehow his father knew.

"And then I go upstairs to my bed and Rebecca's scent, the scent of roses I know so well when she enters the house, the scent of rose petals is all over our sheets," he paused. "You need to be careful, Andreas."

"Careful?"

"I am not blind and neither is anyone else. Your mother says nothing. She looks down at her sewing and chooses not to see what is right in front of her."

"But... ," Andreas started to protest.

"No." His father raised his hand. "Let me finish. The two of you cannot do this. It will come to no good. When you think I am not looking, I see how you gaze at her, how the two of you gaze at each other with such love, as if the rest of the world does not exist. But it does exist. That morning, I pulled off the sheets and told your mother I had soiled them with my boots. She would have been beside herself if she knew the truth. And today, for the first time since that day, you will be together with Rebecca and her family. You must wear a mask, Andreas, a mask of indifference when you look her way. You do not want her family to see what I see in your eyes, on your face. I pray Rebecca has the sense to do the same."

Andreas looked at the pebbles on the ground.

"Do you understand me? I fear what would happen if the Solomon family knew what I know."

"I love her," Andreas said quietly.

"I'm sorry. You must find some nice Greek Orthodox girl in Athens and marry her. That will make you forget this insanity between you and Rebecca."

"I don't want anyone else, Patéra. I have loved Rebecca ever since I was a child."

"Son." His father put his arm around his shoulders. "When the two of you were little and I'd watch you play at the castle and the aqueduct, I could see the joy you found in each other. And I knew you were grateful that she brought you to us. You were so serious all the time, and such sadness weighed on you. No matter how Eleni and I tried, the sadness was always hanging over you like a terrible cloud. But you would see Rebecca and your face would light up. You would smile. For those first few years it was the only time you smiled. So how could we discourage you from playing games with her, from sharing your books with her? I hoped and prayed as you grew up, those feelings you had for each other would change, would lessen."

"Well, they didn't. I know we have no future. But we can't help how we feel."

"It's too bad her marriage did not work out."

"David Tiano was a scoundrel. She deserved better."

"Well, that doesn't matter anymore. I know you try not to be in the same room with her. Ever since that morning, you find an errand that will get you out of the house when Rebecca is there. Your mother thinks you must have had a falling out. She laments that you used to talk about books and so much else."

Andreas gave his father a weak smile. He pulled a cigarette from his pocket and offered one to his father. Yes, he would force himself not to make eye contact with her. He didn't want to get her in trouble. As much as he wanted to make frequent visits to Kavala to see his parents, to see Rebecca, he had to fight the urge to talk to her, to touch her, to be warmed by the look of love on her face.

"I'm going tonight. I need to be there for Joseph. I will barely speak to Rebecca except to say hello. You needn't be concerned about me tonight."

Rebecca was settled into a comfortable chair, and a little girl, sporting dark curls, was seated on her lap. Everyone was socializing, drinking, eating and trying not to talk about how life had gotten so difficult under this rule by the Bulgarians. *"Anyos munchos,"* everyone wished Joseph a happy birthday. Rebecca looked at her cousin and his family, trying to show good humor and appreciation for family and friends who had come tonight. But the undercurrent of sadness, a man's livelihood being taken away because he was a Jew... The family would pull together and try to help them. But what further restrictions might be placed upon their community? The Jewish men, women and children, along with their Christian neighbors and friends, tried to put those sad thoughts aside for a few hours.

Conditions in Kavala were not as dire as last year. At least food was more available. During the winter of 1941-42, there had been famine all over Greece. In Athens, people had dropped dead in the streets of malnutrition. The British had blockaded the ports of Athens and the wheat that came from abroad to feed the people of Greece had vanished. People were eating grass to stay alive. But in the winter, there was no grass to eat. If you had connections in the black market, there were ways to survive. But without those connections, the Greeks had faced a terrible fate. Here in Eastern Macedonia, food had been hard to find, but the situation was not as dire. During the spring and summer, the food supply had increased. Everyone hoped this year's winter would not be as harsh as last year's.

She had seen Andreas across the room and forced herself to ignore him as he usually ignored her. Whenever she came into the shop, Andreas made a point to find an errand to go somewhere else. When he returned, he either stayed with his father in the cobbler shop or went up to his room. She knew he was trying not to be near her. Just as she tried not to be near him. It required all her will not to reach out to him.

She smiled as the little girl with black curls reached over to get another sweet. "Lina," Rebecca cautioned her. "Too many sweets will make your tummy ache."

The little girl pouted, but then her attention was caught by Andreas coming across the room with his mother.

"And who is this?" Kiría Eleni asked with a big smile on her face. "Such a pretty little girl."

"This is Lina Petratos. Her parents are over there with their other children. Her actual name is Galina, off the official Bulgarian list of approved Bulgarian names, but they call her Lina,' said Rebecca.

"Can you imagine not being able to give your child a name of your own choosing? Having to pick from a list of approved names?" Kiría Eleni muttered, her voice filled with disgust.

"Her name is Lina?" Andreas asked in a hushed voice.

"Yes," Rebecca answered. Something was wrong. Andreas was looking at the child so intently.

"May I hold her?" he asked.

"Of course," Rebecca answered and watched as he bent down to take the little girl who smiled up at him. But he stopped, his expression frozen.

"I... I," he stammered.

"What's wrong?"

"I had a sister who looked just like her, Baby Lina," he whispered.

"But the sister you have been looking for is Maria." Kiría Eleni frowned.

"I had another sister. I had forgotten her and what happened to her." His eyes were filling with tears. "I had another sister, Baby Lina. She got sick." He turned and walked away toward a bank of windows.

"Here." Rebecca handed the child to Kiría Elena and followed Andreas who was staring out the window.

"Andreas." She put her hand on his arm. "Andreas, tell me."

"I had forgotten. I couldn't remember. Can you imagine that I had forgotten? What kind of person forgets he had a sister? I had a little sister, Baby Lina. She got sick and we had no medicine. I remember now. My mother was holding her and Baby Lina was crying and then she wasn't crying anymore. Maria and I used to tickle her to make her laugh. There were so many people all around us. We were on the quay in Smyrna. I had forgotten. But seeing that little girl, I remembered. I remembered." He looked down at Rebecca and her hand on his arm. "You shouldn't do that," he warned in a soft voice.

"I don't care," she told him, her heart squeezing at the anguish on his face.

"It hurts, Rebecca. It hurts so much to remember." He wiped the tears from his face with the back of his hand.

Rebecca reached inside her dress pocket and pulled out an embroidered handkerchief. "Here," she touched his cheek tenderly and handed the handkerchief to him.

He took it from her and gazed at her with so much love in his eyes.

"Rebecca," it was the stern voice of her mother. "Come with me. This isn't proper."

"Mamá, I don't care. Andreas is upset."

"You are no longer children. Now come away before everyone sees your behavior and the gossips start talking." Mamá grabbed her arm and pulled her away forcefully.

Rebecca gave Andreas one last glance as he tucked her handkerchief into his vest pocket. She followed her mother meekly, knowing she was going to be chastised for her immodest actions.

"What were you thinking, Rebecca? You are a grown woman, a grown Jewish woman and he is a Greek Orthodox man. I'm glad your father is in another room and didn't see this kind of behavior."

"Mamá, he was hurting. He was remembering things that happened to his family."

"It's not your place to console him. Where is Kiría Eleni? Why hasn't he taken a wife? Is there something not right about him? His mother told me he vows never to marry. What kind of man doesn't want a wife?"

"It's because of what happened to his family when he was a boy. He is afraid that anyone who married him would have back luck and suffer a catastrophe."

"That doesn't make sense."

"I know that. But such terrible things happened to his family, his thinking is confused."

Rebecca and her mother heard a shout across the room. Someone yelled. People gasped. Women cried. What happened? Rebecca hurried to where a young man was handing out sheets of paper. People stared at the paper. Others ripped it to shreds and stumped on it. What was it?

Rebecca looked down at the official-looking paper.

To all Jews:

All Jews over the age of ten years, must wear the Star of David pinned to their clothing.

The head of the family must submit a record of family wealth to the Bulgarian administrators.

No one can go out of their house after five in the afternoon until morning.

Jews cannot use the telephone.

A photograph of everyone in the household must be presented to the authorities at which time a yellow identification card will be issued.

All shops owned by Jews need a sign outside to indicate Jewish ownership.

Jews cannot walk on the main streets of the town.

"Rebecca. It's getting worse." It was Andreas at her side. "Those fake identification papers my parents are keeping for you. You must use them. You must leave here."

Rebecca watched her parents' reaction to this awful proclamation. No one paid any attention to her and Andreas. "Leave? Leave my family? I will never do that, never." She tried to walk away from him, but he grabbed her hand.

"Please, Rebecca, please. It's the way things began in Nazi Germany. Then Jews were thrown out of their shops and beaten on the streets. I couldn't bear it if something were to happen to you," he whispered to her, his voice filled with anguish

"Nothing is happening to me. Yes, these restrictions on the Jews are terrible. But my whole family, my whole community will suffer under them together, united. We will bear what we must. I shall wear a yellow star. That won't hurt me. What could possibly happen to me that would make you so worried?"

"Rebecca I remember vividly my father telling us everything would be alright. There was no reason for us to flee. He was a man of great intellect and he was wrong, so wrong."

"These are Bulgarians, not Turks and not Nazis. Andreas. I don't know why the Jews are being singled out. But Papá has often told our family that Jews have been persecuted over the ages. My mother's family are Sephardic Jews, whose ancestors were forced to flee from Spain hundreds of years ago. We persevered then. We will persevere now. We will all be fine."

Kavala, Greece: March 3, 1943
Rebecca reached inside her skirt pocket, pulled out a handkerchief and wiped her nose. She hoped this miserable cold was finally going away. She'd been up night after night with a terrible cough and felt exhausted this morning.

Her mother frowned as she poured chamomile tea into her daughter's cup. "Have more tea. It can help your cold. I heard you coughing all last night."

"I'm sure I'm getting better. Are you still upset about our cousins?" Rebecca asked, although she already knew the answer. There was so much sadness and worry in their family and she didn't want anyone to be burdened with concerns about her.

"How can I not be upset?" Mamá asked and looked at her husband. "Another cousin's son was taken away for forced labor. Who knows when he will return and who knows which other young man in our family will be taken away?

"The Bulgarians have taken it all. Everything that made our home such a comfort is gone. The wedding presents from my family... I now have to pour tea from a porcelain pot. I had the finest tea and coffee silver service. The most beautiful candlesticks, finely engraved silver trays. All my silver, all my jewelry that was left after we had to sell so much to keep food on our table... They have taken everything, Isaac. Those horrible Bulgarians have left us nothing."

"Esther, what is most important is we have each other. We're fortunate that none of our sons-in-law have been taken for forced labor. But we grieve for our cousins who have borne such a terrible burden. Silver, jewelry, they are only possessions. I know it hurts you, Esther. It hurts me to see you so sad. But someday these Bulgarians will be gone, and I promise to give you more beautiful jewelry and more silver pieces. I promise." He smiled at her.

Rebecca observed her parents and the love they showed for each other. That was what a marriage could be. When Rebecca was little, before she realized she would never marry, she hoped for such a match. David, her wayward husband... She rarely thought about him anymore.

Some of her sisters had found love in their marriages, though most of them just tolerated the husbands who were matched to them. As long as the men were good people, earning a decent living, that was all a woman could hope for in an arranged marriage. The love, like Papá and Mamá had between them, was rare. Her mother had assured all her daughters that couples developed a kind of love between them as the years went by.

Rebecca finished the hot tea her mother had poured and got up from the breakfast table. "I'm due at the Matsakis shop early today. We are finishing a bridal gown with intricate beading. Even with her glasses, Kiría Eleni has trouble doing fine stitching. So it's up to me to complete this gown. I'll try to get home early."

She got to her feet. "Mamá, I sewed a dress for Julie's dolly. When she comes over today, make sure you give it to her. I made it from leftover silk scraps in a beautiful pink color."

"I'll give it to her. You're such a good Tia, Rebecca." She smiled fondly at her daughter. "Now take your warm winter coat. It's freezing outside."

Rebecca bid her parents goodbye, grabbed her woolen coat and hurried down the street toward the Matsakises' shops. She hoped fervently that she could finish the beading and return home early. Even though it was morning, a night of coughing had exhausted her and she was tired.

Andreas was in the kitchen with his parents. He gave her a perfunctory smile in greeting and went back to eating his breakfast.

"Rebecca," Kiría Eleni called out. "We have good news today. Andreas has decided to move to Salonika. He will be closer to us and maybe he will come to visit more often."

"That's nice," Rebecca commented.

"He is moving there because there is so much need for help in the refugee community," Kirios Vassilis explained, as he spread his quince jam over a hunk of bread. "There has always been a huge number of refugees from Asia Minor in Salonika and now, with so many being forced out of the Bulgarian Zone, it's bursting with new refugees."

"And he is also moving because our son can sometimes not take care with his words." Kìrios Vassilis frowned at him.

"You're right, Patéra. I should have been more careful."

"What happened?" his mother asked.

"I was out in a taverna in Athens one recent evening. I was enjoying myself with my friends, when a man, who I didn't know, started speaking drivel about my people, about the refugees from Asia Minor. He said that soon the Germans would rid our country of the Jews and next they should turn their attention to the seeds of Turkey.

"I spoke up when I should have just been quiet. I told him what I thought of him and his ideas in no uncertain terms. I didn't know that he was a highly placed collaborator. The next day, a good friend visited me and warned that I was going to be brought to Merton Street to be interrogated by the Gestapo and then probably sent to the Hadari prison. Athens is no longer safe for me. Patéra says he is sure his brother

Constantine in Salonika will smooth things over with the authorities if need be."

"Andreas. We know you love your people. But these are dangerous times and you must take care."

"Yes, Mamá. I will take care."

"Rebecca." His mother turned towards her. "Can I get you anything before I clear off our breakfast?"

"No, thank you. But maybe if you have some *faskomilo* tea? I'm still suffering from this terrible cold. Well, I need to get to work."

"Of course, I'll heat up some tea and bring it to you."

"Eleni, remember you don't have to prepare an evening meal for me and Andreas." Kìrios Vassilis folded his napkin on the table. "We're going over to visit Odyessus. My friends and I have been looking forward to tonight. We're going to talk about the old times, the good times before this occupation. We'll be late."

"Late?" Kiría Eleni said as she gathered the breakfast dishes. "When you go to Odysseus, you forget the time. I don't expect you and Andreas until way after midnight. Just be sure you have your papers with you in case you are stopped by one of those Bulgarian beasts on the street."

By late afternoon, Rebecca had almost finished her work with the beads. The sound of the door opening and the heels of a woman walking across the floor made Rebecca look up. Kiría Eleni had promised the dress would be ready tomorrow. Why was the Bulgarian matron here today?

"I have something wonderful to show you," Boyana Alexandrov told them as she laid a small box next to the Singer.

"What is it?" Rebecca asked politely in Bulgarian.

"Look." The older woman opened the box to reveal beautiful iridescent pearls that shimmered in the afternoon sunlight.

"They are beautiful," Rebecca said with admiration.

"I ordered them months ago, but they just came in this morning."

"Perhaps you'd like me to add them to the neckline?" Rebecca offered. "I think they would be a wonderful addition."

"No, of course, I don't want them only on the neckline. I want all the pearls on the dress replaced by these."

"But you need the dress by tomorrow, isn't that correct?"

"Are you stupid? Of course, I need it by tomorrow. And you will replace every single pearl of inferior quality with these."

"We can try, but... that will require many additional hours of sewing."

"I'm already paying you more money than you deserve for my daughter's dress. We will be here first thing in the morning. See to it that all those inferior pearls are removed. Do you understand? Or are the two of you too ignorant to understand what I am telling you?"

"Of course, it will be our pleasure." Rebecca forced a smile. She held her cough until the Bulgarian left the shop. She didn't want the woman to yell at her for coughing near the bridal gown.

"Rebecca." Kiría Eleni hurried to her side. "I don't understand Bulgarian that well. But was she saying we needed to redo all the pearls on the dress?"

"Yes," Rebecca sighed and wiped her nose with a handkerchief.

"Why do I have these old eyes? I can't do that work anymore. You have to be home before five o'clock or you could be arrested as a Jew on the streets after curfew. You'll never get it done before then."

"I'll just stay here until it's finished. I can sleep overnight in your spare room and I'll go home tomorrow morning."

"I'm so sorry, Rebecca. I'll go over to your parents and tell them you won't be coming home tonight. If Andreas wasn't home, you could sleep in his room. That spare room isn't very comfortable. But I'll prepare it for you."

"I wish I felt better. I haven't been sleeping well with this cough. I'm so tired. I think I could sleep anywhere tonight."

"I am sorry you are forced to work late tonight, Rebecca."

"It's not your fault Kiría Eleni. Let me get to work. When you go to see my mother, please remind her to give my niece Julie the dress I sewed for her dolly. My mother has been so upset. I reminded her this morning, but she has been so distracted with the terrible things that have been happening. Yesterday we heard another cousin was taken away for forced labor. He is the third cousin that has been sent away from the family."

"These are terrible times," Kiría Eleni sighed.

Andreas looked up from his game of backgammon. It had been such a wonderful night, surrounded by their old friends. They drank, argued politics, ate *moussaka*, enjoyed *ravani* and played backgammon. The only thing missing, the only thing that made tonight different than those nights in the past, was the absence of any of their Jewish friends, who weren't allowed on the streets after five o'clock.

"How are Joseph Rouso and his family doing?" Artemis asked.

"His pharmacy was taken away. That was his pride and joy. How is it for a man when he can barely provide for his family?" his father answered.

"I worry about our Jewish friends," Andreas said and took another swallow of *ouzo*. "It's not just wearing Stars of David or having so much confiscated… I think about Germany and that time called *Kristalnacht*, when the Jewish businesses were broken into and people pulled out into the streets and beaten. Is that the next step? We don't have Nazis in our streets, but the Bulgarians are no better."

Andreas thought of Rebecca. How often he thought of her, every day wondering how she was, what she was doing... It was so hard to come back home for a visit, to see her and to pretend they had no feelings for each other. Today, his mother told him about a Bulgarian woman who was demanding last minute changes to a gown. The changes would require Rebecca to work long into the evening. She would have to spend the night in their spare room, because she couldn't leave to go home after 5 o'clock. Her eyes were runny and she had a cough. She should be home in her own bed tonight.

Andreas pulled out the watch from his vest pocket. It was almost two o'clock in the morning. "Time for us to go home," he told his father.

Kìrios Vassilis got to his feet and everyone gave hugs to their dear friends before they grabbed their heavy coats and walked out the door.

"It's cold," his father looked at their breaths frozen in the night air. "Let's hurry, before we freeze."

They were walking quickly in the frigid air when they suddenly were stopped by a line of troops blocking the entrance to their street. They walked cautiously toward the young men standing with rifles barring their way.

"Papers!" a short young man barked at them. "Are you Jews?"

"We are Orthodox Christians." They handed over their identification papers.

"You, this Andreas Sefaris. It says you are from Athens. What are you doing here in Kavala?"

"I am visiting my parents."

"Hmph." He handed their papers back to them. "Hurry on home and lock your doors when you get there."

"What's going on? Why are the streets blocked?"

"We are cordoning off this area to keep any Jews from escaping. We are taking away the Jews. This does not concern you. Now get going."

Andreas and his father tried not to break into a run. Taking away the Jews! Andreas's heart thundered in his chest. They stopped in front of the Solomons' house. Andreas watched in disbelief as Rebecca's brother, sister-in-law and small children came rushing out of the house. A soldier was at their back, pushing them with the butt of his rifle. "Please," Ephraim pleaded. He was silenced by a kick of a boot in his back.

"Shut up and go. You don't have time. The trucks are waiting for you."

Ephraim's children and his wife Sara were crying as they hurried toward the crowds of people who were streaming through the streets: women, children, infants, men, the old, the young and the sick.

Andreas walked up to a young soldier. "Why are they being forced out of their houses?"

"They are Jews. We don't want them in our country."

"Where are they going?"

"We have orders to take them to the empty tobacco warehouses."

Andreas and his father watched as Isaac and Esther came rushing out of their house, a soldier pushing them to walk faster.

"Your names?" A soldier peered down at a long list through his wire-rimmed glasses.

The Solomons gave their names and the soldier appeared to mark them off. He frowned at the paper. "Tell Rebecca Solomon to come out!"

"There is no one else in the house," said another soldier.

"Check everywhere, under the beds, in the closets! My list says Rebecca Solomon lives in this house. Twenty-nine years old."

"We will check again." The solider saluted and ran back into the house.

"Hey you, Isaac Solomon," the soldier addressed the older man. "Where is your daughter hiding in your house? Do you have a secret cellar in the floor?"

"My daughter is not home. You won't find her in the house. She left today to visit family in Drama."

"Jews are not allowed to change their residence. Who gave her permission to leave?"

"She is a headstrong girl," Isaac tried to explain.

"You should take better care of your own daughter." The older soldier took out his whip and lashed at Rebecca's father who tried to block the blows with his arm. "Dirty Jew! Hurry up! The trucks at the end of the street are waiting for you."

"Papá!" Rebecca's sister Klara ran to her parents. "What's happening?"

Her husband Carlo was carrying both their daughters. The child, Julie, who Andreas knew was Rebecca's favorite, was shrieking with terror.

"My dolly! I don't have my dolly!"

"Shh," Isaac tried to soothe his granddaughter as he offered to take her from her father. "We will get you another dolly where we are going."

"But I don't want another one! I want dolly!" she continued to scream.

As the crowd began to move, Andreas and his father hurried along with them.

"Where are you going!" a trooper yelled at them.

"We want to say goodbye. Please."

"Make it quick. "

Andreas and his father had stripped off their coats. They placed them over the shoulders of Isaac and Esther Solomon, who, in their haste, had only put on thin coats. As Andreas bent over to drape the coat around the older man, Isaac leaned toward him and whispered hoarsely in his ear.

"Take care of her, Andreas. Keep her safe." The man's eyes filled with tears. "Promise me."

"I will. I promise."

"Get away from them!" The trooper menaced Andreas and Patéra with his baton. "If you are interested, there will be an auction of all the household items tomorrow. Those Jews have such wonderful things in their houses. Maybe we will find the gold hidden in their walls."

"Where are they being taken?" Andreas asked again.

"To the tobacco warehouses."

"Why?"

"Because they are Jews. You are acquainted with this family?"

"They are our neighbors."

"I have a list of people in this house. It says there is a girl twenty-nine years old, Rebecca Solomon. Do you know where she is?"

"She is not at home with her family?"

"Stupid Greek! I would not have asked you if we found her! What can someone expect of you Greeks? Look at the Christian women weeping, giving small gifts to the Jews. What a pathetic sight. You must all be communist trash."

Andreas and his father eyed his mother, who had come out of the house, tears streaming down her face as she grabbed onto the hands of her Jewish neighbors who were being loaded into the back of trucks. Their eyes were wide with shock and terror, mothers clutching their babies against themselves in the frigid night air.

As Andreas watched the crowds of people streaming out of their houses and down the streets, a memory rose up before him. He was running beside his mother and Maria. His mother kept saying, "Run, don't look down," keeping their gaze away from the dead beneath their feet. Horses charging blindly in flight. No, no, he told himself and pushed the memory aside.

Rebecca. He must find her. Andreas felt the bile rise up in his throat. He hurried to his mother's side. "Mamá, where is Rebecca?" he whispered in fear.

"I forgot all about her. When I heard the commotion in the streets, I ran outside. My God, Rebecca!" his mother gasped. "I think she is still asleep. But maybe she heard all this commotion and she's out here, rounded up like an animal."

Andreas turned and ran back to his house as fast as he could. What if she woke up and saw what was happening to her people, to her family? Was she already outside being thrown into a truck?

CHAPTER 14

Bulgarian Zone of Occupation, Kavala Greece: March 3, 1943, 2:30 AM

ANDREAS DASHED PAST the sorrowful, terrified people, who were being herded through the narrow street. He tried to avoid their eyes filled with horror. Help me, help me, they seemed to be reaching out wordlessly to him. But how could he help them? He had no weapon and even if he had, he was only one man against the countless Bulgarian soldiers in the streets. He forced himself to look away as a feeling of helplessness and dread washed over him.

What had happened to Rebecca? Rebecca was gone. He knew she was gone. She had seen what was happening to her family and she had rushed outside to be with them. Maybe she couldn't find her family and she was all alone. Was she standing in a truck, shivering in the cold air with no one to warm her? He'd go with her. Wherever they were taking the Jews, he would go with her. He'd demand the soldiers let him go with her.

He reached his house and steadied himself on the door frame. Stirring from his buried memories, he saw himself on the quay and he heard the sound of a Turkish cavalry officer on his horse. And then he saw the soldier on horseback and his mother was holding onto his boot. She was sobbing, pleading for Maria. Andreas couldn't catch his breath. That night so long ago, what had he done? What had he not done? Had he tried to save his mother? As it flashed in front of him, he remembered. He had curled up into a ball and prayed that the soldier wouldn't kill him. A coward. He was a coward. He hadn't tried to save his mother and Maria. Why didn't he shoot the soldier on horseback? Why didn't he use the gun? What was wrong with him? His father always told him, "Make us proud of you. The name of Sefaris should only reflect honor. It should never be shamed."

And tonight, he had stayed too long with his friends, drinking and laughing, while Rebecca was being taken away. He was too late to save

Rebecca. Would he ever see her again? Ever hold her in his arms? He'd go to the tobacco warehouses and find her. He'd bribe them, anything, he'd do anything to save her. But it was too late. He knew it was too late.

He took a deep breath, opened the front door and ducked beneath the door frame. Inside the house, he grabbed a lantern to illuminate his way up to the spare room and raced up the stairs two at a time. He felt as if his heart was going to burst in his chest. He couldn't catch his breath and he clung to the stair railing, sweat dripping off his forehead. No, he couldn't let this happen to him. That feeling of panic and anxiety that would immobilize him. It had happened to him before. No, no, not now. He needed to see if she was there or not. He must start searching for her. Rebecca! She had heard the commotion outside. She was gone! Everyone he ever loved was gone. He was a curse on them. A terrible curse! He took a deep breath and continued racing up the stairs.

The door to the spare room was closed. He threw it open and raised the lantern. Under the quilt there was something, someone was there... he wasn't sure.

"Rebecca?" his voice filled the small room.

She stirred and opened her eyes filled with bewilderment.

"*Efharistó Thee mou.* Thank God," he whispered a prayer of thanksgiving, and made the sign of the cross across his chest. "Rebecca," he breathed in relief.

"Andreas?" She sat up in the bed, a quilt pulled up to her chin against the cold air of the room. "What's the matter? What's wrong?"

He rushed to her side and gathered her in his arms. Rebecca was safe. "Rebecca," he breathed in relief, "Rebecca."

"You're hurting me. Don't hold me so tight. Andreas, you're shaking. Why are you here in the middle of the night? You can't be up here. It isn't...."

"I'm sorry. I didn't mean to hurt you." He loosened his embrace and stared down at her face, her beautiful face. She was safe. She was here. He could breathe again.

"What's happened?" Her eyes widened with fear.

"It's alright. You're safe."

"Of course, I'm safe. What's happened?" she asked again.

"You need to come with me. You need to look out the window."

"Why do I need to look out the window? It's still dark. Isn't it the middle of the night? You're scaring me."

Andreas held the lantern and grabbed Rebecca's hand, guiding her to the shuttered window.

He pulled back the shutters and revealed the street, illuminated by glowing lights.

"*A Dio!* My God! What's happening!" Rebecca gasped. "All those people in the street! All those Bulgarian soldiers! Are we supposed to go out? Do I need to get dressed?"

"No, no Rebecca. The people in the street are all Jews. They have been roused out of their beds in the middle of the night, forced to walk in the streets until they reach trucks that will take them away."

"Why? Why are they doing that? What about my family? Surely they are okay, safe in their houses. They haven't done anything wrong. I need to go home and make sure they are alright."

"Rebecca, all the Jews in Kavala have been rounded up."

"All of them? My family? Mamá? Papá? That's not possible. You're wrong. But what about the children? Who will take care of the children? I need to get to them and take care of them. Surely they can't have made the children come out in the middle of the night? Why? I need to go to the children and help them. Why didn't they take me?"

"You don't understand, Rebecca. Every Jew in Kavala was thrown out of their dwellings... old, young, sick, everyone, even babies. The Bulgarian soldiers have a list of everyone who lives in each place and they are checking them off so no one will remain. No one can hide from them."

"No, Andreas. You are wrong! That can't be! What about me?"

"Your name is associated with your parents' house. When they asked for you, your father said you had gone to Drama."

"My father said that? How do you know?"

"I was able to spend a few minutes with him before he was forced down the street with the others."

"I don't understand. I need to get dressed and go outside. I have to be with my family. If they are being taken away, I have to go with them." She turned away and reached for her clothes.

"Your father tried to shield you Rebecca. He doesn't want you to be with them. He told me to keep you safe. He made me promise," Andreas said with anguish in his voice.

Rebecca stood still. "Andreas, what's happening? What did the Jews do? I have to be with my family. I have to. The children, they must be so frightened. I have to help with the children. Julie, I made her a new dress for her doll." Tears started to stream down her face. "I have to be with my family."

Andreas took her clothes away from her gently. "No, Rebecca. You aren't going anywhere. You are staying right here." He put his arms around her.

"Give me back my clothes!" she yelled at him through her tears. "I am not staying here!" She tried to push away from him.

Andreas grabbed hold of her shoulders. "Look at me. You are not going down there. They are taking everyone to the tobacco warehouses."

"Then I will go to the tobacco warehouses to be with my family. My parents are getting older. I need to be with them, to help them!" She again tried to push away from him.

"I told you, your father asked me to keep you safe. Do you understand what I'm telling you! Rebecca, the soldiers are treating everyone brutally, forcing them out of their houses in the dead of night in the freezing cold. Bulgarians have evil intent toward them. I don't know what is going to happen to them in the warehouses. But you aren't going there."

Rebecca stopped pushing against him and collapsed in his arms. He held her close as she began to sob. "Shh," he tried to soothe her. "I will keep you safe. I will keep you safe. I'll never let anything happen to you."

"Why is this happening?" she asked in between sobs.

"I don't know why they are rounding up the Jews. Why were the Greek Orthodox Christians killed by the Turks? There is so much evil in this world, when one group is identified as being different, less than the others. It never makes sense, but it keeps happening."

∞

Andreas, Rebecca, Vassilis and Eleni sat around the kitchen table with only a solitary candle to light the darkness. The shutters were closed to prevent any light being cast into the street. They didn't want to cause any attention to their house by bright light shining from the windows in the middle of the night.

Kiría Eleni poured tea for Rebecca. "Drink some more. It will help you feel better," she urged.

"Feel better?" Rebecca was bewildered. How could she feel better? Where were her parents, her sisters and brothers, their children? Why had this terrible thing happened?

"It will help your cold." Andreas's mother frowned as Rebecca coughed into her hand.

"We need to have a plan," Kiríos Vassilis began. "Rebecca, we can't hide you here for very long."

"I want to be with my parents. I need to be with them. You said they were taken to the tobacco warehouses. Please, I need to go there to be with them," she tried to make them understand.

Kìrios Vassilis looked down at his hands and said nothing.

"If you don't take me there, I'll go by myself," Rebecca said with defiance.

"Now, Rebecca Solomon," Kìrios Vassilis said sternly. "You are staying right here where you are safe, until we can decide what to do."

"Alright," Rebecca acquiesced. She didn't mean to be disrespectful to this family who was trying to help her.

"Eleni." He turned to his wife. "Andreas and I need to go out for a while."

"Where are you going in the middle of the night?" asked his wife.

"We're going to see Father Leonidas."

"Who is that? Can he help me get back to my people?" Rebecca asked with desperation.

"He is a Greek priest who has gone underground after most of the Greek priests were forced to leave by the Bulgarians." Kiríos Vassilis got to his feet.

"Rebecca, at first light, I will go out and try to find out what is happening in the warehouses," Andreas said. "They may let me in because I am a doctor, even though I am Greek. But you aren't going anywhere now.

Remember, your father made me promise to keep you safe. For now, you need to go back up to the spare room."

It was still dark when Kiría Eleni tapped on the door and told her to come down to the kitchen.

Rebecca's whole body felt numb. In those few hours when she laid on the bed, the quilt pulled up to her chin, she kept seeing her family, the children being pulled out of their houses, thrown into trucks. Tobacco warehouses? Surely they weren't going to live in the warehouses? But where were they going? Andreas would find out. Maybe she could join her family when they arrived at wherever they were going.

Papá had told Andreas to keep her safe. What did that mean? It meant she shouldn't go with them. If Papá told the soldier she was in Drama that meant he didn't want her to be with them. But where could she go by herself? She knew she couldn't stay here. People would recognize her as Rebecca Solomon, a Jewess. She had those false identification papers. But where could she live all by herself? And she didn't want to leave Andreas. She believed when he said he would keep her safe. Their love for each other, though so impossible, seemed the only thing to which she could cling. She stood by the window looking down onto the empty street, now littered with papers, children's toys, pieces of lives interrupted. She hadn't been expelled from her house and taken away. But life as she knew it had vanished before her eyes and was replaced by nothing but a vast hole in her heart. She had been torn from her family because chance, in the form of that terrible Bulgarian matron and her expensive pearls, had changed the course of her life for the near future.

Rebecca walked downstairs to the kitchen. Somehow the warmth of the kitchen didn't matter as the coldness that enveloped her wasn't in the air. It had settled into her soul.

Everyone was again seated around the kitchen table. Kiría Eleni had put out some sweets, but no one touched the food.

"Rebecca," Kirios Vassilis began. "Very soon it will be daylight and people will start coming into the shops. You will have to go upstairs to the spare room and stay there. You could live here in hiding. But I worry that people know how close we are and they might also know you weren't taken in the round up. Someone, who is collaborating with the Bulgarians, will mention something to an official and our premises will be searched. We are trying to find some other way of keeping you safe and honor your father's wishes."

"I have those false papers," she offered.

"Yes, you do. But where would you go by yourself? A lone woman? We have family in many places, but I don't know who we could trust. Who would take you in without asking too many questions? There is another possibility," he paused and looked at Andreas.

Andreas cleared his throat. "Rebecca," he said as he took her hand in his own. "You know that I love you. Rebecca, marry me. If you married me, I could protect you."

Rebecca swallowed hard and looked at the table. Marry Andreas? Her thoughts spun in confusion. Yesterday morning was like any other since the occupation. The worst part of the day was having a miserable cold and having to work until late in the night, resewing all those pearls. She had said goodbye to her parents in the morning, not knowing... Would she ever see them again? And today she sat in the Matsakis kitchen with her world turned upside down. The only reality was the man who sat holding her hand, the look of love in his dark eyes as he asked her to marry him.

"Rebecca," Kiría Eleni spoke up. "Vassilis and Andreas went to visit the priest to see if he would marry you to Andreas."

"What did he say?" Rebecca looked back at Andreas, his eyes filled with devotion.

"Father Leonidas would baptize you and then marry us all at one time. He is a good man. He has known our family for years. He can be trusted to keep your identity safe," Andreas explained.

"I... I," Rebecca stammered, unsure of what to say. "Baptize me? I don't understand."

"You must be baptized as a Greek Orthodox Christian in order for the priest to marry you," Kìrios Vassilis told her.

How could she be baptized, become a Christian? She couldn't do that. She was a Jew.

"I can't. I can't." The tears welled up in her eyes.

"Rebecca, it's the only way to keep you safe. Someday, this madness will be over and you will be a Jewish woman again." She knew Andreas was trying to comfort her.

"But, Andreas, you always said you would never marry," she reminded him, trying to move the conversation from the ominous decision she needed to make. Marrying Andreas, marrying the man she loved... But giving up her faith, becoming a Christian. "Keep her safe," her father had told Andreas. Did she need to become a Christian to be safe? When this terrible time was over for the Jews, she would live as a Jewess again. In her heart, she knew she could never be a Christian.

"My father and I talked about that." Andreas smiled at her and squeezed her hand. "He told me I had to give up these nonsense ideas. That is the word you used, wasn't it, Patéra? I had nonsense ideas that anyone I married was doomed. If I don't protect you by making you my wife, I fear you will suffer the catastrophe that is befalling your people. I know it will be hard to give up your Jewish identity."

"But what if the Jews will be in the tobacco warehouse just for a few days... Maybe they'll let everyone go back to their houses," said Rebecca.

"Rebecca, we were told that tomorrow there will be an auction of the household contents of all the Jewish dwellings. No Jewish family will be coming back to their houses. In the morning, I will try to find out what is happening in the warehouse," Andreas told her.

"I want to be with my family," Rebecca whispered, a tear slipping down her cheek. "I'm a Jew. I can't become a Christian. How can I turn my back on who I am?"

Light began to stream through the shutters. She had to wait through the long daylight hours until darkness fell again. She couldn't go downstairs while customers were inside the cobbler and dress shops. She listened to the comings and goings in the shops as she waited for darkness and the dark shadows which announced the closing of the shops.

A gentle tapping summoned Rebecca to the door. Andreas stood there, alone.

"Did you see my parents?" she asked anxiously.

"I wasn't able to get inside the warehouses. But I did speak to some Bulgarian soldiers. I was told that everyone is crammed inside the warehouses in appalling conditions, with very few latrines. They have almost no food. The rumor is they will be sent first to Drama and then to Poland."

Rebecca felt ill. Her mother, Papá, her sisters, the children... How could this be happening to her family? What had they done to deserve this? Was it because the Jews refused to collaborate against the Greek Orthodox when asked by the Bulgarians? "Why is this happening?" she whispered in despair, although she knew Andreas had no answer.

"I'm sorry my love," he paused. "There is nothing that can be done to stop what is happening to your people. But by the grace of God, you have escaped this madness. Please Rebecca, please agree to be my wife. We love each other. I will be a good husband to you. I will care for you and protect you for as long as I shall live." He held his arms out to her and she leaned against his chest, taking comfort in his nearness as he embraced her. He made her feel safe in spite of the madness that had descended upon the world. They belonged together. They had always belonged to each other.

"Yes." She smiled up at him. "I will marry you. Of course I will marry you."

"I have something for you." He released her from his embrace. He pulled out a piece of cloth from his vest pocket and unwrapped a golden jeweled crucifix. "It is my wedding present for you. It belonged to my mother. I've kept it for all these years. It's all I have left of her. Our maid Sophia gave it to me after my mother was murdered. It's her *stavrós*, her cross. As a good Greek Orthodox woman you must have a *stavrós* and I thought my mother would be happy to know I had given it to my wonderful bride."

Rebecca looked down at the cross in his large hands. She took a deep breath. A cross, a cross for her, a Jewish woman, to wear around her neck? But it was precious. It belonged to his mother and he had kept it with him for all these years. Survive, she thought, I must survive. For my family, I must survive. When this madness was over, her family would need her to help them. She would go to Poland and help take care of them.

"Rebecca," Andreas said in a soft loving voice. "Many years ago you saved my life, even though you were just a little girl. You brought me to the Matsakis family. They loved me and took care of me and gave me a family. I never forgot my family from Smyrna. They live in my heart. And today I give you a new life, a life with me. You will never forget who you really are, a Greek Jew. Someday, you will again be a Jewish woman. I promise you."

⤜❧⤏

"Rebecca," Kiría Eleni had taken her aside after she and Andreas had come downstairs, to tell them they were ready to go to the priest. "You are doing the right thing. We want to keep you safe. I am so pleased to welcome you into our family. You know you've always been like a daughter to me. Someday when this awful time has ended, you and Andreas will be able to come back to Kavala. But tomorrow morning, you will take the ferry to Salonika."

"Thank you for helping me." Rebecca gave her a hug.

"How could we not help you? We had to save you from whatever those horrible Bulgarians had planned for you as a Jewish woman. We promise as soon as we learn more about your family, we will contact you. Andreas said they may be going to Poland. When we find out where they have gone, we will let you know. I'm sure you will be able to write to them. They will want to know you are safe and well."

A wedding dress had been found, a dress intended for another bride. But tonight the bridal gown would be hers. Although Rebecca said it wasn't necessary, Kiría Eleni held up the gown and smiled. "You and the bride are the same size. This isn't the wedding ceremony that you may have imagined, but at least you will have a proper dress," Kiría Eleni insisted. "You look beautiful."

The cellar where the priest was going to meet them was dark, illuminated only by candles. The priest's wife led them inside and left them while they waited for her husband to join them. Kiría and Kìrios Matsakis stood beside them. Rebecca watched as the priest hurried into the darkened room.

"I have all the papers here." He put them down on the small cloth-covered table that served as an altar.

Rebecca looked at the icons on the walls. She forced herself to look away from them as the priest went over the papers he had produced. "First, I have Katerina's baptism certificate, dated from 1915, the year she was born. And I have a marriage decree from the Greek Orthodox Church. It's not recognized here in this occupied area, but once you enter the German or Italian zone, your marriage will be accepted as genuine."

And so Rebecca, now called Katerina, stood beside Andreas after a hasty baptism ceremony. With their hands joined together, the *stephana*, the Greek crowns that had been used many years ago for Eleni's and Vassilis's wedding ceremony, were placed upon their heads. Three times the *stephana* were exchanged upon their heads. They drank from a goblet of sanctified wine. Holding a candle, they walked in three circles around the altar.

This wasn't like the ceremony she had shared with David. Her parents and her family had surrounded them as they stood beneath the *chupah*, the canopy, with the Rabbi chanting the wedding blessings upon them. "*Mazel Bueno*" had been called out to them. "Good luck." But those good wishes had proven meaningless for her union with that self-centered man.

And now tonight, in the dark cellar, away from the prying eyes of the Bulgarians, she had been baptized as a Greek Orthodox Christian. She gathered her strength from deep inside her as she listened to the priest's words and felt the presence and love of the man beside her. All of these people were risking imprisonment or far worse by protecting her and giving her a path for a new life. She listened to the priest bless them and pronounce them man and wife. Rebecca had become Kiría Katerina Sefaris.

Kiría Eleni shed tears of happiness as her husband put his arm around her.

Andreas looked at her. Her husband now... but once, a long time ago, he was a sad boy. He was a part of her and he would always be. Someday when she was reunited with her family in Poland, they would understand the decision she had made today.

◈

Andreas covered her with a quilt as they laid back in contentment within each other's arms. He kissed the top of her head and pulled her closer. His wife. He swore he'd never have a wife, a woman he might love, a woman he might lose. But Rebecca... no, he must remember she was Katerina. He had loved her ever since she was a little girl. He knew the beauty of her soul, the compassion of her heart, her goodness. She was also a passionate woman. And tonight, he told himself, he was indeed the most fortunate of men to have her as his wife.

"Andreas?" she asked as she stirred in his arms.

"Yes, Katerina?"

"How will I ever get used to a new name…"

"You will. That's why I will only call you Katerina, even in our private moments."

"There's something I want to mention. Something in this rush for our marriage that we haven't talked about. I know you are being careful about a pregnancy, but…."

"But what?"

"You know I am not a young woman," she began.

"I'm shocked." He laughed at her. "How could I forget how old you are? You are exactly the same age as I am. I am twenty-nine years old and so are you."

"Don't make fun of me." She smiled at him. "It's just that I might be too old to have children. I'm sorry. I never conceived when I was with David."

"Katerina, you forget that before the war my specialty was gynecology and obstetrics. It's only recently that I have been forced to work as a surgeon or as whatever else the Nazis in Athens want me to do. So you see, for most of my career, I delivered babies. Not having conceived in a few months of marriage means nothing. I assure you I have delivered many babies of women older than you… "

"I know how important it is for a man to have children, especially a son."

"Who in their right mind would want to bring a child into this terrible world?" he asked. A child? Even if the world wasn't such a terrible place, he never wanted to have a child. Someone else he could lose, someone else he might not be able to protect.

"A child means life, new beginnings," she offered.

"This is not the time to have a child," he responded. He didn't need to tell her he would never want a child, not ever. Not even if the Axis Powers were overcome and thrown out of Greece. There would always be some other evil force waiting to do harm, wanting to massacre children, just as he had witnessed so long ago on the quay in Smyrna. The slaying of the innocent, so many innocents.

"I hope I don't wake you up tonight. My nightmares have returned since the occupation. I never used to remember them when I woke up. I was sure they were about what happened in Smyrna. But now I am remembering, suddenly I can remember everything. Katerina, you have married a coward."

Rebecca sat up in bed. "What are you talking about?"

"I've been remembering what I've tried so hard to never recall. In Smyrna, I killed a Turk who had broken into our house. He had stabbed my father with his sword. I grabbed a gun and I shot him over and over again. But when I needed to defend my mother and my sister, I didn't shoot the Turk on his horse. I was a coward. I remember my mother trying to save my sister, pleading for her. I saw the soldier kicking her as she tried to hold onto his boot. I remember falling down on the cobblestones, praying for my own life. I should have taken the gun and killed him. But I didn't. I was a coward. It was because of me that he killed my mother and took my sister. You said I wasn't at fault for my father's murder. But my mother... she was a defenseless woman."

"Andreas, you were eight years old. You were a child. Who knows what happened to the gun. You don't remember that you had the gun, do you?"

"No, but... "

"Andreas, you were eight years old. An eight year old child cannot fight off the Turkish army."

"I should have saved my mother. I was a coward."

"Andreas, you are wrong," she said softly, taking his hand in her own. "Andreas, you were eight years old. You were a mere child. Who knows what happened to the gun after you killed the soldier. You were as helpless as the children who were rounded up by the Bulgarians." She swallowed. "Could one of these children, one of these boys have saved his parents? Think, Andreas, think. You are holding yourself responsible for something you couldn't have prevented," she reached over and smoothed a stray lock of dark hair off his forehead.

"I should have saved them."

"You couldn't have saved them. You were eight years old, just a little boy," she told him.

"That's why I couldn't remember what happened. I didn't want to remember because I couldn't face what I'd done."

"Oh, Andreas, I told you before, the reason you couldn't remember the killing of your parents, the kidnapping of your sister is because that was so terrible. You were only a child who witnessed what no one should ever see. Certainly it was too much for the eyes and the heart of a child. That's why you couldn't remember. Your mind was shielding you from those horrors."

"Katerina, do you really think that's true?"

"I know that's true. I am proud to have you as my husband."

The next day, Kiría Eleni gathered a few dresses intended for their clients who were close in size to Rebecca. Her new mother-in-law contributed some of her own underthings and an old suitcase was found.

"I will be delighted to tell those Bulgarian women that their dresses are being delayed and they will have to wait." Kiría Eleni gave her a huge hug. "Now, put this on." She wrapped a scarf around Rebecca's neck and chin.

Rebecca looked at the woman who was now her mother-in-law, the woman she loved like a second mother. "I will miss you," she sighed and then put aside her melancholy feelings. "I'm feeling a lot better today. My cold is almost gone. Why do I need a scarf? I don't think it's that cold this morning," Rebecca observed. "Why haven't we left yet? Hasn't the ferry started boarding already?"

"You must catch the ferry right before it is scheduled to leave," Kìrios Vlassis told her.

"Why?"

"Because we don't want the authorities who check passengers to have time to look over your papers. Your papers are impeccable, but let's not give anyone too much time to look at them. The longer you are standing in a line waiting to board the ferry, the greater your risk to be identified by someone here in Kavala who might know you. You must bundle yourself up behind that scarf. Make no eye contact with anyone. Once we get to Salonika and depart from the ferry, everything will be fine," Andreas told her.

"But, Andreas, there are many Jews who left Kavala and fled to Salonika. I might meet someone who knows me."

"You won't meet any Jews who know you."

"Why not?"

"Because the Jews were all sent to areas of the city where they are fenced in with barbed wire. They weren't rounded up in the middle of the night, but they had to leave their houses and go to designated areas where they are permitted to live."

"In Salonika? But that is the area of the German occupation. I thought it was only the Bulgarians who were so horrible, forcing Jews out of their houses."

Andreas didn't answer her.

"Andreas," Kìrios Vassilis addressed his son. "I was able to contact my brother in Salonika. I shared that you would be bringing your new bride, Katerina, with you. I know he will have a warm welcome for you."

They kissed and hugged his parents goodbye. "You will come to visit us if the Bulgarians will allow you to travel. We can't come back here because Reb…. Katerina could be identified as a Jew," Andreas told them.

"We know that, son. We will come and visit. Maybe someday you will have a grandchild to show us," his mother smiled at them.

Andreas looked down at his watch. "It's time to go." He picked up their suitcases and they were on their way.

"Look at your feet. Don't make eye contact," he cautioned as they made their way down the narrow cobblestone streets to the harbor.

The ferry bobbed up and down in the choppy water as snow clouds gathered on the horizon. Just as they had planned, there was no line to board, as everyone had already made their way up the gang plank. The ferry blasted its horn. It was about to leave.

"Papers!" the soldier barked at them. "You are late. The ferry is leaving."

"My wife forgot her favorite frock and we had to return home to retrieve it. You know how these women are." Andreas rolled his eyes in exasperation.

"Fine, fine." The soldier briefly glanced at their papers and urged them up the gangplank.

Andreas found them a place to sit, as far away from the other passengers as possible. But the boat was crowded and there weren't many seats available for them to sit with their suitcases.

"Keep your scarf around your face, just in case," Andreas cautioned her.

"Andreas, look over there. That couple, they lived down the street. They are going to recognize me." She looked in the direction of a young couple with a boy who were seated beside their luggage.

"Don't make eye contact. Come, I'll put my arm around you. Cough, put your face against me. Remember, Katerina, you aren't feeling well."

Rebecca did as he instructed. The boat blew its horn again and began its journey out of the harbor, away from the only home she had ever known, away from her family. But she needed to focus on new beginnings... on her husband and her new life. She must not keep thinking about her family or the sadness would overwhelm her.

The neighbors who Rebecca had identified, were looking out at the water, paying no attention to Rebecca and Andreas. He held her closer and she looked up at him.

"I love you," she told him.

"My wife, I love you so," he spoke to her in a soft voice. "It's going to be alright. We will be safe in Salonika. According to my father, my uncle is very well-connected."

"You said the Jews have been rounded up there as well. Can I go to visit, to help them?" she asked in a low tone.

"You can't do that, Katerina. You can never do anything to call attention to yourself. Do you understand?"

"Yes, yes. I understand," she sighed. "If all the Jews are being sent to Poland, do you think they will all be going to the same place?"

"I don't know," he told her.

"My family doesn't speak Polish. It will be hard for them," she mused sadly.

She closed her eyes letting the motion of the boat lull her to sleep. They both dozed on the hard bench and then ate some of the food his mother had prepared for them. The horn blasted again. They were arriving at the port of Salonika. People were pointing at the White Tower, the iconic structure of a cylindrical drum that was perched near the waterfront.

Andreas carried their suitcases to the railing with Rebecca at his side. Down on the pier he saw his uncle, Theo Constantine, flanked by officers of the Nazi Gestapo.

CHAPTER 15

Salonika, German Zone of Occupation: March 5, 1943

AS THEY STOOD beside each other on the ferry deck, Andreas gripped their suitcases. His eyes narrowed in apprehension while he watched the line of passengers disembarking the boat, being met by the Nazi officers who were checking identification papers. And out of the corner of his eye, he continued to watch Uncle Constantine, standing beside two Gestapo officers.

Rebecca moved closer to his side. He gave her a reassuring smile that he didn't feel. But he needed to alleviate her fears, even if he was worried about the Gestapo standing beside his uncle. A mix of emotions... trepidation for bringing his Jewish bride into a city occupied by Nazis, joy at finally being united with the woman he loved.

If only he hadn't had that outburst about the Jews when he was in Athens. But when anyone said something disparaging about his people, the refugees from Asia Minor, he was set off and forgot himself. And then that night in the *taverna* in Athens, he'd compared what was befalling the Jews to what had happened to his own people, and how terrible it was to be oppressed and singled out just because of mindless prejudice. Rebecca's identity would have been so much easier to hide in Athens, which was under Italian control. The Italians had been dismissive of the German demand to round up the Jews. He no longer had the luxury of speaking his mind... He had the responsibility of a wife. They would now be living in an area of Greece under Nazi control and Rebecca would have to be careful to conceal her Jewish identity.

Andreas and Rebecca's eyes widened as an old man with hunched shoulders at the bottom of the gangplank was being shouted at by the Nazi officers. "False papers! You disgusting Jew. I can always tell a Jew when I see one." The tall officer hit him over the head with a baton. "You will be taken to the Jewish quarter immediately."

"Please, sir. I'm not a Jew. I'm an Orthodox Christian. I lost my papers and I paid to have these new ones made." The man tried to shield himself from the blows of the wooden stick.

"Liar! Prove you are not a Jew."

"My *stavrós*." He pulled out the crucifix from beneath his shirt that was hung around his neck.

The soldier yanked on the man's crucifix, breaking the chain. The Nazi sneered at it and threw it down on the pier as the man's face contorted with horror. "Anyone can hang a cross around his neck! Pull down your pants!" the Nazi barked.

The old man looked around in embarrassment.

"Hurry up!"

The man opened his coat and pulled down his pants. "Please, I told you I'm a Christian."

"Hmphh. Pull up your pants. What are you doing here in Salonika?"

"I've come to be with my son's family."

"Be on your way." The soldier pushed him so hard, the old man fell down on the dock. All the other passengers waiting in line seemed frozen... afraid to help the man lest the Nazi turn his wrath upon them.

The old man struggled to get to his feet.

"*Pappoùs*!" A young man from the waiting crowd ran forward to help his grandfather.

Andreas turned his attention away from the sad scene with the old man and back to his uncle standing on the dock, flanked by the unsmiling Gestapo officers.

Rebecca placed her hand in the crook of his arm.

"Dr. Sefaris?" said a young blonde Nazi soldier as he approached.

"Yes," Andreas answered in German.

"Please, this way. Herr Matsakis, your uncle, said to come with me. Do not wait in line." He bowed politely to Rebecca. "Frau Sefaris."

Andreas and Rebecca followed the young man down the gangplank. Andreas watched with relief as the two Gestapo agents gave his uncle a *Seig Heil* and walked away before he and Rebecca reached him.

⁂

Rebecca sat at the dining room table staring in disbelief at the display of food arranged on the lace tablecloth. "So much food," she murmured.

"Wonderful, isn't it?" Theo Constantine beamed.

"I didn't realize there was so much food here in Salonika. In Kavala, we had difficulty getting enough to eat, especially in the winter."

"Oh, Katerina, our household has been blessed by my husband's special connections," Andreas's aunt, Thea Margarita, told them. "Food is no problem for us."

"You are fortunate," Rebecca did her best to compliment Thea Margarita. The woman with curly dark hair, streaked with gray, had been warm and welcoming to her this evening.

"And tonight, in honor of your arrival, we have a very special dish. I had schnitzel prepared for you. It is a special German dish," said Theo Constantine with a smile.

"Schnitzel? We didn't have that dish in Kavala. We were occupied by the Bulgarians, not the Germans. I've never heard of schnitzel," Rebecca told him.

"Pork, my dear. Fried with bread crumbs. So tasty." Theo Constantine grinned. "We are learning to appreciate so much of what the Germans are teaching us, their food, and their customs."

Pork? Never in her life had she eaten pork. Jews were prohibited from eating pork. She could feel Andreas's eyes upon her. Rebecca helped herself to the food on the plates that were offered to her.

"Katerina, please have more." Theo Constantine heaped a large portion on her plate.

"Thank you," Rebecca said in a firm voice. She cut herself a piece of schnitzel with her silver fork and knife.

"Eat, eat," the middle-aged man with gray hair and a clipped mustache urged her.

Don't be a fool, she told herself. It's meat and you have barely had any in months. You are Katerina Sefaris, a Greek Orthodox woman. Would the wrath of God strike her down for this transgression? Nonsense, she told herself.

"We are so glad to have you in our home, in our wonderful city, Katerina. Andreas's father, my brother, feared his son would never marry. Vassilis shared with me how you had to marry in secret to have the blessing of a Greek Orthodox priest. Those Bulgarians are so backward, throwing out the Greek Orthodox priests. You will be much happier living in the German Zone of occupation. The conditions in Eastern Macedonia under the Bulgarians have become unbearable. Andreas, your parents should leave."

"Kavala is their home," Andreas explained as he helped himself to another slice of bread. "They'll never leave."

"Well, my brother is in the minority. If my brother came here, I would find him and Eleni suitable lodging. They would have a good life here. For the others coming to Salonika, it is different. Salonika has been deluged with so many Greeks fleeing the Bulgarian Zone. There is no housing for them. We have already been plagued with thousands of refugees from Asia Minor who came here twenty years ago. And now, to have thousands more descend upon us. What are we supposed to do with them? We had a housing shortage before this influx. The refugees from Asia Minor still live like animals. Thousands more are coming in. Where are they going to live?"

"But... ," Thea Margarita interjected. "The Jews left all these beautiful houses and apartments. The refugees could live in them."

"Most of those houses and apartments are too nice for the likes of them," Theo Constantine replied as he frowned with distaste and took a large swallow of red wine. "In the poorer sections of town, the riffraff ran to the evacuated Jewish houses and stripped the walls, the floors, looking for hidden Jewish gold. Their wanton destruction made the dwellings uninhabitable. You know, of course, I have been honored to have been appointed the head of the Service for the Disposal of Jewish Property. And I have a big surprise for you, nephew. I have selected the most wonderful apartment for you and your new bride. Fabulous windows with a view of the sea, a large backyard and a veranda."

Rebecca forced herself to pay attention to the conversation discussing where she was going to live with her husband... an apartment where Jews had lived and were forced to vacate.

"I have kept several of the better properties intact. For the lesser properties, as I said, the squatters descended upon them, stripping the walls, the floor boards, looking for valuables they were sure the Jews had hidden before they left. But I assure you that your apartment is in pristine condition."

"The Jews were also rounded up in Kavala. Where will all these Jews be going?" Rebecca tried to sound nonchalant.

"Who knows? Who cares? What's important is that soon all of Greece will be *Juden Frei*. No more Jews in Salonika, thank goodness."

Rebecca forced herself to swallow the forkful of pork. *Juden frei*, free of Jews. Would her family be safe in Poland? She remembered the history of her people that Papá had taught her. More than five hundred years ago, the Jews in Spain had been forced to flee for their lives. The head of the Ottoman Empire had accepted them warmly into what was now Greece. Would Poland give them, give her family, a warm reception and a place where they could prosper and flourish? Rebecca took a large swallow of red wine from the fine crystal goblet.

"Such beautiful crystal," Rebecca tried to change the conversation.

"Those Jews had the finest things."

"I don't understand."

"The delicate china we are eating on tonight, the crystal goblets, my Constantine got them for me when the Jews left. It's a good thing they couldn't take everything with them. Just one suitcase."

Rebecca put down her goblet, pretending to examine it. "You're fortunate to have such a thoughtful husband," she managed to say.

Andreas reached under the tablecloth and squeezed her hand.

I'm Katerina Sefaris, a Greek Orthodox Christian woman. I came into existence yesterday, she told herself. Everything before, including Rebecca Solomon, no longer exists, never existed. But she did exist. I can't! I can't! I can't sit here eating forbidden pork off the fine china that belonged to a family who had been forced to leave everything behind. There is a Jewish woman who received this fine china, crystal goblets, and engraved silverware as wedding presents. Or perhaps they were family heirlooms? Rebecca thought she was going to be sick.

Andreas squeezed her hand again. "So, Theo Constantine, tell us about your sons Roilos and Stathis. And are your younger brothers still in America?"

"Our two sons, Roilos and Stathis, have also gone to America. We have four grandchildren we've never seen. They were going to come home for a visit, but since the war began there is no entry into Greece. Someday soon, the Allies will be defeated and surrender to Nazi Germany. Then things will be back to normal, but even better than before the war. Our family has done well in America. My brother Kostos has several restaurants and my brother Nicolas has a son who has become a physician, just like you, Andreas. He lives in Chicago. Our sons are living in New York. They tell us there are many Greeks in Chicago and New York. We're hoping all is well with them. We have no way of knowing, since no mail comes from America anymore."

Rebecca forced another forkful of pork down her throat. She took a swallow of wine.

"So, Katerina, tell us how you met?"

Rebecca was looking down at her plate.

"Katerina?" Thea Margarita addressed her again.

Katerina? Katerina? Yes, of course, that was her.

"How we met? Well, we have known each other since childhood." Rebecca managed a smile.

"And I've loved her ever since I first saw her, with those long braids trailing down her back," Andreas interjected.

"Ah, a love match!" his aunt said with approval.

"So, my nephew, why did it take you so long to propose marriage to your childhood sweetheart?" Theo Constantine chuckled.

"While I was pursuing my education, my Katerina married someone else. And then when I came home to Kavala last month, I learned she had been widowed. This time, I had the good sense not to wait."

Rebecca forced her thoughts away from the Jewish families who had been ordered to give up their possessions. She gave Andreas a smile as she listened to him relate the story they had rehearsed between them. "No, he didn't wait," she continued the narrative. "We found a Greek Orthodox priest who agreed to marry us quickly before we left for Salonika."

"Of course, we could have waited until we arrived here. We wouldn't have needed to seek out a Greek Orthodox priest who had gone underground. But we didn't want to wait a day longer," Andreas explained.

"Or a night longer?" his uncle said with a wink.

"Constantine, stop that," his wife admonished him.

"Katerina," Thea Margarita addressed her. "I must compliment you on that dress you are wearing. It looks straight out of the latest fashion magazines. It's so stylish and well made. Now that all the Jewish seamstresses have been sent to the ghettos, I don't know where we will get fashionable clothes. They were so expert at what they did. There are other seamstresses. Many of the refugees from Asia Minor became seamstresses when they came here twenty years ago."

"Yes, they did," Andreas commented. "When the refugees came from Asia Minor, there were only women, children and old people who survived the expulsion. All able-bodied men were taken away, never to be heard from again. What were those poor women to do to support their families? If they could, they pooled their meager funds together and purchased a sewing machine to start earning a living."

"Well, I must tell you, I haven't found one of those refugees who can sew beautiful fashionable clothes."

"I sewed this dress," Rebecca interrupted the conversation. She knew full well that when someone disparaged the refugees, Andreas's people, it would make him angry. And who knows what he might say that would get him into trouble? It wasn't an option to speak his mind in front of his uncle.

"You made that dress?"

"Yes, I did. Actually if we could afford it, I'd love to have a sewing machine. Do you think that would be possible, Andreas?" Rebecca asked him.

"Afford it?" his uncle scoffed. "We have a warehouse brimmed to overflowing with the sewing machines from the Jews. Tomorrow you two will go to the warehouse and select whatever machine your bride desires."

"Thank you. I look forward to that, Theo Constantine," Rebecca managed to say. Her head was pounding and her stomach was turning over.

"Andreas, your arrival was not anticipated. It was a surprise to receive a phone call from my brother about you and your bride. But I was able to set up an interview for you tomorrow at one of our finest hospitals.

However, I do think it prudent for you to keep a low profile due to your unfortunate comments while you were in Athens. I'm sure in time you will find your way inside one of our best hospitals. I am able to wipe the slate clean for you this one time. But only this one time."

"Thank you, Theo Constantine. I do understand," Andreas acknowledged.

Rebecca took another sip of wine. Her husband had been warned. Theo Constantine could only do so much to help them.

She desperately wanted this dinner to end. Finally, after hours and hours of more food and conversation about all the good things the Nazis had brought with them to Greece, they were given the key to their new apartment.

They were both so tired, they immediately changed into their night clothes and fell fast asleep in their new bedroom.

The next morning, Rebecca awoke early, reaching out to reassure herself of the presence of her new husband beside her. Andreas was still asleep as she moved nearer to him, closing her eyes for a brief moment, enjoying his warmth, her husband. She kissed his stubbled cheek tenderly and slipped out from beneath the covers.

She left the bedroom, anxious to explore her new home. It was a large, beautiful apartment with lace curtains, finely upholstered furniture, and several bedrooms. There was also a baby's cradle in one of the rooms.

Rebecca opened the cupboards. There were fine pots and pans, beautiful painted porcelain dishes, delicate china, and exquisite crystal glassware. In the drawers, she found expertly crafted silver forks and spoons. Her eyes were drawn to the bureau where silver Sabbath candlesticks and a silver seder plate for the Passover holiday were proudly displayed. She vowed she would take good care of what she found in this apartment until the family's return.

She thought of her family having to leave their houses without the treasures of their Jewish life. And now she was living in a house from which everyone had vanished They were sent to an area with other Jews.

Would they be relocated to the same town in Poland? Would they meet her family and not realize that a daughter of this family now occupied their house?

After Andreas awoke, he left for an interview with the Nazi administrators of a hospital. Thea Margarita appeared early in the morning to take Rebecca to the food shops. As they walked along the streets and avenues, Rebecca kept a tight smile on her face while her companion told her about the previous owners of the shops they passed. She confided in Rebecca that she had liked the Jewish proprietors, but her husband assured her that life in Salonika would be much better for everyone when the Jews were gone. "Do you think that's true?" she asked Rebecca as she paid for a purchase of walnuts.

"I leave those matters to the men," Rebecca answered. Remember, she told herself, you are a Greek Orthodox woman. What happens to the Jews is of no concern to you. But the headache that had begun when she walked past the boarded-up shops grew more painful as the afternoon wore on. The stores made her think about what had been the Rouso dry goods store, now owned and staffed by Bulgarians. She thought of all her father's hard work building it into a fine store, now vanished into thin air. Would her parents be allowed to return from Poland someday? Would Papá be allowed to reclaim the store as his own?

Andreas had a successful interview at the hospital. The Nazis had been pleased to have a physician with his expertise join their staff. Andreas sadly realized he couldn't aid the refugees as he had planned without drawing attention to himself. "I had intended to spend much of my time helping the refugees. But my uncle's warning was clear. I think once or twice a month will have to be enough," he said.

Rebecca had been spending her days preparing meals for dinner and reading the books Andreas had brought home to her. Books printed in Greek, with Ladino inscriptions, the language of the Sephardic Jews of Greece.

As she sat in her beautiful parlor looking out the large window that provided wonderful views of the sea, she tried to focus her attention on her book. But how could she focus her attention on her book? How could she banish thoughts of her family and the family who had lived in this apartment, who ate off these plates, who made love in the bedroom she shared with her own husband. She needed to find something to do all day when Andreas was working in the hospital. Otherwise, she was certain she would go mad.

They had been living in Salonika for three weeks now. Yesterday, Rebecca had gone with Andreas for his first visit to the area where the recent refugees from the Bulgarian zone were living. Andreas had been anxious to reconnect with his old friends, in particular the Melidis family. He had been so proud to introduce "Katerina," his new wife. His wife, the words made her smile and warmed her when so much of the time she felt a chill in her bones.

They visited the area where the new refugees had come in flight from the Bulgarian Zone and those areas settled twenty years ago by the Asia Minor refugees. Rebecca's thoughts whirled after visiting the refugee areas and seeing how so many people were still living in appalling conditions, even after twenty years. These people had never fully integrated into the Salonika population, for many reasons including their difficulty mastering the Greek language.

Rebecca thought long and hard about what she had seen before she presented her proposal to Andreas. "Why not help your people by teaching women to sew? I could open a small shop. I'm sure your uncle could locate one for me, and your aunt would be pleased to recommend my work and designs to her friends. Women could help earn a living for their families who had come to Salonika with little more than the clothes on their backs."

At first, Andreas had not been pleased with her wanting to open a shop. "People will think I can't provide for my wife," he had complained when she broached the proposal.

"Andreas, I have nothing to do all day. You are busy taking care of patients. Cooking the food we get from Theo Constantine doesn't occupy me for the whole day. It's been wonderful to read the books you brought me. At least there are books here in other languages besides Bulgarian.

But that isn't enough to occupy my time. I love sewing and I was thinking that we could find some girls, maybe two from the Asia Minor refugee area. I could teach them to sew and surely that would be a good thing. They could help support their families. I'm sure your aunt will sing my praises and we will find customers."

"Well, it would be a good thing to help those families," Andreas agreed as he grabbed the lunch she had prepared for him. "My wife, you are a very smart woman." He gave her a kiss and hug as he walked towards the door. "We can ask the Melidis family for recommendations."

They returned to the refugee area, and Rebecca asked the Melidis family for help in choosing one or two girls who might like to serve as apprentices in the seamstress craft. She had already chosen two beautiful Singers from a trip to the warehouse with Tio Constantine. He had not exaggerated when he said the storehouse was filled with sewing machines. So many women, thought Rebecca, so many women who used to sew. She remembered being so excited when Kiría Eleni showed her the Singer for the first time. All those hopes and dreams embodied in the Singers. All those women now made to live in horrible areas behind barbed wire.

Did that include the people who once lived in her apartment? As Rebecca thought more and more about the former occupants, she wondered about the Christian family who lived above them on the second floor. She was sure they would know something about that family. She was so eager to learn something about the Jewish family that she urged Andreas to invite their upstairs neighbors for dinner.

The couple upstairs had accepted their invitation to join them for dinner tonight and Rebecca was so anxious to meet them. She had only seen the husband, who left early in the morning, but she was anxious to meet the neighbor's wife and the small baby she heard crying during the day.

Giannis Antonopoulos was prompt for dinner, but begged forgiveness that his wife Stella couldn't join them. The baby was fussy and so his wife decided to stay upstairs with him. Rebecca said she would give him a plate of food to take to her, but Rebecca was disappointed. She believed his wife would know something about the Jewish woman who lived here, since as neighbors, the women may have been friends. That, of course, depended on this family's thoughts about Jews. Were they anti-Semites, Nazis sympathizers like Theo Constantine and his wife?

"Thank you so much for a lovely dinner." The short slender man took another sip of his *ouzo*.

"You're welcome. It was my pleasure. As you know, we are new here and I'm looking forward to meeting your wife," Rebecca told him.

"Well, she's really busy with our little boy."

"Forgive me, Kìrios Giannis, but may I ask if you knew the people who lived here before us?"

He leaned back in his chair, as if in deep thought. "I know your family does not have a favorable view of the Jews," he began. "Your uncle has relished their expulsion from their homes and the indignities they have suffered. So, perhaps, if you feel the same, I would not share very much with you. But, you see, Haim Koen was my business partner." He grew silent and waited for them to respond.

Andreas also seemed to be weighing what to say. Rebecca knew they had to be careful, not speaking against his uncle who had provided for them, and who was his father's brother. And they both knew there were fifth columnists waiting to report on people who spoke out against the Reich. "My dear uncle and I don't necessarily feel the same way about the Jewish people," Andreas cleared his throat. "I had many Jewish friends in Kavala while I was growing up and I bear them no ill feelings. They are people just like us, trying their best to provide for their families. They fought against the Italians in Albania. One of our most decorated Greek soldiers on the Albanian front was Mordechai Fritzi, a Jew."

"Well," Giannis gave a deep sigh. "Haim was my dearest friend. We practiced law together for the last ten years. His wife Daisy and my wife Stella were the best of friends. I can't believe what has happened to them. When the Germans first came to Salonika, they didn't treat the Jews very differently than they treated the Greek Orthodox. When they imposed some harsh measures against them, it was nothing that couldn't be tolerated. And then last July, on the Jewish Sabbath, a sweltering hot day, the Jewish men were forced to assemble in Eleftheria Square first thing in the morning. This included Haim. The men were forced to do calisthenics in the oppressive heat, without any water or relief. They couldn't even wear their hats. People collapsed. The Nazis threw water on them, and they were forced to get up. Many men were hurt so badly they needed hospitalization. Then these same poor souls were summoned for forced labor." Giannis took another swallow of his *ouzo*.

"Haim was a lawyer, like me," he continued. "We work with books and pencils. Labor? I couldn't imagine myself constructing roads. The word came back that men were dying from disease, from hunger. Some form of payment was made to the Nazis and the men were finally released. Part of the payment included giving up their cemetery. Can you imagine? That cemetery dates back five hundred years. It was turned into a quarry. People absconded with the marble tombstones. I heard that the Nazis used headstones to line a swimming pool. Such sacrilege!

"While Haim was gone, I took care of his family. When all Jewish property and businesses began to be appropriated by the Nazis, Haim transferred everything to me. I will keep it until his return. Then, to make matters worse, the Jewish Rabbi Koretz, kept urging everyone to obey the Nazis. In early February, the harsh measures began with the implementation of the Nuremberg laws. All Jews, including children as young as five years old, had to wear the yellow star. Then, the Jews were prohibited from changing their residence. They were not allowed to use the trams or the telephones. After they were told they had to vacate their residences for special areas, there were rumors of deportation from Salonika. But their rabbi, Rabbi Koretz, told everyone not to believe the rumors.

"In early March, the areas of Jewish settlement were blocked off. No one could leave for work. In the middle of March, they learned they were going to be deported to Kracow in Poland. Maybe more people would have fled before this so-called round up if they didn't listen to the rabbi. The Koen's eldest son, Aron, didn't report for forced labor. He went off and joined the partisans in the mountains. He should have stayed there, but he didn't."

"Why not?" asked Andreas.

"Because when he heard his family was being sent to Poland, he felt it was his duty to go with them. He came back from the mountains and joined his family in the Baron Hirsch quarter. Did you hear the news today?"

"No," replied Andreas.

Rebecca was trying to understand all Giannis had told them. Some Jewish men in Kavala had also been sent to do forced labor.

"The transportation of the Jews have begun. But it will take quite a while to transport sixty thousand Jews to Poland. And I've heard they are being crammed into cattle cars for the long journey."

"What have the Jews done to deserve this!" Rebecca couldn't keep silent.

"I don't know. I don't know," Giannis shook his head with sadness. "It is good to know our new neighbors are like-minded people. It's time for me to get back to my wife and son. Thank you again for dinner. Stella will appreciate it as well."

Rebecca sat in disbelief after the door closed. Andreas walked across the room and put his arms around her. "What have the Jews done?" she whispered.

"They've done nothing. It's hate, Katerina. Hate that consumes people towards those who are different. Muslims hated the Greek Orthodox and now Nazi Christians are hating Jews. I lost my family to that hate... my father, my mother, my sisters."

CHAPTER 16

Salonika, Greece, Zone of German Occupation: June, 1943
THREE MONTHS HAD passed since their arrival in Salonika.

It had been a glorious spring of beautiful wildflowers and gentle breezes. The dark days of the winter were forgotten as Rebecca breathed in the smell of flowers and jasmine. The sky was a brilliant blue and the sea was the azure color that reminded Rebecca of her home in Kavala. The sea, how she loved to watch the sea from the veranda of their home. The waves, the ships in the distance. At night, the moon shone its light, turning the sea to silver beneath its beams.

But the beauty of her new home could not erase her anxiety as she waited to hear from Andreas's parents about her family. Before she left, they had developed a code they would use about a cousin who had gone to Athens. Once Eleni and Vassilis heard from her family, they would write that the cousin had arrived safely in Athens. Rebecca knew her parents would realize that the Matsakises would be able to get a message to her. But so far there was nothing. She was so anxious to learn what their life was like in Poland.

This morning, Rebecca was going to the small sewing shop she had set up a few streets away from their apartment. Theo Constantine had been pleased to give her a shop that had been vacated by a Jewish proprietor. Of course, the shop was empty when Rebecca and Andreas had first seen it. It had been stripped bare.

As Rebecca walked down the street, her umbrella shielded her from the torrents that fell from the sky that morning. How freeing it was to be able to walk down the street without a chaperone. Life was more liberated for women here in Salonika. As she walked to her shop, she tried to brush aside the sadness of life in this place, of living and working where the Jews had been forced to leave their homes and businesses. She told herself she would keep everything in good repair so that when the Koen family came back they would be happy to see how well she had cared for their property. Rebecca passed the shop of the green grocer. For months it had smelled of rotting produce left behind by the Jewish grocer. But someone had finally cleaned it out and now it was just a boarded-up shop.

The two young women were waiting for Rebecca as she approached them and took out the key. She had stressed to them the importance of promptness. The girls knew they needed to comply with her requests and work hard, as there were so many girls just like them, with no hope of employment, who would be eager to take their place.

They walked in the door and turned on the lights against the gloomy day. Rebecca did not allow the girls to work on the Singers yet. First, she wanted to assess if they had the talents for dressmaking. She had instructed them in pinning and cutting patterns and they were eager to comply. They had also learned basting and some basic stitching. This week, she would give them instructions on dress fittings.

"Kiría Katerina?" Irini asked.

"Yes?" Rebecca answered as she watched them pin a pattern for a dress more complex than those they had worked on before.

"Glykeria and I were wondering how you were able get this shop?"

"My husband's uncle found it for me," she told them.

"This was a Jewish shop?" Glykeria made a face of disgust.

"Yes, it was," Rebecca answered tentatively, appalled at Glykeria's negative reaction.

"Well, aren't we all so lucky that the Jews were thrown out of town? They are like vermin, you know."

"Do you know any Jews?" Rebecca asked, trying not to show her irritation.

"No, I don't, I'm pleased to say. But everyone knows how evil they are. They had everything... so many grand houses and shops. Our people came here twenty years ago and we had nothing. My parents told me all about it. Nowhere to live, no jobs. We were penniless and starving. The Jews had it so good, and now they've gotten what they deserve."

Rebecca pursed her lips, trying to decide if she should say anything. She sighed, deciding it would be pointless to argue with Glykeria. The girl had heard all this from her family, and so although she hadn't ever had any interaction with Jews, she hated them. There were so many others like this family who had been Pontic refugees from Asia Minor. Many had not raised a word of protest when their neighbors were forced from their homes by the Nazis. But many other Greek Christians were very upset. Women had cried when their neighbors were forced out of their homes. And notably, the leaders of the Christian Association of War tried to stop the persecution of their Jewish comrades. They had planned demonstrations, but were told by the Germans that if they went ahead with the demonstrations they would be executed. Most other guilds and associations were silent.

Rebecca felt weary and tired. As soon as the pinning was done, she told the girls they could go home. Everywhere she walked, she saw reminders of the people, her people, who had been evicted from their homes. They were subversives. They were communists. They were dishonest and on and on... she heard bad things about the Jewish people. And she had to keep her silence so not to arouse suspicion, as Andreas kept reminding her.

There had been one ray of hope in the midst of so much horror. The Archbishop of Athens had issued an edict to the Nazis, telling them they could not send the Jews to Poland because they were Greek citizens. The Nazis, of course, paid him no heed and even threatened to execute him. But at least someone was standing up for what was right. Andreas also told her that the Archbishop instructed his priests to help the Jews by issuing false identification papers and that convents should allow Jews to hide there.

But the efforts of that one good man could not stop the Nazi brutality that Rebecca saw all around her. Every day was a constant reminder of the family who used to live in their apartment and would soon be living in Poland.

"I'm sleeping in someone else's bed, eating off their plates, drinking from their glasses, sewing on their Singers. It makes me weary and sick," Rebecca had complained this morning.

"I know, sweetheart," he said trying to convey his understanding to her. But could he really understand? He wasn't a Jew.

It had stopped raining when Rebecca reached their apartment. She saw a woman she thought was her neighbor coming down the street toward their front door, pushing a baby pram. Rebecca had asked Andreas to invite the family for dinner again, but they had always declined politely.

Andreas and Giannis often visited together in the evenings for a drink and sometimes a game of backgammon. And this evening, Giannis had extended a dinner invitation to Rebecca and Andreas for tomorrow evening.

"Hello," she greeted the young woman with red hair.

"Hello." The woman smiled.

"I'm your neighbor, Katerina Sefaris. I live downstairs."

"Yes, I know," she paused with uncertainty. "I'm Stella Antonopoulos."

"Would you like to come in for some tea and a sweet?"

"Well, the baby... "

"Please bring the baby. I can't wait to meet him."

"He's sleeping."

"That's fine. We won't disturb him."

"I'm not sure," Stella hesitated.

"It would be a favor to me. I'm new here and I don't know anyone. I'm lonely for the company of another woman."

"Alright." The woman lifted the baby and cuddled him in her arms.

Rebecca unlocked her door and after indicating a seat in the parlor, hurried into the kitchen to turn on the kettle. She returned with a plate of cookies. She was glad she had learned so much from all the time she spent with Kiría Eleni. She could cook and bake just like a real Greek Orthodox housewife.

"Let me see your little one." Rebecca approached the woman.

"No, he's asleep."

"What's his name?"

"Sebastian. He's just three months old. You don't have any children? But of course not. Giannis said you had only just married. My Giannis told me you accepted an invitation to join us for dinner in our apartment tomorrow night."

"Yes, we are looking forward to it, Stella. It's very kind of you. I wanted you to know that I have many nieces and nephews. So I have lots of experience taking care of little ones. I would love to take care of your son if you and your husband want to go out some time."

"No, no."

"Alright." Rebecca poured the tea.

The woman looked at the china cup. "Daisy's china," she murmured. "I always admired it. It is so beautiful."

"Yes, it is. It makes me feel sad to use it. But we didn't bring any household goods with us when we left Kavala. Can you tell me about Daisy?"

"She was a wonderful woman. She was so nice to me. I came here from Larissa as a new bride and she was such a good friend to me. I lost two children to miscarriage and she was always there for me, encouraging me. Last year, we both were pregnant at the same time. We both had boys. I miss her."

"I know I can't replace her. But maybe you and I could get to know each other and perhaps become friends."

"Giannis told me you aren't like Kìrios Matsakis, with his hatred toward the Jews. My husband said he likes to talk to your husband in the evening. He says you had many Jewish friends in Kavala."

"Yes, we did. Very close friends and I miss them."

The baby started to fuss and Stella brought him to her breast.

When the baby was done nursing he looked at Rebecca and smiled. She held out her arms and offered to take him from his mother.

"No!"

"Alright." What a nervous new mother! In time, like all the new mothers Rebecca had known, she would relax.

"I need to go back up to my apartment. He needs his *pána* changed. And I have to start preparing tonight's dinner." The woman got to her feet with the baby and hurried towards the door.

"You haven't had any sweets," Rebecca called out to her fleeing form.

Rebecca sighed. She dearly missed talking to her mother and her sisters each day. Of course she and Andreas talked in the evening when he returned from work. But women talk was different.

Rebecca was tired and laid down on the bed for a brief moment. The tiredness…. she knew what that meant coupled with the cessation of her flow. Andreas wasn't going to be pleased. He had cautioned her about having a child during this time of war. She had always yearned to be a mother since she was little. She remembered how devastating it was for her when she learned her lack of a dowry would prevent her from ever marrying. And now, despite Andreas's attempts at contraception, her dream was going to come true. How could she convince Andreas that a child would be a good thing? She should be happy she was going to be a mother. But what if Andreas didn't want this child? She'd been afraid to tell him. But she couldn't keep the truth from him for very long.

She closed her eyes and when she opened them, the room had darkened and Andreas was sitting on the bed beside her.

"I just thought I'd close my eyes for a moment." She tried to sit up.

"Lie down for a while longer." He stretched out beside her. "Did you have a long day?" He propped himself up on his elbow and looked down at her.

"Actually, no. But I did meet our neighbor Stella. She was odd. I don't know. Something wasn't right about her. Maybe she is very distressed about the loss of the woman who used to live in our apartment. She is a nervous new mother. I must bring something for dinner tomorrow night, perhaps some sweets. Just because we're living under this vile occupation doesn't mean we shouldn't display good manners."

"Why don't you bring them some of your delicious *melomakarona* cookies," he paused. "Katerina, I need to discuss something with you. I can't tell you much, for your own safety. But Giannis and I have been talking. He is working, in his own way, against this brutal occupation. And he asked me if I was willing to help."

"Of course, you should," Rebecca agreed, without hesitation.

"There are risks, of course. There are always risks. Recently I've been asked to take on the wife of a high-ranking Nazi official as my patient. The officer's wife is due to deliver at any time now and they don't trust the doctors here. My uncle has been singing my praises and so I am to help deliver the baby. But if I can get close to the Nazis, perhaps I can pass on some information. It would be for the greater good."

"Anything you could do to help, you should do."

"I know life in Salonika, all this pretending, is not easy for you," he said.

"Today, I had to listen to some terrible things the girls in my shop had to say about Jews."

"There is some prejudice from the refugees who came here twenty years ago. They left everything behind and arrived with nothing, no place to live, nothing to eat."

"Yes, I know, and they saw the Jews who they believed had everything they didn't have. The Jews had been here for five hundred years. And, of course, many were well-established. But many of them were poor."

"Well, it didn't seem that way to the refugees from Asia Minor. Katerina, not everyone feels that way. I've encountered many Asia Minor refugees who feel a commonality and empathy with the Jews being forced out of their homes. Some have helped the Jews to hide."

"Yes, I have heard that. Well, I can't single-handedly change people's mind. There are other things that are hard for me."

"Yes, I know. Sundays in church."

"Praying to a God who is not my own. Having to make the sign of the cross," she said as she shuddered.

"We may call God by a different name. But the God who brought you and I together is the same God. I have no doubt of that."

"Andreas, if only the world was that simple." She took a deep breath. "I do want to talk to you about something important."

"Something important?"

"I know how you feel about having children now during the occupation. And I also know you didn't want children any more than you wanted a wife."

"But, Kiría Katerina Sefaris, I do have a wife and I do want her. I want her all the time." He nuzzled her neck.

"Please, I'm being serious." She tried to push away. But he held her tight. "I need to tell you something." She felt her eyes welling up with tears.

He released his tight hold and frowned at her tearful eyes. "Don't be sad, my love. I'm sorry I'm making light of what you want to tell me."

"I know you don't want children, but I think I'm pregnant." She held her breath in anticipation of his reaction.

"Yes, Katerina. I also think you are pregnant. You are forgetting I'm a gynecologist and unlike many other men, I do know a pregnant woman when I see one, especially when I'm living with one."

"I'm sorry," she began.

"Sorry? Shh. Don't say such things and don't be sad. I never want to make you sad." He kissed her forehead.

"But…."

"There are no buts. Yes, I feared bringing a child into this world, just as I fear for you, for all of us. I have seen so much... "

"I know, I'm sorry."

"I know how important it is for you to have a child. You told me how sad it made you feel that you would never be a mother, only an aunt. I want this child, Katerina, Rebecca. It will be part of me and you and what could be more perfect?"

"Really?" she said with a great sigh of relief.

"Our marriage has changed some of my thinking. I no longer have those terrible nightmares almost every night. And I don't wake up yelling, when I do have a nightmare. I think it was finally remembering what happened and having you as my wife that has brought me an inner peace. The loss of my parents, my sisters, left a huge hole in my heart and now I feel more whole. I was sure I never wanted a child. But I know how important it is to you. I love you and I will love our child. Having a child will help hold our marriage together, forever."

"Help hold our marriage together? Is there something wrong with our marriage?"

"We love each other. But when you are reunited with your family, what will they say about your marriage to a Christian? You've always been a good, dutiful daughter. You and I both know your parents will never accept our marriage."

"They will have to. I'll explain how our marriage saved me from being deported. You are my husband," she said firmly.

"Rebecca, I couldn't bear if you were to leave me," his voice was a hoarse whisper.

"I will never leave you, I promise. Even if my family disapproves, I am your wife."

"You are my husband," she repeated. "I promise I will never leave you."

"Yes, I am your husband. My love, come closer and let me love you." He started to unbutton her blouse.

"I need to prepare dinner," she said in mock protest as her fingers unfastened his belt.

"I am not hungry for dinner," he said and then covered her lips with his mouth.

The two couples had enjoyed a leisurely dinner in the Antonopoulos apartment. Andreas stretched out his long legs next to Giannis as they puffed on their cigarettes and Rebecca helped Stella clean up the dishes in the kitchen.

"I'm sorry I seemed a little out of sorts when we met yesterday," Stella said as she dried a dish and put it back in the cupboard. "But this is the first time I've had dinner guests since our baby was born."

"It was a wonderful dinner. Everything was delicious."

"Well, it's not like the old days. But with the extra ration cards your husband got for us through his uncle, I think I was able to serve something presentable."

"Uncle Constantine loves to give us more than we actually need. It's his way of showing off, showing his connections to the high ranking Nazis. Dinner was more than presentable. It was delicious. I hope you will share some of your recipes with me."

"Of course," Stella said as she beamed.

The women finished tidying up and brought out spoon sweets, *melomakaronas* and coffee. Andreas sat with his arm around Rebecca, as he crushed his cigarette in a nearby ashtray. "Your son has been so well-behaved during our dinner. Haven't heard a sound from him. You are fortunate."

"He's due to feed soon. I hope his crying isn't so loud that you can hear it in your apartment," Stella said with a tentative smile.

"We hear him on occasion, but we don't mind. Soon our own child will be adding to the sounds at night." He squeezed his arm around Rebecca.

"A baby on the way! *Syncharitiria*, Congratulations! We must drink to that!" Giannis got to his feet and walked over to a crystal decanter.

The four of them were happy to be spending the evening with like-minded individuals. Giannis and Stella talked about what life had been like in Salonika before the occupation. Stella came from Larissa and had to make new friends. Her dearest friend was Daisy, who of course was now gone. They talked about their favorite movies at the cinema. Andreas joined in, but Rebecca merely smiled as she had rarely gone to the cinema. Her friends in Kavala were married and attended with their husbands. Occasionally one of her sisters would suggest an outing. But most of the time Rebecca stayed at home or babysat for her family members. But that was a lifetime away from here and her new life as Kiría Katerina Sefaris.

It was good to relax and to let down her guard somewhat. She realized she still needed to play act as Katerina, not Rebecca. Although the neighbors were definitely not Nazi sympathizers, and Giannis was working against the Germans, Andreas insisted Rebecca keep her true identity a secret. It was becoming easier in her new role of wife and soon-to-be mother to accept her identity as Katerina Sefaris. Rebecca Solomon belonged to another life, another world. Andreas told them about his attempts to find his sister Maria. He had added her name and the name of Sophia, his maid, to the list of people who were being sought through the newspaper in Salonika. Those people who had been lost twenty years ago. They had been lost, but not forgotten, never forgotten.

Giannis poured four more drinks when the sound of the baby's insistent cries came from the bedroom.

Stella put down her glass and hurried out of the room.

Rebecca sipped at her drink as the men talked about politics and the progress of the war. Surely the Nazis would lose the war, especially with the Americans as part of the Allied effort. Rebecca didn't want to hear about the war. She put down her drink and decided she'd visit with Stella, who was nursing her child.

She opened the door quietly, trying not to disturb the mother and child. Stella wasn't feeding him anymore. She was changing his pána.

Rebecca approached her. "Hi, I didn't want to startle you." She stopped suddenly as her gaze fell upon the baby. He was circumcised... Rebecca didn't know what to say.

Stella looked at her and then continued pinning the cloth *pána*. There was silence between them for a long while. Rebecca swallowed and moved across the room toward Stella and the baby. "He's a beautiful child." Rebecca smiled at her.

"Yes, he is." Stella picked him up and held him against her shoulder. "Well, now you know, don't you? And you must promise never to tell anyone, Katerina. Sebastian is an Orthodox Christian boy, baptized by our priest."

"Yes, of course."

"Well, let's go out to the men. I'm glad it's out in the open. I've hated keeping this secret and now at least we don't have to hide it from you and your husband."

It was a Jewish child. Of that fact, Rebecca had no doubt. Greek Orthodox Christian boys were not circumcised.

The women returned to the parlor.

"Stella?" Her husband seemed to sense something was amiss.

"It's been so hard not telling anyone."

"Not telling anyone? Stella, you didn't?" His voice was filled with distress.

"She saw. Katerina saw me changing him."

The women sat down, Stella still holding her son, who was now smiling up at her, making cooing sounds. She handed him to her husband.

"Our son is circumcised," Giannis murmured. "You must not tell anyone, please."

"Why, of course, we won't tell anyone. But how... " Andreas paused.

"I may have mentioned that Daisy Koen and Stella gave birth to little boys at the same time," Giannis began. "Two weeks after our son's birth, Stella went to his cradle to nurse him. We thought we were fortunate that he hadn't woken up in the middle of the night. But he was cold. He had died before he had been baptized. Our grief was overwhelming. We kept our sorrow to ourselves, except for our priest. And we also told the Koens, our dearest friends. Daisy was unwell after giving birth and was having difficulty feeding their child. Stella offered to nurse him until Daisy recovered from childbirth. We all hoped it wasn't childbirth fever.

"And then the order came that all the Jews had to vacate their residences. Daisy and Haim approached us and beseeched us to take their son. They feared for his well-being. There were such terrible rumors about the conditions where the Jews had been crammed into the ghettos. We didn't hesitate. And now he is our son," he paused, "until the Koens return, of course. But we will treat him as our son. Our Sebastian. He smiles at us. We love him as a mother and father love their son. He knows no other parents."

"Of course, we understand. We shall never tell a soul," Andreas reassured them.

"We won't tell anyone," Rebecca paused. "But I don't understand why this must be a secret. He's only a baby."

"The Nazis have even emptied out the Jewish orphanages," Andreas explained.

"Children, babies?" Rebecca was incredulous.

"They are Jewish and the Nazis are determined that not one Jew shall remain here in Salonika." Giannis held the child closer in his arms.

The conversation that had flowed so easily earlier in the evening had ceased. Rebecca and Andreas got up to leave.

"You have promised," Stella reminded them.

"We would never ever tell a soul." Andreas put his hand on Giannis's shoulder for reassurance.

Rebecca and Andreas walked hand in hand downstairs to their apartment. Andreas closed the door and turned on the lights.

He poured himself a glass of *retsina*. "Oh, Katerina, what a world we live in."

"Babies? What kind of people deport babies?"

"I didn't see it or if I did, I don't remember. But I have been told by other people who fled Smyrna that the Turks bayoneted babies for sport. Evil is evil."

"I can't help but wonder what will happen when the Koen family returns from Poland. Surely they will want their son back. Stella and Giannis will be devastated."

From that night forward, the two couples spent many evenings together. During the day, Rebecca would finish working with the two girls in the sewing shop until lunch time. She had decided they could proceed to working on the Singers. She sat in her chair supervising them as they completed the latest orders. As Rebecca had surmised, Thea Margarita told all of her friends about her nephew's wife's accomplishments as a seamstress. The orders were coming in at such a rate that Rebecca had to stop taking any more new commissions for frocks.

After lunch, Stella and Sebastian would join Rebecca on the veranda where they enjoyed the cooling breeze of the ocean. Rebecca placed a small blanket on the floor, so that the baby boy could rock back and forth on his knees. Rebecca delighted in having him sit on her lap, and explaining all about the waves and the ships, and the sun and the sky. He would look at her with such a serious expression on his little face as if he could understand her words. She knew it was just the sound of her voice that seemed to captivate him. Someday, it would be her child sitting on her lap, a child of her own.

Stella was glad to have someone else change his *pána,* hold him and make him laugh. Her nervousness about the possible discovery of her son's circumcision had disappeared and she was able to laugh and relax in the afternoon until her husband returned from the office.

Rebecca so enjoyed when Sebastian saw her and reached out his chubby arms, a huge grin on his face. He was such a handsome boy and so good-natured. Stella referred to her as his Thea Katerina.

❧

Salonika: July, 1943
Rebecca leaned back in a comfortable chair in the grand house of Herr Ziegler and his wife Helga. Rebecca couldn't help but wonder how wealthy the previous owners of this house must have been. But their wealth, no matter how great it was, didn't protect them from the Nuremberg laws that had been imposed on the Jewish population.

Andreas had delivered a fine, healthy son to Helga, and, as he expected, he was offered a position at the most prestigious German hospital in the city. His patients were at the top of the Nazi hierarchy. Not only did he practice obstetrics, but he did anything else he was asked to do, including surgery, the repair of broken bones and the treatment of burns. And he was always alert for information he either saw or overheard from the Nazis at the hospital. Then he would pass it on to Giannis who had connections with the partisans. In particular, he was eager to convey anything he heard about troop movements.

When Herr Ziegler's wife Helga heard Katerina had a small dressmaking business, creating the latest styles from the fashion magazines, the Zieglers insisted the couple join them for a fine German dinner. It would be prepared by the cook they had brought with them from Berlin. Herr Ziegler had procured four tickets for the opera they would attend after dinner.

At dinner, Helga Ziegler was beside herself with excitement. She said she didn't want Rebecca to sew for anyone else. Her husband admonished her for being selfish. "The wives of other Nazi officers shouldn't be deprived of Katerina's talents, especially since her seamstress days may be over after her baby is born."

"I'm training two young women who I hope will be able to take over for me for a while," Rebecca responded.

"Would you like another piece of *strudel*?" Frau Ziegler asked her as the men lit up cigars.

"No, no thank you. The food has been delicious tonight. I must compliment your cook," Rebecca said what she knew was required.

"Yes, Elsa is such a treasure. You have a Greek cook at home?"

"I am the Greek cook in our family." Rebecca smiled. "We don't have anyone else."

"You really ought to find one so that you have more time for your own pursuits and of course taking care of your husband. Once your baby comes, you must insist your husband finds you help in the house. There must be some Greek women you could find who are qualified. I know there were many Jewish women who did such things. But I'm sure you can find a Greek Christian woman to help."

Rebecca had let out her seams last week, but as she sat in the chair, sipping her German schnapps, she realized she needed to let them out again. Her pregnancy... she often had to stop herself from thinking that at the end of the day she would have liked to share news of her swelling body with her mother, her sisters, her cousins. But there was no one except Stella to confide in. She was going to be a mother and that filled her with joy. But her mother didn't know. Her sisters didn't know. They couldn't give her advice and compare her pregnancy to theirs. She tried to brush away those sad thoughts as she focused on the child growing inside of her and the good man who was her husband, who she loved with all her heart.

"We do have to hurry. We're due at the opera very soon. I'll summon the driver," Herr Ziegler advised.

The opera house was a grand, gilded place. Andreas helped Rebecca into her seat. He handed her the opera glasses and smiled as he watched her eagerly take in the sights and sounds of the opera. She was one of those women who glowed with pregnancy. Not all women were as fortunate. Although at the beginning of her pregnancy he told her he was happy about the impending birth of a child, he hadn't been completely honest with her. He worried about protecting both her and the child. No one ever suspected that Rebecca was Jewish. But perhaps, someday in the future, an acquaintance, whom they never expected was actually a collaborator, would hear an innocent word that might cast suspicion on her. Rebecca played her part well. But there was always the possibility of discovery, perhaps a word in Ladino instead of Greek.

"I've never been to an opera before," Rebecca told their Nazi hosts.

"Oh, this is a very special Italian opera. It's Pagliacci, my favorite," said Helga. "What about you, doctor? Are you a fan of opera?"

"I do enjoy the opera. I've been to a few in Athens." Andreas settled back in his box seat overlooking the stage. He looked at the German program and was so thankful for his facility with languages. Rebecca also easily mastered languages, but she had no interest in becoming fluent in German. "I hate the Nazis and I hate their language. I've learned enough to get by, but no more," she told him.

The music was beautiful and he loved seeing how much Rebecca was enjoying herself, forgetting the horrors of the occupation.

The first act was coming to its conclusion. "This is the most famous aria," Herr Ziegler leaned over and whispered to him.

As Andreas began to listen, a wave of nausea swept over him. That song... that song. It wasn't beautiful at all. He'd heard it before. He smelled the smoke, the stench of unwashed bodies and death. He heard the horrible wailing, the pleading, the crying, the praying. He heard his sister Maria sobbing in fear as she tried to hide between Mamá and Sophia.

He had to flee from that horrible music, but he was frozen in his seat, sweat beading on his forehead. There was a constriction across his chest. He couldn't breathe. He needed to escape from the music. He needed air!

"I'm not well," he managed to say, staggering to his feet.

"Doctor?" Herr Ziegler asked with concern.

"Andreas?" He heard the concerned voice of his wife, as he rushed past her out the door of the opera boxes. He held on to the banister as he ran down the stairs. He had to get away from that music.

"Your father took me to that opera." He heard the voice of his mother.

He ran out the door into the silence of the street. He steadied himself against the building, taking deep breaths, wishing away the smells, the sights.

"*Christós*," Andreas prayed, "help me."

"Doctor?" It was Herr Ziegler. "Are you unwell?"

"I think I need to go home. I apologize. I saw a patient who was ill today and I must have caught something from her." He took a deep breath, trying to calm himself. "My wife?"

"I'm here."

"I'll get the driver." Herr Ziegler hurried down the street.

"The music," Andreas said as he breathed deeply, continuing to lean against the wall of the opera house. "They played it at night on the quay. The ships played it... "

"It's alright." Rebecca took hold of his hands in her own.

"Should my driver take you to the hospital?" Herr Ziegler had returned.

"No, no. I'm feeling better already. I just need to rest at home." He straightened his back. The memories were fading, slipping like ghosts back into the graveyard where they belonged. "I'm sorry to have spoiled our evening. Give my apologies to your wife. Katerina and I will go home."

"Thank you, Herr Ziegler," Rebecca spoke up. "He often catches something from one of his sick patients. He just needs some rest."

Andreas and Rebecca sat in the back seat of the car as the driver made his way back to their apartment. Rebecca held fast to his hands.

"Memories, Katerina. Just bad memories. I am alright. Don't worry."

This was the second time they had been invited for dinner to the house of the Germans. Tonight, Rebecca had brought along a sketch book and two of the new dresses she had completed for Helga.

"They are beautiful! I can't wait to try them on. All my friends tell me how fortunate I was to find you. Since the Jewish dressmakers are gone, there has been no one with skills to take their place."

"Ah, Helga. I heard you mention Jews?" Herr Ziegler arched a bushy brow. "Well, soon they will all be gone from Salonika. The problem, of course, is there are so many, almost sixty thousand. We started the transports in March and here it is July and still so many remain. By careful calculation, we believe they will all be gone by August and then we will truly be *Juden frei*."

Rebecca smiled politely.

"But you, from Kavala, you were so lucky. The Bulgarians were fortunate."

"Fortunate?" Andreas inquired as he puffed on his cigar.

"You know, of course, the Jews were also rounded up in the Bulgarian Zone?"

"Yes, that happened before we left."

"Well, first of all, the Bulgarians only had to contend with a mere five thousand in Eastern Macedonia. Then they had the good luck to send them on boats before they got to the rail tracks and the cattle cars that we use for transport."

"Why was it good luck to be sending them on boats?"

"You haven't heard? The ships all sunk. Everyone drowned. What a stroke of good luck for us. Less Jews for us to deal with in Poland."

CHAPTER 17

Salonika, Greece, German Occupation Zone: July, 1943

REBECCA SAT IN a chair on the veranda, staring out at the sea. Andreas had sent word to the two young seamstresses that the shop was going to be closed for the week. Kiría Katerina was not feeling well.

"Sweetheart," Andreas said as he bent down and placed a plate of bread and cheese on the small table beside her. "You must eat something."

"I'm not hungry. You should go to work. You staying home can't change anything," she said, her eyes still watching the sea.

"I'm not going to work today. Someone else will cover for me. I'm staying here with you. Now, eat just a little something. It's not good for the baby if you're not eating."

"I can't eat anything. I'm sorry."

"I know that I can't take away your pain. I know, because no one could take away my pain all those years ago when I fled Smyrna. I love you, sweetheart. I love you. Come, let me hold you." He drew Rebecca to her feet.

"I'm going upstairs for a few minutes to tell Stella you aren't feeling well and you aren't up to your daily visit with her." He kissed her cheek. "I'll try to find out what I can about the Eastern Macedonian Jews. What we heard last night may only be a rumor. It might not be true."

Only a rumor, thought Rebecca. She knew he was just trying to offer her any shred of hope. Andreas always talked about the efficiency of the Nazis. Nothing was left to chance. If they said everyone had drowned, it was true.

Rebecca laid her head against his chest as his arms encircled her. She listened to the beat of his heart against her ear, a sign of life.

But so much death was all around her. Her tears from last night had finally ceased this morning. And now she was left with an overwhelming feeling of sadness and despair.

She heard the sound of the door closing as Andreas left to go up to the Antonopoulos apartment.

Sitting back down in her chair on the veranda, she laid her head in her arms on the table. Papá, Mamá, her sisters, their husbands, her brothers, their wives, their children, the whole extended Rouso family gone to a watery grave. She thought of that last morning, when the misery of her cold caused her to barely say a proper good-bye to her mother. Her father had been long gone to his shop. What was the last thing she said to him the night before? She couldn't remember. The children... the babies. Her sister Miriam was pregnant.

But her sister Roza had gone to Ioannina with her new husband. At least she and her children were safe. She thought of how Roza had been so reluctant to leave Kavala, but her marriage had saved her from a watery grave. There was no one to say *kaddish,* the prayer for the dead. "May their memory be eternal" were the words one said when one spoke of the dead. But who was there to remember them? Only she and her sister Roza remained. Would Roza even know what had happened to their family? If only the family had gone to Salonika instead of staying in Kavala. She thought of her sister-in-law Sara, who pleaded with her brother to go to Salonika with the rest of her family. At least they would still be alive, even though they would have been rounded up and transported out of the city. Going to Poland was better than drowning in the sea.

Last night, her whole world had turned upside down. Everything, everyone had ceased to exist. She barely remembered Andreas making some excuse to the Nazis. She was having some problems with her pregnancy and they needed to go home where she could rest. How had she not started to scream? She didn't remember. But she was home now, safe in their apartment, until someone discovered she was a Jewish woman. Maybe she would say a word in Ladino instead of Greek. Or she would cook a dish she learned from her mother instead of Kiría Eleni. She would be taken away from Andreas. The punishment for hiding a Jew was execution. She had felt safe here in Salonika. But maybe nowhere was safe in a world where thousands of innocent souls were swallowed by the sea.

She would never be reunited with her family when they returned from Poland as she had imagined. She would never go to Poland to visit with them and introduce them to her child. She would never have to argue with Papá and Mamá that marrying Andreas was not a betrayal of her people. At night, she had laid in bed and thought of what she would say to convince them that her marriage was a good thing. That Andreas had saved her from the deportations. Papá had told him to keep her safe. She would explain to them she had always loved Andreas and he was a good man. She would tell them that Andreas had promised he would do anything to remain her husband. He said he would become Jewish and give up his faith if that is what he had to do, to keep her as his wife. All those imagined conversations she had created in her mind... they never would happen.

None of that mattered anymore. Nothing mattered anymore, nothing. The sea didn't seem a beautiful blue this morning, but a monster of water waiting to consume, waiting to kill. And then she felt something inside her. A slight fluttering. The baby? Could that be the baby she and Andreas had created? The descendant of her whole family who was stirring into life, into a world that hated Jews, that threw them out of the country of their birth, where their ancestors had lived for generations. Her child and Roza's children were all who remained of her family. She wiped away her tears with the back of her hand and placed her hand gently over her stomach. A new life. Surely her parents would tell her she must think of this new life growing inside her. She remembered her sisters talking about this strange fluttering when they wondered was this the baby or just their imagination. She wanted to talk to them, to share the stirrings of this new life. And in spite of her resolve not to sink back into despair, she began to sob again.

She hadn't heard the door open, but she felt Andreas's hand stroking her hair. She looked up at him though her tears. "I think I felt the baby," she told him, wiping her tears from her eyes as she struggled to gain control of herself. "We have to keep the baby safe," she told him.

"We will, sweetheart. I promise you."

Salonika, Zone of German Occupation: October, 1943

It was a bright sunny day. Rebecca, swollen with child in the seventh month of her pregnancy, sat on a bench beside Stella and two other women who were enjoying the balmy weather in a local park. One woman held a child in her arms and the other was sitting on a blanket with her two year old. Conversation swirled around babies and recipes to create from the meager available rations. No one ever said a negative or positive word about the occupation or about the Germans. One never knew who might be a collaborator or if a careless word might be overheard by someone who would report this to the Third Reich. There was money to be made from turning in your neighbors or people who were mere acquaintances.

Since Mussolini had capitulated to the Allies last month, Germany had taken over all the areas that were once under Italian control. The relative safety for Jews in Athens and Ioannina as well as the island of Rhodes was now in doubt. Rebecca thought of her sister Roza and her children in Ioannina, her only family members who had escaped the drowning. Would they be sent away to Poland? There had been no word of measures being taken against the Jews in the new areas of Nazi control. But Andreas had told her he didn't trust the Nazis, that being transported to Poland was not a good thing. His connections with the partisans, through Giannis, had provided disturbing news. Although the first Jews had been transported from Salonika in March, no word had ever been received from a single person. It had been almost seven months and the *andartes* interpreted that to mean the Jews had met their death in Poland.

It had been three months since she had received the news about her family. Andreas had made many inquiries, but he never heard that the drowning of the Jews from Eastern Macedonia, from Kavala, from Drama was not true. She willed herself to get through this terrible time. She had their baby to think of, a new life in the midst of so much death. "May their memory be eternal," were the words that kept echoing through her mind. But who was there to remember them, except for Katerina Sefaris, who used to be Rebecca Solomon? She couldn't tear her clothes in mourning; she couldn't go to the synagogue and hear the men saying *kaddish*, the prayer for the dead. Instead, she sat in a park across the street from debris of the synagogue that had once stood there, but now had been demolished by the Nazis. Stella told her there were once thirty synagogues in Salonika. There were only two that hadn't been destroyed.

Stella had become her best friend, as they shared dreams for their children. Rebecca was Thea Katerina to little Sebastian. And Stella would be aunt to her child. Rebecca loved that little boy. He reminded her of all her nieces and nephews who had perished.

Rebecca was happy to use her dressmaking skills to design maternity frocks in the latest fashions for herself and other pregnant women. There was never a problem obtaining fabric as Theo Constantine could obtain any fabric she requested. Of course, she knew who had once owned those fabrics... the Jewish shop owners who had sold fabric, who delighted in seeing the joy it brought to their customers. Shop owners now deported to Poland to an uncertain fate.

Rebecca refused to believe what Andreas had heard from the *andartes*. Sixty thousand Jews from Salonika had been transported all the way to Poland, just to be killed? That made no sense. If the Nazis wanted to kill them, why bother to put them in the rail cars? Of course, the Jewish residents of this city would be returning. And then her poor friends would have to part with their son Sebastian even if it broke their hearts, as surely it would.

And so today, as every day, Rebecca Solomon acted the role of Katerina Sefaris, pregnant with her first child, wife of the doctor who worked for the Nazis.

"It will be so exciting to celebrate Sebastian's Name Day in a few weeks." Stella smiled as she bounced her happy little boy on her knee.

"The first Name Day is so exciting," Kiría Apollonia agreed as she watched her two-year-old daughter Ursula struggle to open a toy box.

Rebecca placed her hand on her stomach as she felt her baby kick and move about. Was that the strong kick of a girl or a boy?

One evening last week, Kiría Appolonia had brought her daughter Ursula for Andreas to examine. She was worried that her little girl was too slow to walk and she barely uttered a word. Andreas had listened to all that the mother said as he carefully examined the child. "I can't find anything wrong that I could remedy with a medicine. She is a very pretty child."

Kiría Appolonia had nodded in agreement. "She is pretty and as a girl, that is most important. Someday we will provide her with a very substantial dowry, and we will find her a good husband."

A healthy baby, Rebecca would turn the words over and over in her mind. Either a boy or a girl, but a healthy baby and with God's help, a good mind. But even if their child wasn't as smart or as good looking as they dreamed, she had no doubt their hearts would be filled with love for their child.

Stella stuck her fingers inside Sebastian's pants. "He's soaked. Time to get him home for a change." She picked him up. "Bye." She waved at everyone and walked down the street.

"I know you're good friends, Katerina. But she is a little odd, don't you think?" Kiría Appolonia commented. "Whenever her boy needs a change, she runs home to do it. We all bring changes with us, especially when the baby is only wet."

"It's her first, you know. I've seen many first-time mothers who were very anxious, just like Stella. She doesn't have any family here, so it's hard for her," Rebecca tried to offer an excuse, hoping they would accept her explanation. "This afternoon, we are going to be baking sweets for Sebastian's Name Day. I hope many people will come to visit. That will help Stella feel more welcome in Salonika, especially with her own family so far away in Larissa."

"Katerina, I forgot to mention that when I went to a gathering last week wearing the new suit you had designed for me, I met a woman, Kiría Skordyles, a tobacco heiress from near your home. They had to leave much of their wealth in Drama, but because her husband owned warehouses here in Salonika, they are still quite comfortable. She thought my suit was so elegant and she wanted to know who made it. She will be getting in contact with you soon. She said she hadn't seen such fine work since she was in Drama and a seamstress and her Jewish helper from Kavala designed many outfits for her."

"I'm afraid I can't take on any more work now with the baby coming soon," Rebecca told her. "Please send her my sincere regrets." The woman would surely recognize her and her secret identity would be revealed. She could be reported to the Nazis, sent away to Poland, taken away from Andreas.

She took a deep breath to calm herself, when she spied a young girl on the other side of the park. The child looked so much like her niece, Julie, and she was holding a doll in her arms. Julie... Had she been able to take dolly with her when she was pulled out of bed in the middle of the night? She needed her dolly to give her comfort. But Julie would never have a chance to learn to be without her comfort doll, to grow up and become a young woman, a mother, a wife.

If only there had been something that Rebecca could have done to help save her family. If chance hadn't intervened with the Bulgarian matron who insisted on new beading for her dress, Rebecca would have been home that night...

How powerless she was, how powerless her whole family and the Jewish community had been against this Bulgarian occupation and now the Nazis. Someday, she vowed, she would not be powerless anymore.

Salonika, Zone of German Occupation: early March, 1944
Elias Andreas Sefaris was born on December 10, 1943. He was named in honor of Andreas's father. He was a healthy, beautiful baby, born after what Andreas told her was an easy labor for a first child. His eyes at birth were a deep blue that turned dark by January, dark like his father's eyes. Having a child was all she had ever imagined it would be. She was so in love with this baby and with being a mother. Her dreams had come true.

Andreas often came home at lunchtime to marvel at his son, to hold him, to delight in his smile. Although he had delivered countless babies, he pronounced their son to be the most beautiful child he had ever seen.

Eight days after his birth, there had been no circumcision. Andreas had promised her that when these terrible days of the Nazi occupation were over, he would personally circumcise their son. "He will be a Jew. I promise you. You told me if a child's mother is Jewish then that child is a Jew. A Jewish boy needs to be circumcised. He will be. I promise."

But because they were under the Nazi occupation, today, her son Elias was to be brought to the Greek Orthodox Church and baptized in the faith of his father. She knew it was necessary if they were not to arouse suspicion.

As the day dawned, the darkness of the sky and the threat of snow in the air matched the sadness she felt in her heart. She needed to smile today when everyone gave her congratulations. Just as she was forced to smile when her new friends as well as Theo Constantine and Thea Margarita had come to visit and see the new baby, bearing gifts of silver and gold as was the custom. She knew, full well, that the gold and silver items had once been in a Jewish household. Theo Constantine had proudly given her son a beautiful silver kiddish cup, engraved with the Star of David. "Isn't it a fine piece of silver work?" he announced. "When I locate a good silversmith, I'll have that sign of the Jews taken off. But I just wanted you to see it."

"No, please, it's so beautiful. Leave it with me and I'll find a silversmith to work on it," Rebecca told him.

Rebecca had taken the gifts and put them away in a drawer. She had no intention of letting her son see what was stolen from her people, his people.

"Katerina." Andreas said as he placed his hands on her shoulders before they left for church. "I know today will be difficult for you."

Rebecca didn't answer.

"We have to do this," he reminded her as he looked down at her, his face filled with love and sadness.

"I know," she whispered and closed her eyes as he pulled her against himself.

"Is he ready?"

"Of course, he is dressed and ready for his baptism." God forgive me, she thought. I need to keep our son safe. I have no other choice.

Rebecca stood beside her husband as she faced the priest on the altar. Andreas held her hand and helped her feel less distraught as the priest baptized their son Elias. Theo Constantine and Thea Margarita, his godparents, smiled down at their great nephew as the prayers were said and she heard people comment on how remarkable it was that Elias didn't cry. He was such a good baby. The love she felt for her child was fierce and strong; she knew she would do anything to keep him safe, to keep him from harm, even having him baptized as a Christian. Someday, Andreas tried to reassure her, this nightmare would be over and she could live again as a Jewish woman. She pasted a smile on her face as her son's Nazi godparents gave Elias back to her.

Andreas let go of her hand as he went to greet many of the well-wishers from his hospital. Stella and Giannis were the first to congratulate Rebecca. They gave her huge hugs. Little Sebastian, who had just taken his first steps, was struggling to be set free from his parents' arms. He wanted to walk around the church. Stella put him down, but didn't let him stray from her hand.

"Katerina," Stella said in a low voice. "If only my son's baptism could have been celebrated like this. Fortunately, Father Georgios agreed to a private christening. Giannis found two people who could be trusted to serve as the godparents. Having him baptized without a stitch of clothing made anything else impossible. But he is a Greek Orthodox child."

Stella grabbed her son who was now sitting on the floor. "Little Sebastian needs his *pána* changed. I'll take him into the back room of the church. I'll be right back."

"Na sas zése, Kiría Katerina," one of the women Rebecca often saw in church on Sunday, gave her best wishes.

"Efharistó," Rebecca thanked her. She tried to remember the name of this older woman. Yes, now she remembered. She was Kiría Veta, who was employed to clean the church. She was a poor widowed woman who would surely be out in the streets if she wasn't paid to clean the church. Her only son had been lost in the Albanian campaign and now she had no one to care for her. The priest was a kind man, who had suggested she clean the church for the congregation.

"Well, I have to get to my duties today. Lots of cleaning with this crowd. I didn't know you and your husband had so many friends in Salonika."

"Actually, many of the people here are friends of my husband's uncle." Rebecca said as she nodded toward all the men in Nazi uniforms. They stood with epaulettes on their shoulders and hats in their hands. Rebecca

Solomon was in a Greek Orthodox church, surrounded by Nazis. She held Elias closer.

Rebecca watched as Kiría Veta walked toward the back room of the church where Stella had gone to change her son's *pána*. Rebecca rocked Elias as she watched the door where the cleaning woman had entered. In a few minutes, Stella walked out with Sebastian.

"All nice and clean now," Stella told her and put Sebastian down on the floor, holding his hand.

"Did you see Kiría Veta, the cleaning woman?" Rebecca asked with concern.

"No. I made sure no one was there when I changed him."

"She must have gone to another room in the back of the church," Rebecca replied, hoping what she said was true.

April 1944

Today Andreas had brought her ominous news. Those areas that had been under Italian rule, but had now been taken over by the Nazis, were no longer safe for the Jewish people. The Germans had begun the roundup of the Jews who lived in those towns. The people were gathered and deported to a "new life in Poland." No one with any sense believed those Nazi lies anymore. She worried that her sister Roza, her husband and her family... might all be sent away now that Ioannina was under Nazi control. Was it true that the Jews were killed when they got to Poland? But why not kill everyone in their own towns and not have to transport them? Again, Rebecca tried to console herself with that logic.

After Rebecca had told Andreas about the woman from Drama wanting to see her about designing a dress, they agreed she should spend less time at the shop. And when she did go to the shop, she would stay in the back room. The girls now excelled at stitching and using the Singer. Rebecca could easily do her sketching from home. She never attended any large social gatherings for fear there might be someone from Eastern Macedonia who could recognize her. However they did have a small circle of friends, including the Antonopoulos family as well as a surgeon and his wife.

After Rebecca heard the news about other Jews being deported, she wondered if she were to be the only surviving member of her large family. Ioannina was home to members of her father's family, the Romaniote Jews. They had lived in Greece for over two thousand years. How could such a well-established community cease to exist? When the war was over, they could come back and rebuild their lives. Rumors of death were just that, only rumors.

It was early morning. Rebecca and Stella were sitting on the window seat in Stella's apartment with their baby boys. Elias was fast asleep in Rebecca's arms and Sebastian was eating a piece of bread and jam. He stuffed the bread in his mouth with his sticky fingers and smiled up at his mother and Rebecca. He was such a happy little boy and so smart. He already spoke several words.

The women were enjoying the beautiful spring morning under a cloudless blue sky. The waves broke against the shore and the sea was a brilliant turquoise. Such beauty, thought Rebecca, as she sipped her coffee and looked out of the window. How can the world be filled with such beauty when evil was lurking everywhere?

The stillness of the early morning was suddenly broken by the sound of screeching tires down the street. Thundering footsteps ran up the stairs to the Antonopoulos apartment.

Stella clutched her son against herself. "Who is that?" she gasped.

There was a banging on Stella's door.

"Open up!" A voice yelled in German.

Rebecca's heart began to race. She was found out. Someone had recognized her on the street. She and Elias were going to be taken away or perhaps executed right here in Stella's apartment.

"Open up!" The pounding grew more insistent.

With dread, Rebecca watched as Stella walked to the door. She opened it to find a tall Nazi soldier scowling at her.

"Are you Kiría Antonopoulos?"

"Yes," Stella answered with a quiver in her voice.

"And who are you?" He frowned at Rebecca as she held tight to Elias.

"I'm Kiría Katerina Sefaris."

"This does not concern you. I was told you live in the downstairs apartment. You are from the Matsakis family and no harm will come to you."

He turned to Stella, who had paled in fear as the soldier reached for his revolver and pointed it at her.

"You are the one with the Jew baby!" He sneered at her.

Sebastian was frowning at the soldier who was yelling and then he started to cry. Stella held him tightly against herself.

"Please, sir," Stella began in a timid voice.

"Take off his clothes. If he isn't a Jew, I will leave. Did you hear me?" He raised his hand and slapped Stella across the face.

Stella gasped and with trembling hands took off Sebastian's clothes. The little boy continued to wail. There was no hiding what his naked form revealed.

"Aha! Just as was reported. This is a Jew baby and you know the penalty for hiding a Jew."

"He's just a baby," Rebecca pleaded with anguish.

"Mind your own business."

"Please," Stella started to cry. "He is my son. He has been christened in the Greek Orthodox Church. I have his baptismal papers. Let me get them."

"A Jew is a Jew and there must not be even one left in the Third Reich. Not one."

He grabbed Sebastian out of her arms and put a pistol to his head. "Say goodbye to your Jew baby." And with that he shot the wailing child in the head, spattering blood and gray matter all over his mother.

Stella could not stop screaming.

The Nazi threw the bloodied child on the floor like a piece of garbage and stomped on him with his leather boots.

"You," he addressed Rebecca. "I want you to watch what happens to Greeks who hide Jews. Tell all your lady friends." He pointed the revolver at Stella.

Stella bent down toward Sebastian's lifeless form, sobbing uncontrollably.

The door to the apartment burst open. Giannis and two other men, revolvers in their hands, ran toward the Nazi. There was a burst of gunfire and the Nazi dropped to the floor.

"Giannis!" Stella screamed. "Sebastian, my Sebastian." She clutched the child's bloodied, lifeless form, to her chest.

"We need to leave. Now!" Giannis grabbed her hand and tried to pull her away from the baby.

"No, no," she sobbed.

"Now!" He scooped her up in his arms and carried her protesting form towards the door.

"Katerina," he said to Rebecca who was standing in the shadows. "Run down to your shop. You have seen nothing this morning. Hurry! Run!"

The men and Giannis, holding Stella in his arms, ran out the door and down the stairs. Rebecca, clutching Elias, hurried after them. She watched as they climbed into a car and sped off. She did as she was told and walked at a quick pace toward her shop. Her heart was beating so hard she thought it would burst from her chest.

Clutching Elias against her bosom, she fumbled with the key to the shop. Her trembling fingers made it impossible to open the lock. She ran to the back of the shop and, still holding Elias, vomited in the alleyway. She placed the baby next to her on the ground and vomited again and again.

Rebecca withdrew a handkerchief from her skirt pocket and wiped her mouth before she bent over to pick up her son. She rocked him back and forth. Sebastian, such a lively wonderful boy. Sebastian... and the tears slipped down her cheeks.

Andreas had finished his morning surgeries and a delivery which had not gone well. The woman, who had been so malnourished, was found on the street already in labor. Not even her tiny baby had a chance of survival. Hospitals should be places of hope and healing. But these days, they were sad places of death. All the Jewish doctors who had practiced here were now gone and with them, their expertise.

As he walked along the hospital corridor, he was jostled by a young boy who slipped a note in his hand. The *andartes* usually did not contact him. He had always been the one who initiated contact. Andreas dropped the note into his coat pocket and went inside the hospital director's office for the scheduled monthly meeting. The director was a high-placed Nazi with no medical expertise, but a great love of efficiency.

Andreas was a few minutes early and the meeting had not yet begun. He went to the toilet for some privacy to read the note from the *andartes*.

Antonopoulos and his wife have been taken to the mountains for their safety. There was a raid this morning on their apartment and their son was murdered in cold blood. Antonopoulos and his wife are safe. Katerina Sefaris was a witness to the child's murder and to the murder of an SS officer. She was sent to her shop. We are confident no one knows she was a witness. Do not attract attention to yourself. Proceed as if all is normal.

With trembling hands, Andreas took out his cigarette lighter and burned the note.

Rebecca barely spoke to the two girls who were busy on the Singers.

"Is something wrong?" Irini asked her. "You've hardly said a word all morning."

"Nothing's wrong. It is a beautiful day isn't it? But Elias is very fussy," she told them, as she rocked her son who sensed her anxiety and despair.

Stella's son was gone, brutally murdered because his circumcision identified him as a Jew. Although Rebecca reminded herself over and over that her son was not in danger, she knew she was fooling herself. The Nuremberg laws stated plainly that anyone with one Jewish parent was considered a Jew in the Third Reich. A Jew in hiding and anyone hiding a Jew could be executed on the spot.

What if a former customer from Kavala was now living in Salonika and recognized her? What if the tobacco matron from Drama passed her on the street one day? There was money to be made for turning in a Jew. As she sat in the rocking chair Andreas had given her as a special present after the birth of their son, she tried not to transmit the fear and anxiety to her nursing baby. But it was of no use. He was inconsolable this morning.

It was afternoon. Surely she could go back to her apartment now. She gave up trying to comfort her baby and told the girls to stay and finish their sewing. She needed to go home and attend to Elias.

She walked home, her feet leaden. She didn't even attempt to comfort Elias who was wailing so loudly and she was greeted with stares by people she passed on the street.

As she unlocked the door, she was startled at the sound of a German voice behind her.

"Frau Sefaris, I have come to question you about your neighbors."

Rebecca turned around. Please, she thought, don't take me away for questioning. Would she survive under the torture, for which the Nazis were notorious? What if they tried to hurt Elias in order to force her to talk? Would they kill her child right before her eyes, just like they killed Sebastian?

She fought to conquer all her anxiety and terror as she summoned the strength within her. She would be strong. She had no other choice.

"Please, come in," Rebecca tried to sound hospitable toward this vile Nazi.

He brushed past her, his leather boots loud on the polished wooden floor.

"May I put my son in his cradle? He is very out of sorts today."

"Can't you stop his crying, woman? It is grating on my nerves."

"I have a sleeping draught my husband gave me for him. I'll give it to him, to calm him."

"Before we proceed with my questioning, take off your boy's clothing. He is a boy isn't he?"

"Yes, but... "

"*Mach shnell*. Make it quick. I don't have all day."

Rebecca felt a calm descend upon her as she pulled off his pants.

"I need to see his naked body!" he told her with irritation.

She opened his *pána*.

"Alright. Put him in another room and close the door so I don't have to hear him."

She placed Elias in his cradle and put a few drops into this mouth. Andreas had brought the sleeping draught home weeks ago, but it had never been used until now.

Rebecca closed the door and walked toward the Nazi. "May I offer you some refreshment?"

"This is not a social call, you stupid Greek woman! Where were you this morning?"

"I had breakfast and then I went to my sewing shop as I do most mornings."

"And your husband?"

"He left in the middle of the night to deliver a baby."

"Did you hear anything out of the ordinary this morning from your upstairs neighbors? Gunshots?"

"Gunshots? We often hear gunshots in the middle of the night, but nothing from upstairs. Has something happened to my neighbors?"

"Do you know them well?"

"Kiría Antonopoulos and I often walk our babies together. The men sometimes have a drink at the end of the day."

"Have you ever seen their baby without his clothes? Do you know he was a Jew, a circumcised Jew?"

Rebecca gasped in what she hoped appeared to be surprise. "A Jewish child? Why would they have a Jewish child? They are devout Greek Orthodox Christians, aren't they?"

"The penalty for hiding a Jew is death!"

"Of course. Everyone knows that."

"And besides hiding a Jewish child, they killed one of our fine officers... The Antonopouloses are nowhere to be found. They are obviously members of the resistance. You deny knowing they were traitors to the Reich?"

"Oh my! My husband and I had no idea! And to think we shared our residence with members of the resistance! Hiding a Jewish child? What a ridiculous and dangerous idea."

"Ridiculous and deadly. We are on the lookout for them. When we find them, we will make them give up the names of their accomplices in the resistance before we kill them. If they try to contact you, it is your duty to report it to Nazi headquarters."

The Nazi turned to go, but stopped in mid-step. "You understand how fortunate you are, don't you, for having the protection of Matsakis? I find it hard to believe you didn't know the truth about the Antonopoulos vermin. But Matsakis said we were to leave you and your husband unharmed."

"Of course, our uncle knows we would never be involved in such activity."

"Hmphh." The Nazi clearly had his doubts, but saluted *Heil Hitler* before he walked out the door.

Andreas stayed at the hospital, not daring to leave until his usual time. "Do not arouse suspicion," he had been told over and over by his contacts in the partisans.

When he entered the apartment, there were none of the usual smells of dinner cooking on the stove. Rebecca was seated in a chair, clutching Elias in her arms. She only glanced briefly at Andreas.

"Katerina," he said as he ran to her side and knelt in front of her.

"Sebastian was murdered this morning. He was just a baby," she whispered, looking into Andreas' eyes.

"I know. I was sent word. Stella and Giannis have fled to the mountains."

"What about us? What about our son? He isn't circumcised. But his mother is Jewish. His mother... "

"Shh." He placed his fingers on her lips. "His mother is Katerina Sefaris, a good Christian woman who goes to church every Sunday."

"A Nazi came to question me. I know he didn't believe me when he asked if I knew about Sebastian. He said I had the protection of Theo Constantine."

"We do have his protection."

Although the threat of discovery never left Rebecca's mind, life continued. Church every Sunday, the beautiful crucifix that had belonged to Andreas's mother always around her neck. There was a meal on Sunday after church with Theo Constantine and his wife, where they listened to the praise of all that the Nazis had done in Salonika and the assurance that the Allies were losing the war. Rebecca and Andreas smiled politely and never uttered a word of disagreement. For they knew Theo Constantine had protected them the day Sebastian had been murdered.

Rebecca had joined a church woman's group that engaged in communal good deeds. Elias seemed to grow bigger every day. He had his father's dark hair and eyes. When he was six months old, Rebecca realized she was carrying another child.

Although Theo Constantine had painted a positive picture of the war, Andreas's contacts told him the war was going badly for the Germans. As Rebecca and Andreas waited to hear good news, they had learned all the other Jews of Greece had been rounded up and transported. In Athens, some Jews had gone into hiding from the Nazis. Family members were often split up to make their hiding easier. To avoid discovery, many Jews had to move from place to place. The Christians who hid them were risking their own lives. One day, many of the Athenian Jews had been lured into a synagogue with the promise of flour for making Passover matzo. And in this way they were rounded up and deported. The Jews who had gone to Poland were never heard from again. And although there seemed no logic for transporting everyone somewhere else to kill them, there was no other explanation for their silence.

One day, Andreas brought her news about the island of Zakynthos, where every Jew had been hidden in the mountains. When the Nazis asked the Metropolitan Bishop Chrysostomos and the Mayor for the list of the Jews, they gave them a paper with only their own names. There was goodness in the world, he told her.

Rebecca couldn't see goodness when all around her were the signs of the Jews of Salonika who had been taken away, their shops, their houses. She thought about her dear friend Stella. Were she and Giannis safe? She tried not to think about the horror of Stella watching her son murdered before her eyes. But often at night, she had nightmares that it wasn't Sebastian who had been murdered, but it was Elias. And in her dream, there was nothing she could do to stop it.

CHAPTER 18

Salonika, German Zone of Occupation: September, 1944

IN LATE SUMMER, Rebecca gave birth to a girl. Andreas held their little girl, with tears of joy in his eyes. "She is so beautiful, just like her mother."

"I guess I was wrong when I said I might not be able to give you children," she said softly, exhausted from childbirth, but so happy to have delivered another healthy child.

"Yes, every once in a great while, you are wrong. Are you sure you don't want to name her Esther after your mother?"

"Esther is an easily identifiable Jewish name. Maria is the right name for our little girl. Doesn't she look like a Maria? And she will go to school, won't she? I want her to go to school."

"Our Maria will go to University, I promise you.

"Now, why don't you rest? I'll take care of our little girl and show her to her big brother."

"I am tired." She closed her eyes. Another baby she thought. She had her own small family, but it would never replace all those who had been lost. She was determined to look ahead. There must be a future for herself and her husband, but most importantly, her children.

Theo Constantine made sure that they were never again bothered by the Nazis. Andreas reassured her they were family, even though he wasn't of the Matsakis flesh and blood. Constantine Matsakis would take care of his brother's only son. Family was everything. Rebecca knew Andreas often thought of his family from Smyrna. There was no one left of the family into which he had been born. But now, since their marriage, since the birth of their children, a peace about his past had seemed to settle over him. Most evenings he slept well, without the nightmares. The night of the opera, after they were driven home, Andreas told her about the memories that had been triggered by the music of Pagliacci. He described the horrors of the quay, the smells, the sounds and he told her tearfully about the murder of his mother. Rebecca had held him in her arms that night, trying her best to give him comfort.

With two young children to care for, Rebecca never went to her sewing shop anymore. She sketched fashion designs at home. Her customers were now all the wives of Nazis and collaborators. Greek women did not have enough money for clothing when food was still so scarce. Of course, that didn't affect the high level Nazis and the collaborators who were well fed from purchases on the black market and had money to spare.

Rebecca was often filled with guilt when Andreas brought home a bountiful basket of food and extra ration coupons from his uncle. "Katerina," Andreas would admonish her. "You need to eat. Elias and Maria need nourishment to grow. We distribute so much of our food through the church to the less fortunate. Even if we gave away all this food, it wouldn't feed all the poor of Salonika. In these days of so little food, it brings back to me the months I ate from garbage cans when I was a boy. How well I remember the terrible feeling of hunger in my belly. I see the malnourished people on the streets and I fight to keep those horrific memories in the past where they belong."

And so Rebecca didn't protest as she prepared the food he had brought from his uncle. Their little boy, Elias had grown plump while so many other children were stick thin. Each day Rebecca ate well to ensure an adequate production of milk for her baby girl.

October 1944: Salonika
Mainland Greece was liberated from the Axis occupying troops. German garrisons still remained in control of Crete and other Aegean islands. This terrible war would soon be over. Europe would be free again.

It was hard to believe the occupation by the evil Nazis and Bulgarians was finally over. Would any of her people be coming back from Poland? Was it true that the silence from the Jews who were sent to Poland meant no one would return? Rebecca kept telling herself when the Koen family returned, she and Andreas would immediately give them back their apartment and find another place to live. Andreas had mentioned he might like to return to Athens. Initially Rebecca said she wanted to go back to Kavala, her home. But was it her home when her family had vanished as if they had never lived there? Did she really want to dwell among the ghosts, walking past the houses and shops she had known so well?

Now, Katerina could be Rebecca once more. She had stopped attending church on Sunday, except for the occasional holiday that was important to Andreas. There was no Jewish community to welcome her back into their midst. She kept the crucifix of Andreas's mother in her skirt pocket. She wanted it with her, not as a symbol of Greek Orthodoxy, but as a remembrance of the woman who had given birth to her husband, who had surely loved him as fiercely as she loved her own son and daughter.

The first Jews who came back to Salonika had been hiding in the mountains. Rebecca asked Andreas to find the whereabouts of men who had come back from hiding. She had made a list of all her family members from Kavala, hoping she hadn't forgotten anyone. She brought the long list with her when she knocked on the door.

"Who is it?" came a gruff voice.

"*Me yamo* Rebecca Solomon. I am Rebecca Solomon," she answered in Ladino, the language of her family, for the first time in so long.

The door opened a crack and then opened fully, revealing a short man with a dark beard.

"*Por favor.* Please, I have a list of my family's names. They were from Kavala. There is no one left, everyone drowned, and I want someone to say *kaddish* for them."

The man with the beard looked at her with an intense gaze. "You are a Jewish woman?"

"Yes, I am Rebecca Solomon," she repeated.

"You don't look like you spent the war in the mountains. Where have you been these past few years?"

"I... I've been here in Salonika."

"And how did you evade the Nazis, woman? Did you offer yourself in trade?"

Rebecca resisted the urge to slap his face. "How dare you!" She stiffened her spine as her hands fisted at her sides.

"How did you manage to live in Salonika when all the Jews were shipped away?"

"I lived as a Christian," she told them.

He grimaced at her. "Well, give me your list. *Kaddish* will be said for them."

"*Grasyas*. Thank you," Rebecca said firmly and turned to leave.

"Rebecca Solomon," he addressed her. "I had sisters your age. They had families, children. They were taken away and I may never see them again. Who knows what happened to them in Poland. My parents, my grandparents. I urged everyone to follow me to the mountains, but they wouldn't go. Why are you still alive? How did you manage to live as a Christian in Salonika?"

"I will appreciate you saying kaddish for my family, may their memory be eternal." She turned and started to walk away.

"One moment, Rebecca Solomon from Kavala. There is a rumor that all the Jews from Eastern Macedonia didn't drown on the barges. Only a few boats went down. The other boats continued on with their human cargo which was sent to Poland to a place called Treblinka."

"My family could have survived?" Rebecca asked with excitement.

"I didn't say that. I just said they may not have drowned. The information on the barges going down came from the Bulgarians. They are wonderful liars about everything."

"What do you know about this place called Treblinka?"

"Are you sure you want to know?"

"Of course I do."

"Rumors, of course. No one knows yet for sure. But it's said no one survived Treblinka. It was a place of death. Now I have things to do. I will say *kaddish* for your family."

Rebecca slowly walked back to her apartment, a heaviness upon her. To have had her hopes raised and then suddenly, cruelly, to have them dashed again. A place called Treblinka.

⚜

Rebecca tried several more times to make contact with those few Jews who had come back from the mountains. She brought them food, clothing, all she could spare. They took what she brought them, but there were always the silence or at times the questions. How had she lived through the war in the city? She didn't owe their hostility an answer. There were some women who thanked her effusively for her help, but for most people she was an enigma, a Jew who had survived in the middle of their city when thousands had been deported.

She was now Rebecca again. But something was nagging at her, especially when Andreas told her he would circumcise their son. She had disagreed. "Not now," she told him. She couldn't get the image of Sebastian's murder out of her mind. "We can do it later."

"Alright, Rebecca. But the sooner we do it, the less difficult it will be for him. I'm sure we could find someone in the small Jewish community who has returned from the mountains who could do it in the traditional way with the proper prayers, if that's what you want."

"No, let's wait."

In December, Andreas brought home news that there had been a demonstration on the streets of Athens. There were snipers on the roof and many people were killed. Corpses littered the streets and hence there seemed to be the beginning of a civil war.

Once mail was restored, Andreas started reaching out to Vassilis's brothers in Chicago. Andreas was a son of Greece, but America represented a beacon of safety in his eyes, safety for his wife and family, who he swore he would protect and keep safe.

Immigration into the United States was very restricted. But he hoped when the war was over in Europe, his uncles could pull some strings, know of some avenues that would make their immigration easier.

In the meantime, Andreas and Rebecca made plans to take their small children to see the Matsakis family back in Kavala. Rebecca was anxious to visit with Andreas's parents, to show off her children to the only grandparents they would ever know. But at the same time, she was filled with the dread of seeing the houses of her family, now occupied by strangers.

It was January when they disembarked from the ferry.

Eleni and Vassilis were beside themselves with joy as they embraced them and the children at the harbor. It seemed there weren't enough kisses and hugs, as they made their way back to the house.

The grandparents spoiled Elias with treats and never let Maria out of their arms.

"Our next children will be named for you, I promise," Rebecca told Kiría Eleni as she unpacked their belongings.

"No, they should be named for your parents."

Rebecca looked at her mother-in-law. The silence grew loud between them as the memory of Isaac and Esther Solomon seemed to rise up and envelope them in sadness.

The next day, Andreas expressed his desire to go down to the harbor.

"You go," Rebecca told him. "I'll stay here and help your mother with the cooking. She wants to hold Maria all day long, so she'll need my assistance in the kitchen." Rebecca turned away from him and looked out the window down to the street.

"I thought you and I could go up to the castle and the aqueduct for a little while this morning. My parents can take care of the children."

"No, you go. I'm staying inside."

"It looks like a lovely day."

"I said no. I'm staying inside," she raised her voice as she continued to look down at the street, remembering the night she had watched everyone rounded up by the Bulgarians. Today it was a peaceful street with everyone going on about their normal activities.

"What's wrong, Rebecca?"

"I'm remembering the night all the Jews were taken away. Why was I spared that night? If I hadn't all the sewing to do, I would have been taken away. Why am I alive when everyone else is gone?" she asked with anguish.

"Oh, Rebecca," he sighed. "We can't answer those questions. But you are alive. I am alive and we have two wonderful children."

"Maria and Elias will never know my Papá, my Mamá, all their aunts and uncles and cousins."

Andreas put his arms around her. "I know. I know. But we must look forward, for the sake of our children."

"It hurts so much to be back here in Kavala." Rebecca fought to hold back her tears.

"I understand. Let's leave the babies with my parents and go off to the castle. It has always been a wonderful place for us and I think we could both use some fresh air."

Rebecca followed Andreas on a roundabout route to the castle that avoided passing her old home. They climbed up on the castle and looked down at the sea. Andreas stood beside her and held her hand. "I remember the first time I saw the castle all those many years ago."

"And what did you think then?"

"It was so big and frightening. But I was hungry and it didn't look like anyone lived in this castle, so there wouldn't be any food for me." He laughed. "And then through the goodness of God, I found a warm shed one night and I was rescued by a little girl with gray eyes, brown hair and a big shovel in her hands. She was going to hit me over the head, as I recall."

"I should have," she teased.

"I'm sure you don't remember that first time I kissed you," he turned to her.

"Of course, I remember. We had gone for a jaunt with your British friends and being that they weren't Greek, they didn't know they needed to guard my honor. So they let us go off on our own. How could I have forgotten that day and all the wonderful things you said to me? You know I'd always loved you, all the while knowing we had no future together."

"Life has given us more than we could have dreamed when we were children. God has given us each other and hope for the future in the midst of so much tragedy."

❧

The children had been put to bed and they were all sitting in the kitchen drinking some *ouzo*.

"When we go to America." Andreas cleared his throat. "Patéra and Mamá, you must come with us."

"We are set in our ways. We don't speak English. This is our home. We are too old to start over again. But you must promise to return and see us and we will come to America to visit you and the children. It will not be easy for your family to emigrate. We would have no chance. You are a doctor and I am a simple cobbler. You and Rebecca will have a new life in that good country with your children. The civil war that is sweeping our country, communists who were the resistance, now being vilified... these are sad days for Greece." Vassilis shook his head in dismay.

"I have never heard a word from my brother Constantine. I don't know what happened to him."

"I've been making inquiries about him. He protected us from the Nazis. I'm sure he saved our lives," Andreas sighed. "But it's as if he vanished into thin air. Many collaborators faced penalties and many did not. Some are finding new roles in the new government."

"And now this civil war, with so much bloodshed and violence on both sides. As bad as the Nazis and the Bulgarians were I never could have imagined such a thing, one Greek brother against another. Andreas, I hope they don't examine your background too carefully when you try to emigrate to America. Your connection with the *andartes*, the communists, would make you ineligible to be admitted."

"Rebecca, are you sure you don't want to see your old home? The people who live there now are very nice. I'm sure they would let you come inside," Kiría Eleni changed the subject. "The Bulgarians of course are gone and a large Greek Orthodox family with many children are living there. Your father's store was abandoned by the Bulgarians and a new Greek shop owner has taken it over."

"No. I don't want to go inside. I just want to remember our house the way it was," Rebecca told her politely. She didn't want to go by the house and think of her family, all the memories of them living and loving and singing and cooking and praying. They were all gone, vanished like ghosts, like wisps of smoke.

"My father's family lived in Ioannina for over two thousand years. Do you think anyone could have imagined that someday they would be thrown out of their homes, out of their communities? Who can know the future? But I will make sure my children are safe. Even if we are able to go to America, I will make sure no harm comes to them."

"Of course, they will be safe. In America, no harm could come to them," Andreas reassured her.

Salonika: March, 1945
Andreas returned home earlier than usual from his hospital duties. Little Elias shrieked with joy as he always did when his father opened the door. "Baba!" The little boy took tentative steps toward him and then collapsed and crawled the rest of the way. Andreas bent over and picked up his son.

Rebecca stood smiling holding their daughter, waiting for Andreas to give her his usual kiss and hug of greeting after his long day at the hospital. But her smile vanished as she sensed something was amiss.

"Andreas?" she asked, placing her daughter down onto a blanket on the floor. "Something is wrong. What is it?"

Andreas had a newspaper tucked under his arm. He put Elias back on the floor and sat down in a chair by the table. "You always know what I'm thinking, don't you?" He placed the newspaper on the table and unfolded it, the front page facing upwards.

"What is the matter?" She swallowed. She felt fear rising in her chest. The war had not totally ended in the rest of Europe. "It's something in the paper?" Had the progress of the war against the Nazis been halted? Could the Nazis be coming back to Greece?

"Sit down," Andreas told her. Rebecca took a deep breath and seated herself on a nearby chair. "The newspaper has terrible news. I don't want to read it to you. You must read it for yourself. It is a report of a man named Leon Batis, who has returned from Poland."

Rebecca looked at the paper. The headline seemed to scream out at her. **"They Burned All The Jews From Thessaloniki in the Crematoriums."**

The first man had returned from Poland, telling terrible stories of camps where Jews had been exterminated en masse, killed in gas chambers, thrown into crematoriums. Babies had been burned alive. People had been tortured.

A few weeks later, more returning survivors from Poland had reported sterilization and medical experiments performed on many women. Of the sixty thousand Jews deported from Salonika, no one had any idea of how many might actually return. By August of 1945, only a few hundred Jews had returned.

When the survivors did return, they found their houses had been taken over and in many instances, the new owners refused to give up their newly acquired property. The Jews were temporarily housed in the remaining synagogues.

Rebecca had hoped to return her apartment to the Koen family. She and Andreas would find lodging elsewhere. But no member of the Koen family ever returned. The owner of her sewing shop did not return.

Rebecca and Andreas volunteered their help with the relief agencies who were trying their best to aid the survivors. Rebecca enlarged her staff to five women who were kept busy sewing clothes for the people who had nothing but the clothes on their back when they arrived in the city that had once been their home. Rebecca increased her staff by hiring several girls who had been liberated from the camps.

Andreas had tried to make contact with the Antonopolouses. It seemed an impossible task, until he had finally received word that they had moved to Larissa to be near Stella's family.

Eventually Rebecca and Andreas had received approval for immigration to the United States. During their interviews there had never been a mention of Andreas's connections with the communist partisans and when asked about communists, he had pleaded ignorance.

Rebecca was so happy to be leaving Salonika, where the remains of the Jewish cemetery that had been destroyed were strewn around the town. Tombstones had been used for paving driveways, urinals, the floors of tavernas. On occasion, she had been forced to walk past Jewish skulls and bones that were littered about as a reminder of the people who had dug up the remains of the Jews in the cemetery looking for hidden gold and valuables.

Andreas and Rebecca had made inquiries in Ioannina, hoping some members of her father's Romaniote family had survived and returned. But no members of Papá's family or her sister Roza and her family were on the list of survivors.

Rebecca was ready for a new life in America, where she could have a fresh beginning for herself and her family. Greece would always have a place in her heart, but her future was in the far off land of America, in a place called Chicago. "We won't be living by the sea," Andreas had told her. "But there is a very big lake there. I'm told it looks like an ocean."

"I don't need to live by the sea," she told him. It was hard for her to enjoy the beauty of the sea when she thought about her family drowning. She never heard the confirmation of the rumor the Jewish partisan had told her about that place called Treblinka. It was better for them to have died at the bottom of the sea than to have been burned in a crematorium.

◈◈◈

Andreas was sitting in a comfortable chair, smoking his cigarette after dinner. Rebecca had just placed the children down for the night. Andreas was paging through the final immigration papers, a frown on his face.

"Rebecca? What have you done? I'm checking over the papers before we bring them to the consulate tomorrow. Why are you filling the papers with lies?"

"I will keep my children safe."

"You wrote here that your name is Katerina and you were born in Smyrna. You were an orphan who fled in '22. That is my story."

"Well, now it is my story as well. I am Katerina Sefaris, a Greek Orthodox woman and my children are Greek Orthodox. No one will ever persecute and murder my children because they are Jewish."

"The Nazis and the Bulgarians are gone. Jews aren't being persecuted."

"Perhaps not now. But who knows the future."

"We are going to America."

"I don't care where we are going. Jews lived in many countries. All is fine and then they are persecuted. Thrown into ovens. Not our children, not my children."

"Rebecca," he began.

"I am not Rebecca. I am Katerina. My papers were all burned in the torching of Smyrna. That is why I have no records." Her voice grew louder.

"Your people have such a rich history. Don't turn your back on who you are, please. You shouldn't do that."

"Is it for you to tell me what to do? You can't do that. I won't let you do that. Andreas, I have made up my mind. When the Bulgarians came and then the Nazis came, my people were powerless. I am not powerless. I will do whatever I must to keep Elias and Maria safe. Do you understand me? You weren't there when Sebastian was ripped out of Stella's arms. You didn't watch the Nazi fire bullets into his head and stomp on his sweet little innocent body."

"No, I wasn't there." He sighed with resignation. "No, I won't tell you what to do."

"Then the subject is closed and our son will never be circumcised."

"If that's what you want. But if you change your mind…."

"I've made up my mind. This is a chance for a new beginning, for me and for my children. I will keep my children safe."

"As you wish." He put down the papers and placed them in a folder.

CHAPTER 19

Chicago: 1963

"MAMÁ, WHAT? WHAT did you say?" Maria gasped.

Rebecca saw the shock and disbelief spread all over her daughter's lovely face. I can't do this, Rebecca thought. Not even for you, my only daughter. I didn't want you to know. I never wanted to burden you and your brothers with all the horrors of war.

"Mamá, what did you just say?" Maria asked again.

"I said I am a Jewish woman," Rebecca replied in a quiet voice.

"How could that be possible? Why would you say such a thing, just so I don't have to convert? But I want to convert. I want to become Jewish," Maria's voice was filled with determination. "The Jewish people have a long and rich history and I want to be a part of them."

"You already are Jewish," Andreas told her. "Because your mother is Jewish."

"How could that be possible?" asked Maria.

"In order to escape the Bulgarians and the Nazis, I hid my faith," said Rebecca, as memories of marriage to Andreas flashed before her. The priest and his wife, the Matsakises, and Andreas standing beside her. Greek icons on the walls and her fear and confusion.

"I don't believe you. If that were true, you would have told us. You said you were orphaned in Smyrna just like Patéra. Your Greek Orthodox family was killed by the Turks, just like Patéra's family."

"I adopted your father's history as if it were mine. But it wasn't. I was born into a large Jewish family in Kavala, Greece."

Maria sat back in her chair. "I…. I can't believe this."

"I left my past behind, Maria. That's all you need to know," Rebecca explained in a quiet voice. She didn't want to say any more. She didn't want to revisit the past and those memories…. so much death, the loss of everyone.

"Your past? What about being Jewish? Why aren't you Jewish anymore? When the war was over, when you came to America you could be Jewish again. Why did you turn your back on your faith? Didn't Patéra want you to be Jewish?" She looked accusingly at her father. "Why didn't you tell him no, I'm Jewish. I'm not Greek Orthodox."

"Maria, no, no. You don't understand." Rebecca shook her head. How could she allow Maria to blame Andreas, when he had repeatedly told her not to turn her back on her people?

"Rebecca, she doesn't understand because you haven't told her. You must tell her everything." Andreas reached across the table towards Maria, but she pulled her hands away and put them in her lap.

"No, I don't want to tell her everything," Rebecca said in a soft voice. "The past is the past. Isn't it enough to say I am Jewish and Maria does not need to convert?"

"Drew, Rebecca," Leonard smiled as he said her name. "We have heard such stories. I don't know what to say except I am so sorry. No one can judge the decisions you were forced to make during such horrific times. We will speak to our rabbi, Rabbi Goldman. We belong to a Reform Synagogue that is very progressive. I don't think the Rabbi will have a problem marrying our children, understanding that Maria is indeed Jewish because she was born to a Jewish mother."

"That would be fine," Rebecca agreed. Yes, she thought, for you, Maria, I will do this. I will stand before a rabbi and try to convince him I am a Jewish woman. He will be an Ashkenazi rabbi who may not understand my Romaniote-Sephardic traditions. Perhaps he won't even know there were Jews in Greece. Yes, I will do that, no matter how humiliating it might feel.

"Your family needs time alone. I think we should go now." Leonard got to his feet. "It was lovely meeting both of you. Drew, I'll be in touch about working in that clinic."

"Next time, you will come to our house for dinner." Estelle stood up in front of Rebecca. "But before that you, Maria and I can talk about a bridal shower and registering at Marshall Field's for wedding gifts."

Rebecca got to her feet, taking her eyes away from her daughter, whose face had grown pale with distress.

"Yes, that would be lovely," Rebecca told the woman. The two of them embraced. In spite of Rebecca's initial misgivings about the Strausses, she was grateful for their understanding and compassion. They had raised Steven to be a fine young man. They were good people.

"Your Maria is a lovely girl, and we are so pleased they are getting married. Welcome to our family, to all of you," Estelle told her.

"Steven," Maria spoke up. "Steven, don't go. Can you stay here with me?"

"Of course, I'll stay if you want me to. I drove here in my own car."

The Strausses had gone and a silence settled over the room.

Andreas walked over to the liquor cabinet and took out a bottle of *raki*. He held it out towards everyone. But they all shook their heads no. He poured himself a glassful and took a huge swallow before he sat down next to Rebecca.

"Why, Mamá? Why weren't you Jewish after the war!" Maria broke the silence.

"Maria, your mother became a Greek Orthodox woman to save herself and she remained one because she was terrified something would happen to her children if they were identified as Jewish. She did it to protect you," Andreas explained in a patient voice.

"I don't understand. Why didn't you tell us, Mamá? We had the right to know."

"I don't want to discuss this anymore." Rebecca felt a headache beginning across her forehead. "I told you I was Jewish. That means you don't have to convert and you can get married very soon. That's all you need to know."

"No, no, no! That is not all I need to know. If you weren't orphaned in Smyrna like Patéra, where is your family? Why haven't you been in contact with them for all these years? You just came to America and walked away from everyone? I have cousins, aunts and uncles whom I've never met? Do I have grandparents in Greece whom I have never met? Do they even know that I exist? Do they know about my brothers? Was that fair to us, to my brothers, to cut us off from our Jewish relatives, all so you could pretend to be a Christian?"

Rebecca fought back tears. "I didn't pretend, Maria. I was baptized by a Greek Orthodox priest."

"Does Elias know? Did you tell him and not me?" Maria shouted.

"Maria, do not raise your voice to your mother." Andreas placed his arm around Rebecca's shoulders protectively.

"Maria." Steven got to his feet. "Why don't we go into the kitchen and brew some tea? Maria, come with me."

"Yes, that's a good idea," Andreas agreed. "Then we will all sit down in the living room where we can be more comfortable,"

Maria pursed her lips in displeasure as she followed Steven into the kitchen.

"I can't do this, Andreas," Rebecca whispered. "I can't. I wanted to spare our children the horrors of what happened to my people. I didn't want them to know."

"You have to tell her. You don't have a choice now. You are strong. You have always been strong. And now I can say Rebecca again, my Rebecca, my love. I'm going to get the special box in our bedroom closet. I'll bring it out and it will help you tell her about your past and your life in Kavala."

"I'm not ready to show it to her. Please, Andreas, don't bring it out here," Rebecca pleaded.

"Rebecca, I know this is hard. But it's best for the truth to come out. Sweetheart, I love you. You can do this."

"I don't know what to say. Where do I begin? I don't think she'll understand. Can't you tell her?"

"It's not my place to tell her. It's your family, Rebecca. It's your story."

Maria and Steven came out from the kitchen. She placed the tea cups and saucers on the coffee table. She had also assembled some butter cookies that the Strausses brought for dessert. She avoided looking at her mother and focused her gaze on the tea pot.

Maria's free spirit had always reminded Rebecca of her sister Miriam. In Greece, that streak of independence in a woman was contained and almost stifled. But here in America, it blossomed and grew.

Rebecca started to pour from the teapot, but her hands were trembling. She put down the pot.

"Maria, why don't you pour?" Steven told her.

"Mamá." Maria took a deep breath. "I didn't mean to be disrespectful. Steven told me I needed to apologize. But I was so shocked. We always had

Jewish friends and you never said a word. Where is Patéra?" She noticed her father's absence.

"He is getting something from our room. Here he is." Rebecca watched as he appeared, carrying a large box and placing it on the coffee table.

"What's in there?" Maria asked.

"I think it will help your mother tell you about her family. Open it, Maria."

"I hope there are photographs of your family in here." Maria untied the string and raised the lid.

"There are no photographs," Rebecca said in a soft voice.

"There is something better, much better." Andreas reached inside and withdrew a large thick tablet. "The Solomon family had photograph albums, of course, but they are all gone. Your mother made sketches of her family so she wouldn't forget their images."

Maria took the tablet and began to page through the sketches. "There are so many sketches. This one looks a little like me," she paused at the likeness of Rebecca's sister Liza. "When can I meet them? Can we go to Greece and meet them?"

"That is my sister Liza and you do resemble her, the eyes, your smile... " Rebecca stopped speaking as the tears began to slip down her cheeks. "You can't meet them. They were all killed in a place called Treblinka, a death camp. At first we were told they all drowned. But later we learned they were sent to Treblinka. They were all killed by the Nazis, my parents, my sisters and brothers, my nieces, nephews, cousins. There is no one left from my family. "

"No one?" Maria replied in a terrified whisper.

"Only myself and you, my children." The tears slipped down her cheeks.

"Oh, Mamá, Mamá." Maria moved beside her on the couch. "I'm sorry." She put her arms around her mother.

"My family was rounded up in the middle of the night and thrown out into the streets by the Bulgarians. They were taken away and I never saw them again. I didn't want you to know. I wanted to shield you and your brothers from what happened. I didn't think it would do any good for you to know. We can't undo the past. I needed to look forward, not behind." She wiped the tears with the back of her hand and took the handkerchief Andreas offered to her from his pocket.

"Why weren't you rounded up with them?"

"I was staying at your *Yiayia* Eleni's that night. It was just a twist of fate that allowed me to survive," she paused. "I became an Orthodox Christian the next day. Your father married me and saved my life."

"You told me you loved each other since you were children. And now you are saying Patéra married you just to save you from the Nazis?"

"Wait, wait, Maria. You are jumping to conclusions," Andreas answered with impatience. "Your mother and I loved each other since we were children. Your mother saved my life when I was a little boy. She found me and brought me to your grandparents who took me in and raised me as their own. Since our childhood, your mother meant everything to me. I told her we were going to marry when we grew up. Mamá laughed at me. She said we couldn't marry because she was Jewish and I was Christian," he paused, looking at Rebecca, his face filled with loving emotion.

Rebecca sat in silence. It was too painful to visit those memories.

Maria turned her gaze back to the box and looked at the cloth-covered objects on the bottom and unwrapped them one piece at a time. "What are these?"

"This is a seder plate and this is a kiddish cup."

"They belonged to your family?" asked Steven.

"No, I have nothing from my family. When we lived in Salonika, where you were born, Maria, we were living in the apartment of the Koen family. They left them in their apartment."

"Left them?" Maria was puzzled.

"Fifty thousand Jews were deported from Salonika. They could take very little with them and I don't think the Koen family was very religious. So they didn't take the kiddish cup and seder plate. We were going to return their apartment and everything else back to them after the war. But they never returned. Only two thousand Jews returned in all of Greece. When we came to America, I brought the kiddish cup and the seder plate with us."

"But if you are Jewish where are the things from your family?"

Rebecca sat with her hands folded in her lap, looking at her daughter and Steven Strauss. She saw the love between them and hoped their love would endure and grow as her love with Andreas had grown stronger over the years.

"Rebecca," Andreas was calling her the name she had abandoned. She wasn't Rebecca anymore. She was Katerina. But by calling herself Katerina could she really erase Rebecca, erase her life of almost thirty years. Yes, she was afraid for her children. But was Andreas right? Were Jews safe here in America?

"Maria, your mother will tell you everything. Won't you, Rebecca? It is time."

Rebecca took a deep breath. He was right. It was time. "When my family was rounded up in the middle of the night, it was winter. All their possessions were auctioned off the next day. I saw unspeakable horrors inflicted on babies for the mere fact they were Jewish. I swore to myself that would never happen to my children. That I would do whatever I must to keep my children safe. Your father said in America I didn't have to hide our Jewish identity. But I was afraid, so afraid.

"My father's family lived in Greece for over two thousand years. Their language was Greek. My mother's family came to Greece five hundred years ago. Their language was Ladino, a dialect of Spanish. When you walked the streets of Kavala, you heard the sounds of Ladino everywhere. But it didn't matter how long they had lived in Greece, how much Greece was a part of their heart, their homeland. Almost all of them were murdered. From 76,000 only 10,000 survived. When your father told me Jews were safe in America, I couldn't dare believe him. Do you think my parents could have imagined they wouldn't be safe in Greece? They thought the worst that could happen to them is what had happened in Spain. But annihilation? Who could have imagined such a thing? I wasn't going to allow myself a false sense of security like my parents, my family had. I was powerless to protect my family in Greece. I vowed I wouldn't be powerless to protect my children. I would do anything to keep them safe.

"I was one of ten children, seven sisters, two brothers," she began. "We can look at the sketches together one by one and I'll tell you all about them. Let's begin with Liza. You do have her eyes, her smile. She used to tease me so much when we were children. But as we grew older we were so close…." It wasn't as difficult as she might have imagined. Maria asked no questions, as she sat mesmerized by her mother's words.

"Mamá." Maria took her mother's hand in her own. "Mamá, I'm so sorry. How terrible for you to have to hide your identity for all these years."

"It was my choice. The Greek Orthodox community is very welcoming. Your father's people are so warm."

"That's why you don't go to church very often on Sunday?"

"Yes."

"And when you said Patéra didn't like pork and that is why you never prepared it for us…. that wasn't true."

"No, it wasn't." Rebecca smiled at her daughter.

"For Passover we always went to the Rubensteins, Patéra's partner. Even when it was so close to Easter and you had so much cooking to do, you insisted we go. I thought how nice it was for us to go to them for Passover and for them to come to us for Easter dinner."

"Their Passover seder is celebrated differently than the one in my family. But it felt good to be there to hear the story of the Exodus from Egypt."

"Maria." Andreas pulled Rebecca closer to himself. "It hasn't been easy for your mother. She has never forgotten her family. All these years your mother has struggled with a darkness that can descend upon her when thoughts and memories overcome her. There were mornings she struggled to get out of bed and send you and your brothers off to school. But she did get out of bed and she smiled as she sent you off. And then it was time for you to come home, and she would greet you with love and smiles. She never wanted you to know. She felt you must be protected from the past that continued to haunt her."

Rebecca wiped the tears from her eyes as Andreas continued. "We did not sever your mother's connections with the Jewish people. Your Mamá and I have kept her connection to her people in many ways," Andreas explained. "We contribute to Kehila Kedosha Janina, a Greek synagogue in New York. They say memorial *kaddish* prayers for Mamá's family. We give large donations to many causes in Israel, especially to orphanages."

"Steven," Maria turned to her fiancé. "I don't think we should go out tonight. We shouldn't go to that party. We need to stay here."

"No, Maria," Rebecca told her. "You and Steven should go out and have a good time."

"But you're upset, Mamá," Maria said with concern.

"I'm alright. Your father is here with me."

"Well, are you sure?" Maria asked.

"I'm sure," Rebecca told her. Go on, Maria, she thought. I don't want to keep showing a braveness, I don't feel.

"Yes," said Andreas. "You two go out and enjoy yourselves. But don't come home too late."

They both watched the door close. Rebecca steadied herself next to the table, as she picked up the seder plate and the kiddish cup that had belonged to the Koens. "I'll put them…. I'll put them on display in our…. breakfront," her voice broke.

Andreas put his arms around her. She dissolved into tears as he held her. "Shh, shh. It's for the best that she knows. You had a wonderful, loving family, Rebecca. They shouldn't be hidden from our children."

"It's so hard. It hurts so much," she sobbed.

"I know." He held her closer. "But I'm glad our daughter knows about her mother, who she was, the Solomon family. Maria and our boys need to know about them and the rich history of the Greek Jews."

"Was it so wrong to turn my back on who I was, on my family? But I was afraid."

"I know. I know. You did what you felt was right. You wanted to protect your children."

"Will they forgive me?"

"There is nothing to forgive. You'll tell them all about your family, the Solomons, the Rousos. Rebecca, my Rebecca. I know it is painful. But it is for the best."

After she told all the children about her heritage and her family, it seemed to lift a weight off her shoulders. Her nightmares of the deportations grew less frequent and then they stopped.

The twelve-year-old twin boys, Isaac and Victor, tried to understand the consequences of the news that their mother was Jewish. According to Jewish law, they could be accepted as Jewish if they wished. "Does that mean we don't go to church anymore, and we don't have to go to Greek school in the afternoon?"

"No, that doesn't mean you don't have to go to church and Greek school. But we will go to some synagogue services and I will tell you about my people, your people. Maybe we can begin to celebrate some of the holidays I celebrated with my family."

"Can we have a seder like the Rubensteins have? We like going to their seder," said Isaac.

"I'd love to have a Passover seder for our family. The Rubensteins are Ashkenazi Jews from Eastern Europe, so their customs are different from my family's. My family came from Greece and Spain. We serve our own special Passover foods and we conduct our seder differently. But I'm sure you will enjoy it. Let's have our own seder next spring." Rebecca smiled at her sons. The holidays, Purim. Passover. It would be so good to teach her children about them, to celebrate with them and hope that someday they would pass on her traditions to their own families.

"Ok," Victor and Issac chorused and ran out to the backyard to play ball.

Their oldest son, Elias, had recently returned from his backpacking trip through Europe. He did not try to hide his anger. "Why didn't you tell me? Why was it a secret? Don't you know if you keep something a secret it means it is something bad? So is it bad that you are a Jew? Are you ashamed? You know that I have many Jewish friends."

"Elias, show some compassion and understanding for your mother," Andreas urged him. "Those were terrible times and she fought to protect you."

"Well, World War II was like a million years ago. The world has changed and pretending to be an Orthodox Christian when you are Jewish is ridiculous. There are no Nazis in America."

"I didn't pretend, Elias. I was baptized by a Greek Orthodox priest."

"I don't want to talk about it anymore." Elias turned his back on them and slammed out the front door.

Andreas walked out after him.

Through the front picture window, Rebecca watched Andreas and Elias standing on the front lawn. It was obvious they were having an argument. She waited for an end to their heated words.

They finally came back into the house.

"Mamá. I'm sorry." Elias approached her, hanging down his head in embarrassment. He enveloped her in his arms. "Patéra told me how difficult it was for you when you couldn't have me circumcised after I was born and how hard it was to see me baptized. You know I often speak without thinking. I'm sorry. I think it's kind of cool that I'm descended from both Greek Jews and Greek Christians." He smiled sheepishly.

It was agreed the wedding should be held very soon, so that Maria and Steven could be wed before they left to do voter registration in Alabama. Both sets of parents were convinced it would be alright for the young couple to miss the fall semester in college if they promised to be back by the next semester. Then they would be able to finish their studies.

Rebecca knew she needed to meet with the Strausses' Rabbi before the wedding plans could proceed. Rabbi Goldman was a very nice young man and Rebecca appreciated that he didn't question her about the decisions she had made in the past. He had some questions about her mother's and father's family. He completely accepted her Jewish identity.

Rebecca and Maria spent countless hours at the dining room table with dress sketches strewn across the fine wooden surface.

"What was your wedding dress like, Mamá?" Maria asked, as she studied the three designs she liked the best.

"My wedding dress? It wasn't even mine. Patéra and I got married so quickly, I didn't have a wedding dress. But *Yiayia* Eleni insisted I have one. So we borrowed one from the rack of our customers' dresses. I wore the dress of a prospective bride who never knew her dress was worn by another woman."

"What did it look like?"

"I don't even remember. I was scared that day. Actually, I was terrified. The night before, I watched the entire Jewish community herded into the streets, the crying, the terror... Was I going to be discovered? My name was on a list for my parents' house and the Bulgarian soldiers were looking for me."

"You were so brave."

"Not really. What choice did I have? And I loved your father."

"There is one thing I don't understand. You keep mentioning the Bulgarians. But everyone knows it was the Nazis who went after the Jews."

"Yes, the Germans destroyed so many Jewish communities in Europe, so many innocent people. Unfortunately, they had willing accomplices. In the country of Bulgaria, at the urging of the clergy, the king did not follow instructions to deport the Jews in Bulgaria. The area of Greece that my family lived in was given to the Bulgarians by the Nazis. When the Nazis directed the Bulgarians to deport the Jews in the Bulgarian Zone of Occupation, the Bulgarians were quick to comply with their orders. All the Jews were deported to Treblinka and no one returned except for those who had gone into hiding.

"Oh, Maria, those were bad times. But they are over. Let's not talk about that anymore. I'm going to sew you the best, the most exquisite bridal gown. You've narrowed your choices to these three. Now you must choose." Rebecca gathered up the other sketches and left the remaining three for Maria to make her final choice.

⁂

The Strausses told Andreas and Rebecca to invite anyone they chose to attend the rehearsal dinner. The only Sefaris family was Andreas's uncles and their children. Eleni and Vassilis had both passed away several years before. Andreas and Rebecca felt their absence keenly as the day of the wedding approached. Rebecca knew how much it meant to Andreas to have the American family of Vassilis at the wedding. Cousin Nicolas Matsakis had been instrumental in arranging for the family's immigration into the United States and they would forever be grateful to him. They also invited some close friends and Marty Rubenstein, who was Andreas's partner in his medical practice.

Rebecca was seated next to Phil Nachman, one of Leonard's law associates. He explained to her how he met Leonard in law school.

"Phil," Rebecca began tentatively. "Do law schools accept older students?"

"Older students with their life experience are a wonderful asset to any law class."

"Asia Minor... " she heard the words from across the table where Andreas sat beside an older man who was talking to him. "You are from Izmir? I was in Izmir several years ago, quite a charming place. I was working for the State Department. When did you live there?"

"It was called Smyrna when I lived there," Andreas answered.

"Oh, then you must have lived there before the Greeks burnt it down." The man took a sip of his wine.

She watched the color deepen on Andreas's face. Rebecca excused herself from Phil Nachman, who was still talking to her. She no longer was listening to him. She quickly got to her feet and went around to the other side of the table where Andreas was inhaling on his cigarette, his dark eyes focused on the man who was talking to him.

"Control yourself, Andreas," Rebecca shouted silently, as if she could convey her thoughts to him.

"Excuse me?" Andreas gasped.

"I learned all about the fire when I was stationed there with the State Department. Never made any sense to me why the Greeks burned down their own part of the city."

"No, that doesn't make any sense, which is why it isn't true," Andreas said in measured tones.

"But it is true. The Turkish officials I worked with told me all about it."

"And what did they tell you?"

"The Greeks didn't want the Turkish army to have their wonderful houses and businesses, so they burned them to the ground." The man grimaced in disgust.

"Really? And did they tell you about the Turkish soldiers who poured gasoline through the streets and then ignited them into a river of fire?"

"Well, they didn't or I would have remembered that. How fortunate Attaturk took over the emerging Turkish Nation. He performed miracles in

Asia Minor. Asia Minor was a backward place before he came on the scene. He was such a great leader, a true visionary."

Rebecca put her hand on Andreas's shoulder as she prayed he would not make a scene at this celebration for their daughter's impending marriage.

"Smyrna was not a backward place. And sir, I was there when the Greek quarter was burnt to the ground by the Turks," Andreas paused. "And did your sources in Izmir tell you of the soldiers who slaughtered innocent people, who raped women and young girls, or did they leave that out?

"I... I had no reason to doubt them," the man sputtered in his own defense. "I never heard of such things. I'm sure those are just ugly rumors."

"Andreas," Rebecca said softly. He was under control now. But how long until he erupted?

"Ugly rumors? I watched my father stabbed to death by a Turkish soldier. I watched my mother murdered by a Turkish soldier and my sister kidnapped. All under the direction of Attaturk, Kemal Mustafa. Am I telling you lies?"

"I didn't know. I'm so sorry,"

"Andreas," Rebecca bent down towards her husband. "Come with me, please. Your cousin Nicolas wants to talk to us."

Andreas looked up at her.

"My husband needs to come with me," she told the man who was looking flustered.

"I apologize. I meant no offense," the man said as Rebecca motioned for Andreas to get up from the table.

Andreas followed her across the room.

She turned and faced him. "You can't let that man's ignorance ruin this special evening for us."

"Why do people believe such things?" His voice shook with emotion.

"They don't know any better. If the man was in Turkey, what do you think the Turks would tell them? The Turks have never admitted the slaughter of the Armenians. Why would they take responsibility for the horrors they inflicted on the Ottoman Greeks? They've changed history and people believe them. Andreas, there are those who claim there was never a Jewish holocaust, that six million Jews were never killed."

Andreas sighed and looked at his wife.

"Andreas Sefaris, tonight is for celebration. Tomorrow is Maria's wedding. Don't let anything spoil it for us."

"Rebecca, I wanted to celebrate tonight. And then Smyrna... I had to listen to such blasphemy, lies that make what happened to my family... " his words failed him.

"We will celebrate and be happy tonight. You and I will make sure our children, and some day their children, will know the truth about what happened to our families. They will live in our memories. They will not be forgotten. Now sit down next to me. Dessert is about to be served."

∞

The rehearsal dinner was over. Andreas told her he didn't want to go back home just yet. Rebecca slipped into the front seat and he closed the car door.

"Where are we going?" she asked him. "We shouldn't stay out too late the night before the wedding."

"We're going down to the lake. I know it's dark and cold, but we have our warm coats and we both love to look at the vastness and the majesty of the lake. I wanted us to have some time alone, just the two of us." He drove down the street, the dark expanse of Lake Michigan on the right side of the car.

He opened the car door for her and they walked down to the waves crashing against the shore.

"Come, let me put my arms around you and keep you warm," he said.

Rebecca rested her head on his shoulder.

"Well, it's not the sea," he commented.

"No, it isn't our beautiful Aegean. Maybe we should think about taking the family back to Greece. We've never gone back."

"You've never wanted to go back. Too many ghosts you used to say."

"I know I used to think that. But now, since I've been telling our children about my history, I don't think of my family as ghosts. They live in my heart and our children need to know them. Greece is our homeland. Our children should see it, experience its beauty, its sights, its sounds."

"I can arrange to take time off next summer. While I'm making out my schedule I need to know if you are serious about leaving to help voter registration in the South, and if I need to arrange for help in the house," he paused. "Rebecca, you really aren't seriously thinking about joining Maria and Steven in the South to register voters, are you?"

"No, I'm not going to join them. I'm staying here with you and the boys. But aren't you proud of our daughter for wanting to help in this fight for civil rights?"

"Yes, I am very proud of her."

"To think the Black people aren't able to vote as all other citizens can do. You and I know how important it is for everyone to have a voice. How well I remember when the rights of my people and your people were stripped away by the Bulgarians.

"Andreas, I have been thinking about what I can do to make a difference. I wouldn't leave you and the boys, I promise. In two years I'll finish my undergraduate degree. I was thinking about going to law school. I could help with voting rights and housing discrimination. No one should be second class citizens in this country. In Greece, there was nothing I could do. But here in this country, I can do something."

"I think that would be a wonderful idea and as a lawyer you would be a force to be reckoned with."

"You don't think I'm too old?"

"No, you aren't too old."

"We ought to go home soon. Tomorrow is the big day."

"Just a little longer, Rebecca," he paused. "I can't help but wish my Baba and Mamá were here to see their lovely granddaughter being married to a fine young man. Rebecca, I've been thinking about them so much. I have you, the children, this good life in America. But I miss them."

"I understand, my love. I understand," she said in a soft voice.

The day of Maria's wedding had arrived. She would wear the dress Rebecca had designed for her and labored over for countless hours, making sure every detail was perfection.

Maria and Steven were going to spend their honeymoon registering voters in the South.

Rebecca joined Andreas, who was standing in his place waiting for the bridal procession to begin. She put her hand in the crook of his arm. He looked so handsome in his tuxedo. She remembered what he had told her when she asked if it bothered him that their daughter was not being married in a church. "It doesn't matter what we call God or how we worship him," he told her. "He will bless our daughter's marriage and that is all that is important."

As Rebecca listened to the wedding march, she took a deep breath. She was in a synagogue. Her daughter was being married in a synagogue. "I am Rebecca Solomon Sefaris," she said to Andreas.

"Yes, you are, my love. You are my Rebecca Solomon Sefaris."

They walked down the aisle and waited for their daughter to join them. The music for the bride began playing. And there she was, in a beautiful white dress, her face veiled. They escorted Maria to Steven, whose face was animated in a wide smile as he waited for his bride in front of the Rabbi.

Tears of happiness welled in Rebecca's eyes as she watched her daughter Maria wed in a Jewish ceremony performed by a Rabbi. She wiped away the tears from her cheeks as she felt the presence of her family surrounding her. Maria and Steven stood under the ceremonial canopy, shared the glass of wine, and then exchanged rings and repeated the Hebrew marriage vows.

"Mazel tov!" The crowd chorused as Steven stepped on the glass and crushed it.

"Mazal bueno," Rebecca whispered in Ladino.

Mamá, Papá, she thought. I'm so happy, I'm alive. I have told our history to my children. You will not be forgotten.

And now it was time for celebration and dance.

"Come, come." Andreas beckoned to her, his hand outstretched. "They are going to play music for the *Kalamatian*. We must show everyone how to dance at a Greek wedding."

"I'm here," she laughed, and joined him in celebration of this wonderful day.

THE END

Author's Note

Light and Shadows is a work of historical fiction. The Solomon, Sefaris, and Matsakis families are entirely products of my imagination. The events described in Smyrna, Drama, Kavala and Salonica (Thessaloniki) are based on historical depictions of those terrible events.

Due to Western government interests in obtaining oil and maintaining good relations with Turkey, the details of Smyrna's destruction were suppressed. The Jews of Bulgaria were spared from death, but it is a little known fact that the Jews who lived in the zone of Bulgarian Occupation in Greece were all sent to their deaths in Treblinka, a Nazi death camp.

Mustafah Kemal or Attaturk (the father of Turkey) is looked upon by many as the hero of modern Turkey. He was responsible for ushering Turkey into the modern 20th century through secularization. However, he was the leader of the "Young Turks," whose motto was "Turkey for the Turks." This resulted in the elimination of the Christians by expulsion or genocide.

Between 1914-1917, more than 500,000 Ottoman Greeks were expelled and deported to the interior of Anatolia, which resulted in their deaths. In 1923, due to the Treaty of Lausanne and the resulting population exchange, more than one-and-a-half million Greek Orthodox were expelled from Asia Minor and sent to Greece after living for centuries in Asia Minor. Before the Population Exchange, twenty percent of the population in Asia Minor was Greek Orthodox. After the exchange, only two percent remained.

Two thousand years ago, the first Jews, called Romaniote, settled in Greece. After 1492, a large number of Sephardic Jews came to Greece.

Greece has the sad distinction of being home to the largest percentage of Jews annihilated in Europe. Eighty-seven percent of Greek Jews were murdered. Salonika lost ninety-seven percent of the Greek Jews who lived there at the beginning of World War II.

In Eastern Macedonia, the area that fell under Bulgarian rule, ninety-nine percent of the Greek Jews were annihilated

Rabbi Zvi Koretz of Salonika remains a figure of controversy because of his actions during the war.

Metropolitan Bishop Chrysostomos of Zakynthos and Archbishop Damaskinos of Athens are actual heroes who lived in Greece. Their brave deeds are recognized by Yad Vahsem in Israel in The Garden of the Righteous Among the Nations.

During the Nazi occupation, 80% of Greek industry and 90% of ports, roads, railways and bridges were destroyed. Twenty-five percent of the forests were also destroyed. More than 1000 villages were burned to the ground. Forty thousand people died of starvation in Athens.

For facts and the description of burning of Smyrna, *The Great Fire,* by Lou Ureneck, is an invaluable source and I highly recommend it for anyone wanting to learn about what happened in Smyrna to its Christian inhabitants and the shameful response of the "Great Powers."

The following are some of the many sources I used. Some of the information is conflicting, but I did my best to recount an accurate portrait of the terrible toll inflicted on the Greek people during the 20th century.

Bowman, Steven, *The Agony of Greek Jews* (Stanford, California, Stanford University Press, 2009)

Fleming, K.E., *Greece, A Jewish History* (Princeton, New Jersey, Princeton University Press, 2008)

Halo, Thea, *Not Even My Name* (Picador, 2001)

Horton, George, *The Blight of Asia: On the Synstematic Extermination of Christian Populations in Asia* (2015)

Mazower, Mark, *Inside Hitler's Greece* (New Haven, Connecticut, Yale University Press, 2001)

Shirinian, George N., Editor, *The Asia Minor Catastrophe and the Ottoman Greek Genocide* (The Asia Minor and Pontos Hellenic Research Center, Inc., 2012)

Ureneck, Lou, *The Great Fire* (New York, New York, Harper-Collins Publishers, 2015)

About the Author

Karen Batshaw is an author living in Washington, D.C., and Williamsburg, Virginia. Karen has a Bachelors degree in Anthropology and a Masters Degree in Social Work. She has used her training in social work to explore issues of trauma presented in her books. Her previous novels include *Love's Journey, Kate's Journey, Echoes in the Mist* and *Hidden in Plain Sight*.

Immersion in Greek culture as part of her research for *Echoes in the Mist* led her to the tragic story of Greece during World War II. *Hidden in Plain Sight* was her first book of serious historical fiction.

As she delved into Greece's World War II history for *Hidden in Plain Sight*, she learned about the plight of the Greek refugees who had been expelled from Asia Minor and the historically neglected Ottoman genocide. Batshaw also learned about the unknown history of what happened to the Greek Jews under the Bulgarian occupation during World War II. Both of these events formed the basis of *Light and Shadows*.

To inquire about booking Karen Batshaw for a speaking engagement or Skyping session, please see https://kbatshaw.wixsite.com/home.